Praise for

· · · · · · · · ·

A Dangerous Age

"This novel is the crown jewel of Kelly's extensive career in fashion. I am so proud to have been able to see her morph from a young, fresh-faced twentysomething into the woman she is today. This novel is a celebration of past, present, and future set against the fabulous back-drop of New York City!"

—Calvin Klein

"Kelly Killoren invites us behind the seams of three industries she knows a heck of a lot about: the fashion world, the art world, and the magazine world. Fashionistas, you are in for one fab ride!"

—Giuliana Rancic, *New York Times* bestselling author and host of *E! News* and *Fashion Police*

"[*A Dangerous Age*] explores the New York art, fashion, and publish-ing world[s] few women have access to. Kelly is an insider; Lucy Brockton is, too."

—Zac Posen

"This is the next beach book, especially for chick-lit fans and those who enjoy the TV show *Sex and the City*."

—*Library Journal*

"Intriguing and twisty."

—*Kirkus Reviews*

"*A Dangerous Age* walks us hand in hand throughout the inner sanctum of the New York social world only few are privy to. The clothes, the food, and the pampering are right out of a *Vogue* magazine must-have . . . [a] fun read."

—Melissa Odabash, American swimwear designer and former fashion model

"Kelly is back on the scene in a major way. Iconic, sexy, and smart, this supermodel redefines the rules of the game for all women of a dangerous age."

—John Demsey, executive group president of Estée Lauder

A Dangerous Age

Kelly Killoren
with Teresa DiFalco

GALLERY BOOKS

New York   London   Toronto   Sydney   New Delhi

Gallery Books
An Imprint of Simon & Schuster, Inc.
1230 Avenue of the Americas
New York, NY 10020

First Gallery Books trade paperback edition February 2017

GALLERY BOOKS and colophon are registered trademarks of Simon & Schuster, Inc.

For information about special discounts for bulk purchases, please contact Simon & Schuster Special Sales at 1-866-506-1949 or business@simonandschuster.com.

The Simon & Schuster Speakers Bureau can bring authors to your live event. For more information or to book an event, contact the Simon & Schuster Speakers Bureau at 1-866-248-3049 or visit our website at www.simonspeakers.com.

Interior design by Akasha Archer

Manufactured in the United States of America

10 9 8 7 6 5 4 3 2 1

Library of Congress Cataloging-in-Publication Data is available for the hardcover edition.

ISBN 978-1-5011-3613-9
ISBN 978-1-5011-3611-5 (hardcover)
ISBN 978-1-5011-3614-6 (ebook)

Thank you to my daughters, Sea and Ted,
who constantly inspire me to try and be the best I can be.

....

Thank you to my cowriter, Teresa DiFalco, who challenged
me in myriad ways and helped me celebrate my future.

....

Thank you to Chief,
who made me see possibility out of impossibility.

Kelly

Illusion is the first of all pleasures.
—Voltaire

JUNE

1
. . . .

Billy Sitwell's apartment
167 Ludlow, Lower East Side
Tuesday, June 3
Girls' night

L u, we're listening," Sarah said. "Go."

"Okay, first question: underwear. Are you boy shorts, G-string, or commando?"

We were sitting on the floor of Billy's apartment, legs crossed Indian style like some nursery school powwow. There were sticky spots on the floor that we were all—except for Billy, because they were her spots—trying to subtly avoid, and the apartment was unbearably hot. Lotta had already raised an eyebrow at me about it more than once.

"Other," Billy said.

I was making us take a sex quiz for a fluff piece I was writing for *Cosmo*. "'Other' isn't an option," I replied.

Long-limbed Lotta with her deep-blue Nordic eyes and smoky accent gave a dramatic sigh. "How many questions are there? And are we ordering anything? I'm starved."

Billy was already on top of it, making a charcuterie plate from the oddball things in her refrigerator and the crackers and crudités we'd brought.

"There's just a few," I said to Lotta, who nodded but wasn't listening because she was texting, or on Snapchat, or commenting on her Instagram feed. "It's nothing big."

Life doesn't unfold: it pops open, the way a man rips off lingerie. That's a thing my mother, Cheri, likes to say, and she's right. Twenty-four years ago I was seventeen, sitting in first class on a flight from Chicago to JFK. I was drinking champagne because Cheri said we deserved it. I was leaving my small Midwestern town to be a model. I had an agent, I had a contract, and I was sitting across the aisle from Titus Brockton, one of the most famous artists in the world. Picasso-like famous. I didn't know who he was but Cheri did. He was dipping a tiny spoon into a small tin of caviar. I noticed this right off because it was the first time I'd seen anyone eat caviar. It was also the first time I'd been on a plane. The dream was right there in front of me. Love, adventure, career—I was ready for all of it.

Fast-forward to tonight at the start of a restless New York summer. I'll be forty-two next month and I didn't see this coming. I'm sitting in the same apartment with the same friends, having a version of the same conversation we've been having for twenty years. The rearview mirror looks more like a halfhearted quickie than the sultry, slow striptease I'd imagined.

The four of us get together every Tuesday—we've done it for years since we all found each other here, when we were young and eager and fresh. We're not so fresh anymore. We share two divorces and two failed careers, among other things. We're in staggered states of disarray.

Billy's unemployed and broke. Her mortgage check just bounced, again. She's trying to finish and sell the cocktail-entertainment book she quit her job for, which hasn't seen one full draft that I know of, and she's running an "adventure supper club" out of her apartment for extra cash. Strangers pay to come to her home and get drunk while she feeds them kinky foods they can tell their friends about—

things like fermented eel bisque and sheep's bladder *au vin*. She's a high-end foodie hooker.

Lotta's recreational drug use is turning into a full-time job. She's forty-five and still closing down Marquee. Every night. It's become more than she can manage, and we're not sure what to do about it. It's not a good long-term plan.

Sarah's filthy rich with an adoring fiancé and six frozen embryos, so she *seems* the most solid, but now she wants to be a "socialite." We don't quite get it. She's going to galas and funding philanthropies, and she's assembled a "team" whose sole job, it seems, is to keep her on Page Six. She's also now completely obsessed with her hair.

Me? I'm a cliché. I married young, I had so much time. I thought I'd have two kids, a doting husband, and some sort of intellectually fulfilling career by now. Instead I have a set of outdated head shots, a pile of underwhelming clips, and my marriage is falling apart. Not in the Burton-Taylor way, either, with passion and smashed plates, but quietly, without fanfare. *Like it never even happened.* We've fallen out of love or lust or something or everything, I'm not even sure. It's the oldest story in the book.

Tonight, though, it's the girls. We're all here. We're all good.

We have a system with our Tuesdays. The first one is fitness. We take a class until we get bored or exhausted by it, then move on to something else. We switched from Bikram yoga to SoulCycle last month because Lotta could not stand the heat. Before that, we did Barry's Bootcamp, climbing subway stairs and jumping park benches. We got in fantastic shape but it nearly killed us. Sarah was sidelined with an ankle sprain for eight weeks.

Second Tuesdays are cocktails. Locations vary, but Rose Bar and the Standard are our go-tos. Third Tuesdays are always a proper dinner out, where we are seated at a table and handed menus. Until three months ago, Billy was the restaurant critic for *Gastro Eat* magazine, and she can get us in anywhere on no notice, which is no small feat in New York. Then on the fourth Tuesday we stay in, rotating apartments. If there are five Tuesdays in a month, we skip the fifth, and that's how it works.

Tonight is first Tuesday. We've switched it around, which sometimes happens, so they can help me with my piece. So instead of a park run, we're at Bill's and on edge. It's eighty-five degrees outside and she doesn't believe in air-conditioning. Billy is always saving the environment in small and insignificant ways, and one of those is refusing to *artificially cool* her *air*. That's how she puts it.

"It makes no sense," Lotta reminds her each time we're here when it's hot. "You won't *artificially cool* your *air* in June, but in December you artificially heat it. What's the difference?"

If we were a TV show, all of it would look great. Cocktails, witty lines, a minor drama to resolve, and then we'd shop. We could do this forever on television.

Sarah pecked at her phone, while Billy judged the wines we'd brought. Lotta cracked a window open and fanned herself with one of the books stacked up on Billy's chair.

"Sarah," Billy said, "are you crazy? This is a two-hundred-dollar Bordeaux. I'm not opening it." Sarah shrugged.

Though it was Bill's night to host, I'd taken charge and there was a growing impatience in the room. After my modeling career, I got a journalism degree and put it to work writing hard-hitting articles for magazines with airbrushed celebrities on the cover—things like "Hair *Down There* Is Back!" and "Kiss Like a Kardashian!" It's not the stuff of dreams. But Noel White had just offered me a column in his magazine, *SNOB*. It's edgy and smart, and they don't do quizzes. He gave it to me because of Titus, I knew, and I was writing on spec, so he had nothing to lose. It wasn't the most promising start, but I was fine with that.

"You guys, *focus*. Come on, it's important," I said.

"It's a sex quiz," Sarah said.

"No. It's not. It's the *experience* of four friends discussing how they think about and relate to men and sexuality through the construct of an exercise that happens to be a staple of every popular contemporary women's magazine. It's a statement."

I caught Sarah rolling her eyes. She should have been. The piece was titled "Are You Hot?"

"Humor me," I said.

"We are, Lu. Chill." This from the girl who is steadfastly anti-chill.

My modeling career was short-lived. Partly because the business throws you curves. I was far from aging out, but I also wasn't new anymore. New is everything. One day I walked into the office to meet my agent and there was a girl at the booking table I didn't recognize. She was wearing my sweater. The same baby-pink Azzedine Alaïa teddy bear sweater that Azzedine had given to me. The one you can't get anywhere else, but in Paris, from his store. From *him*. It was like seeing lingerie that isn't yours on the shelf your boyfriend lets you use in his apartment. Men are careless.

But mostly, it was cut short because of Titus. When we started dating, he took a strong stance on my "career," which is how he referred to it. With quotation marks in his voice. Every man in New York wants a model, but they're not all so crazy about being married to one. So instead of the new Chanel ad, I got a husband, a degree in journalism, and a Master of Fucking Arts (as Billy calls it) from NYU.

Somewhere in all of that, though, I misplaced an entire decade. If I were arrested tomorrow for committing aggravated assault on my thirties, I wouldn't have an alibi. *Okay, yes, Officer. I did it.* None of us would.

"What's the question again?" Billy said. She was up now, standing alone in her cramped kitchen, decanting the reds.

I repeated it. "Boy shorts, G-string, or nothing?"

Billy did a sommelier's pour into four glasses, starting us off with a "crisp" pinot gris. She's a wine snob, though she prefers *aficionado*. She makes a distinction between pinot gris and pinot grigio, she won't let us call American bubblies "champagne," and she tastes hints of pine and charred beet greens in what seem to me the blandest of reds. My point is that Billy is a person who won't drink a pinot gris that isn't "crisp," and there better be some scent of pear.

"Nothing," Sarah said. I gave her a wary look.

"What?" she said. "You're giving me bad options. So, nothing."

If I were to put these women on canvas, like Titus does, I'd start with background.

Billy, like me, is from a small town. She's from my small town, actually: we've known each other since fourth grade. I graduated early to move here and she followed me out the next year. We're like sisters. I know that phrase is overused and everyone says it. I use it purposely, though, knowing that while it sounds trite, we just are. Exactly like sisters. Billy modeled, too, briefly, but mostly for catalogues. Her auburn hair and brown eyes are a great look, but at five-eight, she was too short for the runway. Her passion, though, has always been food. She served a foie gras *torchon* at her twelfth birthday party. Seriously. It took her five days to prepare, and it made two of the girls cry.

Sarah is a New York private school product. Her mother divorced early, then often, and they got by on a string of Mrs. Porter's husbands, and then afterward, their settlements. She has four stepfathers, whom she refers to by number. As in, *I had dinner with Three last night.* Or, *Two just got engaged, again.* Sarah has an uncanny knack, like her mother, for pulling money and suitable men out of the air. This socialite thing, though. It's one of the most cutthroat vocations in New York and she's jumping into it now? At forty? Is she crazy? We aren't sure.

Lotta is Swedish, literally. As in, she hasn't bothered to get her citizenship yet, even though she's lived here for twenty years. She's outrageously beautiful—bone-white hair that most girls in this city would kill for and Julie Christie's pouty lips. She loves men and she loves sex. She should. She has a man's attention span, and a man's insatiable appetite for stimulus. She's an art dealer, and she's good, but she loses focus and it gets her in trouble. If she put half the amount of energy into her career as she does into getting stoned by four o'clock, she'd be on *New York* magazine's list of power brokers every year.

"Billy. Come on. Boy shorts, G-string, or nothing?" I prodded.

"I'm with Sarah," she said. "I don't like the choices. What if I just like white cotton?"

"It's not a thesis dissertation," I said. "It's a quiz. Pretend you're killing time in a waiting room. Just pick an answer."

"Boy shorts."

Lotta gave me another dramatic sigh. I put her down for G-string. I took "nothing."

So that's background. As for palette, we're all over the place. Billy's the earthy one, she's a Hopper. I'm a Rothko. (Titus would cringe to hear me say that, he hated Rothko, but I am.) Lotta, wearing a skintight black dress tonight over her six-foot-long body even though it was just us, the girls, is definitely a Klimt. Sarah is a Modigliani. She was wearing, right then, feather slippers.

Sarah had a quick divorce in her twenties, but is now engaged to Brian Banks (yes, *Banks*) of Goldman Sachs. He's conventionally handsome, conventionally dressed, and has conventional money, a lot of it. He helped underwrite the Twitter IPO. He can afford to fund her new hobby.

Billy, single, dumped her last serious boyfriend at the same time she dumped her job. He was a city tour guide who mumbled. No great loss. She most recently dated Marcus, a musician she found on PlentyofFish who had four roommates in Queens. He was good in bed but not for much else, and, as Billy pointed out, it wasn't even his bed. When he started to leave things at her apartment—first a toothbrush, then his dog—she ended it quick. "I'm not a sugar mama," she told us. She has an online dating habit she can't seem to break. She updates her profiles compulsively, the way some people bite their nails. It turns up odds and ends. Mostly ends.

Lotta's divorced, too, from David—a music producer who now goes by Danielle. They never lived together but they were married for five years. *He* helped her get her apartment, and now *she* still steps in when Lotta slips on the rent. He was nice, we all liked him. He's the only stability, I think, she's ever had besides us.

Me? I have Titus. We've been married for eighteen years. And it's complicated.

"For his birthday, what do you give him: a watch, skydiving lessons, nude selfie?"

"See?" Billy said. "These answers are limiting. Because it depends on how long you've been together, and then the age spread, what he does for a living, and why you're even bothering with him at all. If he's just a sex fix, then the selfie. If he's older, then you get skydiving lessons to make him feel young, and a watch? He should already have a watch. The watch is too personal. Who am I to buy a man a watch?"

"I don't even get it," Lotta said. She was still working her phone, flipping from Tinder to Snapchat to Tinder. She obviously had later plans.

"Well, if I'm just screwing him," Billy continued, "if I'm just with him because I'm lonely and he doesn't knock me out but I'm fine with the sleepovers, then I'll give him selfies. You have to be really into someone to jump out of a plane."

Sarah cut in. "But nude selfies should be just in the beginning, or maybe the middle if you think you're losing him. It's tricky because you have to send them before someone else does, I think. Once someone else starts sexting him, you're screwed. You have to preempt with selfies. There's a strategy."

See? This is what I wanted. Smart *are you hot?* repartee.

Billy refilled my glass. I stopped her halfway. The crisp pinot gris with its notes of pear was a little too sweet. It was making me dizzy.

"Luce," she said. "You have to play, too."

"Okay, I am. Let's keep going. You're talking to someone you're interested in. Do you twirl your hair, lick your lips, or look away?"

"Look away."

"Twirl."

"Lick my lips."

That was Sarah, Billy, and Lotta in that order. I was "twirl." Which celebrity did we most want to be like out of Jennifer Aniston, Taylor Swift, and J-Lo? Aniston. Aniston. Aniston. Even Lotta.

"Okay. Here's a good one. What kind of girl are you? Lotta? Are you naughty and nice, dirty and perverted, or flirty?"

Lotta laughed; she almost spit out her wine.

"Dirty pervert, all the way."

"I think I'm flirty," Sarah said. "I'm definitely not naughty."

"Hmm," Billy said. "I'll take dirty pervert, too."

In bed, Lotta talks sexy, Sarah is playful, and Billy takes control. If we were jeans, Lotta would be skinny, Billy would be cutoffs, and I, too, would be skinny. Sarah took "boyfriend."

We were on to the reds now, and the room was not quite as hot. I cleared my throat, took a drink of my wine.

"Okay, last one," I announced, through a mouthful of bread. "Is love more important? Or sex?"

Lotta was up and helping herself to Billy's liquor cabinet. A methodical *clink, clink, clink* of ice and a generous pour of Grey Goose. "If you love sex, and then you find great sex, bingo, you have both," she said.

Sarah said, of course, love.

Billy smirked. "I mean . . . really? I think love would be nice if he has his shit together. Nothing against sex. Sex always comes first, though, so it's just a nice bonus to get love. Luce?"

Lotta had downed the first drink fast and was refilling her glass.

"I don't know," I said. "They're both tricky."

"Don't ever make us do one of these again," Sarah said.

A man and a woman were shouting on the street. "No, fuck *you*!" the man yelled. We got up to watch out Billy's window. A few seconds of angry-looking gestures and then the woman, head down, walked quickly across the street. He didn't follow.

Sarah turned away. "What was that about, do you think? Love or sex?"

"That was definitely love," Billy said. "Luce, pass me the wine."

2
· · · · · · · · · ·

Brockton town house
802 Greenwich Street, West Village
Wednesday, June 4

Once a month, on the first Wednesday (today), Titus hosts a little drinking binge in his studio. He considers it a reward for whoever's modeling for him and anyone else he might like to see. Thirty years ago (before me), they were loud, raucous things—Liz Smith used to report who was there. Actors, rock stars, artists. When we were first married, I used to go. I'd listen to his stories, breathe the linseed oil, and watch him rule his kingdom. They've become more sedate over the years, and now I don't go, though that's not why. I just . . . don't.

The rotating collection of young girls, the art models who "inspire" his work—every one of whom would love to take my place, by the way—will be there. A handful of artists and critics will stop by, too, and a few random collectors will come to gawk. It's no small gesture to be let into the artist's studio. Especially this one.

He'll be preoccupied with it this morning when he comes down. *Lulu,* he'll say. *Where is my Tati, why isn't she here?* Tatiana is his assistant. Lulu. Tati. We sound like cigar girls at a Vegas poker game.

Titus is sixty-six. When I first met him on that flight from Chicago, he was forty-two to my seventeen. That sounds a bit *Lolita,* but I looked older than seventeen. I was tall and long-limbed, with a model's lean frame. Thick glossy hair, high cheekbones, and wide-set eyes—I had the *look*. Men didn't just glance at me anymore, they stared. On the outside, I was a woman, and I was on contract with Model, one of the hottest agencies in the world. I didn't feel seventeen. But I was.

Sometimes I wonder if my mother ever resents not having the aisle seat that day. I wonder if she thinks the whim of a computer-generated assignment cost her a good fling. If I hadn't been in the way, the two of them might have had a nice time. It was Cheri, after all, who knew right away who he was. They might have been a better match, and not just because of their age. Cheri is the kind of woman who would not let a man like Titus get bored.

He invited us to join him for dinner that night and sent a car to the St. Regis to pick us up. He had a regular table at Cipriani, and the owner and waitstaff all fussed over us. No menus; different courses just appeared. Titus ordered by subtle gestures and nods. He was a practiced conversationalist, curious and solicitous. He charmed Cheri right off the edge of her seat. I wasn't sure what to think. It was my first night in New York.

The next morning he sent a gift to our hotel, to me. A Cartier diamond necklace shaped like a heart. It was outrageous. I'd known him for twenty-four hours. But that's the kind of thing Titus does.

The card read:

Thank you, sweet Lucy . . . for the awakening. You have a passion-filled journey ahead of you. Embrace it.

Cheri was thrilled. She collects people. And here we were, our first night in New York, and look what we'd found. If she couldn't interest him herself, she was happy to sacrifice me. But he didn't call. It was five years before I saw him again.

Now, for better or worse, we are here, sharing a stunning four-story town house in the West Village. I suppose in a way it's a very evolved sort of arrangement. Some women might love it, but I feel like I'm at the precarious end of a seesaw, on the verge of a hard, fast fall if he gets off. Women have come and gone over the years, I'm sure. I don't like to kid myself. He was a scoundrel with his first wife. Not even her closest friends were off-limits.

Titus is the kind of man who puts much of his self-worth into women. Into *chasing kitty,* as Sarah tactfully puts it. But if *kitty* hadn't been there all the time offering itself up—his models, the gallery girls, the wives of friends—then there would be no point to any of it for him. I think he'd die. Models make art out of their bodies to achieve certain ends. Titus paints to achieve his. He's the kind of man whose id overrides whatever else the ego and superego might, in an ordinary man, grapple with.

I sound wise now, but I was absurdly naive when I met him. He was a *man,* and not just any man. Some men have the ability to make you think you're what God had in mind when he took that first stab with Eve. Titus is one of them. He *knows* women. He should— they're his life's work.

I should mention that he's handsome. Tall and solid, even now, in his mid-sixties, with thick, slightly peppered hair and a confident, rugged look. He has the kind of face that makes strangers pause and try to place him. They can tell he's someone, even if they're not exactly sure who.

"Lulu," he said now. He was making his way down the stairs because we have breakfast together at nine every morning. Just the two of us, but proper, at the long table in the dining room. Titus needs structure when he's working; this is part of it. Breakfast, yet we don't share a bed. It's not a conventional sort of structure, but he's not exactly conventional.

"Where is Tati?"

Jesus, I thought. *Who cares?*

I handed him his coffee—espresso with cream, one cube of sugar. If we didn't have this, I might not see him for weeks. I'm not kidding.

"She's coming, Ti. Don't worry."

Tatiana is Portuguese and stunning. She hasn't aged one minute since I met her. It's annoying. We've developed a mutually understood awkwardness over the years—I'm awkward around her and she understands it. She exists to serve my husband. *Their* relationship is solid. She's never going anywhere, and she'll be gorgeous until she's dead.

He was in a mood that morning. I could tell by how he walked to the table. Slow and deliberate, like a pout. As if he'd suffered a great indignity. To be fair, he had a show in four months and it would be his first one in four years. It was weighing on him. I knew this. Also, to be fair, he's a Gemini and I'm a Cancer. Cheri gave me a reading from her psychic for my wedding, which was enlightening, if perhaps a bit late. Gemini, it turns out, is my worst possible love match.

He skimmed the papers—we still subscribe, the old-fashioned way—while I set out our meal. Picasso had a Bloody Mary with toast each morning before he worked. Titus is much less austere. Everything has to be sensual. The food on his plate must be evocative, whether he consumes it or not. He is particularly fond of the egg, as both *object* and *sustenance* (his words.) So I've mastered the skill of preparing them. Shirred, coddled, soft-boiled—hen, duck, and goose. I can do a proper French omelet with my eyes closed.

In our first years, I brought breakfast to him in bed on an antique silver tray. I spooned caviar atop quail eggs and fed him fresh berries with champagne. In the first years, everything was foreplay. He couldn't get enough of me. I used to wake up with a red peony tucked behind my ear, and the warmth of his gaze. Now I wake alone. Titus sleeps one floor up, in a guest room or, more often, lately, in his studio one floor above that.

"She knows there are instructions, I wish she'd come early. She knows this."

"She'll be here," I assured him. "It's still early. I'm sure she's on her way."

He was sullen over his food, poking the eggs with his fork. I don't really mind his moods. He's more Rockwell than Pollock. Not that I want him to brood, but he's an artist. They have moods. And it's better to have them quietly than to cut off an ear.

"Zeirdra is here today, and there's only a small group this afternoon but I want it to be nice. Luc is coming, for instance." Zeirdra poses for him, she's new. Luc Sante is a critic, one of the few he actually likes.

Titus's studio is on the top floor, three up from where we were sitting now. He renovated it himself when he bought the house, long before me. It's a large open space with wide-plank, paint-spattered floors. A wall of windows is dressed with long velvet curtains and custom rods he designed himself, along with the lighting. There's a vintage oak bar and a long sofa by Jean-Marie Massaud that Jean-Marie sent, as a gift. It's beautiful. And of course there's the back staircase and private entrance.

"I need Tati. I need to instruct her. She needs to go to the markets. She can't be doing this today at one in the afternoon."

"She knows," I said. "She'll be here any minute, I'm sure. I can tell her whatever you need."

He was repeating himself, agitated. Like a bank robber going over and over the plan.

He wasn't upset with Tatiana. He wouldn't scold her—there was nothing to say. She's been with him longer than I have and she's never let him down. But Titus can't manage anxiety when he's working. He rattles and his nerves shake, like a dog unused to a crate.

"Make a list for me, then."

He absentmindedly put a hand on my arm.

"And if she's not going to come—"

"She's going to come."

"—if she doesn't get here, then I will want you to pick up certain things. I can't have this at nine in the morning on the day I'm having guests."

I picked up a pen and notebook from the table.

"She will be here and it will be fine," I tried to assure him. Because she *would* be here and it *would* be fine.

Longed for him. Got him. Shit. I saw this, once, on a T-shirt. That's not what I felt, though, in the beginning. It's not how I ever thought I'd feel. He seduced me, he loved me, we married. We lived happily ever after, for quite a while. He was romantic. He had extravagant gifts delivered to me on the afternoons of our dates, even after we were married. He dressed me up the way he wanted me to look, and he had impeccable taste. He told me how to wear my hair. He was the Pygmalion to my Galatea and he made me think I made the sun rise. Before we had sex the first time he said, "Lucy, I need you to know how much I love you." I knew.

We've been married for eighteen years now, and there is none of that anymore. James, my hairdresser, says that attraction and repulsion are the same. In other words, what I'm bothered by now is what I was madly in love with then, it's just part of the deal. Okay, James. Touché.

"I need a good collection of nuts, first of all. And I'm not referring to the guests," he said, and winked.

He's flirtatious from habit. Titus Brockton thrives on charm. But we have not shared a bed in three years. We haven't had real intimacy in almost one, and I'm not sure that was even enough to count. He will work, sometimes, all night, and some nights I hear him leave the house. For over a year now, he's hidden behind the looming threat of the show. Of producing new work. But it's up to me, my mother thinks, to keep him here. *Men get bored, Lucy,* she tells me. *There's no way around it.*

"I need to have a preserve: a quince, fig, maybe something with spice. Then a nice bread from Bouley—gluten-free, and the Dean and Deluca prosciutto sliced very, *very* thin."

He touched his thumb and forefinger together to show me.

"And then stop at Cheese Bar and bring back whatever they've showcased today."

He took two careful bites of food and chewed them thoughtfully.

"For wine, you can pull the house white from the cellar and a Chablis, which we're out of. You'll have to get that."

He paused for a moment, drummed his fingers on the arm of his chair. There was a plate of fruit and he took a peach and bit into it with confidence. I'm tentative about fruit. I take a small bite to test for sweetness and texture before I commit. Titus doesn't take a tentative bite of anything.

"Write down Santa Margherita for white."

I wrote down Santa Margherita, for white, which Tatiana would pick up when she got here, along with the rest.

"I think we need to call her."

"We don't need to call. She'll be here in minutes." As would Zeirdra.

When Titus is working it feels like a harem with all of the women who come and go.

I handed him the list and he read through what I'd written.

" . . . add a fruit," he said. "A guava or mango, unless there's something seasonal that looks fresh." He was composing a still life in his head, adding color.

As we finished our meal—shirred eggs, poached salmon, and grilled triangles of bread—he performed his warm-up. He wanted to talk about *A Rake's Progress*, which was on loan at the Met. He wanted to talk about how the life of an artist informs his art. The routines, the financial conditions, the marriages and children. The affairs and the madness. He wanted to talk about the Dadaists and how they corrupted realism. It would put him in the right mood for a day in the studio. Also, he's got press coming up and he's been out of practice. He needed to have a good store of solid things on hand to say.

Because he's an artist, Titus says things like "Reality is a false image." And "Art is a half-truth." And "Lucy, you have to *feel* your life; you can't just simply live it." He uses the semicolon when he speaks. Orally, I mean. You can hear it.

Tatiana came in without fanfare at nine thirty, squeezed into a DVF wrap dress that made her look like Salma Hayek. I mean, come on. Does any woman need this paraded in front of her husband every day?

We lingered at the table until ten, when she appeared with a shot glass and set it in front of him. Deer blood. Chilled, served neat. He drinks a glass every morning. Norman Mailer started him on it. Virility, Mailer said. He claimed to have five orgasms a day. What did he need with five orgasms? There are things these men do just for the biographers, I think.

"Tati, Lulu has a shopping list for you, for this afternoon. You'll serve *croques-madames* at four. I'll mix up the martinis for those."

Vodka and a French ham and cheese. I secretly hoped the béchamel dimpled every one of those girls' thighs.

3
· · · · · · · · ·

I moved into Titus's house very properly, on the day we were married. He actually carried me over the threshold. It was his nod to propriety. We were sleeping together, I was spending my time there anyway, but I didn't officially move in until we were blessed by an official in front of three hundred people at the Frick.

He sent a group over the next week to clean out my apartment and pack my clothes. We'd already decided what would come with me, what would go to Cheri, and that anything left, if she wanted it, was Billy's.

He bought the town house with his first wife, Karina. He married her at thirty-two. I can't imagine the sort of hell she lived through. Titus was just hitting his stride then. He'd had shows at MoMA and the Whitney. He'd been profiled in *Artforum* and *ARTnews*. And he was a fixture on the Sunday society page of the *Times*. I don't think he ever imagined he'd find that sort of success when he came to New York, but when it happened he took to it quick.

Karina's father was a wealthy art broker. They met and married in three months. At the time, every woman in the city was ready and willing for Titus Brockton, and he was ready for them. There were rumors, there were adoring young girls always around. Karina tired of it quickly. Their divorce became official on their fifth anniversary and she married her lawyer a week after that. They live in Los Angeles now, with three kids, and she has what I imagine is a very full life. Soccer games, carpool schedules, Sunday barbecues. Her days, I think, have a shape to them that I can't seem to find for mine.

I didn't picture anything like that for myself, at first. We were enjoying the moment, and we had the rest of our lives ahead of us. Titus was forty-eight, but I didn't think of that. I didn't think about what we might look like in eighteen years when he was sixty-six, and I wasn't.

I stopped modeling before we got married, but I was still well known and he liked that. The artist and his glamorous model bride. We traveled and went to openings and galas. He talked to me about his work. I inspired him.

He was consumed with me. He wanted me with him all the time. Our intimacy was off the charts. There was no reason to think it would end. Why would it? We had money, we had time, we had each other. He'd done his years of fooling around. He was ready for me, he said.

We used to drive to the beach sometimes, on a whim, rent the tackiest motel we could find and behave like giddy tourists, walking the boardwalk, playing the carnival games. We were madly in love. We were happy.

It was like this for at least the first five years we were married. Which isn't bad, really. Many New York marriages don't even make it to five years. It tapered off, a bit, but so slowly that I didn't see it happening. I went back to school and finished my degree. I started working again, writing freelance for magazines. I started spending more time with friends. All distractions from him, from us. That's how it starts.

And then his work wasn't good. There are ups and downs in any career, but it's a unique kind of down for an artist when he can't paint, or write, or make music, or create. Titus didn't need to prove himself anymore, but he was losing the thing that had defined him. He didn't have a plan B. We traveled less. We went out less. In the early years we'd talked about children, but that stopped.

And then after his last show four years ago fell flat, he withdrew. He was having bouts of insomnia, so he began to sleep in a separate room some nights, the one above ours on the third floor. He didn't want it to affect me, he said. And I didn't protest. You don't see what is happening until it's done.

He gradually moved most of his clothes into his new space. He eventually went to sleep there every night. He wasn't trying to make a statement—he was trying to slip out unnoticed.

We drifted apart in the way a house shifts over the years, in such small measure that you don't see it until the foundation is cracked. I don't know if he still loves me. I don't know what sort of life I want with him now. I know I want more than what we've settled into. I want more than a 9 a.m. breakfast slot.

I'm close to becoming a woman who goes to lunch and fills the rest of the time with upkeep. I've seen women fall into this and not find their way out. I want that to terrify me. The thing that scares me is, it doesn't.

4

· · · · · · · · ·

Brockton town house
Wednesday, June 4

uuuucy!" Billy called out in her best Ricky Ricardo. She'd warned me earlier in the morning that she was coming, and bringing work.

"Good morning, sweets." She dropped an insulated backpack on my kitchen counter and started to unpack. She was wearing cutoffs and cowboy boots and her hair was pulled back in a messy braid. You couldn't airbrush more chiseled legs, the product of her fierce commitment to gyms. She power-walks the two miles here from the East Village. Her exercise style is like a New Jersey diner: anything goes, twenty-four/seven, every day.

"I need you to drink with me."

She set out three bottles of liquor and a shaker.

Billy and I met in Mrs. Critchlow's class. She was smart and aloof, with a mass of wild red hair. I was gawky and shy. We hit it off right away. We spent our days after school making elaborate antipasto plates to snack on while we skimmed through stacks of her mother's *Cosmopolitan*s to learn about boys.

In sixth grade, we snuck into *Heartburn* at the mall and after that all Billy wanted was to live in New York and write cookbooks. I wanted to be Nora Ephron. We haven't quite made it yet.

"Right now?" I said.

"Yep. I have a date tonight. And I have a cocktail piece due Friday. I answered your little sex questions, you can do a few shots."

Titus had the music up loud in his studio. We could hear it through three floors. Billy raised one of her perfectly groomed eyebrows in the way that always makes me laugh.

"God, what *is* that? And can't you do something about it? Can't you soundproof the room? It's like you have a bad renter."

"It" was Bartók's *Hungarian Sketches*. Not exactly Wednesday morning pick-me-up stuff, I agreed.

"Can he seriously paint with that shit blaring? I bet it's just a cover and he's on Pornhub. Or getting stoned. When was the last time you saw something he actually did?"

Pot, maybe. Pornhub, no. Titus is too old-school. Whatever he watched would be French anyway, so therefore art. Plus, who needs porn when you have twenty-year-old art students undressing and posing for you all day any way you like?

"Stop. His show is coming up, it's a lot of pressure. He might be drunk today by three, but he's working."

For some artists, the life overshadows the work. Like Hemingway. Everyone knows about the bulls and the women and all the cats. But has anyone actually read *The Torrents of Spring*? I think Titus worries about this. He worries he will be defined the way Billy sees him this morning, by his life and not his work. An annoying roommate who plays Bartók full blast and leaves his dishes in the sink. There's a lot riding on his show.

"If you say so," Billy said with a dismissive wave. "Anyway, I'm writing 'Nine Knockout Autumn Cocktails' for *Bon Appétit*. So I need your help."

"Bill, I'm not drinking before noon. And I don't have a cocktail palate. Especially not autumn."

"You're not drinking before noon, you're *tasting* before noon. This is work, Luce. And I can put these in my book."

By now my counter was crowded with bottles, containers of syrups and garnish, her cocktail gear, and small plastic bags of herbs. She shook a combination of all of them up and poured it into a Christofle tumbler she pulled from my cabinet. This was why we were doing it here. She likes my glassware. You spend money on different things when you're married. The tumblers were two hundred dollars apiece.

"These are all grain-to-glass artisan spirits. So this will be a very organic drunk."

"I don't know that it matters," I said. The dull orange tone of the drink did not look appealing.

"Okay, so I have to tell you this. Marcus, the musician. Remember that whole thing?" She handed me the glass. Billy could bartend at any club in the city with one arm behind her back. And it's not even her strong suit.

"Yes, I remember Marcus. Good in bed, too many roommates."

"Yeah. Well, okay. So this is kind of weird—"

"Oh my God!" I took a swallow from my glass and gagged. I tried not to spit it out. "What *is* this?" It tasted like poison.

"Honey, that is a three-hundred-dollar mescal, is what that is."

I gulped down a glass of water.

"Isn't mescal a hallucinogen?" I said. It was awful.

Billy grabbed my glass, took a sip of it and considered.

"I think you're being rash. This is an *artisanal mescal*, and it is not to be confused with *mescaline*, the hallucinogenic drug. Two totally different things." She took another sip and rolled it around on her tongue.

"It's got a nice smoky flavor that maybe—okay, yes—could be tamed a bit. Oranges, I think. It needs citrus, you might be right."

She started rooting around in my kitchen.

"The thing is," she said, "it's a badge of honor to drink mescal. And very avant-garde to serve it. It's like doing one of those warrior mud runs. It's not refined or elegant and it's not supposed to be. It's supposed to make you feel better just for doing it. There's satisfaction in that sometimes, Lu."

She rinsed out both of our glasses and shook up another drink. Same mescal, loaded with orange this time, ice, Billy's special syrup, and a splash of tonic.

"Some things aren't meant to be liked. Or they're meant to be liked *because* they're not likable. Like those wrinkly dogs that cost thousands of dollars."

"Shar-peis, and no one that I know of has choked on one."

"Whatever. I feel like this is going to be an autumn where people need to drink, and this one is good. It's the crack cocaine of tequila. Rough and gritty and . . . yep, I think I nailed it."

She handed me the new drink and jotted down her notes.

"Try it again."

I took a much smaller sip this time. "Okay. This one is better."

"Would you serve it upstairs?" She gestured at the ceiling toward where *Hungarian Sketches* was still coming through.

"Sure. Yes, I would. Finish your story . . . Marcus."

"Right, Marcus. So his friend, or someone he introduced me to as his friend, I guess asked him for my number. Which seems not very cool, but oh, well. His name is George. He called me and, weird . . . he's a matchmaker. He has his own company. They match people up old-school, face-to-face. I'm not sure if he wants me as a client or a date, but we're taking a trapeze class tonight."

"That sounds like a date."

She was mixing the second drink. I was starting to warm up to the revamped mescal.

"Why didn't you say something last night?"

"He just called this morning."

"Billy. Don't go out with him on the same day!"

"Oh, please. You're not out here, Lu. It's a free-for-all. You go out with them on the same day. What's the difference?"

I examined the new glass she handed me, skeptically.

"Relax. This one's easy. It's called *baijiu*, it's the new sake. It's a little boring alone, but imagine it matched with a grilled sea bass or sashimi. It's the Asian grappa."

This one was much better. I held out my glass for more and she tipped the shaker into it.

"What am I tasting?"

"Basically a very hard white wine, that's the ick part. But I added blackberry syrup and Sprite to tone it down and bring out the essence. It's like a primer liquor. It plays up any secondary you want to add, especially fruit."

Billy's brilliant at what she does, but she's writing drink reviews for two hundred dollars a pop, it's ridiculous. She goes out with unsuitable men, ones like the mescal without the orange. She should have her own spot on the Food Network and be married to a nice environmental engineer who likes to hike.

"You should be dating a nice environmental engineer who likes to hike," I said.

"Yeah. Everyone should. Listen, you don't get what it's like out here. I'm competing with twenty-two-year-old Lottas. *Lotta* is competing with twenty-two-year-old Lottas. And that's who the engineer is banging right now. A twenty-two-year-old Lotta. He could care less about the hike."

"There has to be *someone* who wants to hike," I said.

"Sure. They all do. Every single guy on Match either wants to hike or snowboard or kayak with a really nice girl. But, Luce, they don't. They want to screw someone young with huge tits. That's it. That's all they want. They're like rats with cheese in a maze. You can put twenty other foods in their way and they will only ever go after the cheese."

The door buzzed. Tatiana answered it and we peeked around the kitchen door to watch. It was Zeirdra. Like *Deirdra*, but with a Z. She's not Titus's typical model. She has fleshy knees and large, masculine hands. There is very little feminine about her, not even her breasts, which look neither real nor fake but like an unfortunate mistake everyone has been too polite to correct.

"Holy shit," Billy whispered.

"I told you," I said.

Titus has a type, but it is definitely not this. Still, she was marching upstairs to take her clothes off for him while I was swilling baijiu with Billy in the kitchen. Before noon.

"When do you meet with Noel?" Billy asked. Noel White and Billy run in the same foodie circles. Noel religiously reads her reviews, he reads anything she writes—he's a fan. He's a wine aficionado, too. I've never seen it, nor would I particularly appreciate it if I had, but his private collection is said to be worth more than Bacon's triptych of Lucien Freud.

"Friday," I said.

She handed me a bottle. "Take him the mescal. He will love it."

5

....

Uber car
Broadway, headed to Nomad Hotel
Wednesday, June 4

F ull disclosure: I'm having an affair.

It's not the conventional kind. I've never met him. I haven't seen a picture, or heard his voice. I haven't touched him, or felt the heat of his body. I don't even know his name.

I'm having an anonymous text fling with a complete stranger. It's the sort of thing, three months ago, I thought only a desperate person would do. The sort of thing lonely people go to Craigslist for. But he came to me.

Three months ago, a message lit up my phone late at night from a number I didn't know. Titus had gone out, I hadn't heard him come home yet. And I was almost asleep.

> 212-555-0134: Tell me what you want. Tell me all you've ever wanted. I want to know everything.

> Me: I'm sorry . . . who is this? Wrong number?

That's what I replied, and he texted me right back.

> 212-555-0134: No. Not a wrong number. I found you . . .

I tried to trace it. I tried to do a reverse search. I came up empty. I do not know who it is. There is no name, no face, no voice, just words on a screen.

Three months of this now, of these messages. I never know when they'll come. Some days there is nothing. Some days they take my breath away. Sometimes I reply, sometimes I don't. I don't quite know what to do with it. It's exciting, it's strange, it's a little frightening, too. It could all be some weird kind of joke.

At the moment, I was in a cab on my way to meet Sarah for brunch. She was screening publicists and she wanted my advice. But I wasn't thinking about publicists now, because as my mind drifted in the car, here he was again from out of nowhere.

> 212-555-0134: I'm thinking about you. Again. And again. There's no end . . .

I counted to ten, slowly, and then replied.

> Me: What are you thinking?

> 212-555-0134: I want you to wear the yellow dress for me. I want to see you in it.

This is the kind of thing he says to me all the time. I don't even own a yellow dress.

We were stuck on Broadway at Fourteenth Street. Cars were honking, buses were pushing through. There were sirens, whistles, shouts—the pulse of the city.

I texted him back.

> Me: I don't have a yellow dress . . .

> 212-555-0134: Then surprise me with one . . .

I know. It seems kind of creepy, like at the beginning of a good thriller before they find bodies in the Dumpster. But it's not. It doesn't feel creepy. I feel butterflies when the ping on my phone sounds to tell me there's a text. And I'm disappointed if it isn't Him.

I study strangers in crowds. I check behind me when I walk down the street. I've begun to dream about Him at night and when I wake up it still feels like he's there. I'm dreaming about an imaginary person. Someone I don't know, someone I can't see, and still the dreams are so vivid. I can feel him, I can touch him. I think he must be here with me. But I don't know him. And he's not.

He invades my consciousness and then my subconscious as if he's real and he's possessed me. He clouds my mind. Now, in the car, with Disclosure playing on the radio, "You and Me," I was staring at the back of the driver's head and I briefly forgot where I'd asked him to take me. Because I was thinking about Him.

> Me: I'm meeting a friend.

212-555-0134: I will be there.

> Me: How will I know?

212-555-0134: You will know.

It's a game. He teases me. He wouldn't be anywhere. If he were real he would call me. He would let me hear his voice, he'd tell me his name. He would ask to meet me, and it would probably ruin everything. It's imaginary. It's a harmless imaginary crush. That's what I tell myself, anyway.

Yesterday my mother gave me a book she wants me to read. *Mating in Captivity: Unlocking Erotic Intelligence*. It's by Esther Perel, a "relationship expert," according to Wikipedia. My mother thinks Esther Perel can save my marriage. She thinks this book will change my life. She gave me her copy, the one she's already read, with the pages dog-eared, passages highlighted, and notes to me in the margins. She's marked sentences like this: *Desire is fueled by the unknown*.

She is certain there's a message here that holds the keys to the universe. I'm sure there are many important life questions that the book fails to address, but I promised her I'd read it.

She doesn't know about Him. That I am thinking about someone else, and not my husband. It's embarrassing to say it, but I have feelings for him. Real feelings for this imaginary man who sends words through my phone. He could be anyone, a stranger who somehow came across my number. He could be mentally ill, he could be a predator. He could be any number of different versions of deviant. Or he could be something else.

The cab pulled over at Twenty-Eighth Street and my daydream popped like a bubble, just as the feeling in my stomach began to spread. Sarah was on the corner waiting.

6

....

I'm seeing my mother this afternoon," I called out from the kitchen. "She's making lunch, if you want to come."

I was at the stove. I'm not like Billy. Cooking is not rewarding to me in any way, except for breakfast. There's something about the foods for breakfast. I like watching the eggs curdle and take shape, broiling fat bacon strips to a perfect crisp. Omelets today. Some chopped asparagus spears and a handful of shredded Gruyère onto the left side of three barely firm eggs and then a careful flip to put the right half over the top. It's all in the timing and wrist. It takes practice.

I had a wild-mushroom Yukon Gold hash in the warmer, and Tatiana's English muffins, fresh off the stove. I took it out to him and sat down.

"Ti?"

He was distracted this morning. I had to repeat almost everything I said. And he had been staring at the same spot of the paper since I'd brought him coffee.

"Titus," I said, again, impatient.

He put the paper down next to his plate and ran a hand through his hair. "Yes. I'm sorry," he said. "Your mother. No, not today, I can't go. Another time."

I didn't expect him to actually come, but I did expect an excuse.

He picked out another section of paper and started to eat. It was clear I'd have to talk if I didn't want a silent meal, which I didn't. Tatiana was cleaning the studio. There were muffled footsteps overhead, a thump now and then, but outside of that it was uncomfortably quiet. The sounds of chewing.

"She's just back from her trip," I said. "She'd love to see you." The truth is, she hadn't invited him, but his indifference irritated me. Cheri hadn't called me over to rehash her trip—she had summoned me to discuss my marriage, like a teacher calling a struggling student in after class. I wasn't looking forward to it.

"We might see a movie after," I said. "I don't know what time I'll be home."

"That sounds nice. What are you seeing?"

"I'm not sure yet. The Clive Owen, I think. I don't remember the name."

"Ah, *Words and Pictures*. The writer and the artist. That's apt." He smiled. "We haven't been to a movie . . . When was the last time?"

It was last November. We went to see *The We and the I* at the Sunshine. It was the first snowfall of the year, and the city had that soft, hushed feel.

"We went to the one about the school bus almost a year ago."

"That's right. You didn't like it."

"I did, I just thought it wandered." It did. They took what was essentially one strong scene—a group of teenagers riding home on a bus in a Lord of the Flies–style situation—and stretched it into an entire film.

He put his hand on mine for a moment. "After the show, Lulu.

We'll have our life back. You'll see." Then he began making the signs of leaving. He pushed back his chair, set his napkin down, finished off the last of his juice.

"Tati is in the studio," he said. "I'm going out, then. Give Cheri my love."

"I'm leaving now, too," I said. "I have an appointment. Hair."

His expression changed. Minor disapproval. Titus has a thing about maintenance. He wants to have the most beautiful woman in the room, but he doesn't want to know she's had to work for it. It's a breach of etiquette for him, like discussing money with friends.

"I'll see you tonight, then," he said, and kissed the top of my head. Then he walked out the door.

There are too many mornings like these. Frustrating in so many small ways.

7

. . . .

J. Sebastian Salon
390 West Broadway, SoHo
Thursday, June 5

I spend a part of most Thursdays with another man, in a chic little salon next to the Ladurée bakery on West Broadway.

James makes me beautiful. He also gives me spiritual advice and therapy, and he's a fantastic flirt. I've been seeing him since I moved here, and apart from a brief indiscretion at Sally Hershberger four years ago, he's the only person in New York who's touched my hair.

"Bella!" he shouted out to greet me.

He gave me a quick kiss on each cheek and then settled me in a chair.

"What can we do to improve *this*?" he said, stroking my hair and smiling. "You make my job difficult."

See? He's good.

I met James when I worked at Model. He was twenty-one and ambitious and in charge of the rookies, the hopeful wide-eyed girls like me. It was his job to make us hot. He made a name for himself there and it paid off. Now he runs a small empire. He has this shop in SoHo, a second one uptown next to Bergdorf's, and a product line launching at Target in the fall.

Confession: we had an incident once, before Titus. Vodka in red Solo cups and clumsy groping on his futon. But it ended there, as it should have, and what we have now is a longtime friendship. I think. We're flirtatious friends. Friends, who maybe aren't? No, we are. But I'll admit that there are times when it's confusing.

For my wedding, James cut my hair into a beautiful layered bob, like Barbra Streisand's in *Funny Girl*. Our Vows writer for the *Times* spent an entire paragraph on it and on him. I wouldn't say it launched him, but that kind of exposure never hurts. And before he sent me off that day, in my long Calvin Klein slip dress through a room of white roses at the Frick, he got serious. He held my arms at my sides, looked me straight in the eye, and said, "Honey, if this doesn't work out, I will be here. And if it does work out, I'm here, too."

We might have fallen in love. Who knows? James is a Leo, he's a suitable match. He has a type, though. She's twenty.

"Why so quiet, beautiful?" he asked, combing his fingers through my wet hair.

"Am I? I don't know," I said and shrugged.

James is sexy in the way that attracts men and women alike. Men want to be him, and women want to take him home. With his Prada loafers and black blazer, sliding his Ray-Bans on like Hugh Jackman when he steps out onto the street, he leaves people breathless.

He smells of Kiehl's Musk, which he's worn since I've known him. His hands are strong on my head. His biceps twitch in the mirror. My time here feels like an erotic assault of the senses, all while we make small talk like it's not.

He brushed a piece of my hair behind one ear and studied me carefully. I always feel a sense of displacement between the way he speaks to me, very casual and friendly, and the way he touches me and watches me, which is very not. He studies me, because it's his job. To study and then make me a better version than the one who walked in.

It's an odd feeling when almost all of your eye contact with someone is through a mirror. It's not true eye contact, but contact through something else, a filter. Our eyes still connect. We still see, but there's no risk.

"I'm distracted, I guess. Silly things." It was true. I was thinking about my imaginary man, the one sending notes to my phone. I was thinking how nice James's hands felt massaging my head.

"Tell me one of them. One silly thing."

"Just one? Okay. Love. Love is silly."

He raised an eyebrow. He was rubbing my arms. He does this to relax me, but his touch still gives me goose bumps. Even after all these years.

He laughed a little. "Love? Who thinks about love on a Thursday?"

I smiled back at his face in the mirror. "I was just thinking about how much time we spend chasing it. Well, except Lotta. She thinks love is a hit of ecstasy at Tao and a good Tinder swipe. But maybe she's smart."

"Lotta's fine," he said. "She wants what she wants."

"Yeah," I said. Lotta seemed anything but fine lately, but there was no use going into it with him.

"I think a color touch today before we blow it out."

Color touch. I hate that phrase. It sounds like the copy on a box of Clairol. And why? Did he see grays?

"So what about it?"

"What about what?"

"Love. You said love is on your mind. What about it?"

"It's a ghost chase," I said. "It's like a tree falling in the forest when no one's there. If you love and no one feels it, does it exist? Is it real?"

"Honey, I find love every Friday night and trust me, they feel it."

He was teasing. James isn't cynical. I know that and he knows it. He's full of shit. He wants the real thing, too. As long as she's twenty.

"Be serious," I said. "Unrequited love, for instance. What a ridiculous concept. Isn't all love unrequited? You never get it back from the person you actually give it to. It's like that shampoo commercial. I loved two friends and they loved two friends . . . It just keeps shifting."

"Fabergé! That's a throwback. But, honey, that sounds more like a sex club."

"Whatever, it's all a sham. There is no such thing, it's something we made up and we waste so much time on it."

"What's the matter, Luce?"

He sat down in the chair next to me and spun me around to face him. He grabbed my hand.

"If you're bored in your marriage, honey, that's all normal and fine. A lull isn't an existential crisis. You'll come out of it."

He understands me because it's his job to understand women. And also because he's known me forever.

He spun me around to the mirror again and resumed his work.

"Tell me something you want to do in ten years," he said, changing the subject. He combed the color through my hair, moving my head this way, then that. There's nothing like the feel of a man's hands in your hair, caressing your head. I could have stayed here like this for a week.

"Not big. Just a small thing, a change in your routine. Crystal ball, what do you see?'"

"Just one?" I said. "Okay. Ten years. I'm here, in this chair, and I look ten years younger thanks to Billy's kale smoothies. And you're getting me ready for a panel I have to do at the Ninety-Second Street Y, for my memoir. A fascinating work crammed with all the interesting things I'll have done by then."

"Wow." He laughed. I love his laugh. It's genuine, and deep. "That's serious. What's the name?"

"Of what?"

"Of your book."

"*Thursdays with James*," I smiled.

It's so safe here. James plays old-school jazz. Charlie Parker, Billy Strayhorn. *Lush Life*. It's like another world. And he's like an exhibit in a museum: nice to look at, out of reach. I'm married. I don't cheat. I haven't, anyway. Getting texts from a stranger doesn't technically, I think, at least for now, count as cheating.

"Titus won't like that," he said. "He'll want to be in the title."

"Titus is dead in this scenario. I'm a widow."

"Honey. I'm sorry. How'd he die?" James always humors me.

"He choked. It's fine. It was quick and he had a good last line. The biographers loved it."

He smiled.

"Noel gave me the column," I said.

"That's great, Luce. What is it? What will you do?"

"I'm not really sure yet. I'm meeting with him tomorrow."

"Noel White. I do his wife's hair." He tipped my head down so I was talking into my lap.

"You *do*?" I said. "I haven't met this one. What's she like?"

"I don't know. Sweet. Quiet." He leaned down to whisper in my ear. "She's thinning."

"No!" I said. "How? She can't be more than—"

"Forty-three. And already, the hairline."

Oh my God, I thought. *What does he see in my hairline?*

"She's a brunette bob uptown. The girlfriend's a long blonde down here."

"The girlfriend, too, J? Scandalous!"

I suddenly got a queasy feeling in my stomach. Noel's wife is only forty-three, and James had moved her uptown already. Uptown is for women of *a certain age*. When was he planning to move *me*?

"Anyway," I said. "He wants to retool the magazine. Relaunch it. It's kind of exciting."

He was brushing my hair out into long waves. Pulling it to one side and then the other. I couldn't see any thinning.

"They used to be *the* one thing to read for politics, culture, art. Remember? Then *Vanity Fair* passed them and he can't stand it. So he wants to go retro. He wants to do long-form journalism in short-form delivery. He wants sexy and smart, like 'Frank Sinatra Has a Cold.'"

"What?"

"'Frank Sinatra Has a Cold.' It's a piece *Esquire* ran fifty years ago, very famous. It's the kind of writing Noel wants to put out again. Sharp."

"Sounds great, Luce."

"Websites, clickbait, that's all people read now. No one buys hard copy. But Noel thinks he can come back. He thinks people still want a thing, *the* thing to talk about. Not just a celebrity scoop, but something with substance. Something they'll want to hold in their hands."

"You're sexy when you talk shop."

"I thought I was sexy just sitting here."

"That works, too," he said, smiling. Then he pulled all of my hair into his hands and found my eyes in the mirror. "Sweetheart, don't play the game, change it. Remember that. Listen to James."

I closed my eyes while he finished my blowout. When he's doing this I pretend I'm Lee Grant in *Shampoo*. James, of course, is Warren Beatty. Shit. Lee Grant was probably thinning.

His next appointment walked in and helped herself to the champagne at the front desk. Model. All the big agencies use James—Elite, Ford, Wilhelmina—so some days his downtown space looks like a Bruce Weber shoot. They come in whether he's doing their hair or not. They know the back room is coke-friendly and that it's stocked with Veuve Clicquot.

She looked like a runway girl, eighteen tops. Eighteen-year-old body, eighteen-year-old skin, eighteen-year-old hair. Fifty-year-old boyfriend. She wasn't getting a "color touch."

James walked over to greet her and his whole demeanor changed. His body language, his kiss-kiss. He ran her hair through his hands like it was a fetish, not his job.

She's the girlfriend, I thought. *And I'm the wife.*

I pulled my phone from my bag. I had two new texts.

212-555-0134: My beauty . . .

It was Him. And then another one.

212-555-0134: Abandon everything in pursuit of desire. Desire me the way I desire you.

"Fabulous," James said from behind me, grabbing a hand mirror to show me his work. "Lush and untamed . . ." He was pulling hair away from me in thick handfuls, feeling the soft, silky texture he'd just made. "The sun will hit this like a prism. Watch."

It did. God, he is good. Outside, waiting for a taxi, I felt like Talitha Getty stepping off her yacht in Saint-Tropez. Sun-kissed hair, rich highlights, and an ombré the girls were going to die for—warm honey, with acorn-colored roots.

It wouldn't hurt to look stunning for lunch at Cheri's.

James is an *aesthete.*

212-555-0134: My beauty . . .

It popped up, again, on my phone. I looked around me. Strangers.

8

•••••••••

Cheri Bird's apartment
800 Fifth Avenue, Upper East Side

Cheri lives on the Upper East Side, in a rented pied-à-terre off Sixty-First Street. It's chic and it's transient. She sells properties for a living but doesn't want anything of her own to tie her down, of course.

In Rockland, Cheri sold ranch homes with flower beds for Century 21. Now she's at Corcoran showing prewar apartments, some of which sell for more than all the ranch homes in Rockland combined. It's kind of like going from a small-town city council to the Senate. But you could drop Cheri off in front of the Kremlin in a bathrobe and within an hour she'd be drinking vodka spritzers with Putin.

In the cab, I braced for her speech. She thinks Titus and I are in trouble because I made the colossal mistake of telling her that. And now she thinks she needs to fix it. I've listened to her for years, all her philosophies about keeping a man (something she has failed at repeatedly, by the way). *Embrace his sexuality. Let him wander. Men need freedom, it's what brings them back.* For years she has warned me about children, without the slightest irony. *Don't bother him about children, Lucy. Why would you want them? They're the kiss of death.* Now, recently, she's been nagging me to have them. As if they're something you can just order up from FreshDirect.

She opened the door like I was a huge surprise, even though we just spoke this morning.

"Lucy! Honey, I'm so glad you're here! Come in!"

Cheri Bird—first name pronounced like the fruit, like *cherry* pie—is reckless and unpredictable. Ironically, this makes her entirely predictable. There is always some minor drama that typically, by the time she drips out the details in a slow leak, turns out to have been caused by her. There is always a man. She has "friends," a lot of them, but she's careful. She twirls them around the city like a debutante at a Texas ball. So far, no one is quite what she has in mind. She's sixty-two and looks fantastic, like Angie Dickinson in a thirty-year-old body. She does SoulCycle three times a week and works out with a trainer. Your basic grass-fed Midwestern bombshell.

Incidentally, Bird was never my name, Cheri made it up. My father left us just before the corks popped at my christening, as she tells it. Until then we were Danners, and then Cheri switched to Bird. She likes the way it sounds. "It's catchy, people remember it," she says. "And for a bird, you know, the sky *literally* is the limit."

She arranged the table with a plate of small sandwiches, endive salad, and her potato-leek soup, then started in.

"Did you read the book?" she asked. She meant the Esther Perel. Her new bible.

"Yes," I said.

"*Did* you?"

"No."

"Sweetheart, *read* it. You need to listen to me, because you're taking your marriage for granted."

I tried to look attentive. A text came in from Lotta, which I tried not to let Cheri catch me reading.

Lotta: Date canceled. Don't care, not into Viagra sex anyway! :)
Brazilians? 4 o'clocker?

I would much rather be getting a Brazilian wax right now than having this particular conversation with my mother.

Me: Can't. With Cheri. Call tomorrow. xo

"Sexuality feeds the soul, honey, and you cannot have a fulfilling life with one man or one woman, or sustain joy or love unless you embrace it." She's been rehearsing. My mother read Anaïs Nin in college and now it's Esther Perel. She thinks I should have an affair. It's her not-so-conventional plan of a restart. Cheri thinks an affair will renew passion. It will make me irresistible. This is New York mentality and she's adopted it. If your relationship hits a bump, it's nothing a Tinder swipe or OKCupid profile can't take care of. There's always someone a mile away who can make you feel good. Monogamy is for quitters.

"Your hair looks gorgeous, honey. James?"

"Every week, whether I need it or not."

"Why don't you have a little thing with *him*? He's adorable. Where does he live? Is he looking to buy?"

"Brooklyn. Dumbo. He's out of your range." Cheri is not an outer-borough kind of broker.

"They're renovating the most beautiful loft spaces there," she said, trailing off.

I'd rather have discussed real estate, but she stayed on task. I took a bite of sandwich. "Is there cilantro in here?"

"Honey, he's losing respect for you. Titus, I mean. The trick is to not do it for him, but for you. I really think you could use it. You can't offer up the same routine, the same act, day in day out. The passion and desire wanes. A man like that needs perpetual conquest, it feeds his blood."

Cheri thinks I'm a prude. I'm not. She doesn't remember. I had five years here before Titus. I learned a few things.

"Remember Jerrod?" I asked her.

"Yes. I liked him!" Cheri liked everyone.

"Okay, well, he was a jerk."

Jerrod was actually an asshole, but Cheri doesn't like me to swear.

"Remember Devon?"

"Of course I remember Devon. He spoiled you."

"He was pathological," I said. "He left me alone in Southampton once, at a stranger's house in the middle of the night, without warning or a phone or a ride."

Cheri frowned and dipped into her soup.

"Well . . ." she said.

"My point is, what's the point? You can't have a good affair anymore anyway. No one wants to even commit to that."

"There are too many easy options," she agreed. "That's a problem."

"No one knows what they're doing," I said. "There are no rules, it's chaos."

It's true. New York is a city of dreams. Yet a lot of them are big and hollow, and there's more than the occasional nightmare.

"Titus needs to stay virile, honey, for his health. For his prostate. It's important. He either has to masturbate twice a day or have sex. And I think with his ego, it's important to him that it's sex."

It's not charming to talk about prostates and sex with your mother. And Titus wasn't having sex, at least with me. So what did that mean?

"He drinks deer blood for his virility," I said as Cheri lifted a spoonful of her soup.

"For God's sake, Lucy." She pretends to disapprove of gossip about Titus, yet she hangs on every word.

"Maybe it helps his prostate, too," I said.

"This is exactly what I am trying to tell you, sweetheart."

"He says he uses it to keep the 'creative' drive flowing. I suppose I could interpret this in different ways. Of course, I'd like his creative drive to benefit from my La Perla matched sets, but it doesn't seem to."

Cheri ignored me. She delivers soliloquies, not conversation. It's apt—she loves the theater.

"I mean, God forbid you divorce him, Lucy. Then what will you do?"

She made divorce sound like cancer.

"I don't know. Whatever other divorced women do," I said.

"Lucy, trust me. You do not want to start dating as a single woman at your age."

"Why not? You're dating at your age," I said.

"That's easier. Men like the extremes, not the middle."

She picked up a carrot and took a bite. The greens were still attached; she looked like Bugs Bunny.

"Are you taking the pill?" she said. "I hope you're not still taking the pill."

Taking the pill? Who says that?

"Does it matter?" I said. "Children ruin everything."

"You know, you were never a good planner, like Sarah. You should have done your embryos, too. Now it would be pointless." She's relentless.

I walked over to her window and looked down on the street. Nannies and strollers. Everywhere.

"There are plenty of women, by the way, who lead very full and rewarding lives without children. Even without men," I said.

"Name one."

"Diane Sawyer."

"Oh, Lucy, that hardly counts."

"Why not?"

"Because she's *busy*."

"I'm busy, too."

"No, I mean *busy* busy."

I know Cheri thinks I'm the trophy wife who blew it. She's probably right. I should have done my embryos, too.

"By the way," she said. "Not that you asked, but my trip was astounding. And I don't mean in a good sense."

Cheri was just back from Italy. She'd gone with a man named Gerard.

"Positano is beautiful—how could it not be in a good sense?"

"The food was wonderful, of course. The weather? Exquisite. We drank a bottle from the house vineyard every afternoon, and let me tell you, you can *breathe* the terroir. It's not like here. We were drinking grapes that came from the same soil as the arugula. It's very sensual."

She paused, took a drink of her non-house vineyard white. From a case I'm sure Titus had sent. He is good to her.

"The experience itself, though, was appalling. It was an abomination, actually."

"All of your adjectives, so far, start with *a*."

"Well, that's funny, because he had sleep *apnea*, with one very large capital *A*. He snored. I don't mean occasional little grunts. I mean he snored like a tuba section. Nonstop. Every night. Every single one of them. I haven't slept in eight days, that's why my eyes look like this."

I hadn't noticed anything about her eyes. But it sounded like the end of Gerard.

Side note: when I was growing up, Cheri walked around topless in our backyard, on the patio by the pool. No matter who was there. All of my high school boyfriends have seen her breasts, it was one of the perks of dating me. She is comfortable with her sexuality. She moves around her apartment with the grace and flutter of a dancer. Still, at sixty-two. On the "Are You Hot" quiz, Cheri would score off the charts: *G-string, J-Lo, naughty and nice.*

"Do one thing for me, honey. Read the book."

I don't tell Cheri that I'm having dreams at night of a stranger. I don't tell her about the texts. I don't tell her that he is real to me. He doesn't test me, he doesn't dangle hollow promises. He makes it clear that he wants me. Childish fantasy? Maybe. Cheri would certainly think so. But I have dreamed him. I have felt him. I know how he smells.

> 212-555-0134: Lucy. Stay close to me. If you can be patient, I will give you everything.

"What about *SNOB*, honey? When do you start? What will you write about?"

"I don't know. I'm meeting Noel on Friday."

She started clearing away our dishes.

"You know, he'd be fun, I bet," I said.

"Not someone at work, Lucy. I don't advise that."

"Not for me, for *you*."

She paused to consider it.

"You know, that whole magazine thing might bore me."

"I'll pretend that's not insulting."

> 212-555-0134: Patience. If you have it, I will give you your dreams.

I read his texts in the cab on my way home. They had come in at three forty-five, in the middle of Cheri's vichyssoise.

9

· · · · · · · · ·

Brockton town house
Lucy's bedroom

I didn't read the book, I watched the TED Talk, instead, on YouTube when I got home. *The Secret to Desire in a Long-Term Relationship*. It had over three million hits. It's one of the most viewed talks of the whole series. I propped my iPad up against a pillow and hit play, and, like the crowd of hopeful-looking couples in her audience, I tuned in.

Here's what I learned: give her a buttery French accent and a pantsuit, and my mother is Esther Perel.

We need to have novelty, Perel says. *We need adventure. We need risk, we need danger, we need a journey.*

The audience nodded along with her, but they all looked a little nervous, too. Because we also need shelter and food and clothes and shoes and a good eye cream. When you add in danger and a journey, it all starts to add up.

Is it possible to want what we already have? she asked.

I hit pause and played that back. It's a daunting question. If the answer is no, then life is one long futile pursuit. The more I watched, the more frustrated I became. It did not feel enlightening; it made me tired. Yes, we want danger and risk. This is why we have adultery. This is why Ashley Madison is a multimillion-dollar business. Esther's premise is that you don't have to seek the *other*. You just need to create risk and adventure at home. Sure. Easy.

I picked up the book and turned to a page that my mother had marked. She had highlighted four sentences.

Love is to have. Desire is to want. In desire we do not want to go back to the places we've already been. In desire we want to go somewhere new.

How can any two people ever hope to pull it off? It's impossible. Never mind all of the distractions there are even in the best of situations. If you're not on your A-game for one minute, there's someone in the wings waiting to sext, or friend, or Instagram herself in lingerie. Or one day a stranger could just send you a text.

Crisis of desire is a crisis of the imagination.

I get it, Esther, I get it. We're just not trying hard enough.

I wasn't thinking about Titus as I listened to her, or as I skimmed through the passages Cheri so enthusiastically marked for me. *"Lucy! Read THIS!"*

I should be, I knew, thinking about my husband but I wasn't. I was thinking about mystery and adventure and a journey. I was thinking about Him. I've saved every one of his messages.

212-555-0134: I want to look at you, I want to touch you. I want to feel your softness, inhale the scent of your skin.

212-555-0134: Tell me one thing that means love to you. One real thing.

Love is to have. Desire is to want. I don't want love from Him, he's the unknown. I want desire. This is all anyone cares about. Isn't it?

There was a new message on my phone. I hadn't heard it come in.

212-555-0134: Imagine my eyes, as if they were the only way I could speak to you. Imagine what they would say to you each morning as you woke to me.

Me: What would they say?

212-555-0134: Imagine what you would feel.

I have known many women who married young like I did and then married again when that was done. They treated it like sport. When they left, even with children, that was it. Some assets changing hands. But then barely any trace at all of a life they shared with someone.

I didn't want to feel that way. I wanted to panic at the thought. I wanted my heart to race in fear at the thought of a life without Titus. What worried me more than anything was that it didn't.

10

....

I went down to breakfast in workout clothes. I wasn't meeting Noel until midafternoon. Titus had already made coffee.

"You're up early," I said.

His hair was uncombed, in a charming way. Tousled. Boyish.

"Yes, Leo's coming this afternoon." Leo is Titus's agent. "I want to get good work in before then. What do you have planned today?"

Titus hadn't asked me about the column, and I didn't expect him to. He's consumed. With himself, with the show. With whatever. And he also thinks Noel's a fraud, even though he tolerates him socially.

They go back thirty years. They were both young and hungry and found success at the same time. Noel gave life to magazines the same way Titus did to figurative art. Neither of them invented their mediums, but they changed them. There was a time when they were all anyone could talk about. But now their stars have faded. If Titus's show isn't a success, he could be a punch line. And Noel's empire is in trouble because it's 2014 and hard copy doesn't sell.

"I'm meeting with Noel," I said.

"The pompous jackass Noel?" He laughed. "I'm kidding, Lulu. That's wonderful. Don't take anything less than a cover."

"He could give *you* a cover. He could do a retrospective of your year. Everyone loves a comeback."

He brushed it off.

"I've got to work. Tell Tati, will you, to bring lunch at two and then to prepare something light for Leo at four."

"No breakfast?" I said.

"Not now. No, just tell Tati—"

"Two, then four. I will.

"Thank you, love."

He smiled and covered my hand in his, and then went upstairs to his studio.

I wasn't sure what to expect from my meeting. I knew Noel was in trouble. I knew his print circulation had dropped by half in five years. And that when circulation drops, so do advertisers, and when advertisers drop, it's the kiss of death, no matter how many Ellie Awards are in the display case in the lobby. Ten years ago *SNOB* was the most respected magazine in the country. It inadvertently created celebrity culture as we know it today. It took actors and fashion designers, even the foodie explosion with its celebrity chefs, and made all of them relevant—as cultural touchstones, as movements, as political voices. That all started at *SNOB*. It juxtaposed pop culture with gravitas in ways no one before Noel had thought to do.

He'd been doing this a long time, he'd managed bumps before.

I was twenty minutes early, but his secretary took me right in.

"Lucy!" he said, and jumped up from behind his desk. He kissed me once on each cheek, and I handed him the bottle of mescal Billy had given me.

"From Billy Sitwell, with affection. She promised me you'll love it."

Noel examined the bottle and raised his eyebrows—impressed, I could tell. Not so much with the bottle, but with who it came from. One time we took Billy to a Red Thursday. It's a pretentious wine dinner Noel hosts once a month. He borrows a chef from Daniel Boulud to make Kobe beef burgers for an exclusive group of guests each tasked with bringing an overpriced red wine that will knock him out. Billy brought a cheap California cab that he raved about all night. It was a regift. She wasn't even trying.

"Tell Ms. Sitwell I'm flattered she thought of me," Noel said, smiling, still examining the bottle. Noel is on his third wife, the brunette bob who's "thinning," and has a girlfriend. If not for that, he and Billy might be a good match. He put the bottle away in a cabinet and then got serious.

He was giving me fifteen hundred words and he wanted three pieces quick, "in the pipe," he said. He told me it had to be branded right off. He wanted a *concept*. He said we needed intriguing characters and good copy so people would be hooked. He said, "Bang!" with a hand clap so I'd know he meant business. Noel is loud, sometimes belligerent, but he's smart.

He was pacing the room in his black cashmere sweater and stone-washed jeans that belied his years. He has a knack for keeping his style about fifteen years younger than his age.

"I want *Vulture* obsessed with us, Lucy, and everyone at Michael's to be talking about us again when I walk in the door." Michael's is where Noel eats fifty-dollar Cobb salads with the rest of the game changers in town. Deals aren't made at Michael's, they're closed, usually before lunch is half eaten.

His plan is to go retro. Back to the long form that made journalism relevant in the '70s, but deliver it with modern tools. "Write it sexy. Write it short. Deliver it fast!" he said, accenting every third word.

"Dribble it out on Twitter. All my writers maintain a profile now, and they have to cross-tweet, retweet, favorite, whatever, to make the content move."

Ugh. I have to do Twitter?

He threw out new-media words: *TrendSpottr, tracking influencers, visual content, social-media strategy.* Noel doesn't have a "new media" office, though. He's trapped in the luxurious old. Sixty-fifth floor. Stunning view. More square feet than most studio apartments and, of course, a full bar. He has an assistant right outside his door who does anything he needs, including keeping his girlfriends away from his wives, and his ex-girlfriends away from his ex-wives and remembering the birthdays of all their kids.

I scribbled notes down, trying to keep up.

"I'm moving away from the traditional subscription sales approach and focusing on digital and mobile platform rollout, single-copy sales. But the thing is, Luce, no one will care unless the content sizzles."

He had a plan for that, too.

"'Frank Sinatra Has a Cold,' but fast and hot." For Noel, this is the piece that set the bar. "Study it. It's probably the most intriguing profile ever done of the man, and he barely said one word. Gay Talese found the *essence* of his subject. That's what I want you to do."

The *essence* of my subject. I must have looked nervous, because he stopped.

"Lucy. I have *faith* in you. You could really do something here, and it could be good for both of us."

He has faith in my name, anyway. He's notorious for loading his masthead with celebrity names. Titus Brockton's wife on the cover? People would be curious.

"Thank you. I appreciate that," I said.

He walked to the bar behind his desk. "Have a drink with me."

Before I could respond, there was a glass of bourbon in my hand. I was just glad it wasn't the mescal.

"I have some people picked out," he said. "Josh Calloway: hot young chef with the city's three new 'it' restaurants. He's been one of *New York* magazine's Sexiest Bachelors four years in a row. Not groundbreaking, really, but keep him in your pocket."

I wrote it down.

"Then Lauren Spencer. Google Analytics says she's the most sought-after profile on OKCupid. Why? What's her secret? Love in the twenty-first century, moving fast, that kind of thing."

"Okay," I said. I wrote down Lauren Spencer.

"And then, Odin."

He stopped on Odin. One name. Like Beyoncé. Like Cher.

"She writes a blog."

I knew this, vaguely. I knew the name but I hadn't read her. Was he serious, though? A cover profile on a girl who wrote a blog? Who was even still writing blogs?

His whole demeanor changed. No more shop talk. He grinned like the Cheshire cat. He paused for effect. He slowed his pace around the room. He looked smitten.

"Okay, Odin," I said.

"She's the jackpot, Lucy. Google her. Just 'Odin.' Her blog will come up, but you won't find anything else. No last name. No one knows her, no one's seen her, no pictures. Nothing. But I think I know her. I've been reading her for months. I've got her pegged. She's smoky. Mysterious. Think Kristen Stewart meets Angelina Jolie. She's *smart*. Social observation hasn't seen anything like her since Joan Didion. *And* she appeals to the eighteen-to-forty-five demographic, men and women both. Everyone's reading her and no one knows her. If we get this girl—and who knows? Maybe she's not a girl. Maybe she's an old man, some retired publishing exec bored out of his mind who likes being back in the game. Maybe she's Nikki Finke. Maybe she's me. Maybe we're getting catfished."

Noel was doing laps around his desk now; he was wound up. He was alternately speaking to the view of Pearl Street below him, to the giant *SNOB* cover collage on his wall, and to me.

"Did you see it, *Catfish*? Maybe she's catfishing the whole fucking thing, all of us."

"Yes, it's a show. I'm familiar—"

"It was a movie first, a documentary, now there's a show. They play loose with the story, but who cares. The first thing is that this kid falls for someone online. He thinks she's a young girl in her twenties, like him. They make plans to meet and they're always thwarted at the last minute. It goes on for months. Meanwhile, they're falling in love, he's falling in love with her. So he finally shows up on her doorstep one day. Remember, he thinks he's crazy about her. They're probably having phone sex, or Facebook sex, whatever people do. Who the fuck knows. But he thinks they're soul mates. So he shows up, to meet the love of his life in person—"

"And she's married and fifty, with kids. I remember it now."

"Yeah, but that's not— Okay, yes, she's married. But it's more than that. She was playing her daughter, as herself. She was the mother, and playing the daughter, and then playing a younger daughter, too. And also playing the mother! She introduced this guy to the whole family. He's talking on Facebook to all of them, they all love him. But they're all her. The mother. No one else even fucking knows she's doing it. Thwarted artistic dreams. Dreary town, loveless marriage. Et cetera."

Noel air-quoted the "et cetera."

"That's the kind of story I want to get. Who knows what's real and what isn't, that question's older than time. And who's to say it even matters. But why do you think they call the show *Catfish*?"

Noel paused, picked up and scanned a letter on his desk, put it back down.

"I don't know," I said. I didn't.

"Well, her husband's not even upset with any of this when he finds out. He tells the filmmaker—and maybe this whole goddamn story was made up, who cares, it's good. He tells the filmmaker how Japanese fishermen used to ship their cod tanks out, and by the time they landed, the fish were lethargic and made shitty filets. No one wanted them. So then they stuck a catfish in the tanks. The catfish stirred things up, kept the cod feisty, on their toes. Alive. So when they arrived? Firm, fleshy fillets. The fishermen got their money. The husband says the wife is his catfish."

I was intrigued now. Noel was caught up in his story. He was speaking as though he had a full room of captive audience and not just me.

"Lucy. I want *SNOB* to be the catfish."

I wrote, *Old fisherman's tricks: look up*, in my notebook.

"It's smart. If we get Odin, let's just say this: that's a huge fucking get."

I nodded. His enthusiasm was contagious.

"Your job is to find her. Get her to talk. Spin her story into gold." He stopped to refill his drink. "Lucy?" He gestured to his glass.

I'd barely touched mine. I took a drink of it and nodded. I'm in the big club now, bourbon at noon and no more pedicure stories.

"She's all over the board. Highbrow, lowbrow. She's more revered than A. O. Scott. She destroyed the new restaurant of one of the champs of a new hit show, *Foodie*, because apparently he plays with himself and doesn't wash his hands. She got one of Trump's campaign advisers fired for something she wrote and that's all little shit. You know about Jantzon."

I did know about Chet Jantzon. Everyone did. Up-and-coming politician, running for Senate with presidential promise. Then gone. And I know he and Noel were friends. But Noel clearly admired this girl.

He had a smile on his face. Dreamy, staring at nothing. He shook it off and went on.

"People read her because she's a voyeur. Even the people nervous about her love to read her. The mayor's office is going apeshit right now because rumor is, she has something big on de Blasio. But you know what? I bet they love it."

He sat down on a corner of his desk and swirled his drink. "Maybe she's not even real. Maybe she's a whole fucking team, a really brilliant publicity stunt. Maybe the joke is on everyone. Who the fuck knows, just crack it, Lu. High hopes."

"How do I find her?"

"Yeah. Well, that's the tricky part. Listen, if you can't, we'll do someone else. I just think this would be a big one. Maybe the art is a picture of her in a Batman mask, or Catgirl." He took another drink. How did people work like this?

"What if she's crazy?" I said. "Scary crazy."

"Even better! She might be some Wall Street billionaire's kid who just repeats shit she hears at her parents' parties, and bingo—great story."

He rubbed his hands on his temples. Noel clearly needed a great story. No matter how it unfolded.

"The sad fucking truth," he said, "is all those Real Housewives' Instagram feeds get a bigger readership than we do. Even fucking Miami. We gotta kill that. Jesus."

The more worked up Noel gets, the more he swears.

"Hollywood Life gets thirty million views a month. Thirty million fucking people reading about Rihanna's nude photo leaks and some nobody's sex tape. They're running the industry right now when we should be. We need this."

I wrote down *Odin. No last name???*

"I want to run it in October, Luce. So we need it end of next month."

"Okay," I said. It sounded impossible.

"She's *l'amour fou*, Lucy," Noel said. "She is the object of desire. We don't know her, we can't have her, and so we desire her. That's what I want."

Jesus. Was everyone reading Esther Perel?

Noel's parting words to me were, "It's a slam dunk, Lucy. Go home. Read up."

I went home. I looked her up. Odin's website was nondescript; unadorned, on a white background with black type. There was no About, no Bio, no Contact Me. No anything but a stream of cutting blind items and asides.

She had a very artistically filtered photo of a Memorial Sloan Kettering bigwig smoking a blunt. (Caption: "Medicinal?") But it wasn't just that. Exposures are nothing new. There's not a New Yorker worth their cab fare who can't weather a *Daily News* cover storm. They blow over. Politicians come back and start politicking again. Embezzlers take a month on an island, then find new financing. It's the twist she gives.

The entry on Chet Jantzon, for instance, reads like a John Cheever story. Repressed desire, dark choices, and then, inevitably, the broken man. He didn't have a chance.

I searched back to her first entry. January 1, six months ago. How did anyone know she was even there?

She has a Twitter account, which was somewhat more revealing but not much.

Username: **@OdinNYC**
Tweets: **3,178.** Followers: **830,724.** Following: **0.**

Her profile description: "To destroy is always the first step in any creation."

—e. e. cummings

Her tweets were vague rambles. A mix of quotations, a few coy words of her own.

ODIN @OdinNYC   **1d**
Love is not elusive, it's dangerous. Vulnerability is danger, danger is thrilling.

ODIN @OdinNYC   **1d**
"Life isn't about finding yourself. Life is about creating yourself."
—George Bernard Shaw

ODIN @OdinNYC   **2d**
No one can surprise you if you're paying attention.

ODIN @OdinNYC   **3d**
"Be of love a little more careful than anything."
—e. e. cummings

She wrote the mundane:

ODIN @OdinNYC   **4d**
Organic black truffle aioli at Pommes Frites. #beyond.

And slightly ominous:

ODIN @OdinNYC   **4d**
Jean Harris wore a mink coat to shoot Scarsdale in his bed. #style.

ODIN @OdinNYC   **6d**
Our desire, above everything, is a narrative for our lives. Our desire is narration. And it ruins us.

ODIN @OdinNYC
Your secrets patiently wait to undo you.

And then, like a faceless someone lobbing a grenade into a parade, six months ago, there was this:

ODIN @OdinNYC
Chet Jantzon: bit.ly/10ybt47

That was it. One name, one link to a post on her website where Chet Jantzon's actual name is not mentioned once. And it still ruined him.

I reached out to her in the only way available to me at the moment. I followed her, then tweeted her.

@OdinNYC I'm @LucyBrockton. Would like to talk about possible profile for high-end publication. DM me? I'll send my #, your convenience.

11

....

Brockton town house
Sunday, June 8
Morning

H e's here again. It's crazy.

> 212-555-0134: You looked beautiful yesterday, ravishing. I
> wanted to take your clothing off in pieces, one by one. I
> wanted to feed every one of your desires.

I don't respond. Does he really see me? Is he following me? Does
he know where I live, does he know me?

I was at McNally Jackson yesterday. I was looking for books about
spies because that's essentially what Odin is. Did he know I was
there?

I want to tell him about my dream. The one I had last night,
which I should really be telling to a shrink. I should know whether
this is all Jungian or if it's Freud. I should not be falling in love with
someone I've never seen. I should not be falling in love with a text.

In my dream I'm wearing the yellow dress, the one he wants me to
wear. But he's upset. He thinks I'm wearing it for someone else and
not him. We're in a quaint tourist town, it's on the ocean. We're walking around through the shops and small bistros, and even though he's

angry his hand holds mine tight. We're completely anonymous. We enter an open-air café and he rests his hand on my bare thigh as we order drinks, and he keeps it there as we drink them. We don't speak, because we don't need to.

We leave and walk to a small park; it's deserted. He sits on a swing and positions me on his lap and then he enters me. My dress is fanned out by the wind.

Who can I tell this to?

I can't tell Titus, or Tatiana, the first two people I'll speak to today. How can I have breakfast with my husband when I've just dreamed about sex with another man?

12

· · · · · · · · ·

Livia Rothwell's apartment
740 Park Avenue, Upper East Side
Tuesday, June 10

Livia is the last of the great New York eccentrics—a cranky ninety-two-year-old recluse with cataracts. She lives in Sarah's building and I read to her once a week.

I found her in the lobby a few years ago. She was getting her mail, shuffling around in a red cashmere cardigan and Gucci slippers, squinting through oversize glasses. She dropped a large envelope and I snatched it up, then followed her to her door; I was crazy about her right off. She looked like a great story, and she is. Her tales are almost unbelievable. She has snuck into Gracie Mansion, for instance, in the middle of the night more than once. With two different governors.

Livia's second husband was a very wealthy collector, so she knows a thing or two about art. She's known Titus, casually, for decades. Though I've never seen it—she says it's stored—she has a Brockton in her collection. It wouldn't surprise me a bit if one day she nonchalantly announced they'd had an affair. It's not impossible.

I have my own key, so I let myself in. She is always in the same place when I come. On her Paul McCobb sectional smoking Carlton cigarettes, her tiny frame swallowed up in a bright silk kimono. She listens to crime shows on television—an oversize Sony flat-screen that is the only modern touch in her apartment. Livia herself is a piece of art. A Magritte. Witty and provocative, in playful childish tones.

"Close the door, Lucy. There's a cold draft." She said this after I'd already closed the door.

Livia is half out of her mind, too, which I don't think is a bad thing. I don't mind it at all.

"They raised the maintenance again. I can't afford to keep the heat on anymore."

"Livia, it's June. You don't need the heat on."

In the late '80s someone wrote a tell-all book about her. I found it in the dollar bin at the Strand: *Rothwell's Follies*. Very few of the details in the book match the stories Livia tells, but that's fair. She can tell them however she wants. She came here from Chicago seventy-two years ago with a trust fund to dance at Juilliard. She has a photograph of herself on the wall by Man Ray and, next to it, her portrait by Lucien Freud. Both of them are stunning.

We're reading *Sense and Sensibility*, for about the six hundredth time because Livia likes Jane Austen. It doesn't seem like it would suit her, but even Livia at ninety-two is a romantic. Even Livia, beneath her small cranky surface, wants adventure and desire.

"Fanny is a coldhearted little one," she said in her raspy smoker's voice before I started. She dragged out her syllables like she was doing a scene.

"*'He was not an ill-disposed young man . . .'*" I read.

"Oh, good Lord Christ."

"*'. . . unless to be rather coldhearted and rather selfish is to be ill-disposed . . .'*"

"He was an ass," Livia said. Our readings are peppered like this, with her salty introspection. It makes them interesting. I went on.

"*'Had he married a more amiable woman . . .'*"

"Oh, for God's sake. Is it *her* fault he's an ass?"

"Maybe," I said. "You can't stand her. So maybe it is."

"Fanny's a moony-faced miserable woman, but that doesn't excuse *him*." She started to cough, and I poured her a glass of water from a pitcher on the table.

Livia hates men. She hates everyone to an extent, but especially men. She's had bad luck with them. She married three, one of them twice, and they were all horrible by her account and now they're all dead. She has two children she doesn't talk to; she has her house-keeper, Marta; and she has me. There are accountants and lawyers, of course, but most of the family and longtime friends she was famous for feuding bitterly with are also dead.

Before I began chapter two, I went to the kitchen and pulled two cans of beer from her refrigerator, one for each of us. Cigarettes and cold beer—two vices she's still committed to. Aside from the beer, her refrigerator was bare. A container of yogurt, a protein drink, and a bowl of chicken salad that Marta must have made that Livia probably wouldn't touch.

I poured the cans into tall glasses and handed her one.

My phone began to buzz, three new texts. Livia has no patience for phones or gadgets or technology of any kind, so I tried to talk over it, and then glanced down.

Lotta: Doll. Dead here, bailing on work. Grab your Blahniks. Let's hit Morandi!

Billy: Drinks piece in. Editor loved mescal! Date sucked, tho. Call. :)

212-555-0134: I want to watch you. I feel you like you're here with me. I want you near.

"What are you doing? Why did you stop? I don't pay you to sit there."

Livia doesn't pay me at all, and I know she'd be perfectly content if I did just sit here. Sometimes, when I stay late, that's what we do. We listen to *Law & Order*, and just sit.

I replied, discreetly, out of order.

To Him: I want you near, also. Very much.

To Lotta: Yes on Morandi. Headed to Whitney first. Meet me there? In 30?

To Billy: Recap at Morandi? I'll text on the way.

13

· · · · · · · · ·

The Whitney Museum of American Art
Madison Avenue and Seventy-Fifth Street, Upper East Side
Tuesday, June 10

It's a short walk to the Whitney from Livia's, so I often stop there
before I head home. They're moving downtown in a few months,
which will feel strange.

I like to come here the way some people like to go to Mass. On
weekday afternoons, it's often empty and hushed. It's almost spiritual.

Lotta, though? Not empty, or hushed. Certainly not spiritual. She
waltzed in like a Simon Doonan display, colorful and showy in white
trousers that matched her hair, an oversize Céline trench, and kelly-
green Brian Atwood stilettos. There weren't a lot of heads here, but
the ones that were snapped around fast.

"I've been up to my hair in art all day, Luce. This is not where I
want to unwind."

"I know," I said. "Humor me. I was in the neighborhood."

"Honey, you look so serious." She reached into her handbag and
took out a small envelope of small orange pills. She swallowed one
quick and held another out to me.

I waved it off.

"It's Xanax, Lucy. It's not *drugs*. You could use one."

"I don't think you're supposed to pop them before happy hour, Lot."

"Don't be a nag."

We meandered around.

"All of this is gone in October," I said.

"But the new place is *sexy*," she said. "Renzo is almost eighty, I think, and I'd screw him in a minute."

"That's sweet," I said. "I'm sure he'd like that." Renzo Piano is the "starchitect" who designed the new museum. It *is* sexy, she's right. Modern design anchors the High Line and it's a ten-minute walk from our apartment. It's just a big change.

"You're too sentimental, Lu."

"Everything just feels precarious," I said.

"Everything *is* precarious. All the time. It's supposed to be. Is this because they picked Koons?"

The Whitney chose Jeff Koons for their last exhibition before the move. It's right before Titus's show and it was a huge slight. It's all marketing, though. And Titus isn't good at that.

"Luce, I think after October—after you play glam artist wife for the press and do what you do—you should disappear for a while. Go to Mumbai and let some gorgeous raja knock you off your feet. You're just treading water."

"I was thinking Texas."

"Great. Texas. Big, steak-chewing oilman."

"And then what?" I said.

"And then what *what*?"

"After I get knocked off my feet. Then what?"

I was thinking of Esther Perel and how she'd made it sound like so much work! Anyone can manage the knockout; it's the long road after.

Lotta was laughing. "Who cares? Then whatever. You're existential today."

"I'm nostalgic. Different."

We were in front of the Hoppers.

"You need to meet this girl I just signed," Lotta said. "She sold out her first exhibit with us and she's got something at MoMA already in March. She's hot right now. *Molto alla moda.*"

"Hopper depresses me," I said.

We went upstairs to the room Titus shared with Richard Prince. Lotta is suspicious of anyone with permanent collection space. She works with conceptual art, avant-garde. She thinks Damien Hirst is conventional, so she was clearly just here to be nice.

"I like seeing his stuff as a stranger," I said. "I like to pretend I don't know him. Or pretend we're not together anymore and think about how this would look to me then." It would be odd to see his paintings if we weren't together. If we stopped "mating in captivity." If we gave up on the whole thing.

"Okay, let's try it. Look at this." She walked over to Titus's area. "Think of the work from the outside in. Like you're a stranger, just what you said."

The Whitney has twenty-four Brocktons, which include a series of twelve that Lotta was giving her attention to now. *Les femmes et la mort,* Women and Death. Twelve paintings of women who murdered, who committed gruesome acts for their lovers. Titus worked from mug shots and newspaper clips. The contrast of his interpretation of them and of the horrible things they did is stunning.

Lotta was studying *Karla: #2.*

"You know . . . if he comes up with shit like this again, he's back on top. This is what they want to see, doll. *L'artiste brillante.*"

She was right. This collection gives me chills. Not because the backstories are so horrible, but because of how beautifully he painted them.

"The thing about it is that beneath every piece in this building," she said, "is a raging storm of madness and pain. Not just from the artist, but from the collateral damage he inflicts. On his lovers, his wives, *their* lovers and children, all of it."

My phone vibrated and I glanced down.

212-555-0134: Be with me, be my love.
212-555-0134: Where are you, and who is on your mind?

"Take this one," Lotta said. "This chick picked up girls and roofied them for her boyfriend, then cut them into pieces when he was done."

Karla had a languid pose, in a high-backed chair dressed in a gown.

"I mean, this is fucking insane. Look at her. Like the Madonna. She looks like she's waiting for a lost soldier to return. Dressing for him every night and wandering an empty house. It's madness."

She moved on to *Diane: #3*.

"You know, he shouldn't take it personally, about Koons. They needed a spectacle. Titus is too serious, you can't have a big party around him."

"Everything is personal right now."

"Sweets, if that's his biggest problem, he's not trying hard enough."

My phone vibrated again, twice.

Billy: No on Morandi. Headed to gym—B.

Lotta had wandered away. She was impatient. It was almost four o'clock and she wasn't at a table with drinks.

212-555-0134: Give me your heart.

I texted Him back.

Me: I can't give you that. It's dangerous.

212-555-0134: A thing is only worth doing if there is risk.

The moment I stop thinking of him, he comes back and my pulse races. He has recently started using my name. *Who is he?*

212-555-0134: Lucy, tell me what you dream of at night . . . tell me what you feel. Tell me when you think of me.

I think about him more than I want to admit. But I don't tell him that. And I don't tell him what.

"Lu, I got an Uber. Ten minutes. Meet me outside."

14

. . . .

Brockton town house
Monday, June 16

S arah showed up at my place Monday night dressed from cleav-
age to toe, all five foot nine and 120 pounds of her, in Saint
Laurent. Sometimes New York feels like one big long costume party.

"Okay, honey," I said. "Talk."

"What?"

"Um. The outfit? We're staying in."

It was trash-TV night. We were going to watch a three-hour mara-
thon of *Snapped*. Three hours of sex, lies, and murder.

"Well?"

She made a vague reference to a meeting she'd just come from—
cocktails, producers—then walked past me and settled into one of
the cushy chairs in the library.

She took a Buzzfeed quiz on her phone to find out which Gossip
Girl she is while I started the popcorn, which I was cooking the old-
fashioned way, on the stove. "Serena!" she announced, thrilled.

"Hey, Luce," she called out. "Can I tell you something you won't
repeat until I'm ready?"

I stopped shaking the pan and she came into the kitchen.

Uh-oh, I thought. "You're not pregnant," I said. "Are you pregnant?"

"No. No, no. No." She laughed. "It's worse."

My eyes got big. "Brian closed your Tom Ford account?"

"I mean, not worse for me. Worse for *you*. You guys will hate it."

She took a deep breath. Popped kernels started pinging against the lid of the pot.

"I'm auditioning for a reality show. I'm on the short list, too. I actually might get it."

It took me a few seconds to understand. What? *Why?* It's one thing to watch them . . .

"Wow," I said. I wasn't sure what to say. I ran through the brief list of shows I could think of that were local. What *was* there?

"Luce! Just 'wow'? It's new and they're casting right now. It's five Upper East Side private school girls who are grown now with careers or kids or husbands or ex-husbands, or whatever, but still live in the same neighborhood. They've already picked two women. I know them. They went to Chapin. So the thing is, I have to be really visible right now. I have to show the producers I have a life. You know, it has to be interesting. They have to be able to see my story in scenes."

"Wow," I said again.

"Stop saying 'wow'!"

"Okay, but wow. I mean, I can't picture it . . . I can't picture you. A reality show? So you're going to run around all day with cameras everywhere?"

"Not all day, not every day. You only shoot for three months. I'm excited about it."

They would eat her alive. Would she be filming this conversation right now? Had she even thought this through?

Sarah grew up with the *real* gossip girls. That was her world. She had the kind of childhood that made up for in money what it lacked in stability. She'd gone to Chapin, and after her parents divorced, she shuttled between London and Park Avenue. Hers was a family, even as the stepfathers rotated through, more concerned with finding an interesting way to pass the time than with jobs or careers. She's bounced around a little, from one thing to the next. But for a year after she graduated from Brown, she hosted a short segment called "News Breaks" for MTV. She loved the camera.

"Okay. That's great, then. But I'm not going on TV. I mean, are you going to bring cameras to SoulCycle?"

"Let's figure that out when we get there. Okay? Jeez." She laughed. "I won't embarrass you. Not seriously, I mean. You might like it."

She was thumbing through a back issue of *SNOB*—Noel's office had sent me two years' worth. I finished popping the corn and paired it with vodka sodas. Parmesan cheese on top of Sarah's bowl, truffle salt on mine.

"I have to go to everything now. There's a thing next week," she said, her mouth half full of popcorn. "It's just a book party, but Patrick will be there. I have to show up."

Patrick McMullan is a photographer. He has the largest photo archive in the city. If you don't know Patrick, and he's not taking your picture, then in the world Sarah wants to live in now, you don't exist.

"What is it?"

"*Glamour Girls*. That's the name of the book. Don't laugh. I know you think this is silly."

We moved the popcorn and drinks into the library and stacked up pillows. I turned on the television.

"So, you'll be . . . a reality star?" I still wasn't processing it.

"Yeah, but don't jinx me, I have to get hired."

"Do you know how mean they get on those shows?" I asked her.

"Oh, come on, Lu. That's all fake. When the cameras are off it's just like any normal job."

"But the entire job is when the cameras are on," I said.

She shrugged her shoulders.

"What about Brian? What about your wedding?"

She looked at me, horrified.

"Seriously? I can't get married *now*. My profile needs to be higher. I have to think about the show, too. If I get on, that's a good story line for next season."

"Right," I said. Story line? "So he's okay with this."

"Of course. He loves it. He said if I do it, we're in it together. I mean, he'll support me."

"He's going to film scenes?" I tried to picture telling Titus that I'd gotten a new job and that it was one where cameras would move into our house and film what we did, every day.

"Well, yeah. He has to, because there's no kids yet. You know? Though I could do a scene where I visit the embryos. Anyway, he's my main story line. 'Will they, won't they,' blah blah."

"But you guys don't even fight. Don't you have to fight? I mean, you don't have any adversity at all. And before you even go there, I'm not fighting with you."

"Lu, relax. I got this. There's always a nice girl: I'm doing that one. I'm the one who comes home to the sweet, rational boyfriend and complains about how crazy the rest of them are. I'm trying out for Voice of Reason."

I thought about this. It was what Oscar Wilde did. He showed up to all the parties, he had all the good lines, and that was what he got famous for. If Sarah wanted to be whatever she wanted to be in this city, it was as noble a pursuit as any.

"Okay, but, Sar, don't try to be Brooke Astor." I had a handful of popcorn in my mouth. Truffle salt is my weakness; I will eat the whole bowl. "And don't try to be Tinsley Mortimer, either," I said. "Remember the wheel. Someone already invented it and it's flawless. There's nothing else to do with it."

"Right," she said. "Focus on the chassis."

I was thinking of how Noel wanted something fresh and new, but old. Odin hadn't responded to my tweet.

"If Brooke Astor were alive, she'd have a show," she said. "But I get it."

She adjusted a pile of pillows and flopped down.

"I want to do something great, Lu. This is perfect for me. And seriously, don't say anything yet," she said.

I wasn't sure if a reality show was something great, but what did I know?

I turned the volume up. *"Tonight on* Snapped: *A love triangle. Lisa Walker, her lover, and her husband."*

While they laid out the tryst, I tried to picture Sarah doing tequila shots with bitchy women she'd gone to high school with. I tried to picture us all having drinks at Rose Bar, on film. Outfits. Hair. Lotta on camera? Who was ready for that?

Oh, dear God.

15
· · · · · · · · ·

D oll, what are you doing?" It was Lotta.

"Tweeting," I said. "I can't think of anything smart."

"No one tweets anymore, Lu. Instagram. Sexy photos."

"It's for the magazine. No sexy photos. What's going on?"

"She's here today, my newest star. Come meet her. Come in. Like right now."

I had a stack of reading I wanted to get through, but a gallery stint with Lot is never dull.

"Okay. Where?" Lotta's gallery has six different spaces in the city.

"Chelsea. You can be here in ten. Hurry, we're getting snacks."

When I got there, Lotta was in high gear. This is her element—finding new talent, then helping them figure it out. She's like their gorgeous and hip, edgy aunt. She finds them boyfriends, apartments, and drugs, and lends them money she doesn't have. And she is fierce with their careers. When she's focused, she's one of the best dealers in town.

The space was empty but Lotta was still dressed for an opening.

"Honeycomb!" she said. "You look sparkly and fresh. Satina's in the back—come here and look at her stuff."

She led me to a room with five giant canvasses staring down.

Simulated phone screens with text bubble conversations, but not just any conversations. Angry ones. I was trying to absorb it.

"So she does these *sick* collages of text fights," Lotta said. "They're beautiful. I mean, this is how love starts and ends now, in silence on a screen. No voices, no touching, no eye contact. You can have the nastiest, soul-crushing breakup while you're in the checkout line at Citarella. Dead quiet—it's horrifying."

She was right. Just a glimpse made me queasy—I saw a "fuck" and a "whatever" . . . all of it so big and menacing in white and blue text bubbles.

"Jesus," I said.

"I know. Right? Passive-aggressive evil shit.

"Here," she said. "This one's the nicest, look at this. It's called *Fuk has a "c."* I love this girl."

FUK HAS A "C"

. . . hey, babe. I know ur still mad. Want you 2 know I luv you and hope ur having a great day.

                                                                    . . .

Wut does ". . ." meen ?
Oops "mean"

                    It means, "Good. I hope 'ur' day's great, too."

Okay . . .

                              What does "okay . . ." mean?

Listen I know ur pissed . . . No big deal.

                              Really? Ok. Cool. No big deal.

Jesus jule . . . I said I was sorry!!

I know and you "luv" me and blah blah.

yeah. Ok. Well like I said I hope ur day is good and maybe we can talk when ur ready.

Who said I'm not ready? Listen, I'm just not into crazy anymore. Like all that bullshit on FB. You still haven't even fucking explained it. No worries.

It was a jok I told you that. A fuking Jok!

Whatever Josh. I think you're great, so maybe you should just go be great.

Ok, jule. You no I luv you. i get it. Sory it went like this.

You fucking moron. It's "know" not "no" and "hop" has an "e" on the end. I'm not even going to bother with "sory."

Yeh ok. whatever julie.

Right. Whatever, Josh. "Luv" ya.

Fuk u

"Fuk" has a "c."

Lotta was watching me. "Serious, right?"

"Disturbing. Are they real?"

"Of course they're real. And these are all sold. She is hot."

Lotta lit a cigarette and we heard footsteps headed toward us.

"Sat, come here," Lotta called out. "I want you to meet my friend."

"Sat" loomed large, just like her work. She towered over the room; she had at least five inches on me wearing flats. She was stick thin and suntanned, with wild blond beach hair. She could have been Fabio's daughter.

"This is Lucy, she's a writer. Lucy, this is Satina."

Sat took a puff of Lotta's cigarette.

"I was just telling Luce how wicked you are, honey. How huge you're going to be."

Sat stuck her hand out and I shook it.

"Nice to meet you, Satina."

"What?" she said.

"She can't hear in that ear," Lotta said to me. "Talk to her other one."

I aimed at her other side and tried again. "It's nice to meet you."

She smiled.

"We have fried chicken in the back, Lu. Plus bubbles. Sat is from Alabama."

The back room was a beautiful modern art-deco event space, wide open and airy. Lotta had a table laid out with sparkling rosé—one bottle was opened, two were on ice—and platters of food. Fried chicken, deviled eggs, and deep-fried little balls Satina informed me were boudin.

"Sat's grandmother knew Capote. Like, as a kid," Lotta said.

"Really?" I said.

Lotta was beaming at her new find.

"Grandma's dead, though," Satina said. "I haven't been back there in a while."

"I'm sorry."

"Don't be. She's been dead for a long time. Everyone's over it."

"Well, I love your work. It's intense. I couldn't look very long, it rattled me." I picked up a boudin.

"What are these?"

"They're kind of like doughnut holes," Satina said, "but spicy not sweet. There's an art to how you make them, everyone has their own secret. My aunt Jen makes the best. These are good, though, Lotta."

"Birds and Bubbles, East Village. When my girl wants Southern comfort, I get her Southern comfort."

Lotta filled three glasses with champagne.

"Okay, so listen, Luce. This totally hot piece of work has been coming around. He's a collector, Russian. Sat met him. He is take-your-fucking-breath-away gorgeous and all chill about it like he seriously has no idea how beautiful he is. He comes in, and knows his art but he's not an asshole. Says he's in town for a couple months and is shopping, can I show him something, blah blah. A-*maz*-ing piece of work. I'd clear out a floor just to display him. Right, Sat?"

"He's luscious," Satina agreed.

"Russian?" I said.

"Yeah. Like he lives there Russian, but has a place here. He does something with electricity. I forget what he called them, but those windmill things."

Our glasses emptied fast. Lotta filled them back up and our first bottle was gone.

"Wind turbines. He's, like, an *oligarch*," Satina said. She laughed at the word.

"Oh, he's an oligarch, definitely," Lot said. "He's as oligarch as they come. Anyway, I showed him some pieces and bingo, sold him Satina right off. A commission. He wants her to do a piece in Russian, with the special characters and everything."

"I should do them in every language," Sat said.

"It's very *il bel inconnu*, Lu. The handsome stranger showing up out of nowhere. No one referred him, there was no appointment, no his people calling our people. *Très mystérieux*."

Satina had an appetite. She had eaten three pieces of chicken before I finished my first.

"Lucy, by the way, is Lucy Brockton. As in Titus," Lotta said into Satina's good ear. "As in, they're married."

I narrowed my eyes at her.

"What? Wow. Seriously?"

I smiled and nodded. "Seriously."

"Holy shit, that must be a trip."

"It is. It's a trip," I said. Poor, tall, gorgeous Satina. Here she was, just one degree from Titus, and stuck with me.

"They don't have sex anymore, though. Luce needs a foxy new man."

I glared, and Lotta winked at me. Satina was bent over her chicken. She had announced that to the bad ear.

"Honey," Lotta said, "pack up a care package for Bill, will you? Can you stop by there? This is the best fried chicken in the city. She'll appreciate it."

"Sure."

She turned to Sat.

"Doll, let's get out of here. We need some treats before the party."

Treats. Right. Art wasn't the only thing Lotta got high on. She turned to me. "Wild opening tonight. Come with!"

"I can't, sweetie," I said. "I need my sleep. I hope to see you again, Satina. Keep her out of trouble."

16

· · · · · · · · ·

ODIN OF NEW YORK
MONDAY, JUNE 23

WRITE THE BOOK OR SELL THE JEWELS . . .

That is what Ava Gardner said when she was old and broke. It was time for her to be practical and those were her options, literally, if she wanted to keep the lights on. Spill her secrets or unload the gems. What would you do? I'd tell the secrets. Every time.

Ava moved to London to get old—she was smart. Don't wilt beneath the spotlight, ladies; do it quietly and out of town.

What do the women of New York do when they feel that first stab of faded beauty? When maintenance isn't just a fun girls' day anymore but a full-time job and your husband is having his first blatant affair, the kind where if you call him on it he'll leave, and if you don't he'll probably still leave, just not as soon.

You have to think of money, of course. But men are good. Don't kid yourselves. Women who come out ahead are as rare as a good book advance. You hear a lot about the one or two who get one, but everyone else starves.

And the options for second husbands get depressing fast. Best to get that first divorce behind you quickly. Don't get caught still waiting for it at forty-two.

Men can always make money. They don't need gyms or dermatologists. They don't need fillers or caps or waxes or extensions, because they can always make money. When they lose it, they can make more. And as long as they have it, they will have women. Ladies, you're disposable.

So what do the beautiful women of New York do when the offers dry up and the divorce settlement is nowhere near what their Miami lawyer led them to believe, and when the parties they're invited to are the same ones He goes to with his—*God, that was fast!*—next wife, who might also be your former best friend's niece . . . what does one do?

No access to the yacht or jet. Avoiding the shame of flying commercial means having friends who'll still take pity. Assuming they don't get dumped before you rebound.

I would try to find a modest flat in Paris. You can have a nice life there on a reasonably small income, and you can go incognito on the Champs-Élysées, wearing Topshop knits and dark glasses. You can always dim the lights strategically when the infrequent suitor comes to call.

Look around. The woman I'm describing is at your dinner party tonight. She's there with her husband, but he's just started screwing the new "face of J.Crew." She knows it, the whole table knows it, but it's not for anyone to say yet. Not until she has a plan, anyway. She doesn't have a plan.

They lose interest, girls. And they aren't sentimental; they don't come back. And sad, I know, but now no one cares about your smart Wellesley degree, or your languages, or your ability to pull off a sit-down dinner for twelve on a day's notice.

You have spent years perfecting entire skill sets that are worthless.

In her better days, Ava Gardner swam nude in Hemingway's pool. He watched her climb out once, and ordered his staff to never drain it. Such power she had. Such brief and fleeting power. Then she died alone with the lights dimmed, trying to sell her secrets for cash and grateful for the occasional check Sinatra sent her way.

Get the jewels while you can, girls. Then put them away for a small flat in Paris.

God, she's depressing. I wanted a drink after reading her. This is Odin. This is what I'm working with. I'm working with the *idea* of a woman. I have to figure out a story to tell about her, even if she's not there. She's everyone, she sees everything. And she's invisible.

JULY

17
· · · · · · · · ·

SoulCycle
384 Lafayette Street, NoHo
Tuesday, July 1
Girls' night

It's hot and we're moody. I'm worried about this piece. I'm supposed to find someone no one's ever met and write something amazing in four weeks. Impossible deadline. Nothing to work with.

It's fitness night, so we're at SoulCycle on Lafayette. This is Billy's pick. It's a tough-love workout, intense, like her. They hold the class by candlelight, which appeals to her green side, and Lauri, the instructor, has the best playlists of anywhere we go.

"I called her. Left a message," Sarah said and shrugged her shoulders.

"And I texted her," Billy said. "Nothing back."

I hadn't seen Lotta since the gallery, and none of us had talked to her in a week. It wouldn't have been so unusual if we hadn't had the sense something was off. We took three bikes in the back.

I'm not overly ambitious with my workouts. I have no great dreams of running marathons, but I do feel like I'm in above-average shape. I can carry on a conversation through the entire class, for instance. Sarah struggles. Billy, of course, is a fiend. She wouldn't even feel this.

"Okay, state of the union, Lu. Go," Sarah said as we strapped in our shoes.

"I met with Noel. I'm profiling some blogger he's obsessed with who no one knows how to find."

I checked to make sure my resistance was set to one.

"*And* I handed in our little 'Hot' piece. September issue. Don't worry, I only used first names."

I started pedaling slowly to loosen up.

"Thank God," Billy said. "I don't need publicity about my lack or abundance of hotness, whichever one it is."

"Also," I said, "Cheri already dumped her new boyfriend. He snores."

"Ew. That's bad. Can't he take something for it?" Sarah asked. "Seems like an easy correction."

"She doesn't want to have to work that much this early. She's not ready for the fix-it-pill stage."

"What about Mr. Man?" Sarah asked between breaths. The class hadn't officially started and she was already in workout trauma. "What's new there?"

"He's working. He's moody. He's obsessed with this one piece for the show."

They exchanged looks.

"It's not a big deal. He's under a lot of pressure. Billy had a date," I said. "Let's talk about her and George the Matchmaker, and their trapeze."

"Let's not," Billy said.

We were still in warm-up, but she had her resistance already set at three.

"Fine," she said. "First, trapezes suck. I didn't know I was afraid of heights. Now I do. Then afterward I thought I'd be nice and feed him, so we went back to my place and I made steak frites."

"Okay," Sarah said. "So far so good."

"Well, he's a matchmaker. Right? But a really shitty one if he was trying to match with me. He took his iPad out while I was seasoning the frites, with a very expensive *fleur de sel*, by the way, that he definitely did not deserve, and he pulled up a porn site. And cranked up the sound! He sat there on my couch waiting for me to feed him and watched porn. It was gross—the lights weren't even dimmed. We hadn't even had a drink."

"Wow," I said.

"No jokes, Luce."

"Can you still use him professionally?" Sarah asked. "Can he still match you up with someone else?"

"I don't think he's in the right line of work," Billy said.

Lotta strolled in then, casually. We were just ending warm-up, so she was technically very late. She was supposed to be stretched and locked in already. She took the empty bike next to Sarah, who was incensed. Sarah gets frustrated with Lotta's nonchalance.

"You can't just walk in after warm-up!" she hissed. "I'm surprised they even let you. Where have you been? Where were you?"

"Shopping," Lotta said, with her mischievous Swedish grin. Lotta is as reckless with money as she is with men and drugs. With everything. "I left it behind the front desk—they're watching it for me. Bag to die for, girls."

"Ooh, what is it? Tell," Sarah begged, her disapproval instantly gone.

We're all a sucker for a new bag, but Sarah's the worst. She could feed a small country with what she spends.

"Chanel. You'll see."

"Why didn't you call me back?" Sarah asked her. "I left a message. And why didn't you answer Billy's text?"

"Phone died."

"For a week?"

Lotta shrugged her shoulders, flipped her hair into a high bun, and strapped in her shoes.

Then the lights went out and we were awash in candlelight.

"Welcome to Tuesday *SoulCycle!*" Lauri announced through her mic.

"Today we ride with the spirit and *energy* with which you *learn* to *live.* Breathe through the *nose.*"

We stopped talking. The mood was set. Hard, sweaty, yet sort of romantic, too, in a weird way, with the candles and Lauri's soothing voice. You can get lost in it. Billy and my mother are both addicted. I can see why.

"Another *turn* to the *right.* Reach *down* and put it in that *third position,* angels."

Billy moved hers to five. You can cheat and stay at a low resistance the whole class. But what's the point of that? Sarah was still at one.

"Get in a *rhythm* with the one in *front of* you and get in *tune* with the *person* next to *you. Concentrate* on that *view!*"

There were some nice views in the room.

"Let your Tuesday *go!* Let it *fade away* in this first ride and open yourself up to the *awesome* possibilities you see right now. *Today!*"

The music started blasting. Lauri began to shout at us above it. Her assistant, a sleek blonde with a butt you could serve tea on, was yelling at us from the back. "SoulCycle, *bitches!* Get off that saddle!"

Sarah hated it; I saw her wincing.

We were all wearing the same Lululemon leggings with matching black tanks. I know, cute. It's just a thing we do. Our little nod to solidarity. We were also all sans makeup except Sarah, who even had her eyelashes on because in her new social pursuits, she had to be camera ready, everywhere, all the time.

Billy was wearing a fat headband, with her long wild hair pulled back tight. She looked like she was taking a road ride from Southampton to Montauk. She takes her workouts seriously.

"Eight more. Right here, Lucy. Look at me!"

Lauri doesn't let anyone coast.

"Lotta. You're holding back, babe. Let it go!"

"This is bullshit," Lotta said.

Taylor Swift came on, and watching Sarah "shake it off," I started laughing so hard I could barely pedal. Lauri closed us down with "Empire State of Mind," and the entire room sang along to it.

Concrete jungle where dreams are made of. There's nothing you can't do, now you're in New York.

Forty-five minutes later, we were sweat-soaked and hopped up on endorphins. The room cleared out slowly, but we jumped out first. We skipped stretching.

"Okay, who's up for margys, dolls?" Lotta asked in the locker room. "*Après*-workout drink? Yes?"

"Where have you been, Lotta?" Sarah asked her. "Seriously."

"Come on, Sar. I *work*. My Swedish charm does not pay the rent."

Sarah rolled her eyes.

"I'll go, but I only have an hour," Billy said.

"Oh God. Don't tell me you have some sad date with a guy who winked at you on Match."

Billy glared at her but let it go. Lotta's playful like a cat is playful. Her claws come out.

I passed around powder in the locker room and we patted our faces down enough to look presentable.

"*Vámanos*, bitches. Chop, chop," Lotta said, hitting Sarah with a towel. She was toned and taut and ready to go. It's amazing what shopping and a workout can do for a girl's mood. And, of course, whatever she's taking.

"La Esquina, here we come!" Lotta announced, walking out onto the street with a new blue velvet *monster*-size Chanel bag.

"Holy shit!" Sarah said. "It's gorgeous."

She fingered it admiringly. "Lot, who buys a six-thousand-dollar Chanel bag on a Tuesday?"

"That's *exactly* when to buy a Chanel bag, sweetie. On a Tuesday."

Walking up Lafayette, from workout to drinks, in our matching leggings and coordinated tops, we looked like a movie trailer. Four cool girls taking over the city.

La Esquina is a big dark vault of a restaurant with a NO ADMITTANCE sign on the entrance and a long windy labyrinth of a maze to get in. The club vibe hit Lotta right between the eyes. She was in the bathroom before we even got a table.

"We should have searched the bag," I said.

"Are you kidding me?" Billy said after the three of us sat down. "She needs a post-workout hit? And where the hell is she getting the money for that bag?"

We ordered margaritas and grilled corn. Lotta found us twenty minutes later. Her eyes were red and she smelled of *l'eau de pot*. She looked stoned out of her mind. We knew the drill.

"Okay, state of the union, dolls. Catch me up," she said.

The music was too loud for anything serious, like a friendly but concerned casual question such as, "Honey? What the hell are you doing?"

Still, Billy, under her breath, managed to get in her disapproval. "You couldn't just *wait*? Until you got home?"

Sarah deflected. "So Lucy got a fabulous ombré, look at her. Gorgeous. Tight-Ass is painting a secret painting, and Billy had a bad date."

"Speaking of paintings, Luce . . . " Lotta said. "People are flipping out over this show. I hope he's ready."

Lotta and Titus are like sparring partners, whether they're in the same ring or not. I'm sure there is a lot of gossip right now about his show, and she's in the industry; she hears all of it.

"Babe," Lotta said, turning to Billy. "Where'd you meet this guy?

Whole Lotta Fish? What's it called, HotSugarDaddy? Where do all the cute virtual boys hang out now?"

Billy gave her a *don't go there* look. "He's a friend of a friend. And anyway, first and last date. I just need to work. I'm shopping my book."

"What? Shopping where?"

Oh, boy. *Drop it, Lotta,* I thought. Lately she zeroes in on one of us every time we get together.

"Selling it. I have the proposal at three different publishers. I'm just testing final recipes, then they'll drop in photography and copyedit. Done."

"Cool, doll."

"It's very close."

"If you say it's close, it's close," Lotta said.

I did a quick assessment. On the surface, four ordinary girls having a drink after a great workout. But you didn't have to dig deep to find trouble. Lotta was stoned. Billy was in a funk. Sarah was planning scenes with her embryos for a show she wasn't even on yet. I was checking my phone every minute for texts from an invisible lover.

I might be carrying on with a stalker. He could be doing this with ten other women, or maybe he's catfishing me. He could be an eighty-year-old man, or a fifteen-year-old kid. He could be Odin, for all I know. If you do a search on my name, one of the images that comes up is a photo of a Calvin Klein ad I shot once in nothing but a strategic pose. Maybe this is just a nut who liked my pictures and is getting some sick thrill.

"So this girl I'm writing about. Her name is Odin, she writes this blog called Odin New York," I said, changing direction. "Have you guys heard of her?"

Lotta's head whipped up from her phone. She'd just ordered a round of Moscow Mules even though we hadn't finished the margaritas. I was already two drinks behind her and done.

"Why?" she said. "Who's asking?" She peeled her sunglasses off. Her eyes went mock big.

"Noel wants me to write something about her, but I have to find her first. All I have is her Twitter name. No one knows how to reach her, or who she is. She's this big mystery."

"Never heard of her," Billy said. Typical. She wouldn't admit it if she had.

"He wants to feature it in a fall blockbuster issue," I went on. "A big bang. Like the fashion issues. Something to send *SNOB* flying off the newsstands. I'd love it if I could get her to do a photo shoot."

"Ha," Lotta said. "Well, that would do it. She's totally fucked up. She's a train wreck. Everyone will read that."

"Lotta, you don't even know her," Sarah said. "Why do you need to say that?"

That was a silly question. Why did Lotta need to say anything? Because she did. She smirked and shrugged her shoulders. "She *is*. She's fucked up. Cray-zee."

"How do you know? I've heard of her. I think she's smart. Everyone reads her blog. How does that make her fucked up?" Sarah and Lotta sometimes bicker like teenage sisters.

My phone was going off.

212-555-0134: Lucy, I am dreaming of you.
212-555-0134: Are you thinking of me?

"Yeah, well. My Russian knows her. The one I told you about, Luce, the oligarch. The hot collector who dropped out of the sky. Unless there's more than one Odin."

"What?" I said.

"Yeah. He was talking about her. Listen, I gotta go." She jumped up, threw three twenties on the table, and blew us a kiss before making her way back through the labyrinth and out the front door.

"Wasn't this her idea?" Billy said.

"At least it was just pot," Sarah offered.

"Yeah. She really toned it down for us," Billy said. She was losing her patience.

"She could have shared," I said. They didn't laugh. We all knew why she left. It wasn't to smoke more pot. Pot was nothing compared to what we were pretty sure she'd be doing later.

Txt me when you're home, love you, I sent her.

xox, she sent back.

"So what are we doing for your birthday, Lu?" Sarah said.

God. My birthday. Forty-two going on fifty.

"Nothing at all. Or something off-the-wall. Like a strip club in Newark. Or the zoo."

Lotta, of course, did not text to let me know she got home.

18

....

Lotta lives in one of the most famous buildings in New York, 43 Fifth Avenue, but no one ever says the "Avenue"; it's just 43 Fifth. Julia Roberts has an apartment in the building. People buy here just for the address. Lotta's ex-husband, David-turned-Danielle, the music producer she never lived with, cosigned the papers for her to get in. Lotta would never have gotten past the board on her own.

I'd been summoned here. She had something for me, she said. She was being coy about it.

Lotta is very similar to Titus in her makeup. I think this is why I'm slightly disapproving of her sometimes, which I feel guilty about but can't help. Or maybe I'm slightly threatened. If one of my friends was going to screw my husband behind my back, it would be her.

She has a man's appetite for everything. Money, sex, booze, drugs. She goes all out on all of it. Her blood type, we sometimes joke, is sex-positive. Her life quest is to lure anyone who comes near. She's a wolf.

"So, your girl Odin?" she said. "Here you go, doll."

She handed me a Cartier note card, and in Lotta's tight, chic scrawl right in the center was an e-mail address.

"Don't say I never gave you anything."

"Lotta! Where did you get this?"

"Oligarch."

"What? Where did *he* get it? Odin's an art whore? She's supposed to be so hard to find. I don't get it—how does he know her? Who is he?"

"It doesn't matter. Sometimes you don't ask, Luce. You just take."

Lotta was smoking Gauloises. She might not die gracefully, but she'll be glamorous as hell on the way.

"Where'd you go after SoulCycle last week? After drinks?" I asked.

"Out. Late night."

"I told you to text me. Even in the morning, I don't care."

She grabbed her phone and started to type. *I'm home, Lu. Kiss.*

"Cute," I said, reading her text on my phone.

"Bättre sent än aldrig," she said, smiling. "Better late than never." Lotta is a smart-ass in four different languages.

The buzzer signaled Billy on her way up. She had a date tomorrow night and she needed an outfit.

She saw the cigarette right away when she walked in and made it a point to cough. Then she made it a point to frown at the state of the apartment. Then she made it a point to point it all out.

"Jesus, Lot, it's like twenty degrees in here." She shut off the air conditioner and started opening windows. "It isn't healthy. It feels like a morgue."

Lotta put a box of salted crackers on the table, with a jar of tapenade, and then emptied a bottle of ice-cold vodka into water glasses for each of us.

"And are you kidding?" Billy said. She was flattening takeout boxes as indiscreetly as she could. "Lotta, the place is a mess."

"À ta santé," Lotta said, lifting her drink.

I spread some tapenade on a cracker. It was stale. The cracker, I mean.

"You can't put glass in the garbage!" Billy yelled from the kitchen.

"Jesus, I hope she gets laid," Lot whispered. She lit another cigarette in defiance.

"So listen, Lu. If you talk to her, be careful," she said after Billy walked back in.

"Talk to who?" Billy asked.

"Odin," I said. "Lot got her e-mail for me."

"Wait. You *know* her?" Billy asked. "How do *you* know her?"

Lotta demurred. "I know her *name*, I know of her. It doesn't matter. What does this guy do? Where are you going? What's his story?" Lotta asked.

"He owns a gaming company," Billy said. "That's all he told me. And his name is Max. We really didn't chat much."

"How old?"

"Um . . . twenty-five."

"Billy Sitwell!" Lotta said and laughed. "Jackpot! Is he bringing his skateboard?"

"Don't laugh, that's how it works. They're either twenty-five or sixty-five. There aren't forty-two-year-old men waiting to date us."

"Bri's forty-two," Lotta said.

"Yeah, because of Sarah's apartment. He's an anomaly. Once you hit forty, the formula kicks in. It's mathematical, you date up or down and his age moves in five-year increments in each direction for every one of ours."

"So wait," I said. "At forty-five you date fifteen-year-olds?"

"It's not a perfect formula," Billy said. "And we're going to Ward III."

We moved to Lotta's bedroom and started rating the options. Her closet looks like a sample sale on steroids.

"So he's young . . . Ward III, I'd do skinny leather, Versace tank." Lotta pulled the outfit, and Billy tried it on.

"Lot, whatever happened to that guy you introduced me to?" I asked her as she pulled out and examined a cropped, fur-trimmed sweater.

Last month I'd been at Rose Bar with Cheri and had seen a long, beautiful blonde wrapped around a very short older man. The man looked completely out of place and it turned out to be Lotta who detangled herself from him. He could have been her grandfather. And when she brought him over, she was clearly smashed. A long, lanky package of chemically induced mess.

"You know," I said. "The one you were with at Rose Bar. *Phillip?*"

She waved her vodka hand around, keeping it skillfully level.

"Oh, he was no one, he's a collector. He comes by the gallery all the time, but he's an investor so he has some ideas for me, too. I need to . . . What do you call it? I need to *diversify*. Mitigate my risk. You know, buy stocks like the other kids do. He just had some ideas."

She was making no sense.

"Bill, I changed my mind," she said. "Wear this one. Show him the abs."

Billy wrapped up the outfit and started scrounging through Lotta's kitchen. There was a jar of olives, a bottle of Dom, and Guerlain face cream in the refrigerator. She pulled out her phone.

"Lot, you need some supplies, honey," she said. "I'm ordering Thai."

"Beef salad," Lotta said.

"I don't care," I said. "Anything."

Across from me, on the far wall framed in Plexiglas, was an original Azzedine Alaïa. A one-of a-kind black leather dress that Azzedine had made for Lotta almost twenty years ago. Lotta never modeled but there was a time when she was everyone's muse. Designers used to fall all over each other trying to give her clothes. Azzedine gave her that dress when she was twenty-five and could still knock out a room with it.

Billy caught me eyeing it. "Remember that?" she said and rolled her eyes. "Hey, Lotta, sweetie. Remember that night?"

"No one remembers that night."

She wore the dress once, to the Costume Institute Gala at the Met, and then to an after-party at Daphne Guinness's. Things got a little wild and she woke up the next morning on Billy's couch, still in the dress, and with no idea how she got there. She was convinced someone drugged her drink. When she showed up at Billy's at 4 a.m. she said she'd lost her keys even though she was clutching them in her hand, and by the time she finally came to the next morning the dress was a wreck. She'd thrown up on it and her makeup was smudged all over. Billy was horrified. She wetted a pile of dish towels and began furiously mopping it off.

I reminded her of that.

"It was an original!" Billy said.

"You were a whole *lotta* mess that morning, honey," I said.

"Whatevs."

"You had a whole *lotta* MAC eyeliner all over everything," Billy added.

It had seemed funny, then. A twenty-five-year old girl with a bad hangover. Now, not so much. She always played harder than the rest of us, but also always assured us she had it covered. Like a tightrope walker who has pulled off his stunts enough times that no one thinks twice about it. Then, when you're not looking, they fall.

"Just be careful, Lucy," Lotta said now, cruising away from the subject. "You're easy to check up on. Make sure your secrets are cleaned up."

"What secrets?"

"All of them. This sneaky texting you're doing, for one."

"What?" I said.

"Wait, whoa, whoa. Back up, everyone. Lucy Brockton," Billy said. "What sneaky texting?"

Lotta was smug. I should have known better. There are no secrets with best friends.

"It's nothing. It's weird, I can't even explain it."

"Haven't you noticed how obsessed she is with her phone? It's first-stage affair," Lotta said.

"It's not first-stage affair, I don't even know who it is. Stop spying on me."

Lotta laughed and snapped her fingers. "Bingo. The handsome stranger!"

"What do you mean you don't know who it is?" Billy asked.

"I mean, I just started getting these texts one day. Out of nowhere. He knows me, he knows my name, and I don't know him."

"Oh my God, Lu. What if he's crazy? You should call the police."

"I'm not calling the police. If he's crazy, he's crazy."

"It sounds hot," Lotta said. "Cock shot yet?"

"No!" I said. "Yuk."

"Honey," Billy said, "you dated a guy for six months who showed the whole city his dick and that was before texting."

"Right, Jerrod. The Polaroids!" Lotta said. "He gave me one—I think I still have it."

"He's not sending pictures. Just . . . okay, yeah, it's kind of intense. I can't explain it."

"Why aren't you fucking him?" Lotta always gets to the point.

"I don't even *know* him. I don't even know his name."

"They're having emotional intercourse," Billy said. "That's better. Dangerous, too, Lu. Be ready to change your number."

"Your last date put porn on full blast while you made dinner and you didn't change your number."

"Touché."

Maybe it was dangerous. I hadn't heard from him in two days. And I hated it.

19
· · · · · · · ·

O kay. Here we go.

To: O@OdinNYC.com
From: LucyBrockton@SNOBmagazine.com
Re:

Dear Odin,

Please forgive me if this seems odd. You don't know me, though I imagine you could. I'm easy to look up and feel free to dig. Anything you can't find I'll tell you.

I'm going to just throw this out. You're the jewel of the city, everyone's talking about you. You've got everyone on edge, but in a good way. A city summer can drag and wilt and you've made this one very cool.

I write for *SNOB* magazine—cutting-edge culture, politics, the fashion scene, that sort of thing. I'd like to feature you in a piece and wonder if you'd be willing to talk. It can be any way you want. I can protect your anonymity. It can be light, we can exchange e-mails. You're in control.

I hope to hear from you.

(I thought what you wrote on uptown/downtown was brilliant.)

Best,

Lucy D. Brockton

(555) 867-5309

The chances of her responding, I thought, were low to none. She'd completely ignored my tweet. I took a handful of jelly beans and played Esther Perel again.

And then, just like that, an e-mail. She responded to my clumsy pitch within minutes. Yes, she would talk. But not in person and not on the phone. Not yet.

Holy shit. What? That's it? That's all I had to do? What was so mysterious? I was beginning to think Noel was nuts. Had anyone else even tried to find her?

I wrote back.

To: O@OdinNYC.com
From: LucyBrockton@SNOBmagazine.com
Re: Re:

Okay, wonderful! Some questions to warm up, then? À la Proust. Take liberties.

Your favorite book?

If you could be any writer who would you be?

What do you look for in a handbag?

Panties and bra: matched set or random?

Reality star or rock star?

Shoe: Jimmy Choo or Brian Atwood?

21 or Bouley?

East Hampton or South?

. . .

Last: What is the first line of your memoir?

Best,

Lucy

God, how cheesy. I regretted it the minute I sent it. Because then I got this.

To: LucyBrockton@SNOBmagazine.com
From: O@OdinNYC.com
Re: Re: Re:

Dear Lucy,

Oh my, what introspective questions! So unique. You won't learn anything about me from them, but I'll answer anyway. Not in any particular order. I'll let you match them up.

First, you didn't ask but I have blue eyes and black hair.

Second, no one can name a favorite book with honesty. It's like trying to pick a favorite feature of your body, it's fluid. Today I might say my legs. They're long and suit my purpose. But tomorrow I could just as easily say my ears. Some days I do love my ears.

Massaro for shoes. You can also say I love Fellini if you want. I don't, but it might play well.

I would be Gertrude Stein, as a writer, because I could be fat and drunk all day and write nonsense that everyone reveres. So on that note, first line of my memoir would be, of course, nonsense.

I don't know about the rest, this has tired me. Maybe later I'll send answers to questions you should have asked.

Be better,

O

Okay, I deserved that. But I could work with it. A little provocative, yes. I don't think she's who Noel wants her to be.

To: O@OdinNYC.com
From: LucyBrockton@*SNOB*magazine.com
Re: Re: Re: Re:

Dear Odin,

Thank you, and point made. Please still consider meeting. I'm a great fan.

Lucy Brockton

20

....

The Standard Hotel
848 Washington Street, Meatpacking District
Tuesday, July 8
Girls' night

O h my *God*, you are serious about this, doll?" Lotta seemed genuinely impressed. Sarah *is* serious about it. Her "team" got her
the August cover of *Avenue*, so we're celebrating. *Avenue* is a magazine for New Yorkers by New Yorkers. It might be meaningless to the
rest of the country, but it's an important step on the social-climbing
ladder.

It's one of those *look at my great apartment* spreads; she showed
us the galley. Her Baker sofa, the Christian Werner chairs. Sarah in
a proper pose, smooth and shiny, her legs crossed like chopsticks beneath her vintage Chanel suit. Every last piece of intellectual clutter
is styled, right down to the antique tea set casually placed on a stack
of Assouline coffee-table books. On the cover she's wearing a Jason
Wu gown that screams *I'm rich and I'm loving it*. She looks drop-dead
gorgeous—the New York dream.

We were at the Standard, and thirsty. "Old-fashioned shooters,
Stu. Line us up," Billy said to the bartender. The rooftop bar has one
of the best brunches in town. At night, though, it's a different crowd.
Gothamist rated it the "Best Bar to See Naked Models on Ecstasy."

It's early, though, just after seven. No naked models yet. Lotta's their best shot.

Stuart lined up four shot glasses of bourbon for us, then set out a sugar shaker and a bowl of orange slices soaked in bitters.

Lotta went first and Stuart watched her, mesmerized, as she unfurled a long, smooth, sculpted arm, licked the back of her hand, and coated it with sugar. She tongued the sugar off like Dita Von Teese, slammed her shot back like a gunslinger, then stuck an orange slice in her mouth and sucked.

Bystanders cheered.

"Jesus," Billy said under her breath. "Is there anything she does that isn't hot?"

No. There really isn't. Sugar. Tongue. Bourbon. Repeat.

She had clearly started beverage service before she got here, though. This wasn't her first shot of anything for the night, and this has been the case, lately, almost every time we see her. Sarah caught my eye and gestured toward her disapprovingly. Lotta's always pushed the envelope, but she's lately started ripping it in half. No one at the bar seemed to mind, though. She had an audience. Who else could pull off an old-fashioned shooter like that?

Grilled oysters mignonette appeared on cue. Billy's always on top of it.

Lotta was laughing too loudly at everything we said. She dismissed the food. She started to bicker with Sarah. She was drunk, and probably high.

"So, seriously Sar," she said. "Do you call the paps now and tell them which hot new restaurant you're going to walk out of?"

I tried to head it off.

"James says you should—" I started, but Lotta cut me off.

"Why talk about him so much, Lu, so incessantly? Just fuck him already."

Even for Lotta, sharp-tongued on her soft days, it felt hostile.

She gave me a long look, sighed, then put her sunglasses on and threw her phone in her bag.

"Listen, dolls, I hate to leave you dry and high but I have a *vee-ry* important client I need to meet. He's buying a fucko expensive piece, huge commission. I can't blow him off."

She finished the shot of bourbon that was in front of her and gave me a quick kiss. Then she waved to the room and was gone.

"She's full of shit," Sarah said. "I think she's just screwing that guy. I know who she's talking about—he's not a client. He's like an 'art john.' He pretends he's going to buy something so she'll keep screwing him. I saw her with him last week, in front of Bilboquet. Loaded with shopping bags and she looked out of it. She didn't even see me. She was all over him, though. I'm sure he bought her that Chanel. Maybe he's getting her drugs. He's sure as hell not collecting art. And he's *really* old."

"Okay, so she has an older boyfriend," I said. "I think I met him."

"Really *old* older boyfriend. She's broke because she's snorting all her money. Or giving it to those little gallery kids she hangs around with. I bet she's already blown the last commission she made. She hasn't talked to her father in six years and she pretends everything's great. She'll be couch surfing in Brooklyn if she doesn't get her shit together."

Livia always says there are two things you don't want to be in this city if you're a woman: broke or old. God forbid, she says, if you're ever both.

"Plus she meets all these guys on Tinder, and they totally take advantage of her," Billy added.

"She's Tinderella," Sarah said. "And you should talk, Bill."

"Whoa," I said. "Let's just relax."

I'd seen Lotta roll through Tinder. One guy sent her a selfie from his bathtub while Billy and I were at her apartment. She showed it to us. He wanted to read her poetry, he said. "Something hot and sexy, like you." This was less than ten minutes after she'd swiped him. Who says that? Is this *really* the way people date? No small talk, no dinner, even. Just straight to bubbles and dark poetry.

"How can she be broke? What about the Dalí?" Billy asked. She air-quoted "Dalí."

Lotta's family had had in their possession, at one time or another, some very expensive art. She didn't just stumble her way into the business. But the story around each piece always ends with her grandfather gambling it away, or giving it to a mistress, or losing it somehow in a drunken blackout. All of Lotta's stories seem to have a gambler or a drunk. We've heard various versions of the famous art dealer grandfather in Sweden, and though minor details shift around, the end note is always this: money doesn't last for men who love women and gambling. It's a slippery slope.

The one piece Grandpa didn't lose, though, according to Lotta, was a Dalí self-portrait. It was given to him by Salvador himself, before he had any idea of what he was worth. It was a sentimental favorite, and years later Dalí tried to persuade Lotta's grandfather to sell it back. He wouldn't and Dalí was outraged. Lotta brought it onto the plane with her in a shopping bag (so her story goes) when she came to New York. She claimed to have it in a security box at Chase. Which makes no sense at all. Chase Bank? That's not where people stash a Dalí.

Titus never believed any of this story for a minute. He hates art tales. It's true that no one knows for sure whatever happened to the piece—Lotta could have it beneath her bed. Sarah swore that she'd seen it, which isn't important. What is important is, if she did have the Dalí in a safe box, she had a sizable fortune. It's worth millions. She wouldn't need to sleep with eighty-year-old men.

21
. . . .

Washington Square Park
West Village
Sunday, July 13

O n Sundays in the summer, James is one of the stylists who gives free cuts in Washington Square Park. Sometimes I meet him here, with lunch. Today I asked Billy to make up sandwiches. I brought the ingredients, she put them together. Roast beef with pickled blueberries, tuna salad with beets and ricotta, and a broccoli sub with lychees and feta cheese. Bill's expression of culinary art in its simplest form.

James was standing at his makeshift salon—a towel-covered bench, a leather satchel of tools. "Hey, gorgeous," he said. "I'm just finishing up."

James will cut anyone who stops, but he does this mostly for the transients who make their homes here. They don't know who he is and they don't care. A guy in Prada saving the world one head at a time.

He was trimming up one of the most beautiful men I had ever seen. Chiseled jaw, dark eyes, broad shoulders, perfect stubble. He could have walked in from central casting.

"Lucy this is Alex. Alex, Lucy Brockton. Writer, model, woman about town."

Alex turned his head to me and smiled—teeth, dimples, eyes.

Check. He was so perfect it was unsettling. "Hello, Lucy." It was slight, but I heard an accent. German?

"Nice to meet you," I said. He didn't look like someone who'd wander through the park for a free haircut.

James works fast. He's like a sculptor in a cartoon: a few quick movements you can't really see, then voilà.

"Okay, all good," James said.

Alex stood up and the view got better. He was tall, with an athletic build. There are so many people in New York who are attractive; there aren't so many who stand out—because if everyone looks perfect, it's all the same. This guy stood out.

"Alex is visiting for a few weeks," James said.

"Oh. Really? Do you have plans?"

He grinned—the dimples!—and I blushed. "I mean, are you planning to see some things while you're here?" I caught myself.

"A few things," he said. He was staring at me—it was awkward. I looked away.

"Thank you, James," he said. He took a money clip from his pocket and James stopped him.

"Nope. Free on Sundays, buddy. Can't take it."

"Well, thank you very much." He smiled, then turned to me, grabbed my hand in the two of his, and left.

"Oh my God," I said. "What was that?"

"Not bad, huh?" James said. "I thought I was going to have to give you smelling salts."

"I'd love to know what *his* story is."

James nodded. "Yeah. Interesting."

I watched him walk away. In the movie version of my life, that would be *Him*. The mysterious stranger who chases after me in his chauffeur-driven pumpkin and Armani suit. We sat down and I handed James a sandwich.

"So, what—he was just in the neighborhood?"

"I guess. You heard him, he's just in town for a few weeks. He's Russian. Does something with windmills or something. What's new, love?"

"Windmills? No. The world can't be that small."

"What?"

"Nothing. Lotta just met this Russian guy who's in windmills. Never mind, it's too weird."

I was having a hard time with the transition. From Alex to chit-chat. Lotta's oligarch?

"This girl I'm writing about is . . . interesting."

"How so?"

"She's not nice, for one. I'm not sure how to approach it."

"Don't make her bigger than she is or you won't be able to write about her. Who was that guy, the one who wrote about Sinatra?"

"Gay Talese."

"Yeah, well, you told me Sinatra wouldn't talk. He was being an asshole, right? And this guy who wrote it just took charge of the story."

"Good point."

I snuck a long look at him while he was eating his sandwich. There were wrinkles around his eyes I hadn't noticed before.

"What else, doll? Your mind's racing."

"I don't know. We're all worried about Lot. And that's really strange about that guy."

I took a last bite of my tuna salad—Billy's brilliant combination of texture and taste.

"Lotta's fine, Luce. She just likes to play. You make too much out of it."

He has said this to me before. But James knows Lotta through me. So how could he know if I'm making too much of it? We've all had drinks a few times. He does her hair once in a while. They might bump into each other here and there, but he doesn't *know* her.

The sound of my phone signaled a text.

212-555-0134: Where are you, beautiful? Where do I find you, my
   heart aches.

I looked around. There was no one, anywhere, with their fingers
to a phone in sight. I texted back quick as James started to pack up
his bench.

                    Me: I'm here. You know I'm here. You know I'm waiting.

What was I doing?

22

· · · · · · · · ·

Brockton town house
Bedroom office
Monday, July 14

I had a stack of magazines piled high by my desk—back issues of *SNOB*, *Esquire*, *Vanity Fair*. I was reading everything I could get my hands on. I read Fitzgerald's "The Crack-Up." David Foster Wallace's magazine work, Lillian Ross and everything Lillian Ross ever wrote for *The New Yorker*.

I had started a biography of Mata Hari to try to get inside this girl's head. But, full confession—I was mostly reading TMZ. The posts *and* the comments, *and* all the links within the posts. I was following every Kardashian story, and then the sub-stories. I couldn't keep straight who was doing what, but I couldn't stop. Khloé was working out, Kim was wearing an outfit, Kendall or Kylie was wearing a racier outfit, and one of them said something on Twitter, then someone replied. I didn't even know who half of these people were and I was hooked. How could I write something more compelling than this?

My ringtone went off.

"Luce." It was Sarah.

And a text came right behind it.

212-555-0134: My lovely Lucy . . .

I can't right now, I thought. *On the phone. Don't go.*

212-555-0134: It thrills me to think of you. Do you know that?

"Lucy. Are you there?"

"Yes, sorry. I was just looking . . . at something."

"So lunch, Saturday, wherever you want. Then Lot has a surprise."

Saturday. My birthday. My forty-second. What happened to thirty-five? I don't even remember seeing it.

"Okay. I don't care. Anywhere."

"Lucy. You have to care! You can't just not care, that ruins it."

"Somewhere low-key. Light on drinking. No bickering."

212-555-0134: . . . to imagine the warmth and softness of your skin
. . . to touch the back of your neck . . .

"Jesus," I whispered.

"What? What are you doing?"

"I'm here. Sorry. I'm just reading some things. Okay, text me where to meet."

"No, *you* text us where to meet. Lunch and then the after. Save the whole day."

"You're too good to me," I said. "It's saved."

"Kisses."

212-555-0134: Lucy, tell me one thing you desire . . .

23

· · · · · · · · ·

I picked Charlie Bird for lunch and we polished off three bottles of Pouilly-Fuissé before dessert. So much for low-key.

Titus was in his studio when I left. He didn't seem to realize what day it was. I didn't care. I wasn't thrilled about this birthday anyway, and also, I'd spent every minute since waking up thinking of Him.

I was getting a cheater's conscience.

At the restaurant, I was thinking about him. I missed half of the conversation because I was thinking about him. All I can think about is being anywhere else right now with him, or checking my phone to see if he's there. There is a physical sensation in my chest when I think of him, an ache that lies somewhere between pleasure and panic.

"Okay, pussycats, girls. Let's go. Get the check." Sarah picked up the check and Lotta got us a car.

The four of us squeezed in, giggling and tipsy. Lotta jumped in the front and gave the driver the address. Her surprise? Vagina facials at J. Sisters.

"It's beauty on crack, dolls," Lotta said. "Vag, then a pedi. We'll have the prettiest parts in town when we get out of there."

Vagina facial, for my birthday. And so it goes. Life creeping into one endless maintenance torture session.

I'd been waxed there before. Everyone had, it's a rite of passage. J. Sisters Salon invented the Brazilian bikini wax. But this would be my first va-jacial, which is one step beyond. For an hour, one of the Sisters would strip, pluck, scrub, smooth, and lather my . . . yeah.

"What exactly do they do again?" I asked in the car. I wasn't sure if I'd had enough wine to let a woman spend an hour between my legs.

"Don't worry about it, Luce. Just go with it. It's amazing," Sarah said.

"Vag and pedis. Birthday vag and pedis," Lotta was chanting as we walked single file up the narrow staircase to the second floor. "The pedi hurts like hell here, but it's worth it. Promise."

The J. Sisters are to vaginal maintenance what Tom Ford is to the little black dress. They changed the game. Reclining chairs, recessed lighting, and little tubs of scalding wax make a beautiful kitty accessible to every woman in New York for less than the cost of a cab ride to the airport.

We each followed a different Sister, who led us back to cubicles and ordered us to strip. "Everything off, right? Okay?" mine said to me. Her name was Anna.

Lotta got the bombshell, of course, though they're all bombshells. Any one of the staff could be a centerfold. Anna seemed very nice until her torture session began.

"Ow, *shit!*" Billy said through the wall to my left. The dividers don't go up to the ceiling, so voices carry over.

"Ouch!" I said back and sucked in my breath.

Anna looked up, patted my leg, and smiled. "After? You'll be so happy."

"This is living, girls," Lotta said through the wall on my right.

It is very no-frills. The thing that marks the salon as slightly out of the ordinary is the cluster of signed pictures of celebrities on the wall. I was staring at Naomi Campbell while Anna stripped off my wax.

"I feel like I'm being skinned," I said.

"Don't be a baby, Lu," Billy scolded.

Anna popped her head up from between my legs. "Yes," she said. "I'm making you soft like that, just like a baby."

"How was your skateboarder, Bill?" I said, trying to distract us.

"It's Max. And he owns a *gaming* company, Lu. He doesn't skateboard."

"Ow!" I said. "This is ridiculous."

"He was cute but his ex-girlfriend's a Victoria's Secret model and he wouldn't shut up about her. These guys are so stupid about *models*. If you just say you're a model you don't have to do one other fucking thing. No offense, Luce."

"None taken."

I bet this was fun to listen to from the waiting room. The sound of stripped wax and the four of us yelling in pain.

"I have ingrown hairs!" Sarah wailed.

"No, noo, don't worry," her Sister assured her. There was a pair of sharp gleaming tweezers in every cube.

Anna let me take a break and put my legs down. Hot wax, tweezers, and then a long, intimate pampering. She had a shelf of lotions and exfoliants that she rubbed and moistened and scrubbed with; then she spread on a papaya enzyme mask and set the timer.

"Fifteen minutes," she said. "Then all done. Just like that."

Just like that.

"How's your marriage going, Lu? Now that we got you drunk at lunch. Talk."

"What? I don't know. Exhausting. It definitely needs a tune-up.

It's funny, you start out thinking how romantic it will be, even, to change his colostomy bag at eighty because you just love him that much. But then something happens. And it's like there's nothing you can do about it. Fifteen years, and one day you're just roommates making small talk. Being polite." Having sex dreams about strangers.

"Whoa, Lucy. So dark! Come on, Sarah's getting ready to walk into this. Again," Billy said.

"Ha! She'll be a serial wife, it's in her gene pool."

"I can hear you, Lot!" Sarah said over the wall.

"Lucy, I don't get it," Billy said. "I mean, does he have erectile dysfunction or something? Can't you just go have hot sex?"

"I don't know. This is terrible, but sometimes I like the attention he gets from other women, because it's less to feel responsible for."

"Aren't you attracted to him?" Sarah asked.

"I know he's attractive. I mean, I can see that. He's an attractive man. But I don't even know how I would have sex with him right now. It would be awkward. He's not asking me, by the way. If I walked into his studio in stilettos and a G-string I doubt he'd look up."

Lotta and I were finished first and moved to the foot baths. Anna followed us and pulled out a tray of what looked like archeological tools. She started digging into my cuticles like Kennewick Man was buried underneath.

"So forget Titus, how's it feel?" Lotta asked. "How's forty-two?"

Let's see, my husband forgot it was my birthday. My invisible boyfriend doesn't know. I have no embryos on ice, and I just got my pussy plucked and plumped for nothing. Who'll see it?

"Could be worse," I said.

"So remember that guy Devon you used to fuck?" Lotta said. She has no problem cursing in a salon.

"Barely. That was twenty years ago," I said. "And we didn't 'fuck.'"

"Well, that's probably why you broke up, which answers my question."

This is her way of finding out how serious we ever were, or weren't.

"He bartends at Acme now. I saw him the other night."

"Are you serious, Lot?" Sarah piped in from her cubby. "I hope you didn't talk to him, he was a total jerk."

"He ditched Lu in the Hamptons. Remember? He just left her there, stranded," Billy added.

"Okay. So they didn't click. It was for the best."

I hadn't thought of Devon in years. He'd gone from asshole to anecdote a long time ago.

"He looks great."

No one responded.

"Are you asking for my blessing?" I laughed. "Are you dating him?"

"I just want to comply with code."

"You shouldn't date him on principle," Sarah said. "Jerk code."

"*Den som spar han har,*" Lotta said. "Waste not, want not, girls."

"Do it," I said. "God, if you had to avoid every man I've ever dated in this city it'd be a pretty dry well."

They didn't respond.

"It was a joke," I said.

"You had two boyfriends," Billy said.

"That's why it was funny."

"They both sucked."

"Thanks, Sar," I said. She didn't stop.

"Remember Jerrod?"

"Let's talk about something else," I said. "Sweetie," I said to Lotta, changing the subject. "How do *you* think you're going to like forty-six?"

Her birthday was next.

"It's going to be *fab*-ulous, Lucy-Lu. Year of the Rabbit, which means I am amorous and romantic. What color are you doing?"

"Blue Midnight."

Lotta grabbed Poor Little Rich Girl Red.

"Hey, dolls. Did you know Hemingway wouldn't drain his pool after Ava Gardner swam nude in it?" She winked at me.

I smiled. "You're reading Odin's blog."

"Wow, now that's power," Sarah said.

"Yeah, but it's so fleeting," Billy replied. "What does it get you?"

"A kick-ass memoir, that's what it gets you," Sarah said.

"You know what?" I said. "We need birthday champagne. Moët and caviar. Lot, call Phonemate."

Phonemate delivers anything you ask them to, anywhere in the city, anytime. Including Moët and osetra caviar to a Brazilian waxing salon in midtown. They were there in fifteen minutes.

"Birthday toast, someone." We were smoothed and pedi-ed and fully clothed again.

Billy did a modified saber on the bottle that sent champagne shooting everywhere.

"Bill!" Sarah said, her shirt soaked, laughing. There was barely enough left for the toast.

"To a dangerous age," I said.

"Ooh, Lucy. So noir." Lotta grinned. "To a dangerous age."

We clinked glasses and Lotta used hers to wash down two tiny pills she produced from a small box in her purse.

"Stop," she said, catching me watching her. "It's prescription, okay? Dolls, I think we need sushi. Omar's."

"We just ate!" Sarah said.

"Caviar isn't food. Come on, a tiny bite."

"Tao, then," Sarah said. "I'm not dressed for Omar's."

The house was empty when I got home. But there was an elaborate bouquet on the table with a note.

*Fire lilies, my darling, for your birthday. Like you, they are bold
and beautiful and as priceless and rare as a precious stone. They
are delicate, and fleeting.*

T

24

Kappo Masa
976 Madison Avenue, Upper East Side
Saturday, July 26

Titus and I were having dinner with Cheri tonight, for my birthday. It was a makeup. A week late, but he compensated for it. There was a Tom Ford box on my bed this afternoon. The chocolate-brown Tom Ford box is like the Tiffany box 2.0. It's the next level, for women with either very generous husbands, or very guilty ones.

Masa is small and serene and very nouveau. The banquettes are covered in leather the color of egg yolk. Dishes are served on thick frozen blocks of glass. It's Cheri's style. There are only a few handfuls of tables inside, which is why for most of the world it's impossible to get in. But Masa is Larry Gagosian's restaurant, in the basement of his gallery. Titus is not just another big-spending diner; his work is on the wall.

My mother flirted shamelessly with my husband. When we picked her up in the cab, she leaned into him, grabbed his arm at every jolt. She wears her dresses cut low when he's around—well, really, when anyone's around—and then flutters her hands above the exposed décolletage like a courtesan. She touches him when she speaks, and also when she listens. She's not making a play for him, though. It's not some latent attraction she can't suppress. It's worse than that. It's insulting. She's like a lioness who thinks she needs to teach her grown cub how to hunt.

She's exaggerated with Titus because she's hoping I'll take note. Because flattery and glossy nails on his arm will catapult us back to year-one bliss. Cheri's never been married for eighteen years. And she's never been married to him.

"Darling," Cheri said. She was sitting across from us and had her hand on his arm.

Darling. Now she was British. "Tell me what you're doing. I know there's that artist thing about bad luck to talk about the work, but Lucy says you're in a *frenzy.* Tell us something. Please, anything."

It's true that he doesn't like to be asked about his work. But Titus will never be rude to my mother. He indulges her. I've never seen him behave rudely with any woman, actually.

I broke protocol and signaled the waiter over. Titus watched me curiously while leaning in to hear Cheri. She recently sold a duplex to a couple with a Cy Twombly, she's telling him. No, she couldn't recall which one.

"He's a shapes, lines, and words man," Titus said, still watching me. "Cheap. They'd be better off selling the fucking thing and buying Apple stock than having to look at it every day."

Cheri beamed at this. She's become an amateur art snob with the tidbits he gives her.

Normally, Titus would have ordered the wine, of course. Titus selects the wine, Titus decides the food. But I know a thing or two and I was impatient. I picked a baijiu from the list—the Asian liqueur from Billy's "Nine Knockout Autumn Cocktails." The waiter looked impressed. When he came back with the bottle, he poured it for me to taste. I nodded and he filled three tumblers. Titus was amused by all this, I could tell. You do have to shake it up now and then, I guess. Whether you feel like it or not.

Titus summoned the waiter next. He'll trust me with the wine, but not the food. He's the one hanging on the wall upstairs, this is *his* joint. Besides, it's like a parlor game to him. He knows what women like. He picked our meals like a street magician guessing which card we had in our hands. He knew I would love the uni custard and the tuna tartare. For Cheri, the Kobe beef, and for himself, and for us to share, the *omakase*—chef's choice.

"You were asking, Cheri, about my piece. Of course you'll come to the show, yes? Everything is new. But the star of the collection, I believe, is the best work I've done."

"Ooh," Cheri said.

"Yes, it's about beauty. And the ways we unconsciously interpret it— the different filters and perspectives at play, things we don't even know that are going on. And it will mean something different on each new approach. It may be hard for me to sell, though. I've become attached."

I know when Titus talks like this that Cheri worries he's fallen in love. With someone else.

"Well, I can't wait to see it. How intriguing it sounds."

Cheri has one of Titus's paintings. She's one of very few who've ever received his work as a gift. He's not in the habit of giving any of it away. It's a small piece, beautifully framed, of a woman with a dog in the park. He painted it specifically for her, so there's whimsy. The woman is resting comfortably on a leash as the dog relaxes on a bench with a book.

As the plates arrived in succession, Titus subtly rearranged them after the waiter set them down. Composition. Everything he was doing tonight was composed—the small gestures, the selection, the solicitations toward my mother.

"Did you see the *Time Out New York* piece?" Cheri said.

He shook his head. He rarely reads his press.

"You're in 'Ten Must-Sees This Fall' with a lovely primer of your work and where to see it before the show."

"I read it," I said. "They did a nice job, I didn't recognize the writer but it was a good introduction."

When they start to write the tale of Titus's life, they'll tell all the stories I don't want to know. I'll be the midlife muse, the loyal second wife. Or maybe I'll be discarded. Or he'll outlive me. Or I'll be the one who didn't give him a child.

Picasso, with his wives and his muses, and the women he loved and the women who posed for him and the women he fucked and married and left—he was faithful to no one but himself. Of the significant women in his life, two died and two went mad. When he left Dora Maar, she said, "After Picasso, only God." Can you imagine coming up with a line like that? And then, who wrote it down?

I do not want to know about any women with broken hearts.

"Cheri, you were in Italy. How was your visit?"

"Beautiful," she said. "Positano is just heartbreaking, it's so lovely. Oh, I could live there. You two should get out of the city before the summer ends."

"Maybe after the show," Titus said. He took my hand and smiled.

After they cleared the table, with the city lights twinkling through the window, Titus selected a sake for a toast. Before the waiter brought it, though, he set out two small boxes. One in front of Cheri, and one in front of me. "The secret to a life lived well," Titus said, "is surprise. Especially for a beautiful woman."

There is a famous Cheri Bird adage: "Jewelry comes from men who don't mean what they say." So I was curious to see her reaction, but she looked genuinely touched. "Titus, how *enchanting* you are," she said. I watched their odd dynamic. Here she was, his young wife's mother, a beautiful and vibrant woman his own age. He was the type of man she should be dating, yet she was forced into this quasi-motherly role with him. Still, he was wining and dining her, and plying her with gifts.

Heart-shaped crystal drop earrings. Swarovski. Jet-black for me, pale rose for Mom. I kissed him thank you and then the sake came. Titus picked his up quick and made the toast:

"To our lives. And our loves." He nodded to me. "And to *folie circulaire*. The madness that rises and recedes."

After dinner, we dropped Cheri at her apartment and, out of character, I snuggled up to my husband for the ride downtown, but then he tapped the driver suddenly and asked him to stop.

"Wait. What?" I said. "What are you doing?"

"Something I need to do, Lulu. Don't think about it. You were beautiful tonight."

He gave the driver a hundred-dollar bill, kissed me, and got out. Was he serious? The driver casually pulled away like this was something he did every night. Drop the husband at Sixty-Fourth Street and drive the wife home.

I peered out the back window to try to see where he was walking but he was gone.

I didn't know if it was the baijiu tonight, or the sake, or the unplanned course of the day, but for a moment I'd expected a different outcome.

Damn jewelry. Cheri's always right.

At Fifty-Eighth Street, we were at a standstill. It would be half an hour, at least, before I was home. It was ten, and I didn't want to end the night making bad Netflix decisions.

I fished my phone out and sent an impulsive text. It was definitely the baijiu.

> **Me: Where are you? Have a drink with me? Mercy date.**

I got an instant reply.

> **James: Party girl. Yes! Caught me free. Meet at 7th and 11th.**

I told the driver the new plan. "Take your time," I said. I didn't want to get there first.

James was standing outside the unmistakable red awning of the Village Vanguard when we pulled up. I should have known. And he was holding something in his hand.

"The next set's in forty minutes," he said. "We can get a drink next door while we wait."

"A set? We're doing a *set*? Are we listening to jazz, Jimmy?" I giggled and put my arm in his.

"Not just jazz. The best jazz. It will blow your mind, sweetheart." He grinned.

In twenty years of New York, I had never been here. But I knew that Miles Davis played here. John Coltrane. Thelonius Monk. It's hallowed ground.

We went to the tiny bar next door and he ordered us each a scotch. "To my girl," he said. "Cheers." My second toast of the night. We clinked glasses and the scotch went down like candy. I could feel it color my cheeks.

"What is that?" I said. "In your hand?"

It was in brown paper wrapping, whatever it was, and he handed it to me.

"Happy birthday. I know I'm late."

I tore off the paper.

"It wasn't easy to find," he said.

It was a magazine. The April 1966 issue of *Esquire*. No explanation was needed. The headline was right there on the cover: "Frank Sinatra Has a Cold."

"JJ, how sweet of you!" I hugged him. I was giddy. *It must be the scotch*, I thought. It was just a magazine. I could have found it myself. But I was giddy.

"I was going to give it to you when you came in, but you don't usually ask for a drink late Saturday night. I thought maybe babydoll needs a pickup."

He laughed and grabbed my hand, and then casually let it go. I wanted to cry. Nothing. Right? We're just friends. Saturday night with a friend. Harmless.

My phone made a familiar ping.

212-555-0134: Where are you, my love?

My heart jolted. I quickly shoved the phone back in my bag.

"Okay," I said, taking another drink of scotch. "Who are we seeing? What do I do? When do we clap?"

He laughed. "Christian McBride, and you're going to love them. It's a trio. Piano, bass, and drums. You don't have to do anything. Clap when you want."

The club was in a basement. The ceilings were low, the room small. We sat in a cramped row of chairs with our drinks, a few feet from the music. It was hypnotic. Mind-blowing. When the drummer soloed, every pop, every brushstroke on the snare gave me chills.

Afterward, James called for a car and I assumed we were going home—my drop-off was first. But I didn't want to go home.

"Mr. Chow. Tribeca," James told our driver. Apparently he didn't either. It was almost 2 a.m.

Mr. Chow was packed. And the crowd was eclectic—women in three-thousand-dollar dresses, men in eight-hundred-dollar jeans, and college kids in American Apparel T-shirts.

We sat at the bar. I was suddenly starving, and the smell of chicken satay almost knocked me out. Immediately, plates started to arrive from the kitchen. Satay and a steaming mound of crispy beef.

"Oh my God," I said. "Their peanut sauce. I could bathe in chicken satay."

"Don't give me ideas," he said, and winked.

We drank champagne straight from the bottle, like beer, and

licked the sauce off the plate with our fingers. I was officially drunk when James playfully dropped a spoonful of sauce on my arm.

"Are you crazy?" I said, laughing. I wiped it off and got him back.

Within minutes, we had satay sauce everywhere. The bartender offered us dish towels and another round. I definitely didn't need it. We were acting like two teenagers after prom. We started to clean ourselves up, laughing hysterically, and then James licked off a spot on my arm. I was feeling the Moët, big-time. And the scotch and the sake and the baijiu all at once. He was licking my arm and I couldn't stop laughing. It was the only thing keeping us safe.

"Give me a pickup line," I said when I caught my breath.

"What?"

"Hit on me. Pretend we just went out."

"We did just go out."

"No, I mean like on a real date. You just met me, we went to the club, now it's two in the morning and you've obviously green-lighted me because we're here, you didn't put me in a cab. So what now? Close the deal."

"Close the deal." He smiled his gorgeous smile. I felt a pang of jealousy for the women who actually *were* in this scene with him. The ones who knew they'd wake up in the morning with their head on his chest.

"Okay . . . so, Lucy . . ."

"No, not Lucy. Call me Venus."

"Venus?"

"Yes."

He changed his face and got serious. The shift was so sudden and drastic, it startled me. Then he took a lock of my hair in his hand. Shit. If you find a guy who knows how to handle your hair, do not let him go.

"Look at you. You're messy, Venus," he said. He ran two fingers down a strand of my hair and then licked them off.

"You're going to come home with me. And then I'm going to wash your hair and fuck you until it dries."

His hand left my hair and drifted to my thigh.

I paused, two beats too long. "Whoa," I said.

"Not bad, huh?"

"No. Not bad." I smiled and tried to look game. It was all fun. Right?

We laughed our way out of the restaurant and then shared a car home; he dropped me off on his way. He kissed me good night on the cheek.

The sun was coming up. I was going to hate this in a few hours, but I loved it now.

When I opened the door, Titus was there. Sitting in an armchair, facing me. It was too dark to see his expression, but I guessed he wasn't smiling.

"Oh, boy," I said. I felt like a teenager who'd gotten caught sneaking in. And I did the worst thing I could possibly do in that situation. I started to laugh. Something about it seemed so absurd, and I'd been laughing all night.

"I'm glad to see you're all right," he said. He sounded angry. He started upstairs, and I followed him.

"I'm glad to see *you're* all right, too," I said. "I'm really glad to see you came home. Where the hell did you go?"

"You're drunk, Lucy. I won't do this."

"Of course you won't. Where did you *go*?" I said.

He turned around and looked right at me. He looked like the weight of the world was on his shoulders. He looked weary.

"I went to Waverly. I just needed to sit at a bar undisturbed, have a drink, and listen to the clatter. Sometimes that's the most relaxing thing in the world. I'll assume you did something of the same. Take some aspirin before you go to bed."

I went to my room, undressed, left the Swarovskis in my bathroom, and took three aspirin. I removed my outfit one piece at a time, with great concentration, and laid it all on the ottoman. I doused myself with MAC mineral mist and climbed beneath my cool, crisp Frette sheets. I was too drunk to think about what had just happened, too drunk to care. The sweetness of the night still lingered.

Then I remembered, He'd sent a message while we sat at the bar. I read it and painstakingly fumbled a reply.

Me: I'm sorry. I just read this from you. I am in bed, and I am thinking . . . of you. You'll be in my dreams.

25

········

I slept restlessly, and I dreamt.

It was the same dream I've had before, where I can feel his hands. Where I can smell him and touch his skin. But this time he had a face and it was James. I woke several times, then fell asleep again into an erotic haze. When I woke, I felt him slipping from my fingers. When I fell back to sleep, he was there. James. So now I'm a slut in my dreams.

The alarm on my phone finally rattled me fully awake at eight. I braced myself for the hangover.

My phone showed three new texts.

212-555-0134: I want to tell you something . . .
212-555-0134: . . . I didn't expect this to happen . . .
212-555-0134: I didn't expect to fall in love with you.

And then another came in. I felt a heady warmth go through my body. A heady rush that made me forget where I was.

I felt weightless. Wherever he was, I wanted to be there. Whatever he was doing, I wanted to be doing it. And then my headache hit me like a truck.

212-555-0134: L'amour fou, Lucy. Do you know what that is?

Me: Tell me.

212-555-0134: Mad love, Lucy . . .

212-555-0134: . . . it's the pursuit of desire . . . it is above everything.

212-555-0134: The object of my desire is above everything. It is you.

212-555-0134: You are what I desire.

It felt like he was here, in the room. Watching me.

I got up. My hair smelled like Mr. Chow. I combed it into a pony-tail, threw a sweatshirt and leggings on, and went downstairs. There was coffee, and a note.

L,

Take it slow today. You likely feel awful.
   I'm at the gallery most of the day, with Leo.
   Let's just put this behind.

Me

26

· · · · · · · · ·

Livia's apartment
Tuesday, July 29

Livia was asleep when I let myself in. Her television was on, so I made myself comfortable and watched the end of *Criminal Minds*.

She woke up irritable.

"Who's here? What is it?"

"It's me, I'm sorry. I didn't mean to scare you."

The apartment smelled of cornflakes, though I doubt Livia's ever eaten them. For the last ten years I don't think she's eaten much of anything at all. Her body keeps going, she says, to spite her.

"What time is it?" she said. She looked confused to have me there.

"One thirty. Are you hungry?"

"No, I'm not hungry. Tell me what you've been doing."

Livia likes a story as much as anyone. But she's a daunting person to live up to.

"Well . . ." I said. "I exfoliated my vagina Saturday. Birthday present from the girls." I got up to find her something to eat.

"Oh, good *Lord*," she said. She laughed and waved her tiny arm in the air, an unlit cigarette in her hand, and then she coughed. I brought back a plate of Fig Newtons and a glass of water.

Then I explained the "facial."

"None of you even have any *sense* anymore. You would never have caught me getting up to any of that. They were thankful for what they got, just the way they got it, all of my husbands. Every one. They were grateful."

She started coughing again and took some more water.

I had a suspicion they might not have been as grateful as she thought.

"You're all competing in some beauty pageant, for what? To have sex? With a man? You've screwed it all up."

It wasn't worth arguing with her. She was probably right, we probably had screwed it all up. But don't knock the va-*jacial* until you've had one.

I started *Sense and Sensibility* at chapter six. We didn't need every inner thought and struggle of the Dashwood women. They had just arrived at Barton Cottage after being displaced from much more extravagant surroundings. Mrs. Dashwood's husband had died and had left them in the lurch. They hadn't accepted it yet, but they were broke. Two words next time, Mrs. Dashwood: *estate planning*.

Livia interrupted.

"What are you even doing all of that for? I don't understand it. Why are you running around pulling out your *pubic* hair, for God's sake. There's nothing elegant about that."

I marked our page and closed the book. I sighed.

"Livia, did you ever go on a blind date?"

She started laughing again. I didn't catch the pun. "Ask me next week," she said. "I'll give it a whirl and let you know."

"No, I mean . . . did you maybe ever write letters to someone you hadn't met? Did you ever have one of those wartime affairs?"

"Good God, no. With who?"

"Well, that's what I mean. A stranger."

"Why would I write to a stranger?"

"Well, sometimes you can say more to a stranger."

"Don't talk to strangers, Lucille. Don't tell strangers one damn thing."

Per our routine, I went to get our cans of beer and after I poured one for each of us, I stalled. I didn't feel like reading anything else. It *was* a depressing chapter, she was right. Elinor, Marianne, and their mother, once all so comfortably secure and now crammed into a dingy little cottage with barely enough room for the piano. How were they supposed to entertain?

"Did you ever feel bad when you cheated on your husbands?"

Livia let out a hard laugh, which turned into a cough.

"Lucy, *cheating* is a word for schoolgirls. Grown adult women don't *cheat*. There's a timeless art to the *affair,* and your generation doesn't respect it. You've screwed the whole thing up."

I didn't entirely disagree. Though in our defense, Livia never had to contend with Instagram.

"What is Titus doing? Is he painting?" she asked.

"Yes, actually, he is," I said. "He has a show soon."

"And what are you doing? You need something of your own, you know. Like me. I had the theater."

She did. On top of one Chippendale end table was a jeweled box filled with old playbills from the '40s, from her short-lived Broadway career. She had chorus and backup roles, mostly, but she also had a short run as the lead in *Gentlemen Prefer Blondes* when Carol Channing got pneumonia. She was Lorelei Lee, the star, for six weeks. There's an entire chapter on it in *Rothwell's Follies*. By all accounts, she held her own.

"I'm writing," I said. "I told you, for *SNOB*, for Noel White. I'm working on a profile piece right now."

"Oh God," she said, and waved an arm in the air. "The world does not need more writers, Lucille."

I laughed. "I'm writing about a woman—she's interesting. Very elusive."

"That doesn't sound interesting. Women aren't interesting. You can't trust them."

"You always tell me don't trust men."

Livia sat up straight in her chair and turned her head toward me.

"Don't trust any of them. I've been having bad feelings at night. Get a lawyer, Lucille. I've been meaning to tell you that. Get one before you need one, and don't be cheap about it."

"Where's that coming from?"

"You don't have to take all the money, but take care of yourself. You didn't sign anything beforehand, did you?"

Livia walked out on her second husband, the art collector, with nothing but an armful of jewelry—as much as she could scoop up on her way out the door. She took a cab to the Carlyle and got drunk on vodka with ten million dollars' worth of jewels piled on the bar. That was her settlement. She didn't have enough cash to even pay for her drinks.

"What are you talking about? I'm not getting divorced, Livia."

"Not today maybe, but you will. You should—every woman should at least once."

"Everything doesn't always have to end."

"Lucy Brockton, that's the most absurd thing you've ever said. Everything always ends, but you want it to be on your terms. I don't have a good feeling. And I'm trying to tell you that."

"About what?"

"All of it. Close ranks. It's a queer sultry summer, as they say."

The sky was bright blue out Livia's window.

"Van Gogh was obsessed with himself. Did you know that?" Livia said. "He painted *piles* of self-portraits, more than anyone else ever did, and no one even wanted them. Who would want them? No one asked van Gogh for his portrait. That's why you shouldn't marry an artist. They're vain."

"I'll keep that in mind next time."

"They're all out of their minds. *Starry Night*, for God's sake, was just the view from his room at the nuthouse. He was locked up! There was nothing else for him to paint except the view out the window."

I didn't know where she was going with these asides and I didn't want to entertain them so I reopened the book.

"*'Music seems scarcely to attract him, and though he admires Elinor's drawings very much, it is not the admiration of a person who can understand their worth.'*"

"Edgar is either a bore," Livia offered, "or Elinor can't paint. They're a god-awful match."

You could marry and divorce three men, one of them twice. You could play Lorelei Lee on Broadway, sleep with a Rockefeller, pose for Lucien Freud, and still wind up listening to Jane Austen on a Tuesday in an apartment that smells of cornflakes.

Erotic intelligence. How does it fit in at ninety-two?

My phone buzzed on the table next to me.

212-555-0134: I want to read to you by candlelight.

"Why did you stop?" Livia asked.

"I didn't."

The phone was set to silent, but there was a soft buzz when he came in. Livia was sharp. I went on.

"*'He must enter into all my feelings; the same books, the same music must charm us both.'*"

It buzzed again, twice.

212-555-0134: I want to bathe you in rose petals.
212-555-0134: I want to possess you completely.

"That's ludicrous," Livia said. "Who wants to read all the same things? Who wants to spend all of that time together? You only need to be good in one place with a man—the *bed*. You wind up fighting all the rest of the time anyway."

She sounded tired. She'd be asleep in ten minutes.

"You know, he could have been the greatest artist of his generation if he hadn't died," she said. She was fading.

"Who, Livia?"

"Nixon."

God, how I'd sometimes like to be ninety-two.

27

....

One Vandam
180 Sixth Avenue, SoHo
Wednesday, July 30

Cheri asked me to look at an apartment before she showed it, because she was sure she'd get the sale and she gets attached to her properties the way girls fall for summer boys—wild crush, bittersweet good-bye. She wanted me to meet her crush before he goes.

Cheri is an anomaly in New York real estate, where the dress code is black, black, and black. Her Midwest flair stands out. This is why her clients love her. This is why men love her. This is why she can sell a five-million-dollar apartment faster than a good Birkin knockoff. She's not so much interested in whether her clients buy or not as she is in having an audience. And they love it.

You have got to see our broker. She wears capes!

She also wears tangerine-orange tights to SoulCycle, and when Manolo Blahnik comes out with a feathered stiletto, she'll think she's gone straight to heaven. She's a character. Everything about her is over the top. She is definitely a Miró.

Today, though, no cape. Just a hot-pink sleeveless Ralph Lauren, and toned arms with sculpted shoulders, courtesy of her twenty-five-year-old trainer, Jeff.

"Wow," I said, taking it in. "Not bad."

It was stunning. The floor-to-ceiling view was the first thing to jump out as I walked in, and it opened out onto a huge terrace the entire length of the apartment. The master bedroom was like a suite at the Plaza, complete with a coffee station and bar. And an enormous aquarium separated the dining room from the living space, like a slice of deep sea—5,300 square feet of therapeutic calm for fourteen million dollars. That's about three thousand dollars per square foot.

"I don't know how you do this," I said. "You must fall in love every day."

"They're just harmless flirtations," she said.

"So, honey, these two just got married, they're newlyweds. He sold one of those apps that go on your phone for some crazy amount and *I* think they should have a baby right now, quick, before he gets used to all that new money. You know how nuts people get."

She led me down the hall. The library had a carved wood fireplace. There was a full spa and two oversize bedrooms besides the master.

"Anyway, I want to play up that angle, while they fall in love with the view. Look. See? This would make a perfect nursery."

She glanced over at me. "Have you thought any more about that?"

"About what?"

"A nursery."

"Jesus, Cheri. You've been telling me for forty years not to have children. Stay on message."

"Lucy, don't curse. And yes, that's true when everything's going well. But you need a shake-up right now."

I shrugged and fastened a button on her dress.

She regarded it for a moment and then undid it.

"Too uptight," she said.

"But they might not actually want to stare at your bra."

"Lucy, name me one man on earth who's offended by a bra."

"Your client's wife."

"His wife isn't buying, trust me."

Cheri walked slowly across the long length of the living area, her heels clicking across the floor.

"You know, when I sold to the Litchfields in Rockland, twice mind you—their first home and then the four-bedroom with pool—Glen Litchfield poured me a shot of bourbon. They said, 'We want it,' and he pulled a little flask out of his coat pocket and we toasted right there. Liddy doesn't drink, but she appreciated the moment. Real estate is romance, sweetheart. It's people falling in love. It's all anybody wants. That's the thing you haven't figured out. Everyone wants to fall in love, all the time. Titus is in love with his work, he's intoxicated right now. You need to make sure you get the benefit of that."

"*I* want to be in love," I said. "Who said I have anything against love?"

"Then make it happen, honey!"

"Love isn't tangible, it's made up. You know that, right? It's imaginary. It's an invention, there's nothing real about it. When it's gone there's no proof it ever even existed at all."

"That's a terrible philosophy, Lucy."

"It's not a philosophy, Cheri. It's true. If Titus and I divorce . . ." I used the word on purpose and let it hang there for a moment. It was mean of me. Cheri does not want to lose her glittery son-in-law.

". . . there would be some tangible things about it. There would be property, money to divide, et cetera. And then there would be nothing. He would go on, I would go on. Memories would fade and we'd make something new up with someone else all over again. None of it is real."

"Well, it's a terrible way to look at things."

"It's just how it is." I took a bite out of an apple from the arrangement Cheri had laid out on the bar.

"There's no real physical proof that anyone ever meant anything at all to anyone else ever. It's there. And then it's not."

"Lucy! Make him fall in love with you again."

"Where's the payoff in that? Why can't *he* make *me* fall in love with *him*? Why wouldn't he *want* to? Men are supposed to pursue."

"But they only pursue when they're in love. Do you see what I'm trying to tell you?"

"No, it's exhausting."

"Listen, I have champagne in the refrigerator just in case," she said. "It's so exciting. They've been looking for six months—they might decide this is it today. I don't know how they couldn't."

"Other offers?"

"Two. But it's perfect for these kids. They'll probably have to go over asking, but he can afford to. Stick around for this, honey."

"I can't. I have things to do."

"Are you writing that piece? About that girl?"

"Yes."

"Because I looked her up, on her website, and she seems odd to me. Why can't you just write about a shoe for *Vogue*?"

"I know what I'm doing."

I didn't know what I was doing.

"Well, I hope so."

In the hall, as I left, I passed Cheri's just-married new-money buyers.

"I would kill for that master bedroom," I said. They looked eager. She was smart to get the champagne.

At the elevator I could hear my mother's chirpy voice. *You are going to fall in love with this one. It has you written all over it. Voilà, the view!*

28

....

Noel is nervous about the piece. He should be. I am. And at the same time, he's doubled it to three thousand words, which doesn't help.

"Okay, the good news is I found her," I said. "I got her e-mail address, and she's talking to me."

"Yes, that's good. Bad news?"

"The bad news is she hasn't agreed to meet. I can't do a story without seeing her. And, I'm not even sure she's a story."

He was pacing the room. He was fixated on this woman. To him, she was Helen of Troy, Helen Gurley Brown, and Helena Christensen all airbrushed into one. Captivity. Sex. Intrigue.

He was ready to have me crash it, which means he'd allow me to turn it in past deadline, past the window of time that allows for edits and copyedits. He was going to trust me on this, he said. They'd squeeze it in last minute—no one likes to do that, but they would.

He wanted her bad.

"Where are you getting this feeling she isn't a good story? Where's that coming from? Because you need to trust me, she's a story. And you can write it."

I had to be careful here. Noel was obsessed and so, he seemed to think, was most of the city. Someone would get to her sometime, of course, and if it wasn't him he'd be furious.

"Maybe I'm just not the right person. I found her, and, as far as we know, no one else has. I could hand it off."

"No, Lucy. It's delicate right now and you know that. We don't need her losing confidence in us and we don't need her to preempt us by mocking the whole thing in her blog."

"I've been reading her old entries. Yes, they're interesting. The mystery angle is fun. I'm just not sure she's a *story*. She's young, new, precocious. How is she any different from the chef you wanted me to do?"

"Are you familiar with Lucien Carr, Lucy?"

I told him I wasn't. He enlightened me.

"Lucien Carr was one of the beats—Ginsberg, Kerouac, all that, those beats. And then he killed a man. He snapped. Some weird sex thing, doesn't matter. He stabbed him, dumped him in the Hudson, they found the body. He must have had a hell of an attorney because he only served two years and then went on to be a great news editor, one of the best. Anyway, do you know what Lucien Carr told his writers when they were struggling with a story?"

"No. I don't."

"He said, 'Start with the second paragraph.' So, Lucy, that's the advice I'm giving you. If the first graf doesn't work, start with the second."

"Okay."

"You'll be at Per Se, right?"

Noel's big dinner next month at Per Se. Shit. I'd completely forgotten. I hadn't told Titus and, of course, Titus is probably mostly who Noel wants to go. He won't want to go. We'll have to go.

"Yes," I said. "Of course."

"Good. I'm bringing some potential advertisers in and I want you to meet them. It will be the best dinner you have all year, I promise you that."

In the cab back from Noel's office, I checked my e-mail and I had this.

To: LucyBrockton@SNOBmagazine.com
From: O@OdinNYC.com
Re:

Dear Lucy Brockton,

Okay, let's just do this then. Let's meet. You can come to my apartment. Send me your number and I'll text you the address.

O

Her apartment? Was she kidding? Just like that.

I sent her my number and she texted me right back. She would meet me one week from Saturday. She lived three blocks away.

AUGUST

29
· · · · · · · ·

Brockton town house
Monday, August 4
Artforum interview, part one

ere's some backstory on my husband, for what it's worth. Call it "Behind the Art." It's not much, but it's more than you'll get in the bio material for his show.

When he was a little boy and living in Bern, he was fascinated with cap guns and cowboys. He wanted to be John Wayne. But his father, like his grandfather before him, was an art dealer, a big one. There were expectations. Perhaps what has done the most damage to Titus's psyche was this one early dream to be something else that he couldn't share. He was like a truck driver's son who wants to dance in the ballet. So he grew up restless in Europe. He collected motorcycles and fast cars. Speed gave him courage. Then art, when he finally embraced it, gave him power.

He began painting in high school after his family moved to Paris, and when he graduated, his father gave him fifty thousand dollars and a ticket to New York. "That's all there is. Don't be careless," he told him. By this time, Titus's mother was long gone. She was a dancer, and unstable in Titus's telling. He doesn't really talk about his family, but his father, from what I know, was difficult, and his mother was nuts. Titus came to New York and never saw his father, who raised him, again. He died before we were married.

Titus didn't come here alone, though. He came with a friend. Maybe the only real friend he's ever had. Roman Montreaux. He was an artist, too, a gifted one, but life does what it wants. So Titus made it and Roman didn't. He struggled for a few years, and then he left. I don't know the details, but there was a falling-out about it. They didn't speak again.

Titus sold his first piece that next year. He was twenty-eight. It was called *Woman at Midtown* and it sold for one million dollars, which was unheard of. Leo is a very savvy dealer, so that didn't hurt. But no one thought it was a fluke.

If Titus's estranged mother, or his father, read the press at the time, and of course they must have, he never knew. No letter of congratulations to him, and he was easy enough to find. They were an odd bunch. He reconnected with his mother, briefly, when we first got together. She sent daisies for our wedding. His sister sent a text. Titus's stepmother misspelled my name on a fruit basket. *Lewcie.*

The anonymous buyer of *Woman at Midtown* lent it to several prominent museums for years before retiring it to his own collection, and it's never been seen again.

The first time Titus told me all of this, he was emotional. He'd lost everything. His family, his first work. His childhood friend. I thought he was letting me into his own private world. But with a few clever edits he spins his background into anecdotes and then there's nothing personal about them anymore. So you never know which parts are meaningful and which aren't.

When he exceeded his ambition, he became bored with it. The whole thing. For a long stretch, before he started working on this collection, he called what he was turning out *schlock*. I have to agree. He said it sometimes resignedly, sometimes with humor—the fruits of a man pulling one over on everyone, because he could. Anything of Titus's will sell now. That's just the truth. People are as enraptured by the man as they are with any of the work.

Take his last show, at the Paul Kasmin Gallery in Chelsea four years ago. *Artforum* covered it. Reluctantly, though, like a child forced to visit an elderly aunt. The *Times* wrote it up for Fashion and Style, not Arts. So that tells you something right there. It's not like he can't paint anymore. But anyone who knows his early work, or truly loves art, could see he wasn't really trying.

He could've gone on like that forever, if he wanted. He could shuffle around the city in pajamas, draw caricatures from a stool in Central Park. Artists aren't models, whose careers rise and peak in a predictable cycle. The shelf life of an artist is infinite. If he becomes feeble, if he goes crazy, if dementia sets in, these are all part of the myth. If Titus begins to stumble, it will simply be a new and intriguing chapter. But that's not what he wants. I know he wants this show to be good. He wants to remind people of who he was. He wants to remind himself.

The work he's so focused on now is the pièce de résistance of his new collection. It's the centerpiece of the show, and he's both disturbed and energized by it. I can't remember the last time I saw him like this. He's sullen and gloomy, and then he's like someone newly in love. The tone of his voice, even, changes from one day to the next. He's working like he used to. Furiously in love one day, furiously mad the next, furiously engaged with the art.

Postscript: Five years ago, Roman shot himself with his father's antique derringer. He's dead. We found this out, of course, from Leo.

Richard Train was in our living room today because *Artforum* is doing a long piece on Titus to run after the show. Richard had been shadowing him for months. He'd been to the studio Wednesdays. He'd spent time in the studio watching Titus work. And he's scheduled some formal time, like today, for Q & A.

Titus likes to have me near when he does interviews. Not too close, but near. Close enough so I can put a hand on his shoulder if he's saying too much, or refill his drink, or interrupt when I think he needs to regroup. He feels safe with me here. He knows I won't let him go off course, or lose his temper. In the end, he wants witnesses. He wants someone here to watch.

Tatiana and I had stage cues. It felt like we were performers in an arty off-Broadway production of *Faust*. She sashayed in with the *gougères*, I plied everyone with wine. Faust took questions from the press.

Richard, in his argyle sweater and corduroys, had a reporter's notebook with him and a small tape recorder. Old school. He was clearing his throat, which meant small talk was over and the interview was on.

"I'm starting the tape," he said.

"Good," Titus said. "Start the tape."

Richard noted the time and date on the recorder, then asked his first question.

"What is your mood right now, as the date creeps up? Your first show in four years, and most of the work is finished, I imagine. There are over two months, still, but perhaps it's beginning to feel impending? Can you describe your mood?"

Titus took a large blood orange from a bowl Tatiana had set out and started to peel it. I leaned against a wall across the room, facing Richard but not Titus. So he knew I was there but couldn't see me. A detail I'm sure will be noted in the piece.

"My mood? I'm miserably fucking unhappy, that's my mood!" He knew to laugh after this. Not too serious. "That's redundant, but it needs to be. I've found I can't create outside of that mood. It makes me terrible to live with, but that's how it is. You need to be unhappy to create art. To create anything. Nothing brilliant happens when you're happy. Or sober, for that matter." To make his point, he took a long drink of his wine and topped off the glass. "There has to be release from all of it, too."

Richard jotted some things down and Titus took another drink.

"So by that measure, you must spend a great deal of time unhappy," Richard said.

Titus was separating the segments of his fruit. He took a deep breath and let it out. His presence, he knew, was a character in the piece, as much or more than his words.

"No. Creation isn't the entire process. For instance, I've been working on the pieces for this show for almost three years. And in the beginning, what you start with is just a place to start. And that's a job in itself, to be able to give yourself a place to start, a place to work from. That is critical. It's daunting to start completely over each time with nothing, a blank canvas, but after years you understand how to just get to that place you can create from. The misery comes after, and it hits like a storm. It's unpredictable. You don't know when you'll enter that phase, and it's excruciating."

I'd heard all of this before. My mind started to drift. I checked my phone. I hadn't heard anything from Him for several days.

"Does it get harder? I mean, does it get more intense, more excruciating over time? Is it a more laborious process or place to channel?"

Titus took another drink. The bottle was almost gone. Tati brought out a tray of cheese and cured meat.

"It's a discipline. So, I suppose, like an athlete, who over time must work harder and harder to get to the place where muscle memory kicks in, it's a discipline. Artists break down because they lose the discipline. They look ahead and just do not want to go there anymore. But then the problem is, what else is there to do?"

"Give me an example."

Titus ran a hand through his hair, then filled a small plate with bread and cheese.

"Pollock," he said. Uh-oh. Here we go.

"He shut himself away in the Hamptons, with his wife and his mistress, and he tried to paint and enjoy his life and be happy all at the same time. He thought he could just work and live and be *happy*. This is why we got all that crap he turned out."

I was tempted to discreetly steer him away from this, but Pollock is dead and Titus is big enough to criticize him. I let it go. Richard needed the pull quotes.

"Pollock turned out crap?" he said, smiling.

"Don't get me started. Who gives a fuck about Pollock?" Titus raised a hand dismissively. "And his paint-spattered shit? No one cared. What they cared about were the adornments. He was a raging alcoholic, a ticking bomb with a wife and that crazy woman he was sleeping with. 'Good God, what will happen next,' we all thought. Watch!"

He emptied the bottle into his glass, then emptied the glass. He wasn't exactly distancing himself from Pollock.

"What everyone always cared about with Ana Mendieta weren't her shitty little pieces with tufts of grass, you know that."

Richard was making more notes. I uncorked a new bottle and set it down.

"It wasn't her talent. They bought her work up because everyone knew her husband was going to throw her off the roof. And finally, he did. It took him five years to work up the nerve, and then it made his career."

Titus poured more wine, put his nose over the glass, held it up to the light, then took a drink.

"You can be an unsuccessful artist or a successful one, and some of it is luck, and some of it is maintaining your momentum, and some of it is knowing that you're also an entertainer."

"I wouldn't expect you to say that."

"Why not? It's true. This is another thing. I don't give a fuck about art anymore. I don't care what they say about it, about what I show."

"So the intersection, then . . . between art and commerce—"

Titus cut him off.

"Maybe sometimes the cigar is just a cigar. But art is never just art. What people cared about with Pollock was Lee Krasner, and how pissed off she was about Ruth Kligman. When Ruth came out with that god-awful thing she called her love gift . . . his last work, she said. Well, the 'art world,' as they call it, went fucking mad. Lee is there all these years and supporting him and maybe even has more talent, but the point is, the only interesting thing about Jackson Pollock was that he was screwing this crazy woman and she turned up with his very last piece. No one was interested much in the work itself."

"You're cynical."

"No. I'm a realist. The 'art world' is an industry. It's a business, with a load of money. And it thrives and bleeds and breathes and lives and dies on adornment. Scandal is adornment. Gossip is adornment. Vice is adornment."

"Then we should talk about yours."

"My vice? My gossip?"

"Your scandal. Your adornment."

"Well, it's too late for me to die young. You'll no doubt dig up, and rehash, some indiscretion. At this point, it's the thing people are most interested in. I know. The one thing I don't have yet is *le grand scandale*. And if I did, it's not something we'd discuss in front of my beautiful wife."

He turned around to me and winked.

"Where is it?"

Titus smiled at Richard, but it was strained. He doesn't like to be pressed. And when he doesn't like a conversation, his expression doesn't change but it hardens. Richard was right, though. There hasn't been a great scandal, and what are the odds of a man like Titus completely escaping one?

"For art, I'm a pretty boring prick. But for what they pay for my work now with me alive, I know they're counting on something. There would be no bigger gift I could give the whole world right now than to fail, or for you to uncover something disastrous."

"Fail. You mean the show?"

"Yes. Watching a car win the race is rarely as satisfying as seeing it hit the wall."

Richard had barely taken one drink of his wine, but Titus emptied the last drops of the second bottle into his glass anyway. "Lucy," he said quietly. I went to the kitchen to get another.

"Describe your work. If the casual art lover reads this, they won't understand what a realist is, or what sort of art you create, and they'll look at Wikipedia, which doesn't do you justice. And I'd rather you describe your work than me."

Titus drummed his fingers on the table.

"I'm a figurative painter, which in simple terms means I don't paint lines or shapes or boxes. I paint things you can *feel*. Like Modigliani and like Matisse. Like Egon Schiele."

"Who do you admire? Among your peers, who has influenced you?"

Titus thought about it.

"Otto Dix. I admire him and he has influenced me, although you won't see any resemblance in our work—it's in a subtler way. Otto Dix said fuck you to the abstractionists, and then kept doing his portraits. He was a smart-ass. You don't need me to tell you that—you can see him laughing at you in his work."

Richard nodded and smiled as he made a note. Then he put his pen down and leaned back in his chair.

"Can we talk about Roman Montreaux?"

Titus didn't answer him. He started sliding his wineglass around in circles by the stem.

"He was your friend. You shared a studio. There was a time when—"

"Yes, it's very unfortunate, what happened to Roman. It is tragic. But he wasn't cut out for this business."

Richard let that hang between them for an uncomfortably long moment. Titus drank his wine, finished the segments of his orange, and patiently waited for Richard to move on. Roman was off-limits.

"Surely there was some influence."

Titus remained silent.

"Well, I'd like to revisit that at some point."

I could see Richard was annoyed, in his quiet, polite way.

"Okay. So the show again. Where are you with that right now?"

"Two minor pieces are complete and sold. I'm indifferent to both of them. There is a series in black and white, which I haven't done before, which will show you that even in his fucking sixties, Titus Brockton still has range."

Richard jotted that down, then set down his pen and picked at the cheese and bread Tatiana had put out.

"The whole show, though, is the piece I am working on now, the piece that must be finished in eight weeks. This one is very good. Nine solid months of work for it, like a birth. And it feels good, and I don't care about the critical response."

"You don't care what I think?" Richard asked.

"No. That's how I know it's good. When I am turning out shit, I care about what you think. Because I hope you won't notice. But I know this is good, so I don't give a fuck what anyone says. Lucy told me once that I have constructed my whole life as one big setup for a fall. 'No mediums,' she says. 'You don't have a medium. No one can live a life without medium.' She's right. We need monotony, now and then."

Some of this he had said before, but it is always uncomfortable to hear him comment on me, our life, as anecdote. Right now I wanted my own drink.

"Happiness and unhappiness are both narcissistic. Misery requires its own unique energy to fuel and preserve. Unhappiness requires nurture and care. Some days you should stand in the rain and let your clothes get muddy, just to have a different story to tell. There should be some days where not a single person is aware that you exist. Some work should be mediocre. Some moments should go unnoticed."

No great secrets here, but it will be a good read.

Bottle three was now empty and Tatiana discreetly cleared it, while I discreetly replaced it with a fourth. If this one emptied, I'd worry. Overall, it wasn't a bad part one.

30

· · · · · · · · ·

ODIN OF NEW YORK
TUESDAY, AUGUST 5

YOU ARE ALL A LOST GENERATION . . .

Remember that? It's what Gertrude Stein said to those spoiled Americans in Paris in the 1920s. She said, "You are all lost."

Hemingway and Picasso, Hart Crane and Harry Crosby, and the girls who chased after them. They were artists and writers, and people with money who just wanted a good time. If that's what being lost is, then none of us will be found.

The girls didn't fare as well as the boys. Zelda Fitzgerald lost her mind. Hemingway ran off with his wife's best friend, and Kay Boyle's work was largely ignored. Gertrude Stein was the only one with power, and it had to do with money and her ferocity. She scared the hell out of the men, with her blunt unapologetic masculinity.

Nothing changes. We believe we evolve: we do not. Women fare poorly. Men behave badly. When we tire of things or people, we throw them out. A louse is a louse is a louse.

Consider Z, that's what I'll call him. He's here, right now, among you. He has great wealth and power, and he's on the verge of a spectacular fall, the kind that will send him into self-imposed exile, to a small town in Idaho. It's not even that

interesting, really. It happens every day. We've taken all of
the glamour out of the fall.

New York is an amusement park. Once your admission
price is paid, the challenge is making it on the merry-go-
round. You have to wait, first, for someone to get off.

I know your secrets.

Reasonable people flee the city in August because New York in
August is like a hangover without aspirin. This August, though, I'm
holed up in a closet at a small antique desk against the wall, beneath
a chandelier, reading a blog.

Every closet should have a chandelier.

I'm content here, squirreled away with my ideas. There's a thrill in
creating something from nothing. Modeling isn't creating, it's a pose.
The art is the photography, the set design, the production, the fashion. Here at my desk in my small closet office with the chandelier
above my head, it's all me. I do it all.

My word count is one: *Odin*. Which means I have 2,999 to go.
Here's what I know: she's prolific, a little dark, and she likes the
truffle aioli at Pommes Frites. But who doesn't?

It's the first assignment with teeth I've had in years, about a girl
who might or might not even be that girl. About a catfish, thrashing
its way up the avenues, keeping the city from turning into mushy
filets.

I thought about different angles I could take. Different details I
could pair and arrange and turn into something. So far, all I have to
go on is her writing. But her name, for instance. Her obsession with
e. e. cummings. Her secrecy. Is she an aspiring actress? A model? An
MFA grad fishing for an agent to help sell her sprawling postmoder-
nish first book?

I pictured her drinking bourbon and crushed ice on a porch some-

where in south Georgia, smoking whatever brand of cigarettes South-
erners smoke. Yeah. A tough Southern girl, who thinks she's above all
this nonsense. What was she living on? How do all of these bloggers
and tweeters and social-media "strategists" make any money at all? If
Noel White is worried about collapse after running one of the most
powerful media companies in the past thirty years, how does one-
named Odin expect to make it? On a blog? With no selfies?

I was thinking of a title because I had to start somewhere. "Odin
Takes Manhattan." "Odin and the City." "The Girl Who Knew Too
Much."

Don't overthink, Lucy, I thought. *Don't reinvent the wheel. There
are two stories: A Stranger Comes to Town and A Man Goes on a Journey. Pick one.*

I needed to write it like Titus paints. Realism. No abstractions,
no tricks. No scribbles or dots or pixilated illusions. *Nouns, not verbs,
Lucy. Don't overthink.*

The jar of jelly beans on my desk was supposed to last all week.
That didn't seem likely right now.

31

. . . .

J. Sebastian Salon
Thursday, August 7

I didn't know why I felt uncomfortable, but I did, walking down West Broadway to James's. It was just hair. It was just my regular appointment. I'd thought of a million reasons to cancel this morning, but that would have been silly. We went to a jazz club, we listened to music. Big deal. We went to Mr. Chow afterward because everyone gets hungry. I would have told all of this to Titus, if he'd asked. He didn't ask.

"Beautiful! You make my day just by opening the door."

He gave me his double kiss, led me to a chair, then leaned in and wrapped my hair around his hands. He massaged my head and observed me in his mirror. Same old routine. Still. It felt different today. I could smell his breath. I could feel it on my neck. Goose bumps popped up on my arm. His touch felt intimate. Why? He was rubbing my arms like he always does, studying me like he always does, but I couldn't meet his gaze, not even in the mirror.

We were both quiet. I was trying to think of something to break it. I could feel the fabric of my shirt against my skin. Even when he stopped touching me, I felt his hands.

"Don't move, babydoll. I'll be right back." I grabbed a piece of gum from a pack by the mirror so I'd have something to do with my mouth.

He came back with a glass of champagne, a bottle, and a bucket of ice.

He started trimming my hair and for the first time as he did this, we didn't speak. The music was playing, thank God. It covered the silence. I didn't want us to be quiet. One of us, I felt, should tell a joke. A bad one.

"How's the artist?" James said, taking the lead. Spell broken. "Is he ready? How close is the show?"

"I don't know." I smiled weakly. "I mean, I don't know if he's ready." Were we just going to start chatting? First I wanted the small talk and now I didn't. "He's distracted and moody. That's usually a good sign."

"What about your girl? How's that coming? Did my good-luck charm help?"

I smiled. He meant Odin. I started to relax and he topped off my champagne.

"It's going okay. We're meeting Saturday, actually. At her apartment."

His eyebrows raised.

"I thought no one's ever seen her. I thought she was a secret," he said.

"No one has. She is. I thought so, too. I'm not sure why—it was her idea."

"Okay, so how are you going to knock this thing out? Because I want to put a pile of magazines in the shop and I want it to impress people."

"You mean you don't want me to embarrass you."

We were going to skip over Mr. Chow. Okay, good. Fine with me. Nothing happened, anyway. It just got all muddied in my head.

I closed my eyes and let him pamper me. When he was done, I looked like a '60s Bond Girl. He cut my hair into layers like a lion's mane and I opened my eyes to someone new. I liked her.

"Jimmy," I said on my way out, feeling brave from the champagne, "thanks for the other night. I needed it." I blew him a kiss and left.

32

....

Odin's apartment
105 Bank Street, West Village
Saturday, August 9

S he texted me at eleven and asked me to be there at noon. 105 Bank Street. In a city of seven million people, she literally lives three blocks away.

I had no idea what to expect. I'm not entirely sure why she'd even agreed to see me. If she's going to come out, there are much bigger names to come out to. If she was strategic, she'd have a more coordinated plan. A public relations team, a campaign. For all of Noel's buildup of her mystery, it seemed too easy to find her.

She's on the top floor of a small but elegant building. She buzzed me in immediately, but it took almost five minutes for her to answer her door. It doesn't sound like that long, but stand still and time it. It's unnerving. A reasonable person wouldn't have waited, but I did. I could hear footsteps, and scuffling, she was there. I was ready to leave, when she answered.

She opened the door slowly, like a tease. She made an instant impression; there was no taking her in. Blue eyes, just like she'd said, with jet-black hair and pale skin. Smoky, yes, like Noel had predicted. She could have walked right off the canvas of a Brockton.

She wore a simple white tee with ripped Balmain jeans that skimmed the ground. No shoes. Nice touch, I thought. Self-possessed. Self-contained. Self-assured. With a whiff of anger.

"Lucy," she said. And then nothing. No smile. No *please, come in*. No handshake. Nothing.

I had a notebook of questions in my bag, and my favorite Montblanc pen. I was wearing the engraved gold Rolex watch ("Angel") Titus had given me at our wedding. Talismans.

I almost instinctively kissed her cheek, but caught myself and instead put my hand out to shake hers, which she submitted to, but with petulance. She let me grab it, like a queen might a servant, without enthusiasm. She was young, calm, and unsettling. I felt grossly outmatched.

"Odin?" I said. It came out squeaky. "Thank you so much for meeting me."

She reminded me of the girl in my high school who French-inhaled her cigarettes and flaunted her married boyfriends.

"I want you to know how much I appreciate this."

I stepped into the apartment. High ceilings and spare furniture, but tasteful. Two Eames chairs flanked a small table. A pile of books sat conspicuously on the floor. At a glance, I saw poets. Louise Glück, e. e. cummings, Delmore Schwartz, and the Barbie coffee-table book by Assouline.

A collection of vintage ashtrays lined a space beneath her tall windows. A black spiral staircase appeared to lead up to the roof.

There was a single glass of water on the table. She didn't offer me a seat. She didn't offer me anything, not even a crumb of social convention to put me at ease. She didn't give me a lead to follow or instruct me in any way. She just watched me. I walked into the room and she stayed right where she'd let me in.

I took a chance and sat down opposite the water, and she eventually sat down across from me.

I asked her permission to run a tape.

"Sure," she said. "If you turn it off when I say."

"Of course," I said.

"No small talk, Lucy. Just ask your first question."

"Okay. That's what I'll do."

I fumbled for my notebook. Her silence was excruciating. I thought of Satina—we could text out this awkward encounter, blabbering on my side, empty balloons on hers, and she could blow that up and sell it.

"Okay. Um. Let's, can we talk about your anonymity?"

"What anonymity."

"Well, no one knows who you are, nobody knows where you came from—"

"You know who I am—you're in my apartment. You're writing about me, so how is that anonymity?"

She was going to make me work for this. She gave me a closed-mouth smirky smile. My questions were going to be silly to her. She was amused. But why had she agreed to the interview then?

"Is the city on edge, do you think, since you started writing about it? Do you think New Yorkers have a nervous sense of being watched?"

She took a deep, impatient breath, like an actress at the end of a press tour. I tried to take in the apartment without her catching me doing it. A small room, off the one we were in, had shelves along one wall overflowing with books.

"Do *you* have a nervous sense of being watched?"

"No. I don't think so. Should I?"

"It's the observer effect. Are you familiar with that? And observer bias, as well. I'm expecting a certain behavior, so I'm biased. People have a new sense now of being observed. I get almost a million hits on my blog every day. That many people are checking to see if I've written about them or someone they know. It's titillating. There's a different kind of flattery in being watched. It's secret, so it's unsettling—you don't know when or where you'll be seen, or what will be said—which makes it terribly exciting, don't you think?"

Terribly. There was an accent she was masking; her words were measured. Her diction was deliberately bland.

"We are all, by nature, observers."

She was careful and rehearsed. I suspected much of what she'd offer me would be lies.

"Are you a satirist?" I asked her.

"I'm not an anything. I'm curious."

"To come to New York, though, you must have had some sort of ambition, even small. You put yourself in a public forum." She took a drink of her water. She had props, I had none.

"I wanted expression. I wanted a canvas. There's a huge difference in writing to secure an audience, and writing or creating just to satisfy an innate desire to create."

I thought about this for a moment.

"If it's simply an innate desire, why fulfill it in such a public way?"

Again, the half-smirk smile. These were terrible questions.

"Are you married, Lucy?" she asked. She'd waited four and a half minutes to turn the tables.

I hesitated. My name would obviously come up in even the most rudimentary search attempt, even with typos. She must already know quite a bit about me. If she Googled my name she'd see me on the covers of French and Italian *Vogue* and *Elle*. I am on Titus's Wikipedia page, and he is on mine. There are hundreds of trite little details she had access to.

"Yes," I said. "I am."

She nodded.

"Would you like a drink?" Odin asked.

I did want a drink, and yet I sensed any question or offer from her was a trap.

"I have tequila and I have whiskey."

I wanted water. Like the tall, perfect glass she had in front of her, but I knew better. She hadn't given me that choice.

"Tequila," I said. It was a reflex. I hate tequila.

She disappeared into a small kitchen, hidden to me by the wall. Odin. Opaque. There was little in the apartment to define her.

She reappeared with two glasses of clear liquid and handed one to me.

"Cheers," she said, holding hers up. I raised mine, too, and drank it. I felt like I was in a Godard film. The quiet, the sensory deprivation. Everything felt black-and-white and laced with danger. The tequila could be drugged. I could die here and no one would find me.

There was—and I'm not kidding—a crow outside her window, on the ledge.

"Do you— Is there a significant person in your life?" I asked.

"Do you mean, am I fucking someone?"

"If that's how you want to put it."

"Not consistently. No. Is there in yours?"

It felt like a trick question. We'd just covered my husband. I smiled at her. I'd pretend it was rhetorical.

She took another drink of her water, which made me want my own glass even more.

"John Lennon lived in this building."

"You're kidding," I said. This gave me an excuse to look around. "Does he haunt it?"

She smiled. "I haven't run into him, but people still leave things."

"Like what?"

"Books, notes, bottles of whiskey. Last week there was a small box of perfectly rolled joints. I save all of it and a private curator comes once a month to pick them up."

"Did you know that when you took the apartment?"

"You mean, did I have a vain need to live in an apartment with a backstory?"

It was my turn to smile. "Either one."

"No. I didn't know."

"How do you decide what to write? How do you choose who to write about?"

"The same way you do, Lucy. I trust that if something interests me, it will also be interesting to someone else. Someone finds me interesting, which is why you are here."

"How do you know people's . . . secrets?"

I already hated her smile. It spread slowly across her face after every question I asked.

"It's not hard. People *want* you to know their secrets. The Latin word *secretus* means divided or set apart. Nobody wants to be set apart. So we tell them. Most people do not want to die with their secrets, or anyone else's for that matter. It's harmless. It's a parlor game. People want to be found out. It's a relief."

She finished her drink and went on.

"Which fictional character do you identify with, Lucy? You forgot to ask me that, by the way, in your little quiz."

She put her feet on the edge of the table and leaned back in her chair. Who was interviewing who?

"Anna Karenina," I said.

"Why?"

Why? Because it was the first thing to pop into my head.

"I guess because she had desires that fell out of the conventions of her time. She was trapped because of decisions she'd made when she was young. And then a taste of freedom turned into desperation, desperation turned into despair, and she couldn't find her way out of it."

"She was a smart woman. She could have avoided all of that."

"Yes, if she'd been willing to remain dishonest."

"If she'd been willing to play the game, you mean."

I felt like I was being interrogated, even with her sentences. I was on the verge of confessing things I hadn't done just to release some tension from the air.

"What about you?" I asked. "Your fictional character."

"O. From *The Story of O*. Do you know it?"

"Of course," I said. Anyone who'd taken a women's literature class in college after 1970 knew *The Story of O*.

"Why her? Besides the convenience in names."

"Because a woman wrote an entire book chapter by chapter for an audience of exactly one—her lover. And for forty years nobody even knew who she was. It was only shortly before her death that she revealed herself. I think in the near future, we will long for anonymity and it will be unattainable."

I waited, hoping she'd continue.

"Everything is about greed, Lucy. Always. Right now people are greedy for fame. Everyone wants to be famous until everyone is, and then nobody will want to be. You know what people really want, Lucy?"

"No."

"We want someone to tell our story. We want there to *be* a story, because without a narrative our lives seem ridiculous, just a bunch of pointless unconnected scenes. We crave narration. If no one is telling our story, there's no use in playing it out."

"Yes," I said. I didn't want a philosophical debate, I wanted her to talk.

"There's nothing interesting about Anna Karenina without Tolstoy. There are a million Anna Kareninas out there, all waiting to be explained."

Which, of course, was exactly what Noel wanted me to do for Odin. This was exactly why I was here. She wanted narration, too.

"Where are you from, Odin? Where is your family?"

She laughed. "Slow down, Lucy Danner."

My maiden name. She *had* looked me up.

"You'll get your piece. But don't be lazy about it. Biographical trivia is dull."

That was easy for her to say—she didn't have my word count or deadline. She signaled me to turn off the tape; this was all I was getting today. I thought she'd keep speaking, then. Give me something more, off the record, but she didn't. Instead we shared another uncomfortable silence and then she asked me to leave.

"I'm not completely against meeting with you again, Lucy."

"Okay, good. I'll be in touch, then."

Odin. She's a Kahlo. Surreal and disturbing, and in complete control.

33

· · · · · · · · ·

Brockton town house
Tuesday, August 12
Artforum interview, part two

Let's go back a step, Titus. Talk about something easy. Your career spans almost fifty years now, beginning with *Woman at Midtown*. What can you say about it?"

Titus shifted in his chair and cleared his throat to find his interview voice. He looked tired.

"My first pieces, my early work before I came here, when I was still in Paris, were all shit. Birds and barns. Years of that. Shit. Luckily, I wasn't in the spotlight. No one knew who I was then, so no one saw. I didn't show anything. I burned them. But then there was pressure because I didn't have a portfolio. Oh, I had a dozen pieces, but nothing really. You can't just show up twenty-four years old at a gallery, and show them twelve middling pieces and expect them to drop their kir royals and put together a show. So I knew I had to do something good here. Really good. I met Leo, that was a stroke of luck. And he liked me, so he gave me space and his faith. And then I did *Woman at Midtown*."

"Leo. And he was representing Roman at the time, too?"

"Yes, he was."

Tatiana brought out a pitcher of lemon water and poured each of them a tall glass. Richard tried to be discreet, but he wasn't. I caught him staring at her ass. I couldn't blame him, it is perfect.

"Did you have any idea of the enormity of that piece? Of the reception you would get?"

Titus got up and walked to the bar in the next room. He poured himself a bourbon, no ice. He looked out a window. He swallowed. The quiet went on uncomfortably long. The artist reflecting? Nostalgia? What was he doing?

"I didn't realize the significance of it. No. You never do in the moment."

"Were you happy with it?"

He returned to the table and sat. He downed his drink, and Richard's eyes went to the empty glass.

"I was happy with it, yes."

"You followed it up with something so markedly different."

"Lucy," Titus said. "Love, will you refresh?" He gestured toward his glass. I retrieved it but took my time coming back. Pace yourself, T.

"Yes. I didn't want one piece to define me."

"Sure. I understand that."

Richard jotted a few things down. I could tell he was thinking his next question through; he was off script. There was something here, and he wasn't going to let it drop.

"But . . . it's so markedly different—"

He was referring to the Whitney collection, *Les femmes et la mort*, the murderesses.

"Yes, markedly different."

"So markedly different that it was hardly recognizable."

I set his drink down in front of him and he seemed to regain some composure.

"Thank you, love," he said, then turned back to Richard. "Well, that's what one hopes for. I loved doing that series. It wasn't a tortured sort of art, even though the subject material was unspeakably grim. When I showed the works in progress, the collection, to Leo, he called it an 'exhale.' He studied the collection long and hard, so long it made me nervous, he wasn't saying anything. And then finally he took a long quiet breath and exhaled. Now, when he wants me to know he likes the work, he calls it an exhale—it's his highest compliment. Of course, sometimes he's full of shit."

Titus ran a hand through his hair and then busied it on his chin. He was noticeably uncomfortable. He never enjoyed doing press, but I'd never seen him unnerved by it. Richard, too, I could tell, had picked this up.

"Okay. Good. So, all right, bookends. And I'm not in any way suggesting this is the end for you, but it is a notable moment, because it's been a long time since we've seen anything new or even heard that you might be working on something new. Which is why, I think, this show comes with so much anticipation. And you're far from done in your career, but this is the moment we're in now, and there will invariably be comparisons between your first work and this show. *Woman at Midtown* will be compared to . . . well, how will it compare to what we'll see next month?"

"How can I compare . . . well, let me say this. I'm working on something, finally, for the first time in years that feels complete. And maybe no one will know this except me. And that's fine. There's such a sense of peace when you get the nod from your inner voice. You people could rave and give thunderous applause, but it means nothing if I haven't passed judgment on myself. And for this show I have. There are a dozen new pieces, but to be honest with you, it's just one work I feel attached to. It's the one that lets me sleep at night. I know it's good.

"And there's no worry."

Titus smiled. "Richard, let's take a break. I'm starving, and I know Tati has prepared a lunch. Lucy, can you ask her to bring it in?"

I did and she did. Two flaky and buttery quiches, a green salad, smoked-trout sandwiches, and wine. I don't know how he wasn't drunk. I hoped the food would slow him down. While they ate, Richard went on.

"Okay. Why women? For all these years. Why did you abandon, as you called it, the barns and the birds?"

"I didn't set out with that as my plan. It just happened that way. And I don't do nudes. I *rarely* do nudes, and even then I don't do them in the traditional sense. Instead, I paint women who are naked, exposed. I know the distinction is subtle. My models pose nude for me because it's the setting I want. It forces them to express their vulnerability, show me their scars. It's not their bodies I want to project, it's their essence. Women reflect pain and light like a prism. If you watch them, like I do for hours every day, like I have done for fifty years, if you watch and examine them, you can see everything that has ever happened in the world. Every emotion. Every longing. Every hurt that has ever happened to mankind. I paint them plain, even the most beautiful of my models. What I strive for is to make the fact of their nudity disappear. Their bodies, when I do it right, are inconsequential. It's a cliché to paint nudes—I've been very careful about that. It's already been done and brilliantly. Goya. Botticelli. You can only paint women if you really understand the true beauty in one. You can only know the beauty of women if you understand and then truly love just one."

Naked women all day, I thought, *and he manages to sound like a saint for doing it.*

"And what about the work you're speaking of, the centerpiece of the show? What can you say about it?"

Titus took a long time to answer.

"Woman in Mirror. I don't know what to say about it. I don't. Filters. Perception. It's the idea of seeing everything but seeing nothing, of seeing truth through a prism or through a lens, or through a window or sidelong glance . . ."

I left to get the fruit tart Tatiana had made for dessert. I opened a bottle of Chablis in the kitchen and filled a glass for myself, which I finished off right there, before pouring another. I could hear Titus's voice clearly but not Richard's. They were talking about first Wednesdays—the old days when drinks were spilled, or glasses shattered, or a fight broke out that moved onto the street. He was laughing.

"When the Jaggers would come," he said, "and Bianca and Mick were separating and were not to be invited to the same places, well, sometimes the wires got crossed and they were. So there they'd be in the same small space and it was horrible. Particularly the time that Jerry Hall was also there."

I finished my glass and opened a separate bottle to take out to them. I was bored with this. I needed it.

"There were drugs, then," Titus said. "And everyone ended up fucking someone who was there. I know I sound like an ass, a nightmare of a man. But look, I married a beautiful woman, and I mean not just her physical beauty but her soul. But to love and to be inspired by love, they are separate things and they're tricky to balance. You can eat a piece of fruit every day of your life and some days you will think nothing of it, indifferently removing the rind, separating the sections and consuming it. Other days you can be overwhelmed by how simple and perfect and entirely fulfilling it is."

Right.

"I am not comparing love to a piece of fruit," he said. "But it can become pedestrian like that. A simple and perfect thing that you forget how to enjoy. And then you have to do something drastic, or you'll lose it and to lose it is devastating. Only a weak man can survive that. We could have greater problems, yes. But we don't. These are the ones we have. The pursuit of desire."

I returned with the bottle and the tart, and Richard stopped the recorder so they could enjoy it. Titus switched to his conversational voice.

"Chablis is the stepchild of wines, Richard. It gets no respect, and it's sold cheap with the other cheap labels as if to press the point. Do you drink Chablis?"

Richard laughed. "I am right now."

"It's a pleasurable wine. Simple. It does exactly what is expected of it, nothing more, nothing less."

Richard nodded in agreement.

When he finished his tart and Chablis, he stood up.

"Thank you, Titus. Lucy. Thank you very much for your hospitality. I'll see you next week, then? Last one."

I had the unsettling feeling Richard felt he'd gotten away with something.

"Well," Titus said to me, once he'd left. "That didn't go too badly."

"No. Are you sure? You seemed upset with him at times."

"Bah. They all ask the same thing over and over, fifty years of it. You ask an actor, 'How do you prepare for a role?' You ask a painter, 'How do you get it on canvas?' It's dull. The same damn dull questions every time.

"Come here," he said. "Sit down and have a drink with me."

I didn't feel like a drink. I'd just had two very generous pours of wine, but his vulnerability was sweet, so I had a drink with him. He poured two bourbons and handed one to me.

"I couldn't be any of this without you," he said. He put an arm around me and I leaned on his shoulder. I couldn't remember the last time we'd been like this. It was nice, and I soaked it in. We didn't say anything. He rubbed my shoulder with his hand, he kissed the top of my head, and we stayed that way for a while, until I fell asleep. The last thing I remember is someone tucking a blanket around me. When I woke up, he was gone. It was like coming out of a sweet dream, the kind you don't want to wake up from.

34

......

Il Buco
47 Bond Street, NoHo
Tuesday, August 12
Girls' night

B illy asked me to meet her early, before the other two came, to talk about Lotta. We had been doing this lately, splitting off into twos and talking about the others. Last week, Sarah and I were on the phone for an hour about Billy and the growing gap between her money and her mounting bills. Lotta came by the day after that to talk about Sarah, and, of course, all three of us were talking about Lotta.

Who knows what they were saying about me.

"Gorgeous!" I said and whistled when I spotted her. She was wearing a purple and black Marc Jacobs maxidress with motorcycle boots and a fur scarf. In August. She looked like Lori Goldstein doing a Steven Meisel shoot for *Vogue*. She's the only girl I know who could pull that off.

"The thing is," Billy said. She started in right away once I sat down. "And I'm not trying to fuck things up for anyone, or add anxiety to anything that would otherwise be just fine, but there are *indicators*. You know what I mean? And indicators are something that shouldn't be ignored. And the people closest to you are the ones most likely to ignore them. Which means, in terms of Lotta, us."

Insalata di polpo arrived. Sweet tender boiled octopus with a tart lemony dressing—it's my favorite dish here.

"You're talking very philosophically about a very nonphilosophical subject," I said. I thought, but didn't say, that maybe she was worrying about the wrong person.

"I'm just saying, there are serious red flags."

"Okay. So what are they? Is there really so much that's different? Lotta likes to have fun. She always has. She's always danced on the edge."

"That's fine, if there's a net."

"She's never had a net."

"Okay, but twenty-five or thirty with no net is a lot different than almost fifty without a net, and I'm not being sexist. It's the same for men. Opportunities dry up. Your sense of balance isn't as keen. It hurts more when you fall."

Fuck. We were all screwed, then. Billy was screwed—what was she talking about? This is a girl who impulsively quit her job with no scrap of net at all. Sarah was screwed. I didn't know how yet, but she was. Titus and I and our confusing state of a marriage, and what if he left? Who would I start over with? What would I do? I couldn't imagine.

"Without a net you end up one of those women of 'a certain age' at the Baccarat Hotel with no underwear and a nose full of powder."

"Great. I don't have a net," I said

"Well . . . I don't know about that. But like I was saying, she's having a lapse. She's screwing that old man because she's broke. She's basically trading sex for money, or worse, but she won't be able to do that in ten years."

"She has the Dalí . . ." I said.

Billy rolled her eyes. "Right, the Dalí. Let's just say—hypotheti-cally—that the Dalí doesn't exist. Here's how it looks. The gallery pays her on commission and guess what? She's not selling anything. And what she does sell, she blows in a night. And the gallery doesn't care, they're not losing anything. She's eye candy."

"She just signed that new girl. I saw her work, it's amazing."

"Trust me. Take whatever she says and divide by half. Her eventuality isn't good. She can go home and day drink, or get high and crash on someone's couch. So she does. That's what her life is going to be, so then she'll age out and she'll be broke and I can't even think about it. She doesn't have family here, and none of us will be able to handle her if she stays on this path. I hate drugs. I hate what they do to people. This isn't my first rodeo. Remem-ber?"

I did. Billy had a boyfriend when she first moved here who loved coke. But it was a time when everyone we were around liked coke—or something. It seemed okay. Kevin didn't stand out until he started cheating on her, then started pushing her around. He shoved her into the wall so hard one night she wound up at Lenox Hill. He went downhill fast after that.

"I ordered the *pesce fritto*, too," Billy said. She was studying the wine list now. Billy reads wine lists the way other people read a good book. Front to back, completely engaged, over and over. She can tell you the five best bottles of any restaurant in the city.

"The girls should be here any minute," she said.

"Bill, can I tell you something? Before they get here?"

"Sure," she said without looking up.

"I went out Saturday night a couple of weeks ago. I mean, not on a date, not like *out* out. And not with any of you guys, of course, but kind of the same as if it had been you."

She looked up and eyed me.

"No, nothing like that. I just went to a jazz club. You know, and listened to jazz. The second set. Christian McBride. "

"Okay . . ."

Sarah and Lotta walked in then, together, and talk immediately turned to cocktails. Billy ordered wine for each course, and when the drinks were on our table, she spoke to them and turned to me.

"So, right before you got here, Lucy was saying—"

"Nothing. It's not even a story, it's nothing. I went to the Vanguard, I'd never been there before, that's all."

"The Village Vanguard? You're a jazz cat now, Luce? How the hell did you end up there?" Lotta asked.

"Long story. Titus had to meet someone after dinner, so I got a drink with James. He likes jazz, you know that. No big deal."

Dammit, Billy. I wanted to tell it to *someone*. Not everyone.

Lotta broke the silence with a laugh. "You listened to me, doll! I told you. You should have been fucking him ten years ago."

I glared at her. "It wasn't even close to that. I'd just never been there, that's all. That's it. That's all there is to the story. It's a cool place, we should go sometime."

"Lulu, that's where lovers go. On a date. Did you see four fun party girls anywhere? Sitting all quiet in the dark, elbow to elbow, taking in the smooth, sultry bass?"

She got a laugh out of this.

"What happened to the invisible guy?" Billy said.

I smiled. "Still invisible." He was. Really. He hadn't sent anything in more than two weeks.

"I told Titus I'd be home early," I said. It was a lie. I just wanted to get out of there. I was irritated. They'd ruined the whole thing, and I'd just wanted to savor it, a tiny little bit.

"Okay, let's just do apps then. But I also want a bowl of pot-au-feu." Sarah. Always up.

"I'm sorry. I'm just tired. Let's order. Dinner, whatever."

I wasn't going to be mad. They did me a favor. This was no time to be sappy over anyone, imagined or otherwise.

None of us has a net.

35
· · · · · · · · ·

Livia's apartment
Friday, August 15

W hen Willoughby's around, Marianne starts behaving like an idiot," Livia said.

Sense and Sensibility. Still. It's so painfully slow.

"She's not the first woman or the last to do that, Livia. Everyone's an idiot when they're in love, it's part of the deal. I think that's how you know."

"It's absurd."

Livia has a cold. She has me skipping around in the book, because she has favorite parts and does not want to suffer through any dull ones, with her cold.

"'No,' replied Elinor, 'her opinions are all romantic.'"

Livia is a tiny woman on any day, but today she looked especially frail. Though she was still in command of the room in spite of how little space she took up in it. She was nursing a drink. A hot bourbon with lemon that Marta fixed her before I got here. For the cold.

Ninety-two years old and she still gets up every day and forces herself through the routine. She'd be a hit on Sarah's show, if Sarah gets it. She's colorful and cantankerous; she wouldn't be afraid to say anything on camera. I think she'd love the spotlight. *Rothwell's Follies* has a chapter in it about her rumored affair with Henry Kissinger. It might be fun to hear, from ninety-two-year-old Livia, how the little diplomat was in bed. She wouldn't pull punches, I know that.

We were about to read for the umpteenth time the part where Marianne gets dumped by Willoughby.

"Wait a minute," I said. And I went into her kitchen and made a hot bourbon for myself.

"So you side with Elinor," I said, sitting back down.

"They're both foolish."

"But you're favoring *sense* over *sensibility*?"

I wondered what Livia would think about Esther Perel.

"Let me tell you something, Lucille," she said. "What was it Colonel Brandon just said to Elinor? Read it again."

"*Your sister, I understand, does not approve of second attachments.*"

"You see, they're both foolish. It's not one or the other. I married the first husband for love, the second one for money, and the third one . . . I don't know why the hell I married the third one. But there isn't one or the other. If Marianne had any sense *or* sensibility, she'd marry the colonel and keep Willoughby on the side. One day women will get smart and live like men and they'll be better off."

"Some do. I don't know if they're better off."

"What is your little gaggle doing?" she asked.

Livia is fond of Sarah, who checks in on her often. She brings her trinkets, and then they complain about the board.

"They're all losing their minds. That's what they're doing," I said.

"This is just some dull self-serving stage you've all invented. Don't make it a big thing. You have a lot of years left to kill, Lucy. You girls should make peace with disappointment—the sooner the better."

36
·········

Jivamukti Yoga School
841 Broadway, Union Square
Tuesday, August 19
Girls' night

S eriously, guys. Shut *up!*" Billy hissed at us.

We were being careful to whisper, and we were in the back
of the room, too, but you are not supposed to talk at Jivamukti at
all, and Billy has a crush on Dechen, the instructor. She follows the
rules.

Dechen Thurman is Uma's little brother. He's smart and cute, but
a little serious for my taste. He wants to save the world. Every single
day. So in addition to tree and pigeon pose, he's constantly teaching
Important Life Lessons. Personal responsibility is a constant theme
here. Today he was talking to us about destinies. We're all responsible
for our own, we get to choose our path each day, blah blah, et cetera.

"He's such a *drag*," Lotta whispered. Billy glared.

His yoga, though, is hard. Even Billy was sweating fifteen minutes
in. And I could barely touch my knees today, let alone my toes.

Lotta had lost weight. In her black yoga pants, she looked thinner
than I've ever seen her. It wasn't a good thin.

Inhale. Exhale.

She's always straight with us, though, isn't she? She's not hiding anything. Not anything big. She'd tell us if she were in trouble. Wouldn't she? She won't, on the other hand, tell us where she got her new Céline cross-body bag in hot pink. And I know better than to ask.

Sarah's breathing was so loud it got Dechen's attention and in a second he was by her side to help her get back in line.

"Oh my God," Billy whispered. "Seriously?" She was mortified, and jealous.

"Luce," Lotta said, gesturing toward Sarah with an elbow. "Look." One of Sarah's extensions was lying unattached, separated from her head, on the floor.

"Oh my God!" Billy said again. "*Seriously?*"

They've been dropping like flies since she got them.

There is definitely humor in this, though let's be clear: extensions are no laughing matter. Sarah's are drop-dead gorgeous when they're in, but they're not easy or cheap—five hours, three thousand dollars. Three weeks ago she had a cute but unremarkable shoulder-length cut; today she was Jennifer Lopez. The drawback, though, is the shedding. Sarah tries to scoop them up discreetly, then stashes them wherever she can. Billy found one in her bathroom last week and I found one in my purse.

I grabbed the one by her head and tucked it into my waistband. Sarah was taking up a lot of our life-lesson time. Dechen was still helping her breathe.

"Sex burns more calories than this," Lotta said mid-plank. "Did you know that?"

"Shh!" Billy scolded.

After class, we went to Abraço for *cortados*—espresso with shots of steamed milk served in tall, skinny ceramic cups—and then we sat outside to drink them and soak up some late-summer sun.

"So, Sar," Lotta said. "What's the deal with the show? When do the cameras come? I need some notice." I gave her a dirty look. I wasn't supposed to tell anyone. I obviously had.

"Dammit, Lucy!"

"You had to tell them sometime," I said.

I shrugged my shoulders. Lotta grinned.

Sarah sighed dramatically. "They're still casting right now. I don't know if I'll even get on, which is why I haven't said anything. I didn't want to *jinx* it, Lucy. Thanks."

"Relax, honey," Lotta said. "We had to waterboard it out of her—she was hard to crack."

"I can't really tell how interested they are."

"They're interested. Why wouldn't they be? If you want it, you'll get it," Billy said. "You know that."

We all knew that, which is why we were a little worried. The nice girl never comes out unscathed. They would eat her alive.

"Are you going to make us be in it?" Billy asked.

I laughed. I couldn't imagine one of our Tuesdays being interesting enough for cable television.

"Because if you are, ask Lotta first. She likes that stuff."

"Bill," I said, "she can throw you a party when your book comes out. Remember that when you talk to publishers. Exposure!"

"But, doll," Lotta said, "you need to figure something out about those extensions. You can't have them spilling all over you on camera."

"They have people who worry about that. They won't send me on camera with loose extensions."

"Honey," Billy said, "the whole point of these shows is to make you look like an ass so everyone else who's *sitting* on their ass watching can feel better than you for an hour.

"You guys? Right?" Billy said, looking at us now. "Help me."

Lotta and I did a quick facial rock-paper-scissors and I lost. Smirk beats scowl.

"We hope you get this, Sar," I said. "We're just worried you might be a little naive about what you're getting into."

"Wait. What? Have you guys been talking about this? About me?"

"Duh," Billy said. "It's kind of . . . a little nuts."

Sarah's face went into mad mode. Her eyes narrowed, her lips pinched up, and her eyebrows dropped.

"Listen to me. Lucy, you have your thing, right? Yes. You have this big new thing going on and before that you did other stuff, blah blah. Lot, you have the gallery and your clients and parties and that's all great. Billy, you have your book plus all the weirdos who pay you to eat frog tongue or whatever. I don't burden any of you with my concerns that maybe *you* shouldn't be doing whatever *you* do. I let you do it. And I think it's great. So shut up. I don't want to hear it. I'm not twenty years old. I know what I'm getting into."

There was a good ten seconds of silence. Then, Lotta.

"Don't look over here, I'm solid, doll. It's all good with me."

"Great," Sarah said. "Perfect. Okay, so now my problem is, if I get on, I have to decide between embryos or wedding for my story line. I mean, I'll be forty-one, so I should do embryos first, don't you think? You can't do both in one season—you lose half the material."

"Modern family planning," I said.

"Brian's fine either way, he's fine with whatever I want to do. Maybe we don't even need to get married. Maybe a *non*-wedding is a more interesting angle."

"Sarah. Are you fucking out of your mind?" Billy said. She was annoyed about the "weirdo" remark, I could tell.

"You know they turn into people, right? Your embryos. They're not, like, sea monkeys. And you know Brian's not going to adore you forever, right? There's a window."

"She's right," Lotta said. "Do wedding. Shelf life's shorter on Brian. Look at Lu."

"What is that supposed to mean?" I said.

"You were the one who said it, you told us at J. Sisters. There's a window. It closes."

Sometimes it's a lot of work to have friends.

"We . . . the window didn't close. Who said anything about windows? I've been married for eighteen years, for fuck's sake. That's not a window."

"Girls," Lotta said, "lesson for both of you. Eighteen years or eighteen months, you still only get credit for today."

Sarah passed a pack of gum around. "I don't know how we got on to this."

"Lot's right," I said. "Those couples who stay married for thirty years, then divorce? You think, 'Wow, thirty years. How could they divorce after thirty years?' But thirty years doesn't mean anything more than a year. You shut the door behind you either way. It's a lousy business, Sarah. You never get to coast. Do the embryos first."

"Nothing personal, this is all riveting, but I'm gonna bail," Billy said. "I have to pick up my frog tongue before the tongue store closes."

"Very funny," Sarah said.

Sarah and Lotta headed up the block to get a cab and Billy and I walked in the other direction home.

She went east. I went west. Into the sunset.

37

ODIN OF NEW YORK
WEDNESDAY, AUGUST 20

VARIATIONS ON A THEME

Suzanne Duchamp. Remember her? Of course you don't. No one does, because she was an artist with the problem that her brother was, too. His name was Marcel. Marcel Duchamp. Yes, that one. He rings a bell. Between her brother and her husband (Jean Crotti, another artist), she was completely obscured. Yet it's possible she had more talent than both of them.

Aileen Wuornos? You do remember her, because Charlize Theron made herself hideous to play her in a movie, and then she was thin and glamorous again to get her Oscar in that fabulous Gucci dress. Aileen Wuornos, on the other hand, was hideous the whole time. She got six death sentences for killing those men. Six. It only takes one, but I guess they wanted to make a point. No one obscured her, in the end.

Men are not hard to understand. Most women make it much more difficult for themselves by trying to. There is very little to figure out; it's all right there. They're playful at heart. Think of dogs chasing a ball—they'll chase anything you throw for them. Why? Because it's fun to chase things. They like it. That's it. You could throw a stick, or an old tennis ball, or the jewel-encrusted toy you bought at Posh Puppy. They don't care. They'll run after it. There is nothing more to figure out.

It's important to remember that. You can be a stick, or a ball, or a jewel-encrusted chew toy, and one of them will still chase you.

Let's bring this closer to home. This is a small town. It's a hard place to keep secrets. One of you is in a beautiful apartment right now, sharing a bottle of wine with a husband you'd like to keep. And no, you're not imagining it. Something is different. Something is off. You let him chase tennis balls, because he came back. But that little formula only works for so long. Each time he comes back, his memory of why he comes back fades, until one day he can't remember at all. Is there anything he needs there? Is there anything he really wants? Anything he's missing? No.

Have you found yourself recently, more than once, scanning your mental Rolodex or searching Facebook for names from your past? Names of the ones who got away, the ones you *should* have chosen? Where is that one now and what is he doing? Do you sometimes, at night alone, look through your oversize closet and survey the racks of expensive shoes and wonder—what would I wear if I were meeting him tonight?

Does it feel dreamy to indulge yourself this way? Is it harmless fantasy? Or do you feel panic?

They start out with slicked hair, shined shoes, and confidence. They rule the world. But the shine wears off, and their soles become worn, and the pants lose their crease. They will blame that on you.

Men take what they can get. They take everything until nothing is left. If you're lucky enough to keep their attention, sell your secret. If not, become savvy with Tinder, friend peo-

ple you barely know, start a Twitter account to document the
cute things you do every day, or Snapchat stories no one cares
about. Instagram arty pictures of yourself in black and white.

Be better.

Stay tuned.

38
·········

Omen Sushi Bar
113 Thompson Street, SoHo
Tuesday, August 26
Girls' night

S o, Luce," Lotta said. "You never told us. Did you ever find her?
Did you ever get your *femme mystérieuse*?"

I demurred. I was supposed to be protecting my subject, not gossiping about her. "Yes, I did. Thanks. I found her. We met."

Billy ordered us seaweed salads and sake.

"So?" they all asked at once.

"So?" I asked back.

"Come on, Lucy. Talk."

"I want yellowtail," I said. "I don't care what else."

"Is she crazy?" Sarah asked.

"I don't think so."

"Is she beautiful? Smart? Bitchy?" Billy prodded.

"All three," I said. "She lives in John Lennon's old apartment
building."

"The Dakota?" Sarah asked.

"No. Before that. It's right by me."

"Whoa. How 'right by you'?"

"Three blocks by. Bank Street."

"This is getting fun," Lotta said, grinning.

"Lucy. Come on, spill. Why did she meet you in her apartment, if she's so private? Why would she trust you?"

"I don't know. She's playing with me. She plays with everyone. Lately she's been dropping into the comment sections of websites. She'll just show up, under her name, Odin, and post these blind items out of nowhere. Non sequiturs. Gawker ran a bit about de Blasio a couple weeks ago and she popped up in the middle of the comments with a teaser about Matt Lauer. Only the commenters see it, and who knows if it's real, but then it gets leaked and there's buzz around it and then Page Six and the *Daily News* start trying to guess what sort of scandal Matt Lauer's involved in."

"Oh my God, that's brilliant. She's fun!" Sarah said.

"Maybe she has a thing for you, Luce. She's a lipstick lesbian," Billy said.

"Maybe she's psychic?" Lotta asked.

"Maybe," I said.

"I think it's completely irresponsible for anyone to take anything she writes at face value when no one knows anything about her," said Billy. "She might be a total nut."

"I don't think she's a nut," I said.

"Well, who cares," Sarah said. "I have more pressing matters. I need help."

"Go," Billy said.

"I decided to have a little dinner, for the producers of the show, maybe an assistant and a couple other people. And I need it to be *really* good. I need food, Billy. And Lucy, I need Titus."

Sarah really wanted this show.

"Why don't you need anything from me?" Lotta asked. "How come there's no 'Lotta, I need you to . . .' whatever."

Sarah smiled and flashed her Dr. Weiss caps. "Sweetie, I just need you to be a hot mess. So they see I have interesting friends. I need color."

"Whoa, whoa, whoa!" Billy held up her chopsticks in protest. "I'm not going on your show."

"I'm not *inviting* you on my show. I'm just *asking* you to help me get it, okay? Come on."

Sarah ordered another plate of sashimi.

"Fine, I'm in," Billy said. "Listen, I got the best pickup line last night. I was at Zinc, waiting for Jule, my agent, and she was late so it was just me and this *very* cute guy sitting at the bar."

"I miss pickup lines," Sarah said. "No one does them anymore."

"Because you don't go out, and you're not single," I said.

"Single people don't even go out," Sarah said. "Or they don't meet out. They meet on an app. So there's no pickup line. You're already picked up before you actually meet."

"Whatever," I said. "What was the line?"

"I mean, I should've gone home with him just for saying it. It might have been the last one I'll ever get."

"What *was* it?" Sarah said.

"Okay . . . let me think." She cleared her throat. "His delivery was really good, so that's lost, but it was something like *'You have the face of a Botticelli and the body of a Degas.'* You know what, though, I was on my third vodka tonic."

Lotta started laughing. "Honey, that's a movie line. That's from *The Pick-up Artist*. Was he trying to be funny? I hope you didn't give him your number."

"He probably thought he was being clever; he wanted her to recognize the movie. It was a test. I hate guys who do that," Sarah said.

"Well, whatever," Billy said. "That's what I get for being offline. He was still cute."

"What about my dinner?" Sarah said. "Can we go back to that, please? Billy, I'm serious. I need food, I need you to do the dinner and it has to be amazing."

"Okay. Let me put some ideas together and then let's do a test drive next week," Billy said. "That way you can try everything, see how it looks, see how it pairs, and I have time for corrections."

"Okay. I'm paying you, by the way. This is a paying gig."

"Oh, thank God. I didn't get any supper club bookings this month. So okay, I'll write a menu tonight, we'll shop Friday morning, and do the test run Friday night at your apartment. Good?"

"You're an angel, honey."

"You can pick up my part of the check tonight, too, then. Consulting fee."

"Actually, I got this. The whole thing, on me. I'm in a good mood," Sarah said. "So, Lucy, Lotta—Friday? Test dinner at my place?"

"Yep," I said.

"We're there," Lotta said.

39
· · · · · · · · ·

I left early for Sarah's so I could catch Livia for a few minutes. She doesn't believe in phones, or I would have called to let her know. She *has* one—she just doesn't believe in using it.

She was listening to opera—I could hear it playing before I got to her door. *Tosca.* Major themes? Cheating and betrayal. That doesn't usually put someone in a chipper mood.

"Where have *you* been?" she asked me. I turned off Puccini and sat down.

"What do you mean? I was just here last Friday. I'm going up to Sarah's so I thought I'd stop by."

"What are you doing at Sarah's?"

"Practice dinner," I said.

"What the hell is a practice dinner?"

I went into the kitchen to look for something Livia might eat. She looks smaller each time I see her. I found a tin of smoked oysters, and cheese.

"She's having a dinner party for some people she wants to impress," I said. "So Billy is doing a test run of the food tonight to make sure it all works."

"Practice dinner. That's ridiculous. All she needs are a couple of people to serve and clean up, and martinis. Everyone should be drunk before the main course, anyway, so no one notices the food. The last thing you want people talking about is your *food*. It's worse than weather."

I would have loved to have been at one of Livia's parties.

"Well, she's trying to get on this TV show, so she's having a dinner for the people who produce it. I don't think they'll get drunk."

"TV." She frowned. Livia misses her Broadway days. If the timing had been different, *she* might have had a reality show. She probably still could.

"Why does she have to impress them?"

"Because you know how life works, Livia." I set the cheese and oysters down on a tray beside her. "When you want something, you usually have to kiss someone's ass to get it."

"Do they know who she is? Do they know who the hell lives in this building?"

I laughed. "I don't know. I'll tell them."

Livia stood up and started shuffling her way down one of her hallways into a back room.

"Liv? Where are you going?"

"Come here, Lucille," she called out.

I followed her to a big room full of boxes and sculptures and what looked like decades' worth of artifacts. She could open her own museum.

"Help me. I'm not sure where they are—over by the desk over there, I think. On the floor."

"What am I looking for?"

"The plates."

"Oh." I started looking for plates. That's what she said to look for, plates. The room was packed tight with boxes and random pieces of this and that. I was looking for plates. I didn't see plates. But I did see what she meant.

"Oh my God," I said. Livia went around me and bent over to pick them up. She handed them over to me like they were some things she'd just found at a tag sale.

"Oh my *God*," I said again. "Are they . . . real?"

"Take these up to Sarah. Put them somewhere where the pain-in-the-ass television people will see them."

She'd just handed me three Julian Schnabel plate paintings. She had essentially stuffed millions of dollars into my arms. He doesn't make them anymore, they're priceless. And she had three of them on the floor behind a back-room desk like they were tchotchkes.

"Here," she said. She held out a full-length fur coat that had been lying on one of the boxes. "Wrap them up."

I followed her back down the hall. I wasn't sure what to do. Or say. This was crazy. Livia put a cigarette into her holder and took a long drag off it, unlit. I was standing in front of her, dumbfounded, holding her fur and her plates. She waved me off.

"Go, Lucy. Go on. Have fun at your 'practice dinner.'" She said it singsongy. "You girls. God help you."

I turned Puccini back on for her before I left.

40

....

B illy answered the door with a drink in her hand, in the middle of conversation.

"Entertainment is all in the pairings," she said. "Hi, Lu." She gave me a hug with her free arm. "It's how the food pairs with the wine, how the guests pair with their drinks, how the pre-dinner cocktails pair with the pre-dinner crudités, how the host pairs with the hostess, et cetera."

She ushered me in. "You are never going to believe what Livia sent up," I said.

"Luce, please tell me that's not real."

"Oh God, Billy. Don't worry about the fur. It's from before anyone cared, it's grandfathered in."

"Sarah!" I yelled.

I left the Schnabels, in their fur, on a chair.

They were smart to do this together. Billy had arranged to have *Gastro Eat* do a photo shoot and video of her doing the dinner, for their website. She and Sarah both get the exposure and Billy gets a few bucks.

I followed Billy to the kitchen and she handed me a menu.

ASSORTED CRUDITÉS / PASSED HORS D'OEUVRES
AMUSE-BOUCHE: WILD-MUSHROOM MOUSSE

Soup course: White shallot, chilled
Salad: Foraged-mushroom sauté
Entrée: Veal Prince Orloff
Palate cleanser: Sorbet
Mixed greens, lightly dressed w/cheese course
Dessert: TBD

"I'll add the wines later," she said. "I haven't paired anything yet. I wanted to make sure we were set on the food. I might end up going with duck. Here."

"Billy, oh my God." The mushroom mousse. "Yum."

"I know, right?" she said, pleased. She gave a menu to Sarah.

"So I'm talking to this guy, Mark," Billy said. "From OkCupid. We're just chatting, I haven't met him yet. But he's a linguistics professor at Hunter. That sounds kind of cool, right? Here, try this."

She handed me a stemless Riedel glass filled with something sparkly and pink.

"Yum. What is it?"

"Sar's invitations are pink, so I'm matching the drink. These will be pre-dinner. It's playful. See what I do?"

"Yes. And I love. What is it?"

"It's Hood River, Oregon, juniper berry–infused gin with a shot of rosé and a shot of Korbel. Cheap champagne, cheap wine, expensive small-label booze."

"So what about the guy?" Sarah asked.

"Oh. Right. He's thirty-one, he says. His picture looks older, but who cares. He seems real and serious, which is good. And his picture's cute. No props, no mountain in the background, no dog or guitar, just his face. He's not hot, just cute. Down-to-earth, you know? Real."

"No one's real," Sarah said. "Real people are contrived."

Billy has dating profiles on a dozen different sites. I don't see how you can be on JSwipe and womenwhowantfarmers.com and ChristianMingle all at the same time but she is. Which is why I think she has a problem. We live in New York and she's on Women Who Want Farmers? Also, she's not Jewish.

"Meanwhile, George won't stop calling me. I don't answer them, but I listened to a few of his messages. Apparently he and Marcus think I'm the reason men treat women like shit. Because of women like me. So I apologize, to both of you, and to all women everywhere."

"Whoa. That's a little crazy. Can't you just block him?"

"Yes. I did. But it still goes to my voice mail. I just don't see the call coming in. I'm deleting them all now, before I listen."

"What's this?" I asked. She'd given us each a bowl of ground meat.

"Lamb tartare. It's the new tartare. Lamb and goat are so sustainable, they're all anyone will be pasture-feeding in a few years. Goat, especially. They're the new buffalo."

Raw ground-up lamb. Only Billy could make it taste like this.

"Rafael is doing the shoot, by the way. He's good, I've worked with him before. You'll like him, Sar."

"I'm worried," Sarah said. "I'm really nervous."

"Don't be, honey. It will be a smash—they won't know what hit them."

"I don't think Brian's up for it, though. He doesn't even have anything to wear!"

"Oh my God," Billy said. "You didn't just say that. You need to dial it back a little, Sarah."

"I don't see dessert," I said.

"I know. I'm still not sure about it. I'm toying with butterscotch. What do you think about something butterscotch?"

"Sounds good," Sarah said. "But I'm serious. I have to take him shopping. I don't expect you to get it, Billy."

"Why, because I don't have a boyfriend?"

"No, because you think this is all so dumb."

"Girls," I said, "hug it out. Billy, let's get to the veal, I'm starving. Sarah, come here—I need to show you something. Livia sent something for your party."

I walked her out to the fur and unveiled.

"Holy shit," she said, and then she looked at me, confused. "Okay, I'm sorry, Luce. What are they?"

"Oh, come on, Sarah. They're Schnabels! The plate paintings. They're famous! Never mind, you don't need to know what they are— you just need to be pretentious and pretend to. I guarantee someone will notice them."

"Okay. Wow. That's so sweet of her. I don't like the colors on that one, though."

"Yeah, well. She only had the three."

By the time Billy had the veal done, Brian was home, and the four of us sat down to a nice dinner. Lotta—somehow we weren't surprised—didn't show.

"Thanks, Bill. I owe you," Sarah said on our way out and blew us both kisses. "Call me tomorrow, girls. Good night."

41

. . . .

Crosby Street, SoHo
Saturday, August 30

S arah asked me to go on the shopping spree with her and Brian so
I could take photos for her PR team to leak. That's the excuse for
this trip, the photos, but it's not the real reason. Sarah doesn't think
that, sartorially at least, Brian is ready for his close-up. She hasn't
been cast yet—it's down to her and a woman from Spence—but she
wants to be ready. And she needs him to make a good impression at
her dinner.

Brian Banks isn't your average Wall Street titan. He's nice. Sincerely nice. He grew up in Montana, and I think he would have been
just as happy chasing cows around a ranch as he is underwriting
billion-dollar IPOs.

He has a pure heart and a soul, two things that don't always go
along with money. He's also movie-star handsome, like a young Ryan
O'Neal, and he adores Sarah. Before him she had a series of cute
banker boyfriends and a very short marriage to one of them, Derek. He
took a job in Belgium after their honeymoon and had his stuff moved
out of their apartment the next month. The funny thing was that Sarah
refused to divorce him. So they were technically married for three
years. She wasn't about to have a six-week marriage on her bio.

Brian is nothing like Derek, and he's being incredibly patient about all of this. He helps her brainstorm ways to maximize her social-media profile. He hired a consultant to raise her presence on Twitter and Instagram, and he's interviewing interns. He's basically buying her a whole staff.

And he didn't even flinch when she told him he needed a "refresh." He's a good sport. She's got a strict code of fashion, and I mean *there are rules* strict. No room for personal exploration, no room for expression. She's the fashion yin to Billy's joie-de-vivre yang.

"It's all about branding, Lucy." We were on Crosby Street— cobblestone sidewalks and high-end retail. Five blocks of the finest men's retail in the city. BroHo.

"For instance, I want to be known as the *fashionista* of the group, so I've got to get that out there right away, right now, if I want to be referred to as that in the press. You can't just rely on the media to come up with the image you want. You need to literally give them the language. So everything my PR team sends out—every bio, press release, print interview, whatever—it has to have the word *fashionista*. I've also instructed them to be liberal with the word *muse*."

Brian was beaming with pride, like they'd just had a baby. I couldn't believe these things were coming out of her mouth.

"Sounds like you know what you're doing," I said.

"Film a little while I'm talking, okay? I'll signal when I want you to stop."

I hit the record button on my phone and Sarah's voice went up a chirpy notch.

"So my new blog is at springandlafayette.com, and it's all about fashion, style, and living a life that is *fabulous*. We're all fabulous, but I want every woman to find an even better version of her*self*."

She signaled me to cut. "Okay, wait. That sounds cheesy. Start again, we can edit."

I examined my phone. "How do you edit?"

"I don't know. Who cares? My intern can do it. Start again."

I pushed record. Sarah stretched out her smile.

"Our strength, our confidence, what we project—all of that adds up to our success, which is the point we reach where we can give something back. That's what makes us *fabulous*. I want every woman to *hug her inner fabulous*. That's what springandlafayette is all about. *Hugging your inner fabulous*."

What Sarah wants is to be the new Goop. Which, until now, has been her bible. Gwyneth Paltrow, until now, has been her patron saint. Now Sarah wants to be the patron saint.

"Keep rolling, Lu."

"I'm rolling."

"Today, here's what we're dealing with. I'm sure almost every woman can relate to this. My smart, wonderful, and handsome fiancé Brian needs a refresh. He *wants* one. And who better than the woman he loves to take him through it?"

I was walking backward, in front of them. Brian was smiling and trying to keep his manhood.

"Brian has a kind of predictable Greenwich Yacht Club style. Know what I mean, girls? He has the yacht club look down cold. Not that there's anything wrong with that. Sometimes you just need to diversify."

She pointed to his pants.

"Observe the Brooks Brothers khakis."

I zeroed in on his khakis.

"And standard-issue JM Westons." I zoomed in on his shoes.

"I'm planning a very important *party*—a *V.I.P.*—and I want to see him in a different look for it. Something smart but playful. So we're here on Crosby Street, retail heaven for men, and we are going to change his groove."

I pressed pause. "Careful, honey, you're starting to look like you're in a sugar coma."

She did. Sarah goes into shopping mode and loses it.

"Right. I'll tone it down, okay, thanks. Got it."

I pressed play again as we walked by the stores and she continued her tour.

"There's Superga, great Italian sneakers on your left. Here's Bloomingdale's beauty counter and the MAC store—that's for me, of course. Not Brian." She giggled.

"Mansai, over there, is an *amazing* jewelry designer for men. So ladies—his birthday? Christmas? This is where you go if you want to give him something special and unique. And then here's Saturdays— not only do they have the best coffee bar in SoHo, they also have the hottest line of surfer chic anywhere."

I pressed pause again.

"You're losing extensions again, honey," I said.

"Oh no! God, they are driving me crazy. Where? Luce, pick it up for me."

She turned to Brian while I collected her hair. "They honestly have designers here no one has even seen before, baby. This would be perfect for a scene. Lucy, take still shots now."

Sarah, with her high pony and new red lipstick, was Instagram-ready. She was wearing cropped leather Rag & Bone jeans, half boo-ties, and a cream lace vintage shirt. She looked great. Her publicist would have some good shots for *In Touch*. "Sarah Porter on Crosby."

"Text me the photo from Bonobos, Lu."

I did, and she posted it, with the caption "Retail therapy with boo."

"Sarah. 'Boo'? Really?"

"Lucy, this isn't your thing, you don't know how it works. Text me some more."

I took some more candids of them with my phone, and people passing us craned their necks trying to see who they were. I followed them into Opening Ceremony and watched Sarah fondle the Comme des Garçons wallets, all kelly green and ruby red, set against a staff all dressed in black.

"This is all just practice. For my vlog, maybe. But, Luce, we *could* do a great shopping montage here. Right? I mean, we could actually do this whole thing on the show, where I'm giving Brian a makeover. It's perfect."

"You're up for a makeover scene?" I asked Brian.

"For my girl, I am."

He is way too good for any of us.

They picked Brian out new jeans at Acne, from the huge wall stocked with colors and leg widths. Then we went back to Bonobos and she ordered him three pairs of pants. Two Patrik Ervell shirts from Carson Street, where they also gave Brian a beer while they wrapped them up.

When my phone died, I called it quits. "That's it. I'm tired, I need a drink. Il Mulino, or I'm leaking the bad photos."

"There were bad ones? Lucy!"

We had pasta and truffles and drank Barolo at the bar. Brian stepped outside to take a phone call, in his new jeans, and Sarah watched him, doe-eyed.

"I could eat him in a sandwich," she said.

"Sandwich? That's an interesting metaphor," I said.

If love is a sandwich, then I wonder what desire is. Maybe the Haute Chocolate sundae at Serendipity.

42

. . . .

Per Se
Time Warner Building, Columbus Circle
Saturday, August 30
Noel White Dinner

Per Se is not Titus's scene. Not one bit of it, nothing at all. He hates foodies, for one. He's not crazy about Noel, and he doesn't like being trotted out like a trophy guest.

It is Noel's scene, though. It's Noel in his element. Titus considers preparing a meal a humble craft. Noel treats it like sex. Which is why we're reading an over-the-top tasting menu he put together personally with the chef—ten courses for five hundred dollars a plate. And the kicker? All vegetarian. Turnips "thinly sliced with nori," and "pluots compressed with ginger." To Titus, the words *pluots compressed with ginger* in all lowercase on an oversize menu is an affront to food. And to people.

At the table in our private room, there are: two Google execs, a rich college friend of Noel's, Lorne Michaels (another rich college friend of Noel's), a *Times* reporter, and us. Three billionaires, a magazine mogul, a local celebrity, and the press. Though Lorne is no slouch, Titus is clearly the featured guest.

Per Se has three stars in the Michelin Guide and, according to

Billy, the best wine cellar in North America—and she wouldn't say that lightly. So if you're trying to impress some Silicon Valley investors, it's not a bad place to come.

Noel walked around the table as they served the pre-first-course canapés, to check in with everyone. Then he gave his *set the mood* speech.

"Thanks for joining me tonight," he said. "I'm going to go around the table quickly and tell you who you are, and then I'll talk about this amazing experience you're about to have."

Greg and Steve were the Google guys. Peter was the old college friend. Lorne was Lorne, and Megan was from the *Times* and not here to cover this event specifically, but as part of a bigger piece on Noel for the Sunday magazine.

"And of course, Titus Brockton," he said, "who needs no introduction. And his beautiful wife, Lucy, who I am lucky to have writing for us."

Okay, I'll say it. It was a little intimidating. Actually, a lot. I was glad I wasn't seated by Megan. I dressed perfectly for the occasion, however, which is half the battle. Good shoes, flawless nails, shimmery toes, and a very neat chignon.

"We're doing a nine-course vegetable menu tonight. Not because I'm trying to convert anyone, but because it's brilliant. Jean-Jacques and I worked together to create it and match the wines and I think you'll be impressed."

Noel had done a nice job with seating. Titus was to my left; Peter, the college friend, on my right. Megan was to the left of Titus, and Lorne was to the left of her.

Royal Blenheim apricot compote was the first course. The menu failed to note, though, that the Royal Blenheim is an endangered fruit. I knew this from Billy. I showed her a preview of the menu and she was horrified. There's only one grove left in the world, apparently. It's the vegetarian equivalent of eating shark-fin soup.

Unfortunately for the Royal Blenheim, it also tasted divine.

Noel pulled a chair up beside Titus as they were pouring the second wine.

"My friend. It's been too long. Looks like you're holding up very well."

"Thank you, Noel. It's good to see you, too." Titus reached out to shake his hand. "Vegetables. Clever."

"You'll be amazed what Jean-Jacques can do with them. Listen, I have a Château Margaux for you tonight that will change your life. I'm saving it for the seventh course."

"Good. I'll pace myself," Titus said.

"You're getting nice press for the show."

"Am I?" Titus said. "Good to know. I can't follow all of that. It's noise."

"I don't know if Lucy has talked to you, but we want to do a feature on you for December. We'll review the show, do a 'where Brockton is now' kind of thing. Interview, photos, day in the life of the artist, et cetera. Not just *an* artist, but *the* artist."

Titus hates doing those things, but he did get passed over for the Whitney's last hurrah. There's a reason for that. And *SNOB* is a big magazine. An edgy profile, by one of Noel's hip young writers, of Titus's work and Titus's show in their end-of-year issue wasn't something to laugh off.

"Thank you. Why don't you come by the studio next month. After the show."

"Great, I will. I'll be in touch."

Megan turned to Titus as they were serving the compote, and then Peter turned to me. "So, you're a writer."

Good haircut, dimples, nice suit, no ring. Future boyfriend for Billy?

"Yes. I've done this and that. Noel's doing some ambitious things with the magazine right now. It's a great place to be."

"Noel's tough. He doesn't like to get beat."

"No, he doesn't. What do you do again?"

Peter wiped a napkin across his mouth and cleared his throat.

"I have a start-up company that develops apps. We're lifestyle-themed right now and our flagship is an app called QuikStyl, which we'll be launching first of the year."

"I like the name," I said. "What does it do?"

"Well, it uses a very smart set of algorithms to turn basic data you enter about yourself, plus existing data and profiles on social media sites, to create an image for you."

"What kind of 'image'?"

"Okay, so say you don't have a sense of style."

We were on to the turnip bavarois, and the California pinot noir.

"This is absolutely *amazing*," I said. I turned to Titus, but he was being monopolized by the *Times*. "It's like turnip cotton candy or something. It's so fluffy."

"It's remarkable," Peter agreed. "Anyway, as I was saying, no sense of style, or maybe you do have a style but you're too busy to put it together. You're Joe Johnson and you own two blue suits, jeans, and basketball shoes, some mismatched furniture, et cetera."

"I'm following."

"So QuikStyl creates a user profile—oh yes, wow, try another taste with the pinot." He pointed his fork toward his dish and shook his head in appreciation.

"So QuikStyl creates a profile . . ." I said.

"We create a profile that begins with a basic Proustian question-naire. Then the brilliant thing is, it continues to collect data so that it grows and evolves with you. It can tell you what color and brand of sheets to buy, for instance. What furniture to have, what car to drive, what movies to watch . . . which stores you should shop at, books to read, restaurants to frequent, even what hobbies to pursue.

Now, there is already technology that does these things based on your preferences. For instance, websites with the 'recommended for you' feature.

"But our technology feeds you recommendations based on the image you want to *create*. Not who you are, but who you want others to see you as. And you don't have to think about it. We do the work."

"Wow," I said.

"Yeah. You can even ask it for a list of suggested dinner party topics, for example—talking points that reflect and promote your image."

I laughed. "So, our conversation, right now—was this generated by your app?"

"Nope. It's still in beta." He smiled. I added "cute sense of humor" to my mental list.

"It seems kind of depressing."

Peter's smile grew wider. "Well, yeah. I know where you're going. No individuality, et cetera. But there is. QuikStyl is designed to know you better than *you* know you. It pulls out *your* own personal and unique sense of style, it just makes it . . . easier."

"Sounds like you're going to make a lot of money."

"Yeah. That's the idea. QuikStyl will be a verb by this time next year. Like Google."

Rich. Great smile. Playful eyes. All added to mental list.

"Do you hike?" I asked.

"Um. I guess so," he said, confused. "I mean, I have."

Across the table, Noel was hitting on Steve and Greg. "I've hired new talent. Some fresh names, some old and established ones. We're going back to delivering a magazine people want to hold in their hands. Strong, original narrative pieces. High-end demographic. Sleek, classy ads."

By the time we got to the seventh course, I had veggie rigor mortis. We'd been eating and drinking for three hours straight and had three courses to go. I was staring down a coddled Ameraucana hen egg with truffle mousse when Noel signaled the waiter, who then discreetly produced a separate bottle for Titus and me—a 2009 Château Margaux, just like he'd said. It meant nothing to me, my palate was shot, but I could see Titus was impressed, and Noel was beaming like he'd knocked in the winning run.

Then the wine got the best of the Google guys and Steve shouted across the table, "Hey, Titus. Do you have a Twitter account or anything? Are you online somewhere we can see your stuff?"

No. Jesus. Seriously?

Titus chuckled. His condescending faux-polite chuckle. "Steve, is it? Right? I'm a little past the place where I need to put staged studio shots on Instagram, or whatever the newest thing is. Some of us embrace certain methods, others of us don't."

I couldn't help but think of Satina with her text-fight silk screens. She had a Snapchat piece she was working on now that Lotta said was mind-blowing.

Peter leaned over, around me, to address Titus himself. It was a free-for-all now. This is what eight courses of gluttony and too much wine will do. "So, Titus, this big show coming up. Do these things make you nervous at all, still?"

Peter, can you program QuikStyl, I thought, *to tell you which dumb questions not to ask?* That went in the cons list, on the mental note. But he was still ahead.

Titus dipped his spoon into his chilled avocado-melon soup, followed it up with his wine, and completely ignored him. When I saw Peter take a breath to repeat himself, thinking Titus just hadn't heard, I cut him off. "He doesn't hear well on that side," I said. "He really can't hear you."

"Oh," Peter said, and smiled. *Thank you, Satina.*

After three separate dessert courses, they finally set us free. Noel was taking the Google people to Tao. I couldn't understand how they were still walking.

Peter left me with his business card, which I tucked away for Bill.

Noel pulled me aside before we got out. "Lu, I hate to talk shop. But did you get her?"

"Yes! I did. We met and we're meeting again."

He gave me a quick hug. "That's perfect. Are we on track?"

"Yes," I said. I was lying.

"What does she look like?"

"She looks like a serial killer," I said.

"But a beautiful serial killer. Right?"

"Stunning serial killer, yes. And dinner was unbelievable. I showed Billy your menu, by the way. She was impressed." I didn't mention her horror at the endangered fruit. Noel beamed.

"Give her my best, will you? And send a draft to me as soon as you have it."

"Yes. I will."

43

....

ODIN OF NEW YORK
SUNDAY, AUGUST 31, 2014

NEW YORK IS LIKE A GREAT WOMAN . . .

That's what Woody Allen says, but it's a stretch. I don't see it. Cities are phallic. Men lay them out, men design the buildings, and men erect them in the image of themselves.

I'm thinking today of a man who is the last of his era, maybe the last of his species—the great *artist*. The wealthy and powerful artist. The one who has command of the city. The one people talk about in hushed tones. The one above judgment.

It's not true of them all, even the ones who enjoyed great fame. Rothko died a mess. Pollock got drunk and smashed himself on a tree. Wyeth, etc., the de Koonings. They didn't know they could have anything in the world. Their work didn't even have to be good anymore. But the artist I'm thinking of knows.

He's from a different age and a different set of rules. And, of course, it's been so long since one applied to him that he'd never understand them anyway.

He's the kind of artist who found some enjoyment in his work but mostly worked to enjoy.

Shockingly, his grandfather was a notorious art thief. He produced the family money. So no, it's not all clean. He was a failed artist himself, with an excellent eye and a nose for a sucker. He also had a stable of impoverished unknown talents willing to reproduce whatever he thought he could sell. He kept them well fed and made his family rich. He was a con.

At one point, the great artist hated his work. He had success right off, secured shows in all the right places, and before he was forty had done retrospectives at both MoMA and in London at the Tate. He roams the city like a lion. But how? How did he achieve such great success? Why can't he enjoy it? What will be his downfall? Because there is always a fall. Always.

I don't like New York in the daylight. You can't see anything. It's too industrious. The stories that lurk here sneak in at night.

Someone is writing a piece about me. A drab unoriginal profile for a "prominent" magazine. I can't imagine what she's found to write. Incidentally, she's not a stranger. I know more about her than she will ever know about me. Silence unnerves people, then they reveal. I could write a much more interesting story about her.

If you are ever worried that someone is reading your thoughts, scream loudly in your head. Then look around to see if anyone is startled.

Shit. She's writing about Titus? About me? Is she serious?

SEPTEMBER

44

....

Milk Studios
450 West Fifteenth Street, Chelsea
Monday, September 1
New York Fashion Week

September was a loaded gun. No one was ready for it. It was not the best of times. For one thing, there was Fashion Week and Sarah wasn't invited to one single show. She was a wreck.

"It's a total injustice, it's humiliating," she complained to Lotta and me over a big plate of diner breakfast. She was wearing yoga pants, flats, and a cable sweater—no lashes, no extensions, no makeup—and stuffing forkfuls of French toast into her mouth. She looked completely defeated. It didn't help that Cynthia Braden was on Page Six today and had been on *Good Morning America* yesterday as the newest cast member announced for *Under the Plaid Skirt*.

"I'm supposed to be the fashionista of the group, and I'm not going to Fashion Week?"

"Honey, I hate seeing you like this," Lotta said. "Come with me to Zac Posen on Wednesday."

Sarah let her fork fall to her plate.

"What? You were invited to Zac Posen?"

Lotta laughed. "Crashing it, love. I'm *cra*-zee about him, he always kills."

Sarah looked at her, horrified. "You can't just crash a show."

Lotta waved her off. "Come or don't come. I'm just saying, it's a good show."

I was afraid Sarah was going to snap. This was delicate territory, which is why I carefully thought through what to say before I said it. "Sar. I can probably get us into Jeremy Scott, legit. No crashing. Good?"

"How can you get us into Jeremy Scott?"

"I know his publicist. She's very sweet. One quick call."

I was actually already on the list, with a plus one. But I wasn't going to tell Sarah that. I was also not going to tell her I was on the list for Marc Jacobs and Prabal Gurung, too.

"Of *course* I want to go to Jeremy Scott! Oh my God. Lucy!"

Ambition trumps pride. She was instantly giddy. Jeremy Scott is hard, almost impossible, to get into. None of the other Plaid Skirts would be there.

I'm not so crazy about Fashion Week. It's loud and crowded, there are never enough seats, and everyone's in the most uncomfortable clothing they can find. Plus it's mean. It pits industry people—the fashion editors and retailers—against the bloggers and celebrities, and people like me, who just want to see the clothes. And people like Sarah, who just want to be seen.

It's a pushy crowd. Everyone fighting for space, it doesn't bring out the best in anyone. And it's unbearably hot. The shows are in cramped, airless rooms. The bathrooms are all portables.

But Kelly, Jeremy's publicist, got us a huge win. The second row. We were right behind Kanye and I thought Sarah was going to pass out when we sat down. We could touch him if we wanted to.

"Oh my God!" she said. "There's Susie Bubble!"

"Who's that?" I asked.

"Jesus, Lu. She has four million followers on Instagram! She's an influencer. Very high-end."

You couldn't have asked for a better seat: the cameras were all right here, on us. Selfie flashes were going off like a little fireworks show.

"Oh my God. Oh my *God*." Sarah was name-checking the room. "Miley Cyrus, Taylor Swift . . . Anna Wintour!" And, of course, Kanye, still inches in front of us. In his burgundy hoodie.

"Look, Miley's wearing the collection!" I could barely hear her. DJs were packed tight around the perimeter of the room. It was loud.

"Lu, Bill Cunningham's here! Shit, I should have worn Alexander Wang."

Gigi Hadid and Naomi walked the runway in Jeremy's bright flirty spring wear, along with another dozen girls, all unnaturally thin, tall, and young.

It was over fast, and then we were swept along in a sea of photographers—press and paparazzi. And guess which aspiring Plaid Skirt walked out flanked by supermodels and got her picture snapped doing it?

"That was better than sex, Lu," Sarah said, when we got out of the herd.

"Hmm. I'm not sure what that says about Brian," I said. "Sarah, what are you doing?"

She had a pack of Marlboro Lights in her hand and she was digging around in her Birkin.

"I can't find my lighter."

"Your lighter? Since when do you smoke?"

"Look around, Lu. When in Rome."

There were, at a quick estimate, about seven out of eight people with either a filter between their fingers or a vape.

Sarah produced a small gold-plated lighter and grabbed a Marlboro from the half-empty pack.

"Look at you," I said. "Fresh off second-row Jeremy Scott."

"I need to find a car, Luce. I have to get home and check Wire." WireImage is where the photographers upload all of their photos. It's where you can see who got how much attention.

"Well, there's no way we're getting one right now," I said.

Everyone who'd just gotten out of a show was competing for a car to go uptown, where the other half of Fashion Week is. It was a madhouse. I showed her my Uber app, which had just crashed, to underscore the point.

Sarah managed to find one, but once we got in, it was obvious we weren't going to get anywhere fast.

"Luce, pretend you're Giuliana Rancic and I'm me. Ask me how I liked the show."

"You're scaring me, Sar." I cleared my throat and gave it a shot. "'Sarah Porter! So good to see you here today. So what did you think of Jeremy Scott?'"

"Oh, there's so much to say! It was playful and fun. So colorful! The prints were bold and ambitious, they leapt right off of the models. And I loved the white Mary Janes."

She'd clearly lost her mind. But we'd averted a disaster, for now.

45

· · · · · · · · ·

Billy's apartment
Friday, September 5
Secret Supper Club

S o you'll just hang out in here until I need you, basically. Okay?"
Billy normally used one of the *Gastro Eat* interns when she
needed help with her supper club dinners, but she couldn't find anyone last minute on this one. So she called me.

The dinners have been a pretty steady source of cash flow for her.
She made three thousand dollars in July, after expenses. So they were
a godsend, but she hated them.

"I have to schmooze a little when they get here," she said. "Then
you can help me serve, if you want. I mainly just need you for prep
and plating, though."

"Okay."

"And emergencies. There's always an emergency. Also, they like to
come in here and snoop around, just so you know. They think they're
entitled to. Listen, Lucy, I'm not proud of what you're going to see.
You won't respect me after this."

I filled a big burgundy glass with a huge pour of Sangiovese and
started stirring a sauté pan of crickets.

"Explain the crickets, Bill. Please."

"It's *adventure* eating, Luce. There are a thousand dinner clubs out there, you don't get it. I have to stand out. I can't book a full table on tilapia and sautéed greens."

She was expecting four couples. They were supposed to say "gastrology" into the intercom to get in, like at a speakeasy.

Everything was prepped. The rabbits were roasting, the hen-mousse pâte was plated with bread, and there was a large stockpot of bones.

"Yuk," I said.

"It's bone broth, Lucy. *Brodo*. It's not yuk. And it goes between the crickets and pâte."

Her kitchen was like a mash-up of horror films.

"Can you open those bottles? The members will be here in minutes."

"Members?"

"That's what they like to be called."

I'd only opened one before the intercom buzzed. I answered the door and seated the first two couples. I poured them ginger water while Billy shook up the "adventure" cocktails in the kitchen—Endangered Species: brandy, three kinds of rum, and a little juice. The third rum floated on the top, like an oil spill.

I got the door when it buzzed again, too, because the crickets were at a critical point and Billy needed to watch them. It was the last two couples, so all eight members had their ginger water and gingko nuts now. I checked back in the kitchen.

"Okay, Luce, I need help with this," she said. She had a tray of orange-colored drinks to take out, and she handed me a serving dish of garnishes—rosemary sprigs, mint leaves, Meyer lemons.

Then she pushed open the door that separated her kitchen from the members, and she froze.

"Oh my God," she said quietly, but not quietly enough. "Oh my

God, are you fucking kidding?" Six of the faces were looking at her, confused. Two of the faces were grinning like a couple of playground bullies who'd pulled a very unfunny prank.

She set the cocktails on the table and went back through the door into the kitchen. I smiled and served the drinks.

"Is everything okay?" one member asked.

"Of course!" I said. "She just gets excited when she does these."

They smiled at that. The excitable gourmand.

"Don't you think rosemary's a little strong for—what is this, vodka?" another member asked me.

"Nope," I said. "There's no vodka, it's mostly rum, and the rosemary calms it down."

The bullies looked smug. One of them had already finished his drink. I didn't get it.

"Amuse-bouche!" I said. "I'll be right back."

I shut the kitchen door behind me.

"Jesus, Billy. What are you doing?"

"What am I doing? What the hell are *you* doing? Why didn't you tell me?"

She was bent over like she was either going to throw up or couldn't breathe. And we were whispering because, beyond the door, her members were barely ten feet away. I banged the lid on a pot. Hit a spoon against a glass. I thought it should seem like there was activity.

"Why didn't I tell you what?" I whispered back. I leaned over, too, so I could hear her.

"This is terrible. You have to serve, Lu."

"What's terrible?" I grabbed her shoulders and made her stand up.

"Okay, those people you let in without telling me? One is Marcus . . ."

It took me a minute. "Marcus, the musician guy? From Queens?"

"Yep. And the other one is George!"

"Oh my God. The porny matchmaker?"

"Yes! They're friends, remember? George left the mean messages? I'm why men suck, dot dot dot?"

"Oh, boy."

One of the four men who *wasn't* Marcus or George walked in then and started poking around, opening the oven, lifting the top off the broth pot.

I smiled at him and grabbed a spoon to stir the crickets.

"Is there a fish course?" he said.

Billy pulled it together. "No spoiler alerts, handsome. You'll have to wait." She shuttled him out.

"Lucy, seriously. You have to serve. I can't go out there."

"Why would they come here?"

"Because they're assholes? They think they're funny. Also, I've cooked for both of them: they know I'm good."

"They'll think they're *really* funny if you don't go back out. You can't just stay in here, Bill. How did you not know they were coming?"

"It's a dinner, Lu, not a wedding reception. Strangers go to a website, they buy their seats, they show up. They don't introduce themselves."

She took a long, hard look at the door. It was true, there was nowhere to run or hide—they had her cornered.

"Hand me that," she said, pointing to my wineglass. She finished off its contents, tightened her Hedley & Bennett apron, and twisted her hair up into a bun.

"Gorgeous, honey," I said.

"Crickets, stat. Plate and hand to me."

I did.

"Follow me with the breaded marrow puffs."

I did.

"Thank God they all prepaid," she said.

We traded off serving courses until dessert. I was actually having fun. Billy barreled through, with her riveting descriptions of the origins and source of everything, and it all went fairly smoothly, considering, until I spilled bone broth on George. Or maybe it was Marcus—I wasn't sure who was who.

Marcus, or George, screamed. I can't blame him, it was hot. Then the pair made an angry show of leaving, which included a loud phone call to Joe's Pizza, before they yanked their dates out of their chairs and left.

It didn't seem to faze the other two couples at all. It barely interrupted their meal. Of course, this was in the ticket price, too—side drama. At the end of the day, everyone just wants a good story to take home. One member complained about the texture of the rabbit, and no one finished their crickets, but the mousse pâte was gone in minutes, and there was a lot of discussion about the broth.

We got through dessert and palate cleanser and sat down with the two couples for digestifs. Billy and I helped them finish off a bottle of Fernet-Branca.

"They're going to crucify me on Yelp," Billy said after they'd all gone and we were alone.

"No, they won't, and who cares. You can comment back that there were two asshole egomaniacs here who can't fathom that a woman might not be interested in them."

"Then I'll only get lesbians to come."

We had the dishes stacked neatly in the kitchen, so there was nothing for us to do but finish off the booze. The members had barely drunk anything.

We collapsed on Bill's living room floor with three mostly full bottles of wine.

"Oh my God, Luce. What if you hadn't been here?" Billy said. "What if I'd had to do that alone?"

"What did you *do* to them?" I said. "To make them so spiteful?"

"I seriously don't know. I wasn't mean. I really liked Marcus, too. I could have liked him longer if he'd had his own room."

"No. He's *terrible*! Was he the guy I spilled on? Or the other one."

"The other one. He was great in bed."

"Who cares. It's not worth it," I said. "Although, what would I know?"

Billy poured a white into my glass of red—presto! Rosé.

For some reason, we thought this was hysterical.

"Luce, seriously. Is it that bad? With Titus? Can't you just get drunk one night and sleep with him, to break the ice? It's like first sex—you get it over with, get it out of the way, and then everything's fine."

"I wouldn't even know how to start. It would be awkward. He wouldn't understand where it was coming from."

"Come here, Luce. Look at this guy."

She had her laptop pulled out and was showing me someone from ChristianMingle.

"Ooh. He wants to have kids," I said. She let me read the string of messages they'd exchanged.

"I know. That's bad. I want someone who already has his kids."

"He's cute, though. Right?" I said. It was hard to tell—his face was obscured or far away in all the pictures.

"He told his mother about me."

"Oh, God, Bill. Have you even met him yet? That's creepy."

She scrolled through the photos.

"He has too many pictures," I said. "I don't think that's good. And oh, look. There it is. The guitar!"

This, too, sent us rolling. It had been a long night—it didn't take much.

Billy filled our cups up again. "If he's Christian," I said, still giggling, "what does that mean? Do you have to read the Bible?"

"I don't know," she said. "I had to say I was Christian, though. You have to have it on your profile. Maybe he's not. Maybe it's just a fetish."

It was ninety degrees in her apartment, with the windows open. No breeze.

"Billy, my *wine* is hot, that's how hot it is in here. *Please* turn on the air."

"I can't, it doesn't work."

"What?"

"It doesn't work."

I started laughing. "So it's not about the air, it's about you being too cheap to fix the air conditioner? That's good. Oh my God, wait until this gets out."

"It's not real air, Lu. It's still not healthy, broken or not."

"What's his name again?"

"Who?"

"The Christian."

"Chris."

"Chris the Christian? Come on," I said, laughing.

"Yes, Chris the Christian."

"Okay, so what do you want?" I said. "Do you want Chris to love you or desire you? Because there's something different you have to do, I think. For each one."

"Desire. Duh."

"Okay," I said. "Here's what you do. You need to watch this TED Talk about intimacy, then. And then you'll be intimate"—I could hear myself sounding drunk—"and you'll . . . everyone will desire . . . you, or you'll desire them or something."

We both started laughing again, and I mixed us each a rosé.

"Oh my God, Lucy, you're killing me. Do you desire Titus?"

"I desire the guy who's texting me. I don't even know him. So how's that?" I said.

Billy scooped up our empties and pulled the cork out of another half-empty bottle with her teeth. Then she overfilled our cups—no wonder her floors were always sticky.

"I might just call this guy," I said. "Screw it. Just call him and see if he wants to go for it. Right? I mean, what's with this weird anonymous text stuff. Let's just do it. It's all an act, who can keep that up?"

"You're drunk, Lu."

"You know, if Sar gets the show, she's going to want you to do a dating scene," I said. "And I know I am, but you're slurring."

"I'm not going on the show."

"Why not? It could be fun! Plus, what a great story for Chris the Christian. You go on your first date and it's on TV."

Billy brought out a dish of fortune cookies for dessert. Four each. "Here, read mine for me," she said. "I can't stand to, they're always bad."

"'*Traveling south might bring you unexpected happiness.*'" I said. "Save that one. Here's mine. *You learn from your mistakes. You will learn a lot today.*'"

"That one sucks," Billy said. "It's almost midnight—you don't have time to learn anything. Don't eat the cookie yet! Use it for tomorrow. Get another one. One for me, too."

"Okay, here's yours. *'A dream you have will come true.'* Uh-oh. Careful what you dream tonight," I said. "Here's mine. *'You know the answer to the question.'*"

"What question?" Billy said.

"I don't know. These are terrible fortunes."

"They're just old. Okay, nightcap and then we'll go to bed," Billy said. She disappeared into the kitchen and reappeared with two martini glasses filled with something bright green.

"I did these for the last gastrology party and everyone loved them."

We didn't need anything more to drink, and I especially didn't need anything green.

"What is that? I hate these tests you make me do."

"Relax, it's Chartreuse. It's mild. It just has a nice herbal lilt. It's like an herbal martini—it wards off hangovers."

By the time we finished it, I couldn't hold my head up. Billy fixed a bed for me on her couch.

"You were great tonight, Bill."

"Thanks, Lulu. Sweet dreams," she said.

"Good night, Bill. Remember to be careful what you dream."

46

. . . .

Sarah's apartment
Thursday, September 11

S arah's dinner for the Bravo group was on a Thursday. September 11. 9/11. In retrospect, someone should have picked up on that. Sarah scheduled her dinner on the anniversary of the worst terrorist attack in American history, and on the same day of the week as the Last Supper.

It was more interview than dinner, and Sarah knew that. This night would let the show's producers see what or who she could bring to the table. The other women had been tormenting her in the press, by being constantly in it—*GMA*, the *Today* show, *New York Live*, and every print publication in town, plus the tabs. It was driving her crazy.

Sarah's publicists had planted her own things—rumors she was going to be cast, rumors she'd turned it down—but no one was paying attention. No one was retweeting her tweets, only a handful of comments on her Facebook posts. She only had just over a thousand followers on Instagram. She needed a win.

She needed to nail this. She really wanted to be on this show. So Billy's food had to be off the charts. Brian had to wear his new clothes. Lotta had to be messy—we actually wanted her to be, for once—and the apartment had to knock them out. I just had to bring Titus.

"Panic attack, Lu," Sarah said on the phone. She'd just sent Billy and me a bulleted list of what still had to be done. She'd hired staff from TaskRabbit. We all loved the menu. Chris Benz, from Bill Blass, had practically been living with her the past week to get her ready and Carlos Mota had staged the apartment with loaner furnishings and updated the fabrics on her walls. But although she'd thought of everything right down to the Donald Robertson sketches on the invitations—"Deck This Doll," with a saucy Sarah drawn in a halter—she knew that ultimately it was the people in her room they'd be looking at. This is Sarah Porter's world. Who in it can help her carry a scene?

"Don't freak out," I said. "This is the easy part, Sar. No cameras. No nerves."

"I need color tonight, Lucy. I mean it."

"You'll get color."

Sarah had been coaching us. Who was who, who did what, who to focus on. Scooter Adams was the executive producer. "He's really short, so don't stand close to him in heels, I don't want him to have a complex."

"No worries, sweetie," Billy said. "Have everyone leave their shoes at the door. Barefoot is sexy, and then equal footing."

There was Nelson Rock, the assistant producer. "He has a weird tic, this thing he does with his head that makes him look like he's pecking. Like a chicken. Don't get sucked into it. You'll want to look, but don't, but also don't avoid him."

"Got it," I said. "No one-on-ones. We'll keep Nelson in three-somes for distraction."

Then there was Troy Scott, another assistant producer. "He's really young. He says things like 'totes' and 'right on' like it's a question. He's from Colorado."

"I can handle 'totes,'" I said. Billy concurred.

Those were the three to impress. To round out the group, she had

Vera from her own PR team; Deb Watson, a stylist for the show; and then Lotta, Titus, and me. Of course Sarah and Billy. That made ten.

We weren't the first to arrive, and we weren't the last. We ordered a car and picked Lotta up. She had a flask of Patrón that she put a small dent into on the way.

Brian greeted us at the door with kisses for Lotta and me and a firm handshake for Titus. Clean-cut, chiseled jaw, plus his new Acne jeans with a white shirt and a blazer. He was dressed to kill.

"Shoes off, kids," Sarah ordered from right behind him. "I want everyone to feel like this is home. Billy is literally cooking barefoot in the kitchen."

Two of the Schnabels looked smart but understated on a book-shelf; the other was mounted on a table in prominent view of where we'd eat.

Sarah had the music low; she'd made a Spotify list just for tonight. Coldplay, Rihanna. She had votive candles outlining the apartment like a romantic perforation. The lights were dimmed. You could liter-ally feel the glow.

The table—vivid and artful—looked like it had been composed by Jung Lee. Everything was impeccable. Eighteenth-century French chairs in mixed colors surrounded the Restoration Hard-ware table. Her mismatched china and sterling silver gleamed in the flicker of plain unscented candles. Sarah had even, last minute, ordered playful SIT place cards from the Monogram Shop. Wine was being decanted.

There were plates containing slabs of Parmesan and thinly sliced prosciutto, and bowls of olives scattered around the apartment. And in the kitchen were the night's two stars—the hopeful Plaid Skirt, and Billy, who was working in a floor-length pink velvet Pucci, with her long hair up and her emerald earrings dangling down. Sarah was fluttering around her in a red backless Tom Ford. I was in white leather pants and an oversize white button-down shirt. Beneath that was a lacy black bra. My leopard Manolos sat by the door.

Lotta, though, was the clear knockout, in a navy-blue leather mini. Her black patent thigh-high boots, like all of the rest of our footwear, were at the door.

This room was not hard on the eyes.

"Votives on the stairs!" Deb observed. "I love it. Very Valentino." She was wearing a YSL jumpsuit cut to her navel. Sarah had put together a hot crowd.

"Jesus, is that a Schnabel?" Nelson Rock had made a beeline for one of the plates. Sarah beamed.

"Yes. It's breathtaking, right?"

"His plates are huge, though. I didn't know he made them this size."

Sarah glanced my way, with a look of panic. "Well, he did." She downed a glass of prosecco a little too fast.

We were on to cocktails and hors d'oeuvres. Troy Scott was standing alone with a drink and one of Billy's ratatouille tarts, so I grabbed a Pink Sweater (Billy's gin, rosé, and Korbel) and headed for him.

"So, you're one of the producers?"

"Yeah. This is my first Reality, though. I was an AP on *Law and Order* before this." I filed a mental note to tell Livia.

"I don't know much about the show," I said. "You must be excited."

"Yeah, totally." Troy looked twenty, tops. He still had acne. "It's the first season, you know? So we're still branding."

"What exactly is it? You know, like what meets what?"

He took a moment to finish chewing and swallowed.

"It's prep school girls, but all grown up. *Under the Plaid Skirt*. You know? So they're women with husbands, kids. All hot. All super competitive, and all still in the same neighborhood, so they're taking their kids to their old schools and still kind of slagging each other, but in a different way."

"How different?"

"It's kind of a passive-aggressive bitchiness over who has the richest husband, who has the best nanny, doorman, driver, whatever. It's fucking genius."

He finished off his drink.

It didn't sound fucking genius. It sounded terrifying.

"Holy shit," Troy said. "Is that—fuck, I forget his name." He was looking at Titus, who'd made himself scarce after we came in but was now mixing a martini for Nelson. His famous martini: gin, whiff of vermouth, and a good shake east to west.

From across the room with Troy it was fun to watch. *Here's your color, Sarah. I brought the Brockton.*

"He's huge. Shit. We studied him in art history."

I grabbed an olive between my thumb and finger and took a bite.

"Titus Brockton," I said.

"I can't believe he's here. Sarah knows him?"

I shrugged my shoulders. "You'd be surprised who she knows."

"Seriously."

Billy seated us without incident and we all raised our glass. "Cheers!" Then the staff started serving courses while Bill, in her long pink Pucci, narrated them.

A whipped goat-liver pâté, followed by lamb tartare and then a palate-cleansing crisp arugula after that, with her herbed croutons. A hay-smoked duck confit would be center stage.

I was wedged between Nelson and Deb the stylist. Nelson was interesting. He had a history degree, was a published poet, and bred emus. I was careful not to look at him straight on, like Sarah had warned.

"We're going for public nudity and drunken displays of affection," he said. "That's the show."

We were at a good drink stage—enough for everyone to relax, but not too much. So I hoped he was kidding, a little. We all laughed.

"So, this building," Scooter said. "There's a ton of history here, right? I read the book."

"What book?" Deb asked.

"*740 Park*. It was a best seller. Everyone who's ever been the heir of anything or had any rich scandal has lived here. Robert Durst, the Koch brothers?"

"I don't know," Sarah said. "You don't really see anyone unless you make it a point to. Most of the apartments have private elevators."

Now they were intrigued. There's the Upper East Side, and then there's 740 Park.

"I inherited it from my mother," Sarah said. "I mean, she's not dead, she just moved to Sag Harbor."

"Livia Rothwell lives here," I said. "Four floors down."

Nelson jerked his head toward me. "Livia Rothwell? She's still alive?"

Scooter's forehead wrinkled up trying to place the name. "Who's that? Was she an actress . . . or something?"

"Wow. She must be . . . ninety?" Nelson said. "And she lives here?"

"Around that, and yes."

"She's ninety-two," Titus said out of nowhere. Lest they forget who was right at their table, never mind about the building.

Nelson nodded approvingly at Deb.

"Livia's a good friend," I said. I saw opportunity. "She and Sarah are very close." Nelson was kind of cute. He might be a nice match for Billy, I thought. Better than Chris.

Down the table from me, Titus was flanked by Lotta and Vera. And though it hadn't been a picnic to get him to come, he wasn't holding a grudge about it, either. He was behaving himself with Lotta tonight, refilling her glass, being solicitous. He was playing the perfect gentleman. Of course, she'd gone over and above tonight, and Troy, two seats over, couldn't keep his eyes off her.

It was an oddly cozy group. Sarah's hired hands kept the wine flowing. Titus and Scooter were enjoying Brian's scotch. There was equal talking to the left and to the right, and even across the table. It could have been choreographed. No one said or did anything awkward. Titus told his Susan Kensington story about the night they'd been seated together at a Barry Diller dinner and she handed her panties to him under the table. He never saw her again, to give them back.

"What did you do with them?" Nelson asked, wide-eyed.

"I kept them in a drawer. I thought they were good luck. There's something heroic about a woman you've just been introduced to making that sort of offering. Then I got married, and I suspect my former wife had something to do with their disappearance."

While I can appreciate the anecdotal value in the story, it's not one of my favorites. Titus knows. He leaned back from the table to catch my eye, mouthed "sorry," and winked. He was enjoying our little circus.

We were on the lamb when Sarah gestured me toward the kitchen. She excused herself and I followed.

"What do you think so far, Luce?" There was a half-empty bottle of scotch on the counter so I helped myself to a taste of it while Sarah helped herself up to the rim of her glass.

"I think . . . it's going great," I said, a little alarmed at her drink. "It's a nice mix. Very eclectic. I wouldn't worry about color." I eyed her glass—she had supersized her scotch. Then she took a big gulp from it.

Billy was plating the duck, oblivious.

"Oh God, I'm so glad you said that," she said. "I was so nervous."

She took another big gulp.

"Hey. Easy, honey. You don't need to be nervous anymore, it's going fine. You should leave that in here."

Billy brought over a plate for our approval. "Pretty, right?"

Sarah barely glanced at it. She took another long drink, so that made three in under a minute. "Okay, Sar. Let's slow this down." I took the glass from her hand and gave it to Billy, but it was too late. By the time the duck got to the table, the cat was out of the bag. She was drunk. Brian looked worried. He had a smile on his face, but he wasn't talking.

"Lucy," she yelled, though she didn't need to—she was one chair over. "You have to try the potta cotta when it comes out. It has scotch in it! Bill made it. It's fucking . . . really good."

Blotto. She was teetering in her chair, laughing too late at what everyone said, regardless of whether or not it was funny. Titus could barely contain himself. We'd never seen her like this before. I was stunned. How had it happened? Lotta had kept her cool. And Sarah was wasted.

The rest of the night was a blur for Sarah, but not for us. It played out in stages. There was an angry one first, and she started with Lot, who was engaged in a nice conversation with Scooter about Lichtenstein.

"Oh Jesus, Lotta. You and your musculature *horses* and your big text posters, blah blah. I never see any *plate* paintings when we're at your place." She wagged a sloppy finger toward Livia's Schnabels. She hadn't even known what they were a week ago.

"Jesus," Titus whispered to me. We'd gone off the seating arrangement after dessert—when Deb wandered toward the music, I moved one over. We were coconspirators. "Does this help her or hurt her with these assholes?"

"I actually think it might help."

Lotta, never one to stand down to Sarah, even though Sarah was clearly disabled, fired back.

"When you have a work on loan that you know nothing about, just that someone with knowledge told you it might impress people, that's not the same as appreciating anything about art, my sweet friend. Ask Ti."

"Titus," Sarah said, still addressing Lot. She was slurring. "Doesn't even *paint* his own shit half the time. I heard that." She turned to him. He had his arms crossed in front of him with a huge grin on his face.

"I heard that," she said. "From someone *very* reputable. You have, like, a ghost painter."

Oh my God.

The producers and Lotta were eating this up. The predicament now was how to somehow politely excuse the hostess from her own event. Her dinner, her apartment, her table, her guests, and we needed to bounce her.

Deb commandeered the music and pulled up Sarah's Sinatra list. It kicked off with "The Way You Look Tonight," and all of a sudden it felt like we'd crashed a very bizarre wedding reception. With Brian's approval, Scooter and Nelson moved Carl Mota's carefully placed furniture out of the way, and we danced.

Brian stayed by Sarah at the table. He looked on helplessly as she took a bite of her dessert and spit it back out on her plate. "Ugh!" I almost choked on my laugh. Ms. Hug-Your-Inner-Fabulous Fashionista wasn't quite hugging her fabulous right now. She was a train wreck. It was the best thing to ever happen to Lotta. We had fresh material.

Brian was in way over his head. He had the frazzled half-crazy smile of a parent who's invited too many kids to his toddler's birthday party. He passed more wine around the room but snatched Sarah's glass before she could try to fill it. That didn't stop her. She grabbed a bottle from the table and drank from that.

"Barbara Walters," she said, "couldn't even get *into* this place. Can you, I mean, can you believe that? The *board* turned her *down*. Miss I-Slept-with-Kofi-Annan or whoever. She got the door shut in her face."

We needed a distraction. A big one. Like a bomb threat.

Sarah summoned enough balance to get up and dance, alone. "I Could Have Danced All Night" was unfortunately what was playing. She'd probably taken a thousand dance lessons before she left high school, from interpretive jazz to ballet, even square dance.

Take that technical knowledge and add the misleading confidence of too many tumblers of scotch, and you get one really hot mess. Titus and I retreated to a corner. Lotta slow-danced with Nelson like it was their high school prom. I ran back and forth into the kitchen, where Billy was basically hiding out, to give her updates.

The only people shocked by Sarah were her fiancé and friends. The rest of the group took it in stride. It was a nice time, in spite of the chaos.

Titus and I were flirty, like old acquaintances bumping into each other at a party of mutual friends. But then He found me. Because after Sarah checked out, I immediately grabbed my phone from where she'd stashed them by the door. I had four texts. From Him. Titus didn't make my heart speed up the way He did.

212-555-0134: Where are you, my love, and why so far away?

212-555-0134: You've disappeared. I only want to hold you . . . I'm afraid to imagine where you are, who you're with.

212-555-0134: I want to hold your head in my hands. I want you to be still, and let me touch you . . .

212-555-0134: . . . until you ask me to stop.

I'm right here. I'm at a dinner, in a home with friends, and I can think of nothing but you.

I'd had a little too much to drink, too. Juggling my invisible lover with my husband, while my best friend leaped and pliéd across the room.

If it were just me, Bill, and Lot, the whole thing might be hilarious. If there were nothing at stake and no outsiders around, this would have been the funniest thing I'd ever seen. At one point, when we were all still at the table, she had her elbows up, for God's sake, with her hands cupping her chin. She was talking and talking, and we could not get her to stop.

I found myself unexpectedly alone with Nelson. The music was loud, so I leaned in to hear him, but then I was taken in by his neck and could not stop staring. Sarah was right—he resembled a chicken. His jaw jutted in and out as he spoke, as though he were chronically burping.

And then, on cue, it came. The coup de grâce. Deb asked for the "ladies' room" and Brian graciously escorted her. On her way back, though, she caught a toe beneath Sarah's Feraghan Persian rug, just as Sarah stumbled across the room, arms out, to hug her. It brought both of them down. It was slow and ungainly, and there was nothing to do but watch in horror. They both reached out for something to keep them upright, and then they grasped at each other, and at the end they both latched on to the table displaying Livia's Schnabel plate painting, and all three of them came down. Sarah, Deb, and the Schnabel, which immediately shattered to pieces.

Lotta screamed. Vera shut off the music. And then a terrifying silence filled the room.

No one said anything. We circled the pieces and looked down at them like an exotic bird had just crashed through the window.

"Whoa," Troy said.

Deb started to pick them up.

"No, no," Brian said. "Let's just leave it. I'm sure it's insured, and we'll need pictures of the scene."

"You don't know if it's insured?" Vera said. Her voice was two full notes too high.

"No, I mean, of course it's insured. That's why we need pictures."

I snuck into the kitchen for Billy. "Would you fucking get out here, it's orange alert!"

"Don't worry about this, Deb. Really," I said. She was crying. I put a hand on her back, hoping it was some comfort. "They have it under control." I had no idea if it was insured. I had no idea what I'd tell Livia. "Right, Sarah? We're good. Everything's fine."

Sarah was at the head of the table, her head in her arms. She was passed out.

"Holy fucking shit," Billy said, when she finally ventured out.

"Okay, listen. Everything is fine."

Somehow, the night ended. Lotta danced, there were nightcaps, and at some point in the melée, Titus and I walked out. Scooter was in what appeared to be a very serious conversation with Sarah's publicist. I hoped it was a good sign.

We had the doorman call a car, and I had a rush of drunken sentimentality while we waited in the lobby.

"I love you," I said. Just like that, without looking at him. I held his hand and I said, "I love you."

We looked like a happy couple in our reflection in the polished windows, standing in the plush lobby of 740 Park, waiting for our next place to go.

"Lucy. You know I love you, too."

That was it. We didn't race home to rip our clothes off. There was no magical ending. I fell asleep in the car, then stumbled up to my bed and reread my texts before I passed out. Titus put in a Godard film and poured a nightcap. I was exhausted and he couldn't sleep. I had to be up early; he still had a show. But he'd said, "I love you." *Lucy. I love you, too.*

47

· · · · · · · · · ·

Friday, September 12

"O h God, Luce. It was a *disaster!*" Sarah said. She called the next morning at eight. I was shocked she could already function. "It was a fucking disaster." She was crying.

"No, sweetie. No, no, it wasn't. It really wasn't, I swear."

She paused for a minute, then blew her nose.

"Yeah . . . ?" she said. She wasn't convinced. She shouldn't have been—I was lying. She sounded crushed.

"Yes. You just don't remember it clearly, so you're spinning it bad in your head. Listen, Nelson and Titus really hit it off. I think he's coming to the studio next month. You can come over. Lotta turned into Brigitte Bardot when we hit midnight. She started speaking Swedish and dancing to Francis Lai."

"I don't have any Francis Lai."

"Spotify. Oh, honey, we were passing our phones around like cigarettes. Troy was the DJ. I thought he was going to pass out watching Lot dance."

"In a good way?"

"Yes, in a good way. Billy wore a floor-length Pucci, for God's sake, to serve dinner. The food was phenomenal. The producers got drunk. We broke a Schnabel. You got your color."

"No. It was bad, Lu. There's no way I'll get the show, and this will all end up on Page Six."

"No one's calling Page Six. Let me come get you. Let's get coffee, take a walk in the park. You need perspective, that's all. It was fine."

"What are we going to do about the Schnabel? Oh my God. Brian won't even show me the pieces. He thinks I'll be too upset. What do we tell Livia? Is it insured?"

"I'll take care of Livia." I had no idea what I would tell Livia. "Billy's calling, let me take this. I'm coming to get you this afternoon."

"Have you talked to her?" Billy asked. "Is she alive? Does she remember anything?"

"Yes. Barely, and—thank God—no. Not much."

"She was a mess!"

"Yeah, well, don't tell her that. Because I just got done telling her it was fabulous, the whole night. It kind of was."

"I thought I was going to die when she started pulling her hair out."

I'd forgotten about that. Sarah had briefly come to while we were all circled around the Schnabel, and in her stupor she'd started pulling out her extensions, one by one, with a dreamy smile.

"Stop," I said. "It's not funny yet."

"Troy was cute. So was Nelson."

I couldn't shake the image of Nelson pecking with his neck. "I think I'd go for Scooter. He really wasn't that short."

"Why? Did Lotta fuck Nelson?"

"No! I don't know. How would I know? It couldn't have hurt anything, though."

"There's no way she'll get on the show. Right? I mean, the whole night was crazy."

"I don't know. She wanted color, she gave them color. What if we'd sat there and talked politics? Or art? Or traded stupid boring stories about Fashion Week? They would have run out of there so fast."

"Yeah . . . I guess. What are you doing today?"

"I'm meeting Odin at Washington Square, then going for a power walk with Sarah if she's up for it. She needs to confess, and clear her mind. Come with us."

"Are you crazy? No. No way. She'd see right through me. You break the ice. I wouldn't be able to stop laughing. The extensions!"

The extensions were very funny, I was glad she reminded me. I was starting to warm up to this show.

"How did Lotta get home? She was gone when I left. She's not picking up."

"I don't know, why? I didn't see her there, either, when I left. She took a cab. We were all a little drunk."

"Okay, so she's probably sleeping it off. I'll try her this afternoon. Ciao, sweets."

"Ciao."

48

. . . .

Friday, September 12
Washington Square Park
MacDougal Street entrance

I spent the rest of the morning in my office. I was lucky, no hangover. I had a draft of two hundred words, which is nothing, but it's better than having only one, and I went to meet Odin at noon.

She was waiting for me on a bench on the south side, right where she'd said.

It was odd to see her here, outside, out in public. I felt like there should be snipers positioned along the bank.

"How was the cioppino?" I said. She'd tweeted about it this morning.

"You keep up on me."

"That sort of goes along with this."

"Okay, well, I'm here. It's your move."

"Can I record?"

"Go ahead," she said.

I turned on the recorder. She started walking—I had to run a little to catch up to her.

"What's the last movie you watched?"

"Oh, Lucy. You waste your questions. I'll tell you anyway. I saw a movie called *Breathe*. It's a psychological thriller about two girls. The

nice one becomes obsessed with the not-so-nice one and it doesn't
end well."

Why did everything she say feel so loaded?

"You should see it," she said. "You might learn something."

"Okay . . . I'll put it on my list."

"Did I tell you my favorite color yet?"

"No," I said. "And I wasn't planning to ask."

She was tricky. I decided to just walk with her for a minute and
try to take her in. She wore the same-style white T-shirt and jeans
that she had been wearing when we met in her apartment. A simple
look that she managed to elevate. Her jeans were torn, but it didn't
look contrived or accidental, just confident. She looked like she was
on her way to meet someone for a Ricard and talk about Nietzsche
and smoke French cigarettes.

"Do you regret anything you've written?" I asked her.

She turned to look at me, with her slow, creeping smile.

"Of course not. Regret is self-imposed. It's unnecessary and silly."

She was walking at a faster-than-comfortable pace. I couldn't
check my notes, hold the recorder, and keep up with her all at once.

"I have some idea, because I've read you, but who are your influences?"

From reading her blog, I knew they were far-flung. From Ovid to
Socrates to Perez Hilton.

"I seem to be one of them," I said rather boldly.

She stopped walking and turned to face me. Her look was unsettling.

"I'm rereading the comedies of Molière right now, and the letters
of Jean-Paul Sartre and Simone de Beauvoir. And yes, Lucy. You do
inspire me. I think you're fascinating. Nice Midwestern girl goes to
the city to make it big, then marries the most famous man in town.
Did your life turn out the way you'd hoped?"

"I don't know yet," I said. "I haven't finished it."

"Who are your influences, Lucy? Do you enjoy anyone's work besides your husband's?"

She liked to throw the ball right back. I didn't like the way she referred to my husband. We weren't here to talk about me. Or him. I had already assumed she'd know all the basics about me before we met, but I didn't like her casually referring to them. We weren't friends.

"Well, I'm biased, of course. But yes."

"Who?"

Here we were again. Who was the interviewer and who was the interviewee?

"David Hockney, maybe," I said.

"Of course! You're Mr. and Mrs. Clark and Percy."

If she'd hoped to catch me, she wasn't trying hard. *Mr. and Mrs. Clark and Percy* is a famous Hockney work. A man, a woman, a cat, and an ominous point of view. The woman is standing, dominant. The woman who posed was Celia Birtwell. At the time, she was pregnant, and "Mr. Clark," her husband, was screwing half of London. In the painting, he's seated at a distance from her with a white cat on his lap. The cat is an omen. The cat represents jealousy and betrayal. Titus taught me this. The real Mrs. Clark left Mr. Clark shortly after the painting showed.

"We don't have a cat," I said.

"Do I make you uncomfortable?"

The answer was yes. She had that sneaky way psychiatrists and priests have, of watching, of nurturing silence, then waiting for you to come clean.

"No," I said. "You don't."

"It's a sad painting, isn't it? It captures their one final moment before the end. When you still live your routine, discuss what to have for dinner. When one of you still checks the mail, one of you still turns on the TV. The last moment before everything blows up. Has Titus ever painted you?"

"I don't have anything to say about my husband," I said. "No one asked me to write about him, they asked me to write about you."

I wasn't going to give her anything. I wasn't going to explain. I didn't like her.

"Thornton Wilder once said that if Hemingway ever read his biographies, he'd sleep well knowing his secrets were safe. But if Anna Karenina were to ever read Tolstoy, she'd be destroyed because he knew everything about her and he told the world."

"They say fiction is the real truth," I said.

"Tolstoy knew Anna Karenina from the nape of her neck to the arch of her foot—he knew her darkest secrets and wildest fears. He knew how she acted when she was alone in a room."

"Yes. That kind of goes with the job. He created her."

She was describing the feeling I have when I am with her. I feel translucent. Like we're in some weird science-fiction film where she climbs into my head and reads every single one of my thoughts.

"Which is better to have, success or love?"

"A life is better," I said. "It's best to just have a life."

"Well, I think the catch is that you can have success or love. But you can't have both."

"That's a depressing attitude to have, especially for someone your age."

"Do you know something I don't?" she said.

"Possibly."

"This isn't Illinois, Lucy."

"Thank you for pointing that out."

After she asked me to stop the tape, I excused myself and left her there. And instead of going home, I walked to Billy's.

"I don't like her at all," I said.

"Here," Billy said. "Comfort food." She had a plate of warm chocolate chip cookies. "Okay, talk," she said.

"I can't explain it. She seems to know more about me than I know about her, and I don't understand. Why does she care? It's a bad horror film. If I show up in pieces around the city, remember she lives on Bank Street. One oh five. Send the police there first."

"She has an ego. That's all. She's cultivated this big sense of mystery and she has to maintain it. She watches too many movies, she thinks she's some antihero. She thinks she's interesting. Relax. She's just another girl with a very brief window of fame. You'll publish this thing, and a year from now no one will remember her."

"I know," I said. "You're right. I'm getting too caught up in this."

"Just don't let her rattle you. Listen, you have a ridiculous deadline and you're feeling the pressure. Write something up and turn it in. If Noel doesn't like it, turn it into a book proposal and shop it around. Hire someone to follow her. Maybe she's killed someone."

"She's twenty-four, she couldn't have killed someone."

"Lu. Anyone can kill someone."

"When she looks at me, she looks for too long. She forces eye contact and then she doesn't look away."

"She sounds like a barrel of fun. Just finish the piece and move on."

49
· · · · · · · · ·

ODIN OF NEW YORK
FRIDAY, SEPTEMBER 12

DAYDREAMS AT NIGHT . . .

Do you ever wake up from a dream unfamiliar with your surroundings? Do you ever question everything and fail to find one answer? What makes you afraid? What do you fear?

I see fear in people's eyes every day. It's not a fear of spiders, or of AmEx bills, or a fear of not being loved. It's always the same. Fear of the unknown. I'm unknown. And I know a woman who fears me.

No one has what I have, and no one knows what I've lost. But you could say that about anyone.

I came to this city with a black Hermès bag and a week's worth of clothes. I had enough money to stay for an amount of time, and that time is almost up.

50

. . . .

Livia's apartment
Friday, September 12

There was the plate, and then a dream.

First, the plate.

"Livia, we broke a Schnabel." I practiced saying this twenty different ways, and finally settled on that. It was the first thing I announced when I came in.

She was listening to *CSI: Miami* and didn't respond, so I assumed she hadn't heard me. *I could change course now,* I thought. *Not say it. Or tell her Sarah was robbed. Tell her I put the plates back and then hope she doesn't look.* Instead, I repeated myself.

"Livia . . . we broke—"

"I heard you, Lucy. The first time."

She sucked on the unlit cigarette in her hand. "Pour me a drink, please. Gin. And tonic. Be stingy with the tonic."

I felt like a bad daughter who'd had a party while her parents were in Gstaad and wrecked the penthouse. I dutifully went to the kitchen and made her a drink.

"You only broke one?"

I nodded, yes. Of course, she couldn't see it. "Yes," I said.

"I hate this damned show," she muttered. "They overact."

"Livia. What do you want me to do? We broke a Schnabel. I mean, Sarah will pay . . . I know it's priceless. I'm so sorry."

"Lucille. Did she have a good party?"

I considered whether to tell her exactly how it went. I chose against it and nodded again.

"Yes. She did. I think," I said. "She knocked their socks off. Literally. She made us all go barefoot."

"Then who cares about the plate. It's not even the real damned thing. Do you think I would have sent you off with three original Schnabels? Lucille Brockton, do you think I'm that far gone?"

"I don't understand . . ."

"It's a knockoff. They're knockoffs. Your husband saw that, I'm sure. Expensive knockoffs, but all the same. You should have kept quiet and snuck the two of them back in. How would I ever know?"

A fake. Livia, no surprise, got the last laugh. Sarah, no surprise, was incensed she'd had fakes. But there you go.

And then I dreamed about Odin.

It was late and it was dark and I woke up, in my dream, not knowing where I was and with the panicked feeling that I was supposed to be *somewhere*, and that I was very late. My heart raced, in my dream, and I struggled to place my surroundings. A warm hand fell on my arm, to reassure me. It was a woman's hand. Soft and comforting. *It's okay*, said a voice.

It was *her*.

Why was she comforting me? I know that whatever I had forgotten, wherever I was supposed to be, that it was too late. *It's okay*, she said again.

Then there was another voice from behind her.

I am here, Lucy. I came for you.

And then there was warmth and a body next to me, and it was Him.

I woke up frightened. *This is too much.*

51

. . . .

Monday, September 15

He's gone. I haven't heard from him since the night of Sarah's party. I could just ask him. I could send him a text and say, *What happened? Why did you disappear? Where did you go? Why did you leave me?* But that isn't desire, that's desperation. There's always one who is vulnerable and one who has power, and as soon as the balance is off, it all comes undone.

I have fallen in love with him. There was so much I wanted to say. I was ready for him. And now I'm lost. Angry. How could he do this to me? *What, Lu? How could he do what? He doesn't even exist.*

Esther Perel should have talked about that. There's power, and there's vulnerability. And if the balance tips too far one way, then there's nothing. Where is the TED Talk about how to handle that?

I felt ridiculous. Broken.

I was rereading his texts. It was pathetic, but I didn't understand.

212-555-0134: I will come to you soon.

Me: When? How will I know you?

212-555-0134: You will see me, it will be soon. And you will know.

During our first years together, Titus couldn't bear for us to be apart. He was obsessed with me. He wanted me. It was intense, and erotic. He knew what he wanted me to wear. He knew how he wanted me to walk, how he wanted me to look. He knew how he wanted people to react when they met me, when they saw us together. He composed me. Composition is everything.

He always knew he would be with me, he said. He told me he knew this immediately, when he saw me on the plane. And then one day he asked me to spend his life with him, though I do remember it was just that. His life. Not the *rest* of his life. That one qualifying detail was absent.

I didn't think about the future. I just took for granted that it would be. I didn't consider "fifteen years from now." Because when love exists, it has a weight, it feels like something you can hold in your hand and you foolishly think that as long as you don't let go, you'll always hold it. Like the string on a balloon. If you don't let go of the string, you won't lose the balloon. Simple.

But then the helium leaks out. I held on to the string and then one day, the balloon was empty and I hadn't even seen it happen. And all I had was the string.

Odin is a secret. I don't know how I'm going to get out of her who she is or what makes her tick, but there must be something. If I'm heartbroken over an imaginary man, then she's thinking about something, too. Everyone is driven by something. What drives her? She was expecting a dull profile. I wasn't going to give her one.

52

Da Silvano
260 Sixth Avenue, West Village
Tuesday, September 16
Girls' night

All happy friends are alike, but unhappy friends are unhappy in awful ways.

We weren't okay. But if you go to a restaurant in the city where the staff knows you and you have a regular dish and the room is crowded and the mood is up, you can pretend you are. You roll with it.

We were hungry. We devoured the bread, then the starters—artichokes, octopus, chicken-liver mousse. We were definitely not okay, but we laughed like we were. We were dressed like we were. Lotta appeared to be sober. We were relieved to dodge that for a night. But she was definitely the size-two elephant in the room.

Sarah was going out of her mind waiting to hear about the show. The producers were stonewalling. They'd make their decision soon, they said, and they'd call her either way. Meanwhile, Sophie Layton, who is competing for her slot, was popping up everywhere. The day after the *Today* show, there was a long piece in the *Daily News*: "Sophie Layton Ready for Her Close-Up as Latest Pick for *Plaid Skirts*."

"It's really fucked," Sarah said. "They were supposed to decide last

week, but no one seems to be in any hurry. They've already moved
their shooting dates out a month. Meanwhile, I still have to be out
there. And Sophie's all over the place!"

"Do you have any press lined up?" Billy asked.

"A 'Night Out' story in the *Times*—I still have to figure out where
it will be—and a possible interview on New York 6."

"For what?" Lotta asked. "Interview, 'Night Out' for what?"

"For exposure. If I get cast, it's good advance promotion, and if I
don't get cast, I need it more."

"Oh. Okay." Lotta laughed. It was the trouble laugh. It wasn't
good. "Don't you think you've exposed enough?"

"Listen, I'm not fucking old men for money and pretending to have
some fabulous job. I'm getting exposure. It might get me a book—"

"Hey, girls!" I said.

"A book?" Lotta snorted. "A book of *what*? You have a really expensive fucking apartment on Park. That's all you have, Sarah, so I
get the *Avenue* spread. But why should that get you a book, or a TV
show?"

It wasn't kind. And it wasn't true. Sarah had a lot of things. She
had money, yes. And she had a good relationship, a good heart; she
had energy and spirit and drive.

When had Lotta gotten so bitter?

"Why the hell do you *care*?" Sarah said.

"Girls . . . deep breath, okay?"

Just ten minutes ago we were laughing and devouring the starters.
Da Silvano is a high-profile restaurant, with a sidewalk along Sixth
Avenue. It's a bad place to make a scene.

"And what about you with your bullshit new journalism career?"
Lotta said, turning on me.

It stung, but I didn't reply. This wasn't going to end well. Billy's
head was down as she poked her fork into her salad. I'd given her

a check yesterday, to cover her mortgage for this month. She was behind. She was in trouble. She didn't want Lotta to start on her. For all I knew, she'd asked Sarah for money, too. We weren't so tight anymore, there were secrets. We were in trouble. And when you're in trouble, you say things that cross the line. You can screw things up beyond repair. We were all a little into our martinis, too. It was a dangerous hour.

I could see that Sarah was incensed. Lotta shoots from the hip, and it's usually chemically fueled.

"Come on, we're best friends," I said. "We've been doing this for twenty years. It's the best night of the week. Let's eat and then go see a movie. Okay?"

We hadn't been to a movie together in years.

No one replied.

Here we were. Four women who'd gone through twenty years of lovers, husbands, apartments. At one time or another, we had all wanted different things. But we'd shrugged off the letdowns and somehow ended up here, differently than we'd expected, but still here.

Da Silvano is a popular restaurant for celebrities and the tables are very close. So Richard Gere ended up inches away from us and it lightened our mood. We passed our dishes around to taste. Sarah had the tagliatelle with Bolognese sauce, Billy had gnocchi, and we all shared the penne with lamb ragù. We ordered one last round of drinks, then settled the check and walked to the Angelika to see *The Disappearance of Eleanor Rigby*.

The night was beautiful. The walk was long, but the sidewalks were bustling, so we didn't notice.

Afterward, we hugged good-bye and hopped in separate cabs and went home. We'd managed to save the night, but barely.

53

· · · · · · · · ·

Wednesday, September 17

I believe in second acts, but they don't happen in New York in the fall.

It felt like the end of something. I didn't know what.

Titus's show was three weeks away and I'd never seen him so unsettled. His mood was swallowing up the entire house—there was no escaping it. He canceled his Wednesday. He canceled Zeirdra. No one was coming in. Breakfasts were quiet, gloomy things, as if we were under siege.

I had my own problems. I had to hand in a finished piece in two weeks. That might sound like a lot of time, but it's not if you have no idea what to write. And Noel was checking in daily.

I knew this about Odin. She had money. She had a past. She was twenty-four years old. She was beautiful and alone.

What I didn't know was, why was she here? What were her motivations? Who did she love, what did she want?

I didn't buy for a minute that she was fulfilled by writing a blog, regardless of the attention or intrigue.

There were so many books in her empty apartment. I saw a flash of unhappiness in her eyes. She was lonely.

"Let's go out tonight," Lotta said. "Come with me, Luce." I had only stopped by to see how she was feeling after our dinner. I didn't want any bad feelings to linger.

She looked exhausted. There were dark circles beneath her eyes, nothing that couldn't be hidden, of course, but they were there.

"Let's not," I said. "Aren't you tired? Let's stay in. I'll order something."

I was worried about her.

"It's already late."

"*Leva lite*, Lucy. Live a little."

I knew she was going to go out anyway, with or without me, so I said I'd go. She loaned me a dress so I wouldn't have to go home to change. A Rick Owens that showed everything, and we got to Electric Room at midnight.

She started in right away. Music. Colors. Drugs.

I waved off her offer to split an ecstasy tablet in the bathroom. "Come on, Lot. You don't need that," I said. She laughed it off.

We'd already had drinks at her apartment, neither of us needed anything more.

She followed the ecstasy with a line of coke at the sink. No apology, no embarrassment. We were in her world now and she was going to play the way she wanted.

The club was loud, lights were flashing, the room felt like a carnival ride. I wished I'd eaten. I wished I'd gone home.

"Look, Luce," Lotta said, pointing and grabbing my arm. "Your boyfriend."

I didn't have a good feeling about this to start with. And I didn't want to see anyone I knew, least of all the one she was pointing to. James. I wasn't ready for that. This was Lotta's scene, not mine.

Lotta waved him over and kissed him right on the mouth; then she grabbed his hand and led him to a small space near the DJ, where she moved his other hand to her ass. He smiled at me over her shoulder, sheepishly, and shrugged. *It's Lotta. What do you do?*

Right, I thought. *What do you do?*

I texted the girls.

Me: At Electric w/Lot. She's a mess. Not so fun.

Even on a Wednesday, the club was packed with models. I recognized one of the handlers: he'd been doing this when I was still going to clubs. He got paid to fill the place with beautiful women for all the wealthy older men. That was the crowd tonight, anyway. And then James, in his blazer and white shirt. He had his hand on Lotta's ass. I couldn't watch. What was he even doing here?

I could see the effect of the drugs. She'd screw James right there in front of everyone and not think twice about it.

She brought him back to the table, and a small group followed her. There were eight of us now, crammed into one banquette. Lotta was next to me, with her hand on James's leg. I was wedged between her and a man who smelled like cigarettes and Paco Rabanne. Two girls in tiny Miu Miu dresses sat on the other side of him, and they were all laughing at something, no one seemed to care what. No one was talking, really, about anything. The music was loud and they were all happy. Including James. *What was he doing here?*

"Listen," I said to Lotta, "I think I'm going to bail soon. Really."

"No. Doll! We're just starting. Come on, Lucia. You never play with me." She put an arm around me and gave me her big, sad Swedish eyes. I was torn. I didn't know whether it was concern for her, or that I didn't want her alone here with James.

A tray of martinis appeared. I didn't need one, and I shouldn't have taken one, but I did.

Then Satina walked in. Big, blond, towering Satina with her sky-high legs exposed beneath a tight micro leather skirt. Lotta waved her over. She was with a friend, so that made ten of us squeezed into the tiny space. I couldn't remember which ear of hers to talk into, but it hardly mattered.

The whole table got up to dance. Camparo, that was his name—the man in Paco Rabanne—grabbed my hand. I was feeling the martinis. I started dancing with the girls. And then dancing with James.

When I sat back down, a little less tired, almost wanting to be there now, but wanting to be at home in bed more, there was a bowl of candy on the table.

Lotta handed me a piece, a gummy bear. "Here, sweet Lu. It's cherry." She laughed and held it up to my mouth, then nudged it in. I chewed and swallowed. I hadn't eaten all night. I was starving. I ate another one. I wanted the whole bowl.

Everyone at the table ate one. They were delicious. James gave me an odd look, but everything about the night was odd. How could I distinguish?

I reached for a third and Paco Rabanne grabbed my hand. "Whoa, sweetheart. Take it easy," he said. He held on to my hand, and I let him, and then he dropped it. To say my inhibitions had lessened was to say nothing.

To say the room became brighter in the next few minutes. Well, that was an understatement, too.

The Electric Room, James, Camparo, Satina, and the Miu Miu twins, and my best friend, Lot, were completely transformed into one warm happy rainbow. I saw strobe lights where there were none. I loved strangers in the room. I was touching someone and they were touching me, a light weight on my arm that sent shivers of joy through my heart.

"Honey," Lotta said, laughing. "You're fucked up. My little Lu is fucked up."

I don't know how long we stayed at the club, but then after what seemed like a two-day car ride—during which my life flashed before my eyes on a loop in pastels—I wanted desperately to call Him. I pulled my phone out but could not remember how to get into my texts, how to find him. And then we were at James's.

What were we doing here? I didn't want to be here. There was a voice inside me that couldn't get out, though. It was like the real me was gagged and bound to a chair while the gummy-bear me followed along. Lotta led us into the apartment, laughing. She had the key. The bound-and-gagged me worried how I'd get home. I needed to get home. I needed to get Lot home. The gummy-bear me was just happy.

This was the first time I'd seen James's apartment. It was the first time I'd seen any man's apartment at three in the morning since I'd been married. It was beautiful—a huge restored loft that looked like a cathedral. I heard chimes and choirs, and Lotta's laughter, which sounded like a record on low and far away.

I sat down on a couch and watched her. She moved around the place comfortably. My senses were off, my vision was blurred, but I could still see her walk into the kitchen. She opened up a cupboard and took out three glasses, then opened another and grabbed a bottle. How did she know where they were?

None of us was saying anything. Lotta was laughing, but it sounded like raindrops. Nothing made sense. James was standing behind me, he had an arm on my shoulder. I didn't want it there. I didn't want to be here. But the real me was still gagged and bound. The next thing I knew, Lotta was gone and I was pressed against the wall with James's hand up my dress. And then his mouth was on my mouth.

She was right. It is like sitting in one giant warm bath of love, without any anxiety or unpleasant sensation at all. The perfect temperature. It was fucking amazing.

And I panicked. I wanted out.

"I need to go home," I said. "Now. Right now. I need to go home right now." I was trying to break through. My body, my heart wanted to sleep with him; my head wanted out.

"Where's Lotta?"

"Relax, honey. She's in the bathroom. Everyone's good."

"I need to get home," I said again.

"Okay, Luce. Okay."

My voice was rising.

"I really need to get home. Right now."

He started pacing around. He ran his fingers through his hair—he looked distressed.

"Okay, I'm sorry, Luce. I'm sorry. Let's get you home."

He called a car and then he walked me outside and put me into it. He paid the driver. I'd left my wallet somewhere. I was holding on to my phone. It was four in the morning. Somehow, my keys were in my hand, so I managed to let myself in and stumble to bed.

James found my wallet later that day in his jacket. He messengered it over.

What was I doing? What in the hell was Lotta doing? She'd drugged me.

54

....

Da Silvano
West Village
Friday, September 19

W e were at Da Silvano again, at a middle table, squeezed between the elbows and conversations of a model and one of
the Knicks on our left, a hot gay couple on our right.

Sarah ordered us two martinis, old-school: gin, lemon twist,
two olives, splash of vermouth. Giovanni, the owner, was doing his
rounds—he's an incurable flirt. He rested a hand on Sarah's bare
shoulder. He takes liberties like this, but he dotes on us. We're easy
customers.

He set a bottle of Pellegrino on the table and I poured a glass. The
sight of the olives alone made my stomach turn. Two days later and I
still hadn't fully recovered. After telling Sarah the best dish in the city
tonight was the pappardelle with braised oxtail and that he'd send out
a plate of antipasto, Giovanni moved on.

"Lotta drugged me," I said. "At Electric."

Sarah looked puzzled.

"What? What are you talking about? She wouldn't do that."

"She did that. I'm serious. This is out of control now."

"What do you mean, she drugged you? How? Are you sure?"

I wasn't sure if Sarah was even really listening. She still hadn't lived down the dinner and she was certain she'd lost the show.

"Gummy bears."

"Gummy bears? I don't get it."

"They were all eating gummy bears, and they were laced with something. She knew it and she gave me one."

She took a drink of her water.

"Are you sure she knew? How can you be sure?"

"Come on, Sarah. Really?"

I took a drink of my martini and almost gagged.

Sarah picked at our starters.

"I can't even— She drugged me! She's got all these crazy people around her. They all seem to know her. She has this whole life we don't know anything about."

"Okay. I mean, I don't know what to say."

"I ate two gummy bears because I was starving and the first one tasted really good, and the next thing I know I'm making out with James in his apartment. While Lot is pouring drinks."

"Oh my God. You buried the lede, Lucy! James? Did you sleep with him?"

"No! But it was weird and really awkward."

"Okay, well . . . there's no story then."

"No story? My best friend slipped me a spiked gummy bear—I don't even know what it was laced with—and then I almost slept with my hairdresser. No story?"

"Well, you're fine, right? Lot wouldn't give you anything bad—"

"Sarah. She shouldn't have given me anything at all. And how would she even know if it was bad or not bad? She doesn't care—she'll take fucking anything."

"It doesn't hurt to loosen up a little."

"What is wrong with you? This is crazy."

Sarah didn't respond. She let out a deep breath and looked at the rain.

It had been raining since I woke up Thursday morning, and just then, a ferocious downpour broke out right in front of our windows on Sixth Avenue. It was loud enough to get the full attention of Giovanni's Friday-night clientele.

Autumn rain in New York is a nice respite. It gives everyone a chance to recharge.

"Hail," Sarah said. The staff moved swiftly to relocate two outdoor parties inside. One was a young couple. They looked not quite like tourists—tourists didn't come here—but not quite like locals, either. They were laughing. Her shirt was soaked through, and he asked for a towel. Late twenties, I guessed. And in love. Oblivious. Carefree.

"Come on, let's order," I said.

She got the gnocchi, and though I had no appetite at all, I ordered the veal with prosciutto and bread.

"Sar, I'm really sorry about the show," I said.

Autumn rain never brings anything bad. This is what I thought. But tonight, at Da Silvano, with the young sweethearts laughing, the smell of garlic, and Sarah's spooky calm, the rain didn't seem so refreshing.

"What can I do?" she said. "Nothing, right? Sometimes you don't win. It would probably be horrible anyway, all the bloggers trying to find dirt on me all the time."

She wouldn't meet my eyes. She was making a great show of concentrating on the bread. Drawing a pool of oil on her plate. Breaking a piece off. Dipping it in the balsamic and then the oil.

"Yeah. Maybe."

She took a deep breath and let it back out. "You know what? It's not a big deal. It really isn't."

55

....

J. Sebastian Salon
Saturday, September 20

James had Maroon 5 on full blast when I walked in, instead of his usual jazz standards. It was going to be weird. I knew this.

He grabbed my hand and kissed it like a French waiter; then he efficiently sat me down. Cape. Shampoo. Clips. We did the drill.

"Are we okay, love?" he asked me. *Are we okay?*

No. Of course we're not okay, I thought.

"Of course we're okay," I said.

It wasn't what I wanted to say.

"Things got kind of crazy," I said, and laughed. That wasn't what I wanted to say, either, plus I didn't want to laugh. *"That's* why I don't go to clubs." Again, not what I wanted to say. Strike three.

James smiled but it was an indulgent smile, like a priest listening to confession. Why wasn't he mortified?

He lifted my hair up with both hands, then let it drop. He lifted it up again and held it there. He was looking into my eyes, through the mirror.

"Mirrors," I said.

"Mirrors," he replied.

"Self-knowledge or vanity?"

I wasn't gratuitously changing the subject. The mirror just loomed large right then in front of us, and we were communicating through it. It seemed fair to point that out.

He didn't answer. Instead he twisted my hair up into a loose bun on the top of my head and held it there, so I could see myself. *Okay, not bad,* I thought. Long neck, strong cheekbones. Good eyes, I guess. Pretty okay eyes. Objectively, I saw an appealing image. A perfectly together strong forty-two-year-old woman.

But that wasn't who she was. I wanted to cry.

"Vanity," he said.

"What?"

"Your question. Self-knowledge or vanity, it's vanity. Give them up for a week."

"Give up mirrors?" I said. "How can you?"

"You can. I did it once for a photography class. No mirrors for one week. I turned them all around."

"What was the point?"

"It was an art class. The idea was that self-regard, self-focus, self-anything affects the work, so let's see what happens when you take that away."

I thought about this. I mean, cavemen didn't have mirrors. They never saw themselves. Was that better?

"Van Gogh did over forty self-portraits," I said. "He painted himself forty times from an image he saw in a mirror."

James smiled. "Selfies. He should have painted another forty *without* the mirror. Now *that* would have been interesting."

He started clipping.

"One of my clients teaches psychology. She did a study once, about our need for reflection and affirmation. She said we look for a physical reflection-slash-affirmation of ourselves, on average, a hundred times a day."

"That's impossible," I said. "Who has time?"

"You'd be surprised. Mirrors, windows, a passing reflective surface. The toaster, whatever. It's a reflex."

I studied myself in the mirror in front of me. If I look too long in a mirror, I get nervous. I stop recognizing myself. I see a stranger.

"Mirrors are misleading," I said.

"They're tricky. They sear an image of ourselves onto our brain, and it's not even the same one everyone else sees. So whatever perception you have of yourself, think about it. You're the only one who sees that, and you're reinforcing it a hundred times a day."

I wasn't sure what my perception of myself was.

"If you're confident, you think, 'God, I'm good. Look at me.' And if you're insecure, the reflection confirms your worst thoughts. Either way, we seek it out to prove ourselves right. So anyway, I turned the mirrors in my house around for a week. I dressed, shaved, showered without a mirror. It's a trip."

"Have you ever had your heart broken?" I asked him.

"Yes," he said.

Then he turned me around in the chair so I was facing him. No mirrors.

"Honey, listen to me. It did get out of hand. And I'm very sorry. You mean the world to me, you know that. It was a mistake. Remember this about yourself: you create possibility from impossibility. You're bigger than whatever it is that is happening to you right now. Never mind what happened the other night. Throw it away."

We were okay. I think that's what he meant. Except that I wanted to ask him how Lotta knew where the vodka was. And I wanted to cry.

56

. . . .

Brockton town house
Sunday, September 21

Titus paces around the house now late at night, it wakes me up. At three o'clock, I hear him above me, in his studio. The sound of furniture moving. Footsteps. Why can't he take off his shoes?

Zeirdra came today but he had his studio locked and he wouldn't let her in. I felt bad for her and invited her down. I rarely talk to any of them, his models, but today I did. Which was interesting, because Zeirdra doesn't speak. She has an affliction. It's called progressive mutism. Technically, she's able to speak but she doesn't. She won't. She hasn't spoken, according to Titus, in seven years. She carries a notebook with her everywhere and carries her end of the conversation out on it. She probably has a bookcase full of notebooks of all of her one-sided muted conversations.

"Come downstairs?" I said, and cringed. I do this with Livia, too, sometimes. Talk slower, louder, use smaller words.

She nodded.

"I'll fix some tea. Sit in the library, it's more comfortable."

I put on the water, then changed my mind and grabbed a bottle on the counter. I poured us each a drink from it. I tamed it with 7 Up.

"Okay?" I asked, showing her the glasses. "Bourbon and soda."

She smiled and took it. She would need it if he decided to let her in. I wouldn't want to be locked up in a room with him right now.

"How's the piece?" I said. "Have you seen it?"

She shook her head no. For all of the toughness of her physical appearance, she looked small and vulnerable sitting in the stuffed chair with her notebook.

"Do you know, though? I mean, do you have a sense of whether it's good? Whether he's happy with it?"

It occurred to me that I didn't know how he painted. I couldn't describe it to you. I'd seen him work, of course, but not really. I used to spend time in the studio, but he'd always stop what he was doing and focus on me. I was never a fly on the wall.

She turned to a blank page and wrote.

He's up and down. He'll be happy one day and want to celebrate with wine. And the next day completely silent. Some days, it's as if he forgets I'm there. He puts his music on, he swears, he has conversations with himself.

She showed me the page and smiled.

"I think it's amazing what you do. I understand it, a little. I used to model, but they were taking photographs of me. I wasn't motionless for hours at a time. How do you occupy your mind?"

It's very hard sometimes. It feels like solitary confinement! I play the alphabet game. I go through the alphabet and try to name an animal for every letter, and then a food for every letter, an adjective for every letter. That is sometimes frustrating, though, because I can never get all of the letters. But I have to be careful to not let my mood change, because then my demeanor does and he catches it. What I project affects what he does.

She handed the notebook to me. It's not a bad way to communicate. There are no interruptions. It's thoughtful, with full attention, and back and forth in equal parts.

"Are you going to his show?" I asked her. She shook her head no.

"This . . . might be personal, you don't have to answer, but do you— What is your life like outside of this? Do you have a boyfriend?"

I go to school at night. I'm studying sign language. I want to be an interpreter. My boyfriend's name is Anthony and he's very good to me. He's a computer consultant. We have a studio apartment in Jersey City.

A nice boyfriend. A studio apartment in Jersey City. It sounded like heaven.

57

· · · · · · · ·

Cheri's apartment
Sunday, September 21

Cheri is having an extremely good month, she's the only one of us. She has sold three big properties: a duplex downtown, the terraced place on Vandam, and a two-bedroom on Park. And she's seeing someone she seems to really like, his name is Rolando. She calls him Rolly. Latin, she made a point of telling me. A Latin businessman, which leaves a lot to the imagination.

We were having a late lunch. She'd made us a green salad, and in the oven was a cheese soufflé.

"Honey, so catch me up. Titus's show. The piece you're writing."

"Nothing new with Titus, but speaking of shows, Sarah might be on television. She's still waiting to hear, but she auditioned for a reality show." I didn't want to talk about Titus. I'd had enough with the work and the mirrors and the collections and his show.

Her face wrinkled up like a bad odor had drifted in. "Oh, honey. No. Those shows are *terrible*. Why is she doing that?" Then she whispered, "Does she need the money?"

"No. She doesn't need money. Plus I don't think they even pay anything. It's hard to explain. It's exposure, it's what she wants to do. She has philanthropic endeavors—she can promote them."

"You won't be on it with her, will you?"

"I don't even know if *she'll* be on it yet. But who knows? I might. No one will die."

"Did you finish the book?"

"The book?" I said.

"*Mating in Captivity*, yes, the book."

"Oh. No," I said.

"Did you finish most of the book?"

"Well. No."

I'd read most of Cheri's comments in the margins. But I hadn't read most of the book.

Cheri made a clucking sound with her tongue and shook her head.

"I watched the TED Talk. I think I get the idea."

She took the soufflé from the oven and we spooned into it right out of the dish before it collapsed.

"Isn't this a great metaphor?" I said.

"What, honey?"

"The soufflé. It's this simple, perfect dish, but it's like the Snapchat of food. There's only a brief window of opportunity to enjoy it. If you hesitate, it's gone. It's wonderful and it's fleeting."

"I suppose."

"Is any of it even worth all this work? That's what I'm wondering. The pursuit of desire? How long did it take you to make the soufflé? Was it worth it? Because now it's gone. And if we'd been distracted for one minute, it would have collapsed and been all for nothing."

"Oh, honey. Lucy, you're just so young to be thinking that way."

She was right. She wasn't thinking this way. She was selling apartments and screwing Rolando, and God knows she'd had her share of *what's the point of it all*, too. I thought of what Livia had told me: *You girls need to make peace with disappointment. The sooner the better.*

58

· · · · · · · · ·

Nicola's
146 East Eighty-Fourth Street, Upper East Side
Sunday, September 21

Nicola's is old-guard New York—oak-paneled walls and crisp white tablecloths. The menu is constant and reliable. Men in tailored suits line the bar, accompanied by tall thin girls with big round eyes.

We were here, I'd assumed, because Titus had finished his piece, the last one. The big one. Or enough that he knows he'll make the deadline for the show. And, we were here, too, I'd assumed, because he was happy with it. He knew it was good, and this was his way of telling me. We wouldn't talk about it. To talk about his work at this point, Titus feels, is like courting favor, which in turn breeds patronization. He can't stand that. He prefers his bad reviews to the good ones. He's uncomfortable when they rave. Tonight, though . . . I hadn't seen or felt him this relaxed in years. He was content and enjoying his wine and soup. Nicola's makes a fabulous pea soup.

We have been coming here for fifteen years and he always gets the veal. It's like a comedy sketch. He studies the menu for an excruciating amount of time, he makes the waiter repeat the specials, and then he orders veal.

So I waited to hear Tonio recite the specials—two beef dishes and a seafood lasagna—and then recite them again. I waited, after I asked for a half order of linguine, for Titus to look at the menu one more time. And then I waited for him to fold it up, hand it to Tonio, and order the veal, with the lemon butter on the side.

He was taking in the room and put his hand over mine, reflexively, affectionately, when he talked.

This is nice, I thought.

"We should go to the Cape next week," he said. "We should go away for a few days, before the show."

I nodded. "That sounds nice." I knew that we wouldn't.

"You look radiant tonight," he said. "You're a very beautiful woman."

It caught me off guard. It made me nervous.

"Tell me what you're writing."

He took a bite of his food. It has always fascinated me to watch him eat. He addresses his meals like a maestro does the solo cellist. There are rests and tempo changes. His hands move as though they're choreographed, and he never treats a bite of food the same way twice. He will move the arrangement around subtly with his fork, but with purpose. He's like an actor in a dinner scene.

"It's a profile of a woman no one knows anything about. Noel, though, is obsessed with her. She has this mysterious sort of fame that seems to come from being completely unknown. Which makes sense, I guess, because that's unheard of now."

"Noel just wants to sleep with her. Noel would screw a shoe."

I laughed. It was funny. He laughed at it, too.

"What was going on with Richard the other day?" I asked.

His fork stopped still on his plate and he looked up at me.

"It's just . . . you drank half a bottle of bourbon when he brought up your first piece."

"I don't love interviews, Lucy. You know that. They ask the same fucking questions every time and I have to always rattle off some different way to answer them."

He went back to his veal, then stopped again and this time he set his fork down on the plate. He pressed a hand to his head and didn't say anything for several minutes.

"It's no use."

"It's just a show, Ti. No one's looking to hurt you. Leo will put together your old stuff if you're not ready, he'll make it work, you know that. It's one night."

He looked at me and started to say something, then stopped. He took a deep breath.

"Lucy, there's something I need to tell you."

How many words was that? Seven? Eight? If there was a Buzzfeed list of eight-word sentences you don't ever want to hear, that one would be in the top five.

I knew it wasn't an affair, because he wouldn't tell me about that. Unless he was in love and wanted to leave. So that was it. He was in love, he had cancer, or he'd gambled our money away.

I didn't say anything. I waited, unsure of what to do about my own fork—match his move and set it down? Hold it casually like I was doing now, with a bite of my entrée still pierced on the end? Finish the bite?

I set the fork down. And then, because these few seconds of awkward silence felt like an eternity, I said, "Okay . . . so tell me."

Richard had been right. It did seem a little unusual, and a tiny bit too pat that in all these years in the spotlight, with all of the pressures and temptations and fears that go along with that, there had never been a scandal with any meat to it.

"A woman . . . there is a woman—"

"I don't need to hear this."

"No, no. Please. Listen. It's not that. There is a woman and she's blackmailing me. It's not an affair. It's serious, Lucy."

We were in a restaurant. That was both good and bad. Good because nothing dangerous could happen. Whatever he was going to tell me would be immediately softened by the bite of linguine in its delicate cream sauce, dotted with small scallops and sprinkled with leeks. If you have a bit of delicious food and you can overhear the conversations around you, and if a waiter is fluttering nearby and filling your water, then there's nothing your dinner companion can say that can harm you.

So I finished my bite—one scallop and three expertly twirled strands of linguine—and said it again. "Okay . . . so tell me."

He leaned toward me, the way you do when you want to speak quietly but still be heard. He said, "It's *Woman at Midtown*. I copied it, Lucy."

I didn't respond or react, because I didn't understand, so he kept talking.

"I copied it. It's a copy. It wasn't mine and this woman has the original. I was stuck, I was blocked. So I copied it, and my piece sold, and that was that."

Nicola's has amazing bread, and an herb-infused butter that takes them three days to make. I reached for the bread because doing so required something of my hands. Because . . . what was he talking about? Blackmail? He didn't paint his painting? That was almost forty years ago. I didn't understand.

"I don't understand," I said. I was tearing off pieces of bread, dabbing them with butter, and stuffing them in my mouth. I pulled it off more elegantly than it sounds.

"Lucy. I need you to listen to me. I . . . it was a mix-up. It was an awful sort of thing. That you do, when you're young, and then you go on and it's forgotten. But never entirely."

"You copied it? I don't— How did you copy it? Who painted it, then?"

"It was Roman's painting. It was his work. It was beautiful. I didn't know what I was doing then. I was painting shit. But Roman was painting . . . He painted this woman . . . It was like reading a beautiful tragedy observing that painting. It was truly—"

"Titus. I still don't understand. Then why didn't he sell it?"

"That's complicated."

"You stole his work? Is that— I don't *understand* what you're telling me."

"Lucy. You have to know this. I was young. Stupid. We . . . were both ambitious—what's the word—we were hungry. It was *my* style that made it good. My technique with color. My eye. He was unhappy here, so he left. We were out of money and he felt defeated, so he went back. And then Leo came to the studio and he saw it, he saw mine. I hadn't shown anyone. It was so goddamned frustrating, Lucy, because it was my eye. *My* technique. It was as if *he* had done a knockoff of something I hadn't yet done."

I didn't like this.

"It is *my* fucking style and my technique. It was *my* work."

Was I hearing firsthand maybe the biggest art scandal of the century? There wasn't enough herb butter or baguettes in the city to get us gracefully out of this scene.

"Who is blackmailing you?"

He took another long breath. A hand went through his hair.

"His daughter. It's his daughter. He had a daughter, and her mother died when she was very young. And then Roman died. I can't tell you more, Lucy. She is here. She came here, to New York, to show me she had the piece, the original. I couldn't have this out before the show, so I've met her request. And I don't know . . . what will happen."

He finished and paid our bill, and when the waiter came back with his card, he pushed his chair back and got up. I followed him outside. Though it was Sunday night, there were no cabs. "I should have called for a car," I said and pulled up the Uber app on my phone. Thirty minutes. I raised my hand and gave my best taxi wave. The streets were wet from the rain.

Titus started walking. He hates the humidity of early fall. The swelter of New York sometimes gives him debilitating headaches. I was frantically trying to wave down a cab.

He was halfway up the block, then stopped and turned back to me. "Lucy. Go on without me."

"Go on to where?" I shouted.

He tells me this and then, nothing?

When we were first married, we used to go out almost every night, whether he was working on something or not. Sometimes he'd assemble a group, sometimes just the two of us. He was erratic, though. It wasn't unheard of to have a back table at Morandi set aside for ten and to have his spot empty until they brought out dessert. Then he'd walk in and start a conversation as if it was what he'd intended all along. The things an artist gets away with. And now this one, the one I married, I find out is a fraud.

He walked out of sight. He would go to the Waverly, I was sure. They knew how he liked to be treated there. He could sit at the bar, undisturbed, and observe. I found a cab and went home.

I went to sleep and had a dream. About him. No, not Him. About my husband. Not the stranger I'd fallen in love with, but Titus. It's the first dream I can remember having of him in years. It's disturbing.

It's dark and I see his silhouette in my room. He comes into my bed and strokes my hair. I groggily come awake, what is he doing here? What time is it? Where am I?

"I love you," he says as he brushes the hair from my forehead.

"Do you know what that feels like? Do you know what I feel?"

I am putting my imaginary stranger's words into Titus's mouth. In my dream the two are the same. Titus is Him. He has a face.

He undresses and lies on top of me, positioning himself so he can study me. Then I feel him, and that he wants me. He pulls the sheets away and then my panties to one side, and he kisses me like it's the first time we've ever kissed. Sensually, at first. Then desperately. Fiercely. He whispers my name, over and over. He whispers things into my ear, how he wants me. He touches me everywhere, intimate but intent. Everything that is mine is his. Until finally he comes inside me and collapses. I struggle to breathe beneath the weight of him but I don't want him to move.

I lie there, beneath him, breathless and euphoric. I am trying to understand what has happened. I don't want him to leave.

Not possession, but obsession. Love unleashed. Animal energy. Intoxicating.

Then in the doorway, I see a silhouette. It's a woman, but she's faceless in the dark. She's laughing. Not in a nice way.

I woke up disoriented until I realized where he was. Or where he wasn't. He wasn't in the room with me. I stood up and stared down at my bed, which was empty. What happened to him? What happened to us? It was all just a dream.

59
·········

Brockton town house
Monday, September 22
Artforum interview, final

It was the third and last time with Richard and now, knowing what
I knew, I felt panicked. Now I was matching Titus glass for glass,
secretly, in the kitchen. I knew he was irritated with me for not in-
tervening, for not getting him out of this. But I couldn't. He knew
that. He can be moody, and that's fine, but he couldn't back out of
a commitment to the press, not to *Artforum*, they wouldn't be kind.
And if there is anything at all lacking in the show, one chink they can
expose, then they will if he upsets them. And God forbid they dig up
the other thing. So . . . here we were. Gougères and wine. He had
asked me to be liberal with it, not to let an empty bottle sit.

We'd both suffer through this in an alcoholic haze.

"*Titus Brockton: Mirrors* is the name of your show. Why *Mirrors*?"

"Life mirrors art, love mirrors vanity, self mirrors love. Mirrors are
the ultimate deception."

"Interesting."

"The work is done. And I don't give a fuck how it's received. Ten
new pieces, some old ones. The centerpiece is the one you're all waiting for and I don't give a fuck what you think of it."

"Of course you do. In some way. It's not natural to be completely indifferent to critique."

Titus, to show him it was, shrugged his shoulders.

"Will you start working again immediately, after the show?"

"No. There has to be distance. Space. Each time I approach the canvas again, I cannot create anything unless I have been away. I have to have had stimulation from something else, somewhere else, so that I can return to it and start again. To the same pale, empty white canvas. I start in the exact same place, every single time, and whatever I've done in the past means nothing. It's maddening. And it's where the fucking thrill of it all is, too. The day I can no longer do that, the day that passion fails me completely and there's no desire to start again and create, I'll be dead."

"You make it sound like something evil."

"It is, in a way. Pieces of it. The human soul is dark, Richard, and that is where art lives."

Richard glanced at his notebook, flipped a page back; then he looked up at Titus.

"It was an anonymous buyer," he said.

"What was an anonymous buyer?"

"*Woman at Midtown*. So you . . . Do you know the identity of the buyer? Do you know where it is?"

The dark mood was back, instantly.

"No. Christ, that was forty years ago, Richard. I don't chase my work around. You put it out there and you continue to create."

"All these years, though. It just occurs to me that it's a great mystery."

Titus laughed. "A plane that disappears from the sky is a great mystery. God is a great mystery. Whoever the hell buys any of my work is hardly a great mystery. Artists sell their work, it changes hands, it goes on loan to museums or sometimes stays in private collections for generations. After the artist dies, sure, there's a sensation when a forgotten piece appears. Or a missing piece is found. No mystery."

Like Lotta and her Dalí, I thought. But Titus was right—is it really a great mystery where one particular piece is? Leave it alone.

Tatiana brought out plates of food. I poured more wine.

"Euphoria." That's what you've called the newest work, though the show is titled *Mirrors,* and I think it's interesting what you're doing. The four collections you're going to show seem to make up a certain progression in your life. Can you talk about that?"

"Euphoria is the final chapter of an entire body of work that spans three decades. It is the work that has shaped and defined my life. It has shaped and defined the way I love. This is the reward. I have never felt better about what I am doing. It has also never been more daunting. I have never felt better about my life. And at the same time, to engage in that was daunting, too. You have to live the way you paint. You need to engage yourself in life as if it is art—with great passion, or you won't experience anything. You won't *achieve* euphoria, which is the ultimate quest. Isn't it? It's simple to kill time. But if you want nirvana, you have to engage in your life the same way you approach the blank canvas. Every single day."

I had not heard him talk this way—about life and love, about passion—with this much feeling in far too many years. He looked beautiful.

"What are the obstacles?" Richard asked.

"You know them. Mediocrity. Satisfaction. Status quo. Those are the safe zones. You fight to rise above that and there are people at every turn who want to take away what you have."

"Like what, for instance? What do they want to take?"

"The work. If you have great passion for your work, someone will want to take that away. If you want more and have great passion for love, there will be people in line to take that away, too. It is a daily fight. It can never be conquered. Defeat and loneliness are the beasts we fight until the day we die. They numb you to beauty. They can destroy you."

Richard looked at him for a long moment.

"The new piece—there's a rumor that there is a buyer for that already. Sight unseen."

"No. That is absolutely false." Titus smiled the smile of someone who was done, and Richard knew it.

"A false rumor."

"Yes, Richard. A false rumor."

Richard gave his glasses a quick wipe with his cloth napkin. Uncharacteristically, he finished off his glass of wine, and it was his second. He thanked us both, but he was curt. Tati saw him to the door.

"Well," Titus said. "That is the fucking end of that."

60

·········

Billy's apartment
Tuesday, September 23
Girls' night

"Moët sent me a new bottle of champagne we should try, and these goblets, look. They're insane," Billy said, and started pouring. "You are actually not supposed to drink champagne, or any wine, from a flute. It's an aesthetic tic people have, but it actually works against the wine. Champagne, too, needs to breathe. Even if it's plastic. A plastic goblet is much better to the wine than a two-hundred-dollar crystal flute."

"That should be in your book," I said. *The Gastronomer's Guide to the Galaxy.*"

"What's the status with Odin? Have you written your opus? Has she charmed you?" She handed me a glass and seated herself on the floor.

"Has the seductress seduced?" Sarah asked.

I smiled. "It's been an interesting ride. And yes. I'm almost done."

"Lu, can we do a scene with her if I get on the show? It would kill on television. 'Socialite, best friend of seductress.'"

Lotta called on Billy's phone, to be let in. She was downstairs. I hadn't seen her since the night at Electric, and I didn't really want to see her now.

"Uh-oh," Billy said. "Brace yourself, girls, she sounds completely out of it."

She was. She stumbled into the room. Her hair was a mess and her eyes were wild. She was wearing a black trench coat over leggings and she wobbled.

"Oh my God," Sarah whispered.

"Dolls!"

She weaved her way straight to Billy's cupboard and pulled out a glass. Billy stopped her.

"Sweetheart, sit down first. No rush on drinks."

"No rush on drinks. That's funny, Bill. Get me one, then, will you? Without the rush."

We sat her down on Billy's couch and Sarah and I each stayed on one side.

"What's going on, sweetie?" Billy said.

She shook her head. Then she made a weird noise that sounded like a hiccup at first, and then laughter, and then something else.

"Lotta, what's going on?" I said. "Where'd you just come from?"

"*Phillip.* We broke up. But don't worry. He bought a huge fucking work first."

We could barely understand her, but then she pulled a check out of her pocket. She flashed it at us, grinned, and then ripped it in half.

"Jesus! Lotta. What are you doing?" Billy yelled.

"I don't want his stupid check," she said, and started laughing again. It was scary.

"Phillip from Rose Bar?" I said.

How could someone break up with her if we didn't even know who he was?

"Bill," Sarah said. "Get her water or something. A cold towel."

We had all seen Lotta in various states of intoxication. We had all seen her stoned. We had all seen her high. It was something we were used to. But not like this.

"Honey, what'd you take? Where were you drinking?"

"We went to the fucking *Russian Tea Room*." She was laughing after everything she said, but not in a good way.

"Everyone there is ninety. But the vodka is *very* cold. I don't know why I never thought to be Russian. Their vodka is *very* cold. Billy, pour me a cold vodka, please. Very cold, though. Don't be cranky about it."

Billy came back with a wet cloth and we discreetly cleared off her sofa and tipped Lotta back onto it. She murmured for a few minutes, and then she was out.

"She seriously can't be *doing* this," Sarah said.

"It might make good TV."

It was a bad joke. I apologized for it.

"She seriously can't fucking be doing this," Billy said. "I'm sick of it." Yeah. We all were.

61

. . . .

High Line Park
Chelsea
Thursday, September 25

It was sixteen days and counting until *Mirrors*. Two weeks and counting since I'd heard anything from Him.

It didn't matter, there were things to do. We were all taking turns checking on Lotta, at least one of us at least once a day. We made sure she was going to work, we made sure she was coming home. We made sure she had food. We just made sure.

I met Odin at the High Line, the narrow mile-and-a-half-long park the city had made from an abandoned elevated railway.

"This is my favorite place in the city," Odin said before either of us said hello.

I could see why. It's like a peephole. There is a sense you can't be seen here but you can see everything. If someone wanted to spy on the city's secrets, this would be a good place to do it.

I didn't have a notebook, but I did have the recorder on my phone, which I flashed to Odin to let her know. She nodded her approval and I started taping. She started to talk.

"You're going to find out more about me after you hand in your piece," she said.

"Oh, really? Why is that? You're going to give me the real Odin then? After I'm done?"

She pulled a tin of mints from her pocket and offered me one. I hesitated. I still saw her as the sort of person who would give the journalist a mind-altering drug and leave her here in a place like this, unconscious.

I took it.

"It's just how things work out sometimes."

"I guess I'll have to live with it then."

"There's a writer I like to read, Deborah Eisenberg," she said. "And what I like about her is that there's nothing solid in her stories. They're mercurial. Reading them is like trying to corral a little drop of water and move it from here to there. You want to empathize with her narrator, and she teases you with that, but then she makes it so you can't, and you switch to the antagonist, or to the minor character who should have just come in and out of the scene but against all common sense sticks around. She plays with all of the characters, none of whom stay relevant for more than a paragraph at a time. It's infuriating."

She took a cigarette out of a pack in her pocket and lit it, so there was a pause of a few seconds before she finished her thought.

"Gertrude Stein tried to write the way Pablo Picasso painted. It's annoying as hell. I don't know how he could be friends with her, and she had the power in that relationship, which was interesting. He had the talent, she had money . . . That's the power, I suppose. She offered booze and food and a place to go when they were all broke. She bought their art. Had she not, nobody ever would have printed one fucked-up crazy word she wrote."

"How did you know about Chet Jantzon?" I said. It was a bold question to ask right out like that, but what the hell.

She smiled but didn't look at me.

"He told me," she said.

I was waiting for her to tell me to shut my recorder off. She didn't.

"People want to tell their secrets, Lucy. Remember? Everyone has their lies, and ultimately everyone wants to tell them. The first thing new lovers do is tell each other everything that's ever haunted them, make a full confession. The bad girlfriends, the stint in rehab, the abusive father, et cetera. You tell someone in love with you because they'll justify or forgive anything."

She possessed an unnatural amount of certainty for her age. It wasn't a naive certainty. It's easy to be confident or certain if you've never been tested. It was the certainty of someone who'd survived something—death, heartbreak.

"But why did you want to hurt him?"

We were almost to the end of the trail, where the steps led down to Fourteenth Street and the Meatpacking District, where both of us could easily walk home. Odin stopped and sat down on a bench. She had finished smoking her cigarette, flicked the dead ash in the grass, and slipped the butt into her pack.

"I didn't hurt him, Lucy. You can't live a life of peace if you worry about something you tell someone getting repeated. Neither a borrower nor a lender be. If you tell someone your 'secret,' regardless of how small or big you feel it might be, you can't ever be at peace, ever, if you have any hope that they will keep it. It will torment you night and day. You have to assume once you have said a thing to someone that you've released it and the universe will have its way."

She gestured toward my phone, my cue to shut off the mic. I did.

Then she took another Kool from her pack and this time offered one to me, and I accepted. I fixed it between my fingers and raised it up to my mouth, where Odin then lit it expertly, cupping the flame from the wind.

"Your husband's in trouble," she said after a minute of silence. "Isn't he?"

She looked at me to see how I'd react. I felt her watching. I took a long, sweet drag of her cigarette and said nothing. What was she talking about? What did she know? How would she know anything?

I tried to exhale the smoke like Lauren Bacall and, naturally, coughed. "I'm not sure what you mean. My family is fine."

"Okay," she said.

Okay.

I hadn't smoked a cigarette since my modeling days. The nicotine gave me a heady rush.

"Lucy. You're the frog, in that metaphor."

I shook my head. "I don't know it."

She explained it to me.

"If you drop a frog in a pot of boiling water, it jumps out. That makes sense, right? Of course it does. It's hot, it hurts, it wants out. But if you put the frog into *warm* water, lukewarm water like a sunny pond, it stays. It will stay even as you gradually heat the water to a full boil. It won't try to hop out. The frog will die from the boiling water before it ever occurs to him that he should escape it."

"Interesting metaphor."

"Why do you think it was so simple for you to find me?"

I didn't answer. I didn't look at or react to her or say anything.

"Think about that. Good luck with your piece."

Then she left. She just walked away. That's the note that Odin No-Last-Name from John Lennon's building on Bank Street left me on. An unnervingly coy question, a story about a frog.

I finished the cigarette slowly, savoring it. When it was gone, I wanted another.

I had resolved to drink less—we'd all been doing everything in excess—but I decided I wasn't going to start tonight. I wanted to be home, alone, with Billy's mescal. I had crumbled and texted *Him* earlier. *Why?* That's all I said. It's all I wanted to know. But he didn't respond.

I had the sense someone was near me, so I turned and there was. A man, standing very close. I didn't know how he got so close to me without me hearing, but he was there, and familiar. Tall, handsome. Shoulders I could collapse on.

"Are you okay?" he said. As if my week hadn't already been strange enough. It was Alex, from the park. The man whose hair James cut, the man who looked like there was more to his story. Alex.

"Don't be upset but I've been watching you. And I saw your friend leave. You looked like you could use a drink," he said.

I had nothing to say. I was stunned. I *could* use a drink. Was I in danger? There was no one else around.

He was wearing weathered jeans, a thin T-shirt, and expensive leather shoes. What was his story? He was in town for a few weeks, he'd said. That's it. That's all I knew.

I didn't know whether to run or stay. He was carrying a small backpack and he reached into it and produced two plastic cups, one of which he handed to me. Then he pulled out a bottle. "Champagne," he said. I thought of Billy. Plastic cup, no flute. The bubbly could breathe.

He smiled and reminded me of his perfect white teeth and dimples. Can you fall in love with a smile?

"Thank you," I said and took the cup.

"It's all they had at the Standard," he said. "The red cups."

"Well, again, thank you."

"I recognized you from the park," he said. "The beautiful woman with the sandwiches."

"Right. I didn't offer you one. I lack certain social graces."

We drank from our cups. It was surprisingly good.

"Are you okay?" he asked me again.

"I think so."

"Lucy? Right?"

I nodded.

"Do you have a mirror in your home?"

"Yes." What a funny question.

"Good. Look into it closely, tonight, and pay attention to what it says to you."

I was drinking wine out of a plastic cup in the park with a man who had the shoulders of Hercules. And he was talking about mirrors.

"Where did you say you were from?" I asked him.

He ignored me.

"I'm going to call you a car, Lucy. You shouldn't be here all alone. Where should I tell him to take you?" he said.

"Oh, no. Don't. I live near here. I like the walk."

"Then take this for the trip," he said, filling my cup to the top. And he left.

I sat there alone, without a cigarette, and finished my champagne. I wanted everything in my head to shut down. Odin, Alex, red cups of wine.

It was the strangest day, so far, in a very strange month.

62
·········

Barry's Bootcamp
1 York Street, Tribeca
Tuesday, September 30
Girls' night

None of us is in the mood for a workout.

Lotta was a no-show, of course. After our week of babysitting, she'd slipped away again. We hadn't spoken to her in a week.

So it was just three in Tribeca for Barry's Bootcamp. He put us through everything. Medicine balls, kickboxing, jump ropes, bands. It was miserable and it soured us. Even Billy.

Sarah handed me a kettlebell.

"I talked to Odin the other day," I said.

"Again?"

"Yes, again. At the High Line."

I had their attention. I hadn't said much about her. And I didn't know what to say now. I felt like I was getting played, and I didn't know why and I didn't know how.

"And?"

They were waiting for a scoop. I hadn't listened to the tape. I couldn't remember anything she'd even said except for the frog. And Titus. What did she mean by that? How could I even start to explain it?

And then there was Alex.

"I don't know. It was a strange talk, stranger day," I said. "I need to listen to the tape. She's shifty. I don't trust her."

"Where'd she come from? Where was she hiding until she popped up here, anyway? Is she a terrorist?" Sarah asked.

For a moment, I considered it. Maybe she was.

"I don't know," I said.

They looked at me, impatient.

"She has unreal blue eyes, and she's unnaturally poised and she drinks expensive tequila and seems to have no friends or family or anything. I don't know what else to say."

Billy started her reps. We were on free weights, three sets, twelve reps of each. I didn't even want to lift my finger. I wanted to be under my comforter. I wanted to be reading to Livia. I was tired.

"That's not much of a profile, Lu," Sarah said.

"When Gay Talese wrote about Frank Sinatra, he barely got Sinatra to say one word. The first five hundred words of the piece were just a description of watching him stand in a room, drinking whiskey and glaring at everyone. And it's one of the best profiles ever written." I felt defensive.

"So you're going to describe how she stands?" Billy asked.

I took two ten-pound weights and lifted them straight out from my body. Then down. Then up again. Then down.

"I might."

63

·········

Tuesday, September 30
Deadline

I handed the piece in, almost literally, five minutes before the issue went to press. I "crashed" it. It's risky because there's no space for editorial to review one last time, no chance to fix an overlooked, potentially costly, mistake. There's no time to step back and let it sink in, or think of how it could be better, or which angles I might have missed, and are we sure this really hits.

But I already had a short deadline, and crashing the piece is what I did. I e-mailed it from my bedroom to copy at 5 p.m. and cc'd Noel. Two thousand, nine hundred and forty words.

THE STRANGER IN OUR MIDST

Who is Odin? She has no face, no last name. If you do a search for her on Google, you'll find a cagey Twitter account and a coy, teasing—sometimes unsettling—blog. Odin, New York. And that is all. She's there, and she's not. She's real and she's a ghost. If she's in line ahead of you at Starbucks as you read this—and she could be—you won't know. But everybody knows her name

Odin. If you say this name out loud at any restaurant, bar, or dinner party—the list goes on—anywhere in the city from Wall Street to Harlem (including the outer boroughs), you'll get someone's attention. And not because they're into Norse mythology.

It started with one blog entry—you know the one. She dropped on the city like a grenade. She's a mystery, like the Lindbergh baby and Amelia Earhart's plane and Elizabeth Taylor's last marriage and Bess Myerson's fall from grace.

Who *is she*?

You can't answer this question without answering its opposite. She is not a girl doing a gimmick to get a book deal. She is not a woman who cares about a cause. She is not a mother, or a striver, or a girl looking to trade notoriety for a swing at a TV show.

I shadowed her for more than two months, with imposed conditions, in order to write this piece.

The tape goes off when she says so. The interview ends when she decides it does.

I still do not know her last name. I know little about her past.

I know this. She is a young woman. She has large, blue eyes, like a lion. They're piercing and wise. She sees her surroundings in panorama, she takes everything in. The first instant she glimpses me, I see she's noticed my watch, barely peeking out from a nondescript shirt, and the nondescript white shirt she's registered, too. In less than three minutes of small talk I have the uneasy feeling that she knows everything about me. More than I've told anyone. More than I'll ever know about her.

You can only see her by watching closely, but she doesn't

let anyone watch her closely. This, like almost everything about our meetings, seems a shrewd calculation—she knows how to display herself, to be perceived exactly the way she wants. And then she watches you. Like prey.

I am being paid to observe her, and then to record my observations, and like a force field in science-fiction films, she has turned all of it around on to me. She's a two-way mirror.

Noel called me an hour later, ecstatic, and told me to come in. He had a five-hundred-dollar bottle of champagne, he said, with my name on it. If I drink one more glass of champagne this year, I told him, it might kill me.

It knocked him out. That's all I cared about. I didn't buy any of it. She was just a girl with a blog, who found herself interesting. I told a story. I narrated her. I made her bigger than she was. Next.

OCTOBER

64

· · · · · · · · ·

S arah got the call. I'm ashamed to say it, but my first thought was not of concern. My first thought was irritation. Why was Sarah her emergency contact and not me?

It was exactly what we'd been worrying about but hadn't acted on. We'd been telling ourselves over and over that it would all be okay. That we were making too much of things. That we'd say something next time. We would do something next time. We were overreacting. She seemed better. We would talk to her soon. Then we all got caught up in our own things again.

So now here we were, three best friends in the waiting area of the emergency room in Bellevue, waiting to be allowed in to see the fourth. And I felt horrible, because I was angry with her. And as sick and worried as I was now, it hasn't completely gone away.

"She's in the psych ward," Sarah said when Billy and I walked in. Sarah was there first. "They want to get her stable before they transfer her anywhere."

"Where was she? Where did they find her?" I said.

"God. You don't want to know."

"*I* do," Billy said.

"Sanctum. It's a sex club. It's in a private home. They found her in a town house in the Village. It's just one big crazy orgy, anything goes. I wish I didn't know all of this. They don't know how long she was unconscious. They found her in the bathroom. They had to break the door down."

"Okay," I said. Sex club, no big deal. Drugs, big deal. "What else?"

"She was taking street drugs, that's what the attending physician told me. They see this all the time. She got something laced with hard chemicals. He thinks it was Drano. Apparently, Drano is a very common thing to cut MDMA with because it's cheap and it gets you really high, really fast. And the street dealers who use it aren't exactly chemists. They're sloppy. I'm getting quite an education."

Drano.

This is the kind of urban myth you hear from someone at a party. It's something that happens to someone else's cousin in a small town upstate. This is not a thing that happens to your sweet, beautiful best friend.

When we were finally allowed to see her, it was hard to take. She wasn't awake. There were tubes in her arms. She looked tiny. Tiny like Livia. Swallowed up in her pale-blue hospital gown.

I had a brief flashback of her waking up twenty years ago at Billy's, where she'd passed out in her Alaïa leather dress. I brought coffee for all of us. We recapped the night. It seemed harmless then. A young, wild night out. It wasn't harmless here.

Lotta was at Bellevue hospital. Not Columbia, not Lenox Hill, but Bellevue. Bellevue is where mentally ill people go, and the uninsured go, and where the addicts and the hopeless and the derelicts of the city are brought. There is nothing Lotta about Bellevue at all. Azzedine Alaïa doesn't have a hospital line here, so Lotta was in the same cheap cotton gown as everyone else, we could see the top of it where her blanket was pulled back. It was thin. She had an IV in her arm and an oxygen tube in her nose. Machines were beeping everywhere and there was no space for us to stand. We were wedged in awkwardly. Her face was pale, drained of color. Her body looked drained of everything. She looked so *small*. Like if we touched her, she would break.

She'd have been appalled at her hair. We'd need to do something about that when she woke up.

What if she didn't?

I texted Him again. Not because I wanted to. Or maybe I did. Maybe I was using Lotta's very serious situation to draw attention to me.

> Me: I want to see you . . . I need to see you. I'm falling apart.

This time, after three weeks of silence, he texted back.

212-555-0134: No, love. Not yet. But you will. I promise you will.

> Me: When . . .

212-555-0134: Soon. I promise you.

That was all.

They moved Lotta to a private room and we sat in the waiting area again, and waited. At three o'clock they called us in. She was awake.

"*Syndenstraffer sig sjalv,*" she said. Her voice was weak. Her Swedish accent was strong. We couldn't understand her.

"What, honey?" Sarah said.

"*Syndenstraffer sig sjalv.* The sin punishes itself." She smiled.

She was making a joke. We beamed down at her. Billy and I each grabbed a hand, and Sarah grabbed one of her still perfectly pedicured feet. We weren't quite ready to laugh yet, but it was going to be okay. A tear rolled down my cheek. I looked at Sarah. She had one, too.

65

....

J. Sebastian Salon
Sunday, October 5

It was six days before the show.

I grabbed a smock, I put it on, and I sat down in the chair. I removed the clip from my head and shook my hair out. I barely greeted James when I walked in. I barely said anything at all.

I was angry and frustrated, and I was taking it out on him. I couldn't help it.

He pulled my hair back, held it away from my face, observed. I had no patience for it.

"Let's just do this, okay? I have an event."

Miles Davis was playing: *Kind of Blue*. I was thankful for the distraction. I let James work without talking. For the first time, I watched him work without him watching me.

"What are you doing?" I said.

"Trust me."

He blew my hair out perfectly straight and then he parted it, very sharply, to the side.

"Go with it, Luce," he said. "It looks fabulous."

It looked different. I looked completely different. It wasn't the woman I was comfortable with, the one I knew, who was looking back at me in the mirror. It was a stranger.

When he finished, I handed him my credit card.

"No, sweetheart." He pushed my hand away. "This was for me. Knock them out."

He gave me a kiss on the cheek.

"Lucy. No one can hurt you."

He didn't know that. How could anyone ever say that? Just by his saying it, someone was almost certain to.

66
· · · · · · · · ·

O din had one more surprise for me. It was personal.

ODIN OF NEW YORK
MONDAY, OCTOBER 6

DO YOU WANT THE RED PILL, OR THE BLUE . . .

Girls have silly dreams. I've made a new friend who likes to read the great Russian classics. She is fond of Anna Karenina. They are alike. My new friend is not as careless as Anna was, but she's taking dangerous steps all the same. I find it interesting that it's a fallen heroine she identifies with. She is groping around in the dark.

Anna had silly ideas and silly dreams about love and desire. She wanted to be adored, to be worshipped, to be desired, to be filled with *passion*. These are emotions that are barely controlled or contained. Why toy with them? Why ask for these things? Didn't Tolstoy make it perfectly clear that these things are not only self-involved and foolish but also, more important, *dangerous*? Could his message have been any clearer?

Should you follow the bright lights because they make you feel good? Should desire be your eternal pursuit? Or should you be content to live a suitable life.

Isn't it odd, that Anna was happy until she found desire? It destroyed her.

My new friend, I know you're reading this. Are you interested in knowing the truth?

67
· · · · · · · · ·

The Koons invitation had sat unopened for weeks. October 6, the Whitney.

It had run all summer, but they were having a big send-off before it, and then the old Whitney, closed. His collection was spread out on every floor. His Play-Doh, the porn series. Even *Balloon Dog* was there.

There was a write-up about it in *The New Yorker*. They described Koons as one of the most original artists of his time, which left it up to the reader to guess who else might be in that company. It meant nothing. Only that the Whitney had not asked Titus to be the artist they went out on. Big deal. Okay, it was.

At sixty-six, after everything, after remarkable success, a man can still have petty jealousies. Koons is younger. He has commanded millions of dollars more for some of his work, which Titus calls "drunken playground toys." Titus had had to work hard for his show, and Koons didn't. He isn't even showing new work.

Oh, yes. And Titus forged his first piece.

I know he's angry that we're going—he feels manipulated. But he has his own show in just a few days; it's a bad time to be ungracious. He needs to be seen. He knows that. So I decided we'd go and I'd be stunning. I know what to do, what to wear. I can steal the thunder from a fifty-eight-million-dollar balloon animal. I know what to do with a Saint Laurent smoking-jacket dress—chic, understated, hot. Nude legs, Crème de la Mer bronzing cream, and Manolos with peep toes. Performance art overshadows a still piece any day.

It's Tuesday. I canceled with the girls. I thought Titus and I would have a cocktail before and have a late dinner after. Easy.

He waffled until the last minute, pretending it was an afterthought. Something so insignificant he couldn't be bothered to remember. And then as the time got closer, it was something he decided to blame on me. He was irritable.

"I don't know why you're not wearing the dress I picked out for you," he said. I didn't want to make a thing out of it, so I changed into it. He called a car, and as we pulled up outside the museum he was perspiring. He opened the door and got out without waiting.

I composed myself. I knew this wasn't about me. I'd enter in style, with or without him. Shoes first, then legs. I know how to make an entrance.

"I'm with Titus Brockton," I said at the door. He'd already gone in. "I'm his wife."

The girl in black was unimpressed. She had no reaction to the name. She didn't even look up. "I'm sorry. Mr. Brockton doesn't have a plus one."

I started to laugh. "You've got to be kidding me." It was pointless to make a scene, so I walked away. The fucking *artist* and his fucking artist moods.

I walked up Madison Avenue to Sant Ambroeus, sat down at the bar, and ordered a glass of pinot gris. I took a deep breath and took stock. Dress: Tom Ford. Hair: James Sebastian. Shoes: Blahnik. Nails: Smoke Red. Screw the rest of it. I enjoyed the wine.

68

·········

Fifth Avenue, Manhattan
Thursday, October 9

Billy was waiting for me at the fountain off Fifth Avenue, across from Cipriani. Lotta was still in the hospital, so what should have been a giddy girls' day of shopping had a cloud over it.

But I wanted something to wear, and who better to pick it out? Billy knows how to make a statement, and she knows her occasions. She was wearing a Kanye-style trench, with a gray T-shirt, Rag & Bone jeans, and suede pumps. "This is supposed to be about me today, honey," I said. "You're stealing my sun."

We passed Louis Vuitton and Billy dragged me into Saint Laurent to drool over the patent shoes she's been dying for.

"Something from Dolce," I said. "That's what I want. Simple, but chic."

"Don't play it safe, Luce, have fun with this. I'm thinking rocker look for you. Steampunk glam."

"*No*. Very simple. I'm not even sure I want to go, so let's make me blend."

She wasn't listening to me. It's hard to focus on Fifth Avenue. She paused at the Tiffany window. "I'm doing Harry Winston when I get married," she said.

The show was going to be an event. There would be celebrities, and Titus's peers, and all of the critics and big collectors. Media, of course. It was going to be as much about who was there as it was about his work. And as much as I'd been dreading it these past few weeks, I was very curious to see what he'd done.

"Come on, Bill. Dolce," I said, grabbing her arm to get her attention.

She was looking at the new Polo displays in Ralph Lauren's window. "It doesn't matter what you get, Luce. You just need to enjoy it tomorrow."

So I found something. It was perfect, and we stopped for burgers and Caesars on Fifty-Third.

Sarah called while we were eating, and I put her on speaker.

"Hi, honey," I said. We'd been treating her delicately, like a child who wasn't picked for the team. We were all trying to be up.

"Lucy?" she said.

"I'm on speaker, sweets. Billy's here—we're at Burger Heaven."

"Oh, okay. Well, I just wanted to tell you something."

"Shoot, Sar," Billy said.

There was a pause. We waited it out.

"I got it, I got it! I *fucking* GOT IT!"

"Oh my God!" We both said it at once, then I put the phone back to my ear because she was screaming and scaring the patrons.

"What happened? You got the show!"

She was laughing uncontrollably, or maybe crying—I couldn't tell. She sounded out of her mind. I shrugged my shoulders at Billy.

"Sar?"

"Nelson called me this morning."

"Yeah . . . ?"

"He said there's a lot they've been doing to get production in place, it's been hectic, he apologized. He said there was a time when they weren't sure if they'd use me and Candy Bergen to have six? Or maybe just leave the four."

Her words were all running together, but it didn't matter, we knew the punch line. She got it.

I held the phone out and Billy put her face up close so we could both hear without broadcasting it to the restaurant.

"He said they loved the party! He said in the end, that's what clinched it. They loved you, they loved Lot, they loved your pink Pucci, Bill! Deb Watson was freaking out, she hasn't stopped talking about the Schnabel."

"What about the food?" Billy said. She was starting to pout.

"Who cares about the food, they were thrilled that I was drunk! He said they were worried I might be too uptight."

"Seriously?" Billy said. "I put a lot of work into that."

I shook my head no at her. Ignore it.

"So we don't start until next year, but I have a meeting with Leisha on Monday, she's another producer, we're going over story lines. Oh my GOD!"

Billy rolled her eyes. I shook my head no at her again.

"Okay, see, honey? What'd we tell you? That's what we told you."

"He said that their only hesitation with me was that I might be too nice, too bland. He was *thrilled* that I got drunk. Isn't that funny?"

"Oh, brother," Billy whispered. "She already said that."

"I told you, sweetie. You were a smash. We'll celebrate, promise. See you tomorrow, right?"

"Yes! We will. Wait, what's tomorrow?"

"Very funny, Sarah. The show? And I will see you there."

"Luce. Come on, yes, you'll see me there. I got it, I got it, I GOT it!"

"Jesus," Billy said. "She's going to be impossible."

69
· · · · · · · · ·

Gagosian Gallery
555 West Twenty-Fourth Street, Chelsea
Friday, October 10
Opening night, *Titus Brockton: Mirrors*

The house was packed, of course. Titus had been brooding all day. He likes this part, being back in the game. I know he feels good about that, but he hates this part, too. The marketing of art isn't conducive to the artist. It's a solitary endeavor for the most part. He's had at least two scotches that I know of, but I instructed Tatiana this afternoon to keep him under watch.

We were meeting here. Leo would bring him. He doesn't like to arrive with me. He finds me once his nerves settle. He would never admit it, but he gets rattled. Even a man with his ego and all of his accomplishments is fearful of being found to be a fraud. Ha. How ironic.

My mother was here with Rolando. It had been a few weeks for them now. I like him, it seems promising. Maybe—it's not the craziest idea—Cheri is ready to settle down.

The girls, except for Lotta, who'd been moved to the Hazelden on Eighth, where she'd stay over the weekend, would arrive here staggered. I was early, and alone, and it was nice.

I was wearing the Dolce & Gabbana. Hair up, hoop earrings, and a dress that hugs me when I need to be hugged and lets me be free when I need to breathe. *La dolce vita.*

There are old works here, old collections. Some that he did before me and some I remember well. It's a walk down memory lane. Though there are several single pieces, the show is centered around four small groups. Three of them have been shown before, and one of them is entirely new. He's showing it for the first time tonight. The series, in their entirety, are titled respectively *L*, *O*, *V*, and *E*. From oldest to new. The gallery has done a tasteful job with the print materials. The title of the entire show is, of course, *Mirrors.*

The first collection, *L*, is the collection of murder paintings from the Whitney. The murderesses. *Les femmes et la mort.* L is the name of this series—*Love.*

There are the nudes posed in various settings and situations where he juxtaposed one model's face onto another's body. *Observation*, he called that series. *O.*

There is the series *V—Vitality.*

And then there are the new works. All of which are covered. This is why so many people are here. This new series is called *E. Euphoria.*

The *Times* interviewed him about the new works last week.

"Why *Euphoria?*" they asked him. They all want to know what's in a name.

"It's a culmination," he said. "It reflects where I am, the process I went through doing the work. It was intensely challenging. I had to find my inspiration again. I had to find the love of my craft, the passion. And I had to reach that state, in my life and in my work, where I could transcend the mundane things that keep one mired. So I could rise. And work. And emerge. And find *euphoria.*"

I thought what he told them was kind of beautiful.

The reception wouldn't officially start for forty minutes, but the press were swirling. Reacquainting themselves with him. There were familiar faces here. I stood out in the room. I knew that. I knew Titus expected me to. I dressed for the occasion, and wore a dark smoky eye and James's side part.

I got a glass of wine and found a corner. I felt my phone vibrate from inside my bag, and checked it.

212-555-0134: I will see you, Lucy. Very soon if you are ready. Be beautiful, I'll be watching.

I looked around. What did that mean? Was he here? Does he follow me?

The bulky space was filling up fast. Julian Schnabel walked in. Titus wasn't going to like that. But what did he expect? I hoped he wouldn't see him before they did the unveiling. After that, anything mildly irritating could be dealt with. Taylor Swift, Phil Jackson, Diane von Furstenberg with Barry Diller, and oh, look! Satina. There she was, towering over the room. I waved and she gave me a big smile.

The press was bunched up, but they'd start circling again soon. Right now they had to make sure they got that first good shot. The photographer from *Artforum* came over to say hello. The *Times* Arts staff was here, *Departures*, *Vanity Fair*. Of course, *SNOB*. *Nylon*. *Vogue*.

I wondered briefly if I should have worn the Calvin Klein.

212-555-0134: You are . . . the most beautiful woman in the room.

I looked around again. All of those fluttery feelings came right back. I tried to stay in the moment, for Titus, but all I wanted to do was find Him.

Receptions like this get crowded and are rarely organized, but there's sort of an understood protocol. People will gather around the big pieces, like they are starting to do now. There will be a buzz, with this many, in the room. The hired waitstaff will struggle to keep up with the champagne cocktails and canapés. It's closer to the carnival-like atmosphere of a street fair than the hushed atmosphere of a museum.

When they unveil the night's showcase piece, not everyone will see it at once, there isn't room. But they will eventually. This isn't the kind of crowd that elbows for position. They will quietly get their chance to look, and then move on.

It was five minutes to seven. I knew Titus wouldn't come out on time, which was good for Sarah, who was late. Billy had texted me she was here.

"We definitely made the right choice," she said when I found her. "You look fucking hot."

"There you are! Look at you."

"No, look at *you*. Love the hair."

I spotted someone just beyond her and stopped short. "Oh my God. Bill." I couldn't believe it.

"What?"

"Nothing. There's just a man here . . . who I wasn't expecting to see."

She craned her neck to see where I was looking.

"The one in the black suit, no tie, body like Jesus?"

"Yep." It was Alex. Alex from the haircut. Alex from the wine in plastic cups. Alex in thousand-dollar shoes, unbuttoned shirt, gold cuff links, no tie.

"Oh, yeah," Billy said. "That's Lotta's guy, the oligarch. I met him at the gallery. Wow." She let out a low whistle. "I do *not* understand why she didn't jump on that."

"What?"

He looked our way, smiled, and raised his glass. So Alex *was* Lotta's Russian. The oligarch.

I looked at him quizzically and shook my head. *I don't understand. Who are you? What are you doing* here?

"I swear, you three are the worst hoarders. You keep your little groupies around instead of introducing them to your *single* friend, and then you wonder why I'm online."

I shook my head again. "Weird," I said.

"Not weird. Hot."

Leo walked over just then, and Alex disappeared in the crowd.

"Lucy, love. Look at you. *You* are the real show tonight."

"Oh, Leo. Thank you. You've met Billy Sitwell."

"Of course. My pleasure again, Ms. Sitwell."

It's doubtful Leo remembered Billy—they'd barely ever crossed paths—but he is very old-school about etiquette.

"Lucy, I wanted to tell you that *Woman in Mirror* has a buyer. Sight unseen. You know he has refused to show it to anyone."

"A buyer? Wait, did he agree?"

"Not in so many words. I know he's convinced he won't part with it, but the buyer has offered to house it for five years at the museum of his choice, and he made it known that he was open to other stipulations. I'm hoping you'll help me talk to him."

"Wow. That's interesting."

"I finally met him in person."

"Who?"

"The buyer. Tonight, just a few hours ago. We've been speaking through his lawyer. He's very charming, very sincere. Very real. I was impressed. Truly loves art for the art, he's not looking to flip it."

I didn't understand. This was all . . . Titus hadn't said anything. Did Leo know about *Woman at Midtown*? He must know. Did he know Titus was being blackmailed?

"He's here—"

"Who's here?"

"The buyer, and when I catch him I'll introduce you. Alex Creighton. He's in energy. Russia. Big money in it over there right now."

"Leo. What? His name is Alex?"

"Creighton, yes."

Woman in Mirror is an acrylic on canvas. I know that much. And I know it's seventy-two inches tall and fifty-four inches wide. At that size it will be striking, and I'm nervous. I like to see Titus's work slowly, not meet it head-on. It's like listening to an opera for the first time, or reading a great work of literature, or seeing a film. When there are so many things demanding your senses, all at once, you should approach the work with care.

So when I see there is a crowd and I see the top of the canvas, I take my time to make my way over. Also, I don't like the press to look for my reaction. I know Titus will appear beside me and walk me there. He will take me over and we will have a private brief moment in this crowded room before he disappears back into the hive, to do what he does.

"Leo said he has a buyer," I said when he approached me. "And that he's here tonight and he's willing to do anything you want to close the deal. Including allow you your pick of museums for five years."

"He hasn't seen it. How can he want to buy it?"

"Leo said you knew."

Titus stiffened. "He isn't listening to me," he said. "The piece is spoken for."

"What?" I said. "By whom?" He didn't hear me, it didn't matter, I was within minutes of seeing it and my heart was racing.

I glanced to my left, looking for Billy, and spotted Leo standing with Alex. That Alex. My Alex. Lotta's Alex. This couldn't be . . . It was absolutely too crazy.

As Titus walked me closer to the piece, to where he would unveil it, the group stepped aside to let us through. From the back, even, they sensed him approaching. Yes, it's him. Make way for the artist. Make room.

He was holding on to my hand. This part all felt staged, but I didn't mind it tonight. My mind was wrapped around this Alex thing. Titus stopped me three feet from the work, dropped my hand, and stepped behind the block to unveil it. *Woman in Mirror*.

There was a palpable hush.

At first glance, I saw the back of a woman. Not a nude back, but a beautiful back in a gown that revealed most of it, down to the curve of where it dissolved into her waist. He had managed to capture all the beauty of her feminine form, the way a fashion photographer would. The colors were dark and bold—the feeling I had was overwhelmingly protective. I sensed her vulnerability. Then my eyes moved to the mirror on the wall, the one in the painting, the one the woman was looking into. It was the only place you could see an image of her face. She was looking into a mirror, and meeting our, my, the admirer's, gaze. This is how I saw her. Not directly, but filtered. Making eye contact with me, but not.

And holy fucking shit. *This is how I saw her*. Through a mirror in a painting. Mirrors are deceptive, mirrors are filters. Mirrors are unreal. There was nothing in the world that could have prepared me for this.

The face in the mirror was Odin's.

There was no mistaking her. Right down to her striking Russian Red lip shade of MAC. She was staring at me, through the mirror, with that smile-smirk. Her eyes pierced my soul. It felt like she was laughing at me. Of course she was fucking smirking—who wouldn't be? This was the centerpiece of *E*. Odin was Euphoria.

I scanned the room, panicked. I didn't see Alex's blue eyes anywhere, but I found Titus's dark ones. He looked confused. His smile faded as my face turned to stone. There were gasps, then there were murmurs. It was an encouraging reaction. He'd done it. It was beautiful. He had done it.

I couldn't hear individual words any more than I could pick out a single violin from an orchestra, but I knew the room's reaction was much different than mine.

I felt sick. My skin was cold. No one, of course, was looking at me. Thank God. They were admiring the work. The phenomenal work. His breathtaking, oh-my-God, pricks-hitting-the-ceiling kind of work. It was good and I couldn't bear to look at it. I thought I was going to be sick.

No one was watching me but Titus. Cameras were going off, attentions were diverted. People commented as he walked by, making his way to me. It was a beautiful, beautiful piece of work.

I ran.

I didn't run. No one can run in six-inch heels, and I didn't want that attention anyway.

But I was closer to the door of the gallery than Titus was, and there was a clear path ahead of me. I got there first. And I left.

I'm not sure if you've ever felt this. You're in a room observing someone you love, but no one else in the room knows he's yours. I felt so far removed from where I was, all of a sudden, like an anonymous observer. I felt a sense of desperate loss. I felt a hole, and then I felt like it was burning. How he knew her or why he painted her, was irrelevant. I didn't even want to know.

> Me: Where are you? I need you now.

I waited for ten seconds and texted again.

> Me: I need you now, please. Where are you?
> Me: I'll meet you. Anywhere. Show your face to me.
> Me: Where are you?
> Me: Meet me. Please.
> Me: I need you.

70

· · · · · · · ·

The Roosevelt Hotel
45 East Forty-Fifth Street, room 416

When in doubt, check into a hotel.

I called her before my courage ebbed. Or surged wildly out of control. I wasn't sure, at this point, which way it was going to go.

"What the fuck are you doing with my husband? No, never mind. Who cares? What the fuck are you doing with *me*? Are you sick? Are you mentally ill? Are you completely fucked up, a fucked-up bitch like Lotta said you were all along?"

I couldn't stop cursing. This was no time for Cheri's rules. Have an affair, she'd urged me. I had, metaphorically. And this was how it had all turned out.

The piece would be on newsstands tomorrow. I couldn't say anything. Shit, Noel had been at the reception. I panicked. Until I remembered that *no one had seen her*. No one knew who she was. No one but Titus. And me. And I had never told Titus her name.

Un-fucking-believable.

Everyone in that room, gasping at the beautiful painting. The imagery, the metaphorical symbolism of it. The mirror and beauty and perception and false truth and all of that bullshit. And the big fucking secret—it hit me so hard I could not stop laughing. So hard I started choking. I got it. I got why Titus looked so confused. She'd been fucking with both of us.

"Odin isn't even your real name. Is it?"

"It is my name. Now. It's one I use. I think you and your husband have an interesting conversation ahead of you, Lucy. I don't really feel like explaining it to you. If I'd cared to, I would have done it by now. But I'll spare you some agony, that only seems fair. I'm not sleeping with him. Feel better?"

I hung up the phone. And glared at it. I wanted her to call back. I wanted her to fix this. It was silent.

No one knew the girl in the mirror was Odin. And Titus didn't know that Odin, on the cover of the revamped edgy *SNOB* without a photograph, was his woman in the mirror.

I didn't know what to think. And because I didn't know what to think, I thought first of Titus's reputation. This was his rebirth. If a scandal brought him down, if he was caught in the headlights and the work was lost in the process . . . I didn't think he had it in him to reinvent himself after something like that.

My phone rang. It was Billy. That's when I remembered I had some explaining to do, too. I'd disappeared. There were thirty-six texts on my phone. Seven voice mails. Sixteen missed calls.

Odin and her secrets. She got me. She got us good.

He told me he would meet me anywhere I wanted, so I told him here. Now. *As soon as you can. Please.* And he came.

It was straight out of Jane Austen. Livia would have applauded. No one would have appreciated it more than her.

There was a man at the bar. He was waiting for me. He had the look of a man who was waiting, who knew me intimately, who had fallen in love with me, who had made me fall in love.

He was handsome. He had the kind of face that makes strangers pause and try to place him. The kind of man you can tell is *someone* even if you're not exactly sure who.

"Lucy," he said, "I love you. So much, my darling. Please. Let me explain."

Tall and solid, with wavy salt-and-pepper hair; he had a confident, rugged face.

He was Titus.

71

....

Saturday, October 11

He did explain, and at the same time, I'd figured it out. Odin was Roman's daughter. Odin was who had blackmailed him. It was Odin who could destroy his career. In a way, that would be fair. But instead, she asked for something. She wanted him to paint her. She wanted to be the star of the show. And then she wanted to keep the work.

It was three in the morning. My husband was sleeping next to me in a hotel bed, an arm protectively wrapped around me. I'd never been more in love with him. I didn't care what happened next. We could leave. We didn't need to stay in the city. We could go anywhere and start over. We could be anything.

When my ringtone went off, I looked to see who it was. I quickly shut off the sound. This time it was Odin calling me. I slipped out from under Titus, went into the bathroom, and shut the door. I picked up on the last ring.

"It's late," I said.

"I want to be fair, Lucy," she said. "I'm a fair person. You can ask one last question of me. And I'll answer it, whatever it is."

This wasn't "fair." I had a million questions. How could I only ask one? She had, as usual, caught me off guard. But then it hit me. Yes, there was one. I did have a question. I had one.

"Who is Alex?" I said.

"Alex. That's good, Lucy."

"Thank you. Who is he?"

"Alex is a friend."

"If he's a friend, then why is he trying to buy your painting? Very aggressively, I might add."

I could hear the smirk-smile in her pause.

"Because he's a very *good* friend. He wanted to buy it for me. An early Christmas present, maybe."

"That's one really fucking expensive Christmas present."

"I enjoyed you, Lucy."

"No. Wait. You haven't answered the question. If he's a friend, why was he trying to buy a painting that's already yours?"

Her voice went down to a whisper. "Because he doesn't know it's mine, Lucy. That's a secret."

"I don't understand."

"I made a deal with your husband. He did his part, and I'll do mine. Mine is silence. Now the paintings will disappear. The one he copied, and the one of me. I've answered your question, Lucy Danner. Be good."

And she hung up.

72

. . . .

Lotta's apartment
Tuesday, October 14
Girls' night

We were in various states of disarray. But it was a different disarray than four months ago.

Girls' Tuesday at Lotta's. Her first since she got home.

"Oh my God, dolls!" she said. She was giggling like a little girl. I hadn't seen her look so sweet or so vulnerable in years. "I can't believe you didn't call me, this town is such a *bore* and then all of this goes down and you don't call?"

She had her feet curled up beneath her. Her hair was loose and wavy. She was wearing an oversize sweater and leggings and the apartment was neat. Clean. She'd made us individual chicken pot pies, each in our own little ramekin. Yes, Lotta. Pot pies!

The girls, I knew, would support whatever I told them. It didn't sound so crazy, after all. Not to them. We didn't lead conventional lives—none of us did. We'd all winged it.

Lotta almost died. Sarah almost lost her show. Billy could have easily lost her apartment, and I almost had an affair . . . with my husband.

Titus has a secret that could destroy his career and ruin us. And I don't even care.

"Are you okay?" Sarah had asked. And then Billy. Separately, each of them had pulled me aside in the days after the show. What I told them sounded like a feasible story, but then it almost didn't.

"Yes," I told them. "He doesn't understand women at all, despite how much money he's made interpreting them. He didn't at all think this was weird. And neither did she, I guess. But he's been painting *her* instead of screwing half the city, like I'd imagined. And the piece is beautiful. So I'm okay." I spared them the blackmailing piece. Titus's great scandal would have to wait.

Noel, of course, thought it was the biggest stroke of genius he'd ever stumbled across. I'd been afraid to tell him. Odin had to come out—she was going to come out at some point—and when she did, it couldn't be a surprise. I worried it would destroy his credibility, never mind what it might do to Titus's. I had worried it would smash everyone's work. Take all of us down.

But it turned out to be brilliant. Husband and wife. One wrote the words, the other painted them. The girl in the mirror was the girl without a face. *Brilliant.* Sometimes you get lucky.

Noel used his profile of Titus on the cover of the January issue. There was a photograph of us before the reception. A candid. Titus's hand was on my arm—he was saying something to me. I wish I could remember what it was, it was probably insignificant. *Do you want another wine? Did you see that Laurel is here? Do you remember his wife's name?* But I was smiling at him. We looked united. It was snapped moments before I saw the painting, I do know that. I recognize where we are in the room. I was happy for him. I was excited for him. In the photo, I look . . . in love.

The November cover of *Artforum* was *Woman in Mirror*. It was a close-up of the work. It was a picture of the painting and of the mirrored reflection of Odin's razor-sharp beautiful smirk. She got her first cover.

Odin of New York. The artist's muse.

73

· · · · · · · · ·

The Waverly Inn
Wednesday, October 15

I had questions for Titus, too, of course. I had a lover, my husband.
I'd found adventure and mystery and desire. But I had questions.

He took me to one of his haunts, not a place we'd normally go
together. The Waverly is one of Titus's escapes, I knew that. They let
him sit undisturbed at the bar, they know his drink, they attend to him
when he's alone in the way he prefers—they are discreetly solicitous.
Tonight we sat at a table, not the bar. He took my arm as we exited the
cab. He kissed me on the sidewalk, beneath a full moon, before we
came in. We sat close at the small table, and he rubbed my knee beneath it. His eyes, his focus, his attention were all completely on me.

We'd had the most incredible makeup sex of all time these last
few days. But there were still things to explain.

"I don't really understand all of it," I said. "Why . . . did you do it?
It was a dangerous game."

He grinned at me, mischievously. He brushed his strong, beautiful
fingers across my cheek.

"Why did I do what, my love?"

"Why did you start it? Why did you text me? Why and how and
when did you decide to do it? What did you think would happen?"

The waiter came, then, and uncorked a bottle of champagne. He slowly filled both of our glasses. Titus raised his to mine and we took a drink.

"Lucy, love is the only thing worth fighting for," he said. "You know that. It is the only thing worth keeping. In the end, it matters nothing where any fucking thing I've ever done hangs, or how much anyone paid for it. In the end, it is only love. In the end it's only you. People buy my art because they think it's a treasure. They pay ridiculous sums of money to secure a treasure. They desire, they pursue, they conquer. But I have you. I can't let that die. You are my treasure. It was dying, and I needed it to live again."

It was beautiful, what he was saying to me. How he regarded me. After almost twenty years together, it was beautiful.

"It was sneaky," I said, smiling. "Illicit. You were encouraging me to fall in love with another man."

"That is mystery and adventure, my love. That is what keeps us alive." He winked at me. "I wanted you to feel in love again. I *wanted* you to feel desired. I wanted to awaken those feelings within you. And I needed to awaken those feelings in me. I was never encouraging you to be with another man. It was always me. I seduced you for myself."

He was saying all the right things. He had me weak in the knees. But still, not so fast.

"What did Odin awaken?" I asked.

He sighed and grabbed my hand. "My darling," he said. "She awakened everything. She opened my eyes. She came here to take my life away, and you could argue she had a right to. But instead, she lit a fire that I've been missing for years, and she saved me from losing what I had. I love that fucking piece. I can't remember the last time I've felt so passionate about my work. I painted a woman who is a whore, and a schemer, a liar and a bitch, and yet also so utterly beautiful. In the end, she saved my life. That piece is about love slipping away. It's about evil creeping in. The heart is dark, my love. She gave me the best gift I've ever had, next to you."

He knew what I was thinking before I could say it. He could read, the way lovers can, the subtle shift in my expression.

"Don't hate her, Lucy. We wouldn't be here right now if not for her. You don't truly feel, or live, unless life rattles you. Most people watch life go by without grabbing on. They don't fight, they don't challenge, they submit. This woman threw me a dinghy when I was treading water in a bottomless sea. She gave me a way back to shore. She gave me the way back to you."

He was looking into my eyes, and I looked back. No mirrors, no filter. Just my husband's fierce, beautiful eyes locked on to mine, and they weren't going anywhere. My heart was pounding. The table between us was an inconvenient truth.

The waiter came and, out of propriety, we turned to him. And then we ordered our meal.

JUNE

74

· · · · · · · · ·

Jill Stuart store
466 Broome Street, SoHo
Friday, June 12
Opening

There are three cameras, two producers, one production assistant, and five Plaid Skirts scurrying around Broome Street in front of the Jill Stuart store. Lotta and I are standing at the perimeter, though we're in the scene, too. The premise is that we've come to meet Sarah to give her moral support. She's fighting with the other Skirts and she needs backup. Half an hour ago, they filmed the phone scene of her calling us.

There's a big event at Jill Stuart's new store. That's the stage.

Lotta has gained some weight back and she looks healthy. She's feeling better, too. There is a comfortable ease about her that I haven't seen in years.

She could always wear a designer's clothes better than their own models could and for years she was photographed wherever she went. So she feels at home here. She's wearing an original Jill Stuart piece and looks stunning in it.

James did the hair for both of us, which means we could have worn tracksuits and no one would have noticed, he's that good. Accessorize big, keep the main dish simple. That's a line, by the way, from Billy's book. Which she turned in and sold. It will be out in August.

On set, there was a brief panic and Jill Stuart's PR girl whisked Lotta aside.

"Honey, you are a knockout in that. I love you in it. I've seriously never seen anyone make that dress look *that* good. But now I'm going to need you to change. Anything you want, the store is yours."

"Doll," Lotta said, bemused. "Why?"

"VIP coming in. And she's wearing that dress."

Nine months ago, this would have been a disaster. Lotta would have already been drunk and she would have acted accordingly. She would have left in the dress, after insulting half the crew. But now, eight months into an intensive outpatient rehab, drinking a tonic water and lime from the production tent, she smiled politely and followed the PR woman to the racks in the back of the store.

She reappeared in a white minidress that matched her beautiful pale skin and the Brazilian blowout we'd just gotten together, hours before, from James.

She looked stunning. Literally. Stunning. She sipped at her tonic, leaving a ring of MAC Red on the rim. The waitstaff, young and beautiful, all actresses or models, were entranced.

We went through the paces of what was required for our small scene, and then the din kicked in. There were flashes and shouts. People moved around. We turned and waited to see who it was, who the commotion was for. It wasn't just the production crew here with cameras, there were paparazzi, too. Who was upstaging the Plaid Skirts? Who was wearing Lotta's dress and getting this kind of attention? Gisele? An Olsen twin?

It was Odin.

"Odin, over here!"

She came out and the photographers screamed for her. She looked completely serene. Passersby, recognizing a celebrity in their midst, regardless of whether they knew her or not, asked for her autograph and she obliged. Odin, who hated crowds, who hated to leave her apartment, was holding court like Miss America.

She posed for a photo with Jill Stuart herself, the fashion sweet-heart every actress wanted to wear. Now they were all going to want to look like Odin.

Lotta gave her a big whistle.

"Let's find an after-party for those waiters, dolls." Same old Lotta, the one with fire in her eyes. "No point wasting these outfits."

"I need something to eat," Billy said. "I'm starved."

"No," Lotta said. "I have a better idea. We're not that far from there. Humor me. Let's go see my Dalí."

Billy looked at her dumbly, and I looked dumbly at Bill.

"Come on, I know you bitches never believed me." She grabbed each of our hands. *"Andiamo."*

We went to, of all places, a branch of Chase Bank. Just like Lotta had said. In our defense, it was a private equity branch of Chase, in a beautiful turn-of-the-century mansion. It wasn't a walk-in branch in midtown.

"I need to see Walter," Lotta said at the reception desk. They obviously knew her.

"I'll go get him, Ms. Eklund."

Walter was a kid, thirty-something. He gave Lotta a big hug and shook our hands.

"I need to get into my box, sweetheart. There's something in there I want to show my friends."

"Sure. Let's go."

I wouldn't call it a box. It was a huge, glamorous old-fashioned vault. Walter opened the door. We walked in. And there it was.

"Dalí, dolls."

"Holy— Oh my God," Billy said. I couldn't even speak.

I live with art. I've gone to shows, to museums; one of the best artists in the world creates his work in the space I call my home. But that was different than this. This was a piece no one had seen in fifty years. A piece no one would ever really have believed Lotta *had*. This was one of art's most famous mysteries. Whatever had become of it?

Here it was.

"Okay, girls, don't get carried away. It's climate-controlled in here and I don't need a bunch of people breathing and getting everything out of whack."

"Jesus, Lotta," I said. Titus was never going to believe this.

Back outside, we weren't sure what to do next. Billy was the only one who wanted food.

"My darlings," Lotta said, "I think I'm going to take a walk." She gave us each a quick kiss and headed up the block. "See you tonight, Lu."

We watched her walk away. She rocked that white minidress down Broome Street toward the train, and we watched until we couldn't see her anymore. Then Billy and I headed home.

I had plans with my husband.

So I changed out of the Jill Stuart outfit I'd worn for the scene and showered and scrubbed all over with Fresh sugar scrub. I dried off and put on lotion, then bronzer. Then I slipped into the dress Titus had bought for me. It was yellow. And I put on a pair of black open-toed Manolos and waited for him. He'd been at the gallery all afternoon.

"You look beautiful, Lucy," Tatiana said, smiling, when I came down. Now she was awkward with me, and I understood why.

He walked in and stopped. He met my eyes right away. He looked at me the way a new lover would. With longing. With gratefulness. With desire.

"I'm sorry I'm late, love," he said. He kissed me, then whispered in my ear, "I want to give you everything."

"Tati, I don't need anything else today. Just my beautiful wife."

We had coffee and watched the sidewalk traffic at Sant Ambroeus. Then we took our time walking down the avenue.

"Today is for you, love," he said. "All for you."

There was no talk of Odin. No talk of work. No talk of the girls, or of Leo, or of interviews or of a show. We were discovering each other again. We were touching, I was feeling him. We were learning, as if it were all new, to explore our senses.

He spoiled me with gifts and we committed an unmentionable act in the Barneys dressing room. Spencer, who rarely spoke to me when I came in alone, told me I looked intoxicating.

We went to Cartier and then Tiffany. J. Mendel, Chloé, and then Cèline. We shared a bottle of champagne at Cipriani, and then we ordered another. I have found Him. Finally. He is in love like nothing else in the world matters but my desire. Erotic. Adventure. The unknown.

"I have a surprise for you," I told him. "Humor me. Just follow." We got a cab and I gave the driver the address to Pace. Lotta was there, waiting for us. He looked confused when we got out of the car and I laughed. "Just follow." We walked inside and I took him straight to the back, where there was one single piece leaning against a wall. I took his hand and led him to it.

> **YOU ARE MY DESTINY**
> **I WANT TO BE.**
> **YOUR LOVE MAKES ME BELIEVE**
> **I CAN BE ANYTHING.**
> **YOU CAN.**
> **I HAVE TO WIN THAT FROM YOU**
> **. . .**
> **AND NEVER LOSE IT.**
> **YOU HAVE.**
> **IT IS THE ONLY THING I DESIRE.**
> **IT IS THE ONLY THING THAT I**
> **NEED.**
> **AMOUR FOU.**

I had saved every one of *his* texts. And I had commissioned Satina to put something together.

He spent a long while taking it in. He was expressionless. I didn't know what he was thinking. Suddenly I worried it was too much. And then a tear rolled down his cheek. I loved him in that moment more than I ever thought I would love anyone.

"It's for you," I said.

He kissed me passionately. Lotta walked up behind us and smiled.

We were here and we were good.

We had all the time in the world.

Acknowledgments

My parents taught me at an early age to believe in myself and to believe in love. Jane Austen showed me in her works what love looked like, and Esther Perel's teachings taught me how to show off my superpower so that the one who will love me for me will find me.

I want to thank Luke Janklow and Emma Parry for recognizing I had a novel in me—two, actually. With the help of Emma Parry's critical eye and steadfast nurturing, it was born. I want to thank my Columbia University writing professor, Alan Ziegler, who coached me through my first unpublished novel, which contains the bones of *A Dangerous Age*. My amazing friend Anne Byers drove us from horse show to horse show, while I read her early drafts, and she gave me invaluable feedback. To my mentor and closest friend, John Demsey, words seem so frivolous. Thank you for believing in me when I didn't in myself.

My editor, Alison Callahan, humbled me with her genuine love and enthusiasm for this book right from the start. Her support and sharp eye for a story were priceless, as was Jen Bergstrom's and everyone who worked with me at Gallery Books.

Thank you, Bravo, Frances Berwick, and Andy Cohen, for giving me so many opportunities, and the means to provide for my two beautiful girls. I'm forever grateful. Thank you, Jami Kandel, for pushing me out of my comfort zone. There's nothing more empowering than a friend who truly believes in you.

I owe a debt of gratitude to Jill Stuart and Calvin Klein, who were my first interviews, ever. Thank you for your patience and kindness and for teaching me the tools of how to put my dreams in motion. I am so grateful to Larry Gagosian, who introduced me to the work of so many brilliant artists—Francesco Clemente, Cy Twombly, Jeff Koons, Richard Meier, Richard Prince, Damien Hirst, and even Frank Gehry. That education had an enormous impact on this work. Thank you, Jack Kliger, the man who made me the Editor of *ELLE Accessories*, for your faith. My experience working as the Editor of the first two issues of *ELLE*'s offspring was life-changing. Tom Moore, you guide and protect my girls and me. All I want is for my girls to seek opportunity, and I am so thankful to you for making sure that will happen.

I am truly grateful to Kevin M. Barba, who works tirelessly to build my brand. His vision, adaptability, and unwavering loyalty are rare and so appreciated.

Finally, my beautiful daughters, Sea and Teddy. They have introduced me to an entire world I would never have known. I wouldn't have the courage to take leaps of faith daily, if not for these two angels by my side.

THANK YOU ALL SO MUCH.

Turn the page for an exclusive sneak peek of
Kelly Killoren's next novel

THE SECOND COURSE

Available from Gallery Books August 2017

1
· · · · · · · · ·

East Hampton, New York
Saturday, August 13
Lotta Eklund's Wedding Day

I took a bite of caviar and rolled it around in my mouth, enjoying the crisp saline snap and mineral tang as the tiny eggs exploded over my tongue.

Pop rocks for the rich, I thought to myself, not for the first time.

"Don't you think," I whispered into Sarah's ear, "that this is getting a little fucking ridiculous?"

Sarah took a sip of her negroni and cocked her head. "I think it's kind of sweet."

I took another bite and followed her gaze across the room. "It's like their own private romance novel. I don't understand how those two haven't just melted into a permanent puddle of champagne, rose petals, and empty Tiffany boxes."

We were watching our dear friend Lucy as she sat in her husband Titus's lap. Her arms were twined languidly around his neck as he looked into his eyes with what could only be described as a blazing hunger.

"Maybe used condoms, too. Add that to their puddle."

Sarah wrinkled her nose. "Gross, Billy."

I didn't begrudge them their happiness. They had gone through some rocky times lately and we were all relieved to see them on the other side of things. But it was starting to border on irritating. The two of them had been married for almost twenty years, and they were acting like horny teens who had just discovered dry humping.

We were supposed to be helping Lotta get ready for her wedding. She was due at the altar in twenty minutes, but Titus, legend of the art world and hopelessly besotted husband, had crashed the bridal suite with a tray of drinks, toast points, and a giant tin of osetra.

"Compliments of the groom," he'd said, but I had a sneaking suspicion that he had conjured it all up himself as an excuse to see Lucy.

The suspicion grew even stronger after he'd taken one look at his wife in her semi-translucent slip of a dress and pulled her onto his lap.

"This gown is exquisite on you," he murmured. "Who designed it?"

"Lotta did," said Lucy. "Isn't it wonderful?"

"No, no," said Lotta in her smoky Swedish accent. "Zac Posen did. I just told him the general gist of what I wanted."

"Well, kudos to you and Zac," said Titus.

"Thank you. Now please get out before you further wrinkle my bridesmaid with all your manhandling."

Titus stole one last quick kiss from his wife before he rose to exit. "You all look beautiful," he said, gracing the room with a warm smile. "Most especially the bride, of course."

Lotta returned his smile and then waved him out with an imperial gesture of her perfectly manicured hand. She did look beautiful. The rest of us were wearing filmy white linen, but Lotta was wearing blue silk. The shimmering color turned from summer sky to stormy when she made even the smallest shift in her movement.

"This is not my first rodeo," she had explained when she'd unveiled her gown to us, "and it's ridiculous for me to pretend to be some blushing virgin. You all can wear the white for me; I will wear a color that actually flatters."

Of course, Lotta, with her waist-length, platinum-blond hair, sleepy Nordic eyes, and six feet of Bardot curves, would have looked spectacular in any color—but blue was her particular signature, and she refused to be a generic bride.

The wedding was simple. Which did not mean cheap. It was at the groom's summer cottage. And by cottage, I mean ten-thousand-square-foot mansion with a private Hampton beachfront. It was small—which meant only 250 of the couple's nearest and dearest friends and family. And it was "beach casual," which meant the bridal party would not be wearing shoes.

"Are you absolutely sure about the barefoot thing, Lotta?" said Sarah as she gazed longingly at a shoe box on the floor. "It just seems like a missed opportunity to show off those cute Gucci ankle straps."

"I told you," said Lotta, "you can wear whatever you like at the reception. But no shoes on the beach. I have a vision."

"Okay, then!" said Lucy, bouncing up and dusting off her hands. "Let's get this vision out the door! Only fifteen minutes left to go! Sarah—you do one last hair check. I'm on makeup. Billy, you get that headdress on."

We all sprang into action. There had been a squad of professionals here before us, of course. Hair and makeup, the photographers, and the florist, with the wedding planner hovering over the room like a mother cat tending to her newborn kittens. Lotta had let them do their work and then dismissed them all, demanding a few moments of privacy for the four of us before the ceremony began.

I carefully lifted the fine web of linked platinum chains that Lotta would be wearing in lieu of a veil. The metal all but disappeared into Lotta's silvery-blond hair, just leaving the hundreds of inset sapphire chips glinting through her tresses like the world's most expensive glitter. Sarah moved a few stray strands from the front to the back. Lucy dotted the barest amount of powder over Lotta's chin and nose.

"Enough," said Lotta. "Let's have a toast."

The bridesmaids picked up our negronis. The bride was drinking sparkling water. She'd been 98 percent sober for almost six months now.

When Lotta had first come out of rehab, she was 100 percent sober and had stuck with the usual twelve-step plan. So, we'd tiptoed around her sobriety, thinking of things to do together that didn't center around alcohol or other, more illicit, substances. We doubled up on our already challenging exercise classes. We saw a lot of movies. Took a lot of walks. Drank a lot of coffee. Watched a lot of television. We even took up group knitting at one point, much to my dismay. And then, after we spent our requisite amount of time sober, Lucy, Sarah, and I would kiss Lotta good-bye, and sneak off to the nearest bar.

It ended about six months in. Lotta had marched into Lucy's town house and slammed a large bottle of tequila, and one small, hand-rolled joint, on the kitchen table.

"New plan," she announced. "I appreciate how supportive you've all been. I really do. But I can't live through another fucking night of polite chitchat and Kardashian reruns."

We all looked at each other with alarm. Lotta had been in the teeth of a terrifying addiction before she'd finally gotten help. No one wanted to go through that again.

"This," she said, picking up the marijuana, "is for me. And this"— she pushed the bottle of alcohol toward us—"is for you. You girls are going to party, and I am going to smoke this joint, and you will see that I am not made of spun sugar. I will not melt down or break just because you are having a little fun."

We all stared at her. "But Lotta—" said Lucy.

"No," said Lotta. "I will be 98 percent sober from here on out. I am not going to start snorting coke again just because I smoke a little pot. But I will definitely fall off the wagon if I have to spend one more minute dealing with how fucking boring we've become. Now drink. Please. I beg you. Drink. I can take it."

After that, things went back to relatively normal. We cut back on the coffee and restarted the dinner parties and girls' nights out. We went to all our old favorite bars and restaurants and drank all our old favorite drinks. We tried not to overindulge too much, and Lotta kept her glass full of tonic and lime, and after, she'd go home and enjoy her small daily break from sobriety.

It seemed to work for her. I asked her once if it was hard, and she had shrugged. "Almost dying was hard," she said. "Detox was hard. This . . . this is just maintenance."

I think she meant it. I hope she meant it. But I still couldn't help feeling a pang of guilt as I raised my fragrant glass full of gin, vermouth, and Campari and prepared to clink it against her boring bubbly water.

Lotta paused a moment, looking at us. Then she put her glass down.

"Tell me the truth, you guys. Am I crazy to be getting married?"

I think the three of us must have bitten our tongues in unison.

It wasn't that we didn't like her fiancé. Because we did. There was almost nothing not to like about Omari Scott. If Lenny Kravitz, Jay Z, and a young Quincy Jones managed to combine themselves into one glorious person, you'd get Omari. He'd started out as a neo-soul musician and rapper, which was hot enough, but then he'd switched over to producing and now he owned his own ridiculously successful record label. He was gorgeous, talented, rich, kind, and brilliant, and he absolutely adored Lotta.

But Lotta was barely a year sober. And she had only known Omari for four months total. Plus, he had a college-age daughter who, from everything we'd seen and heard, completely *loathed* Lotta.

Of course she was crazy to be getting married. We had talked about this behind her back nonstop since the day she had announced her engagement.

But before anyone could work up the balls to answer, Lotta laughed and picked her glass back up.

"Fuck it," she said, grinning. "Don't tell me. I don't care. Here's to my wedding!"

And so we all raised our glasses and wished her the very best.

2
....

We made a pretty picture, I'm sure, all lined up at the altar, silhouetted against the sparkling sea, skirts billowing in the breeze: slim, dark-haired Sarah with her strong patrician features and porcelain skin; model-tall, model-gorgeous, model-everything Lucy; and me, doing my best to hold my own, the ugly redheaded stepchild of our little group, just happy that we were all wearing the same thing and that, for once, I hadn't had to borrow my designer clothes. We all smiled and clutched our massive bouquets of lavender and hydrangea and pretended we didn't think this wedding was a disaster waiting to happen.

I will admit that I almost cried when Lotta turned to Omari's daughter, Sage, a gorgeous twentysomething in Adele eyeliner and Bantu knots, and told her sincerely that she wasn't just marrying Omari, that she felt so lucky to be getting such a wonderful daughter—a *family*—as well.

I knew what it meant when Lotta said that. She had been short on a loving family for most of her life. Only the sour expression on Sage's pretty face, and the fact that I could see her just barely managing not to roll her big brown eyes, saved me from completely breaking down.

The reception was in the ballroom (yes, the "cottage" had a ballroom), a huge, soaring space with banks of French doors that opened up onto a mammoth terrace that overlooked the sea.

Lotta had us seated at the bride's family table, right next to the wedding couple's table, because, up until today, we were basically all the family she had. She hadn't talked to her parents in years, and although she kept up a cordial relationship with her ex-husband (who had transitioned after their divorce and was now living as a woman), it wasn't the kind of cordial that necessitated a wedding invitation.

So it was me and my kind of/maybe boyfriend, Brett Hudson (*Brett. Brett. Could I really fall for a guy named Brett?*), Lucy and Titus, who would probably fricking hand-feed each other strawberries dipped in chocolate all night long, and Sarah and her fiancé, Brian.

Though she had managed to cover it up during bridal prep, Sarah was in a shitty mood and was now letting it all hang out. She was pissed at Lotta and Omari for not allowing any cameras in from the reality show—*Beneath the Plaid Skirt*—that she was a cast member on. Her first season had been a hit, and now the pressure was on to top herself. She had initially planned that her second season arc would be all about her own wedding, but now she felt that Lotta had stolen her thunder.

"I can't get married *now*," she said, gesturing around the ballroom. "I mean, we just finished planning all this. It would be so boring to do it all over again."

Brian frowned and buried his nose in his drink. He was known to be a man of endless patience, but sometimes I wondered if the end to that endless was closer than we thought.

"So it's going to have to be the baby first," continued Sarah. "But I'm not unthawing the embryos yet. My doctor wants to see if we can just make one the old-fashioned way. And I think the longer we can draw out the tension, the better for the show, so we're willing to give it a try, right, Brian?" She smiled sweetly at her fiancé.

He cleared his throat and then gave her a smile back. "Of course," he said.

"But we'll need a B-plot while we're trying to make a baby. Did I tell you that Penelope Prettyman is doing a cancer scare this year? I mean, it's a melanoma, for God's sake. Not even real cancer, but she's going to milk it for all it's worth."

I laughed. "Jesus, Sarah, a little heartless, maybe?"

She ignored me. "So I was thinking, maybe I'll sell my apartment and find a new, more kid-friendly place in Brooklyn. We can do a house hunt. Everyone likes real-estate porn."

Lucy's head jerked around. "What? Brooklyn? What are you talking about?"

Sarah waved her hand airily. "Prospect Park. Brooklyn Heights. Hey, do you think your mom could help me? Think what great TV Cheri would be! She's the hottest real-estate agent in New York. She must know all kinds of gossip."

"Leave Manhattan? Why would you do that?" Lucy sounded genuinely bewildered by the idea.

"Matt Damon just moved to Brooklyn for the schools, you know. It's the responsible choice to make for my family, Lucy."

"Well, if Matt Damon says so, it must be true," I drawled.

Sarah turned to me. "You should consider it, too, Billy. I mean, obviously not the Heights or Prospect Park, but somewhere cheaper. I don't see how you're keeping up the rent on your place."

"I still have royalties coming on my book," I said, stung.

Sarah lifted a dubious eyebrow, letting me know exactly what she thought of that plan.

She was right, by the way. I couldn't afford my place. At least not for much longer. I still had a little chunk of money from the initial book sale, but it was disappearing fast, and the royalties were pretty much a delusional pipe dream. It seemed that less people needed a cookbook on obscure cocktails than I had initially thought.

It was embarrassing. Even before Sarah was a quasi-celebrity making huge bank from her TV show, Brian had already been an extremely successful hedge-fund manager. And of course Titus and Lucy had all of Titus's world-famous-artist money plus whatever Lucy had socked away when she was still doing *Vogue* covers and Marc Jacobs campaigns. Lotta used to be my comrade on the edge of poverty— we'd joke about how we were going to end up sharing an efficiency in Queens—but now she was married to Omari frigging Scott, who probably had more money than the rest of us put together. And Brett? Well, Brett had underwritten Instagram—among many other wise investments—so he wasn't exactly hurting for cash, either. With all this around me, being on the verge of broke somehow seemed even more pathetic than usual.

Brett took my hand. "Hey," he said quietly, "if you ever need help . . ."

I jerked my hand away. "I'm fine," I hissed.

I immediately felt bad. I knew he was only trying to be kind.

"I mean, thank you, but I'm fine."

He laughed. God, he was good-looking. Square jaw, clean-cut, with this kind of boyish, tousled thing that got me every time. "Heaven forbid Billy Sitwell admit that she needs any help."

I deflected. "When is the waiter getting here? Lotta promised me that my mind was going to be blown by this food. She said she found this chef when they had a private dinner with John Legend and Chrissy Teigen. It's supposed to be like nothing I've ever tasted."

Brett shook his head. "Hard to imagine there's anything you haven't tasted, B.," he said.

He was correct again. Actually, it was starting to make me a little jumpy, just how well he seemed to know me, but he was right—I couldn't imagine that there was much left under the sun that I hadn't already put in my mouth.

Ever since I was a little girl, food was my everything. My mom killed herself when I was five. She was knocked off this earth by the kind of depression that probably could be controlled with a couple of Zolofts and a gluten-free diet these days, but in 1974, it was basically a choice between being a lithium zombie or shock therapy, so she took what I eventually came to accept as the most sensible way out. My father was left at sea in a million different ways, but cooking was maybe the most tangibly difficult thing for him. So he drew up a never-changing menu, almost entirely based on ground meat. Burgers on Monday. Tacos on Tuesday. Spaghetti Wednesday. Frozen Pizza Thursday. Grilled cheese on Friday. Breakfast for dinner Saturday. And Sunday, we went to Denny's. He was doing his best, but it was unrelenting.

I started out small—changing it up just a little bit. Adding a slice of Swiss cheese to the burgers, a couple dashes of Tabasco to the tacos, making an iceberg salad to eat alongside the spaghetti. But soon I put my precocious reading skills to use by wading my way through the cookbooks that my mother had left behind (starting with *Joy of Cooking*, every Midwestern mom's bible).

I'll never forget the first time I really cooked for my father—like, a full meal; vegetable, main course, and dessert. It was simple. I blanched some green beans, sliced some tomatoes from our neighbor's garden, and broiled a steak. And then for dessert, I made home-made chocolate pudding. Everything turned out great. The beans were crisp and tender. The tomatoes were perfectly ripe and strewn with a smear of salt. The steak was juicy and pink inside, just how we liked it. And even the chocolate pudding—which took real effort on my part—was smooth and delicious.

I was nine. And my father cried after he finished eating.

"Sweetheart, this was as good as anything your mother ever made," he said, smiling through his tears.

I have spent my lifetime trying to recapture the overwhelming pride and happiness I felt at that moment.

I finished high school and followed Lucy, who had been my best friend since grade school, to Manhattan. By the time I arrived, she was already well-established in the fashion world. She was everybody's favorite model, and she assured me that I could be, too.

I thought she was insane. I had frizzy red hair, boobs that were way too big, and an ass that you could serve dinner on, but I also had nothing to lose. It was that, or stay in the Midwest bagging groceries. And to be fair, Lucy supported me in almost every way possible. She let me sleep on her couch, she loaned me her clothes, she introduced me to everyone she knew, and she pulled what strings she could to get me a few small jobs. Me as a model was basically a disaster. Makeup artists labored to cover up my thousands of freckles. Stylists split the seams down the back and then safety-pinned dresses to get me into sample sizes. One hairstylist told me cheerfully that I had the kind of face that was perfect for radio (I still fantasize about punching that hag in the nose). Even with Lucy's sponsorship, I wasn't tall enough, or thin enough, or striking enough to get far. And there is a world of difference between the cover of *Vogue Paris* (Lucy, twice) and modeling clogs and a miniskirt for a Chico's catalogue (me, once. It was the apex of my career, and I was never called back again).

But I still had food. Maybe I wasn't going to get to go to a culinary institute like I had once dreamed, but I had waitressed my way through high school and was more than willing to start at the bottom of the Manhattan food chain.

I bussed tables. I was a hostess. I did time behind the bar, and in a tiny skirt and fishnets as a cocktail waitress. I got into the kitchens anytime I possibly could (which was not very often. In those days, a woman in the back was considered poison). And in my downtime, I read everything I could lay my hands on. I read Calvin Trillin and Ruth Reichl and M. F. K. Fisher and Laurie Colwin. I read Jeffrey

Steingarten and Julia Childs and James Beard and Madhur Jaffrey. I read, and I shopped at the farmers' markets and the Village cheese-mongers and the Italian butchers and the fish places in Chinatown. I cooked in my tiny little galley kitchen with a two-burner stove and inconsistent oven, turning out dish after dish and meal after meal.

And, even more important, I ate. New York City is the best place in the world if you are hungry. And I was starving.

I never agreed to a date unless there was food involved. A man could have had an IQ of twenty and smellled like infected feet, but if he offered me a meal at somewhere above my pay grade, I was in. I cut a swath through the New York restaurant scene, eating out for every meal I could manage. And then one day I went out with the right guy—a guy who watched me put away seven courses while I kept up a running commentary about everything I shoved into my mouth—and who just happened to edit an up-and-coming little magazine that just happened to need a food critic.

Those were the glory years. An expense account and open access to any restaurant in the city. I tried to remain anonymous at first, but word got out fast, and it was a little hard to hide my head of flaming curls and girl-next-door, Midwestern face in a sea of sophisticated New Yorkers. So I gave up and let restaurants do their best by me, and wrote about them based on that.

But, maybe precisely because I was eating the best all the time, I got jaded. It was all so over-the-top. The rich sauces and the strange cuts of meat and the tiny, jewel-like vegetables and the teetering architectural presentations . . . Chefs were tripping over themselves to impress me, and after a while, nothing really did.

So I quit. I got the idea for my book, and I resigned my position at the magazine and I started doing guerilla dinners in my apartment to make ends meet while I wrote it. The dinners were a carefully choreographed freak show and I hated them. Every night I would cook for wealthy voyeurs and aesthetes, people whose palates were as jaded and overtaxed as mine was. They didn't really care about what actually tasted good, just as long as it was new and exotic and they could brag about eating it later. I swear, I could have pissed in a bowl and called it bone broth and those assholes would have lapped it up and asked for seconds.

I thought I was done with all that when my book came out. I thought I had finally caught up—at least a little bit—with my friends. But lately it was looking to be as much of a failure as anything else I had ever tried. It didn't even get a second printing.

And so now here I was, once again having to reinvent myself. But this time I was in my forties. And I was worn down and I was disappointed, and I was tired.

And, honestly, I just wasn't that hungry anymore.

The waiter put a bowl of soup down on the table in front of me. The soup was a light green, almost white. There was a small, brighter-green, quivering square of gelatin floating in the center. I touched the dark blue bowl. It was chilled. I shook my head and rolled my eyes. *Vichyssoise.* Cold potato and leek soup. Not a terrible thing at all, but certainly nothing new.

So much for this chef blowing my mind, I thought as I dipped my spoon in and took a bite.

It was not vichyssoise.

It was . . . it was creamy and cold but also slightly sweet and spicy. There was fruit; I was almost certain it was some kind of melon, but damned if I knew what kind of melon it was. I took another bite. Cucumber? Ground almonds? So, a white gazpacho? No. I wouldn't call it gazpacho, either. I spooned up the green square, which instantly melted as soon as it touched my lips, and my entire mouth was filled with the brightest, most intense herbal flavor. Basil, for certain. And mint. And Jesus, was that lovage? And then, after I took the next bite,

I realized that the green square had changed the entire flavor of the soup. Now the spice was stronger than the sweet, and I could definitely taste apple, not melon. It was like that scene in *Willy Wonka* when Violet chews the gum and she has tomato soup that turns into roast beef that turns into blueberry pie. I scraped the bottom of the bowl, just barely keeping myself from licking it clean. Then I stood up.

"Where's the kitchen?" I called over to Lotta.

She smirked at me. "I told you so," she said.

"Where's the kitchen?" I repeated insistently.

Omari pointed out one of the doorways. "To the left," he said.

I turned and starting marching out of the room.

"Hey, Billy!" Omari laughed. "Please tell Ethan that we very much enjoyed the soup!"

A Dangerous Age

Kelly Killoren

with Tessa DiMiero

This reader's group guide for *A Dangerous Age* includes an introduction, discussion questions, ideas for enhancing your book club, and a Q&A with author Kelly Killoren. The suggested questions are intended to help your reading group find new and interesting angles and topics for discussion. We hope that these ideas will enrich your conversation and increase your enjoyment of the book.